RAISE THE BANNER

The King's Ranger Book 5

AC COBBLE

Cobble Publishing LLC

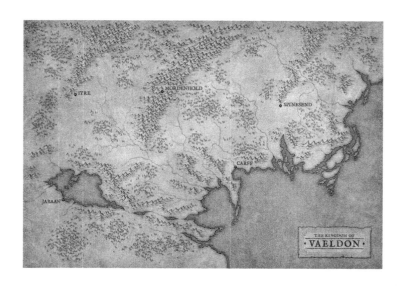

Keep in Touch and Extra Content

You can find larger versions of the maps, series artwork, my newsletter, free short stories, and other goodies at accobble.com. It's the best place to stay updated on when the next book is coming!

Happy reading!
AC

Chapter One

✦

"Are they getting any better?" asked Anne.

Rew smirked. "A little."

There was a thump, a groan, and the dull sound of a body collapsing on loamy soil.

"The progress is slow and painful," added the ranger. He held up a wooden cup. "Nut? Commandant Eckvar roasts and salts them. Good, dense food for a journey, he tells me, but they always make me thirsty."

Wordlessly, Anne scooped a couple of nuts from the cup and popped them one by one into her mouth. As she chewed, the two of them watched Raif struggle back to his feet, rubbing his hip from where it had impacted the ground.

"Yesterday when I came out here, he was doing the exact same thing," remarked Anne.

Between bites, Rew told her, "Aye, it's making me sore just watching, but it's good for the lad. He's gotten used to sparring with Zaine and always being stronger with a bigger weapon. It's not always that way in a fight, and it doesn't hurt to put in a little practice without flirting between each bout." Rew raised his voice. "Let's see another, and Raif, if you don't start putting some thought into defense, I'm warning you it's going to be a long day."

"I'm used to wearing armor," grumbled the fighter, shooting a look at Rew and Anne. "If I had my plate, I wouldn't need—"

"And how would armor have helped you that time?" drawled Ang, leaning on a slender quarterstaff. "Armor gives you a false sense of comfort and makes you lazy. You think you're protected, but against a skilled opponent, there are always gaps in the steel, and if not, there are other ways to neutralize an armored man. All the steel in the world won't stop me from sweeping your legs from beneath you, and once a fully armored man is flopping around on his back like a tipped over turtle, finishing him is easy."

"That swordstaff of yours didn't work so well on Prince Heindaw," accused Raif, shaking himself and raising his wooden practice blade again to show he was ready for another pass. "I don't recall you finding gaps in his plate or managing to put him on his back."

"Fair enough," granted Ang. "Of course, unless you happen to have access to a unique set of enchanted bronze armor and the high magic to power it, that's sort of a moot point, don't you think? Train with the armor and the talent you've got, lad. What we're trying to do is make the best of it."

"Can I put my armor back on, then?" growled Raif, starting to stalk a slow circle around the ranger. "The best of it. Pfah."

"Not even the greatest blacksmith can make a decent sword from tin. People need butter knives, though." Ang gave the fighter a slow wink. "I do what I can with the materials I'm given."

His nostrils flaring like a bull's, Raif charged.

The young fighter had been sparring enough with the former ranger to know Ang was goading him, trying to get a rise, but no one had ever accused Raif of being even-tempered. Chances were, if you tried to get a rise, he would give it to you. It had gotten the lad into trouble more than once, but it'd helped him win some fights, too. Rew had given up trying to talk Raif out of going berserk. It was who he was, but Ang was doggedly determined to break the big lad of the habit.

Raif launched himself at Ang, and the ranger sprang into motion, twirling out of the way and flicking his quarterstaff at Raif's legs, trying to trip the fighter as he barreled closer. Raif jumped, and the wooden staff whistled beneath him instead of cracking against his unarmored shins. He landed and spun, swinging his heavy wooden practice blade after the ranger, but Ang leaned back, letting the blow sail by him.

The moment Raif's practice blade swooshed in front of him, Ang yanked his staff up, catching Raif a glancing blow to the ribs, then reversed course and swept a strike at Raif's head.

The fighter raised an arm, and the quarterstaff smacked meatily against his flesh. Had Ang been using his swordstaff, such a defense would have cost Raif his hand, or maybe the fighter intended to spend the rest of his life wearing his steel bracers, like he claimed. Though, bracers or not, taking the blow on the arm was better than the head.

Cursing, Raif counterattacked, cleaving the air with powerful strikes but finding only air as Ang weaved constantly out of range.

Ang let Raif attack, only dodging and defending. Then suddenly, he ducked a blow and lashed his quarterstaff around. Raif tried to jump it again, but Ang whipped the staff up, catching Raif's legs and upending the fighter so he landed heavily on his shoulders and his head.

The big lad lay on the ground groaning theatrically.

Across the clearing, a slow clap began. Zaine stepped forward, a grin on her face, Vurcell trailing behind her. Her voice dripping with patronizing sarcasm, she trilled, "Very well done."

"The way he moves the staff, it's like fighting two of him," muttered Raif, sitting up and rubbing his shoulder. "Maybe you ought to try—What happened to your face?"

"The young lady attempted a novel new defense and deflected one of my strikes with her forehead," explained Vurcell, his voice cracking as he struggled to stop himself from laughing. "Better than taking a hit to the arm where I was aiming, I suppose. Evidently, her skull is quite thick."

Rubbing a tomato-red lump that spanned her forehead, the thief declared, "We can't learn if we don't try new things, right?"

Chuckling, Ang replied, "That's one way to look at it, or you could just pay attention to the techniques we're teaching you and avoid the headaches."

"Speaking of which…" murmured Zaine, shooting a questioning glance at Anne.

"Come on over," offered the empath. "Both of you."

Dutifully, Zaine and Raif lined up in front of the empath for healing. A gentle smile on her lips, Anne took their pain and then instructed, "Two laps."

"What?" spluttered Zaine, glancing at Rew then at the twin rangers who'd been training her and Raif the last several days. "We already ran this morning!"

"You ran laps for your weapons masters this morning," replied Anne, "but this time, it's for me. Empathy comes at a cost. Unless next time you want to spend a week walking around with that welt across your forehead."

Flabbergasted, the fighter and the thief set off at a slow pace, jogging into the trees, starting on the two-league forest loop that encircled the tiny settlement they'd taken refuge in following the battle against Prince Heindaw in Iyre. The small, nameless village they were staying in was a refuge for rangers who were too old or too injured to continue service in the wilderness. It was secluded, as those men and women preferred peace and quiet, and it was ignored by everyone except the rangers themselves.

Rew had periodically visited the place to seek the wisdom of the elders and to train. The rangers living there might not be able to fight like they used to, but after decades of surviving against the Dark Kind and the monsters of the world, their advice was invaluable. The village was a good place to recover and to grow.

Watching Raif and Zaine disappear into the woods, Rew mentioned, "At that pace, they'll be at it all afternoon."

"Maybe that's their plan," quipped Vurcell. "Jog slow enough that they can avoid the rest of their arms practice."

Ang opened his mouth, ready to call after them to pick up speed, but Anne reached out and caught his arm. "Let them take their time."

The former ranger raised an eyebrow.

Pursing her lips, Anne looked toward the simple wooden huts of the settlement then cleared her throat. "Cinda is reading, and I don't think anything will distract her from it. I wanted to talk without the children noticing us doing it."

Ang and Vurcell glanced at Rew, but he merely shrugged. He didn't know what Anne was going to say, but he'd known something was coming. They'd been still for too long. If he could sense it, she must as well.

Anne dusted her hands off, scattering the bits of salt that had stuck there after eating the nuts. She frowned, as if searching for words, then said, "I feel… a severing. As if people are disappearing from the world. Dying."

Rew frowned, and Ang and Vurcell shared a look.

Noticing the twins glance, Anne asked, "Do you feel it as well?"

Shaking his head, Vurcell responded, "Our noses don't work quite like that. We can feel magic, and yes, there has been a rise over the last week, but it's far away, vague enough that all we can tell is that someone is drawing a lot of power. We haven't mentioned anything because, frankly, I believe this is what we all expected. Valchon will know Rew is coming for him, and the king knows following that encounter, one way or the other, the Investiture will be over. The two of them will gird themselves as best they're able."

"Aye, we've expected it, but people dying?" questioned Rew. "Valchon has no incentive to kill anyone. We have no army for him to face, no territory to threaten. Unless the king… he could be trying to replace the well of power he lost in Jabaan and Iyre."

Her lips pressed together, Anne nodded. "That is my concern."

"We could ask Cinda," suggested Ang. "If there's a surge in deaths that even you can feel, Anne, then surely she would feel it as well. If the king is slaying people to draw power, perhaps she'd—Has she sensed it, do you think?"

Crossing her arms over her chest, Anne responded, "I asked Cinda. She just stared back at me with those cold green eyes. I think she feels it, but she's… unaffected. I wondered if it would spur her to move, but it seems to have elicited nothing."

"You're worried she's frightened, or what?" questioned Rew.

"I worry what made her Cinda is being burned away by what we've asked of her," replied Anne. "She's not the same girl she was. Not grown up, I mean she's lost what made her good, what started us on this journey. I'm not sure she's pursuing this for the right reasons."

Ang and Vurcell looked discomfited.

Rew scratched his beard and cleared his throat. "I, ah, I haven't spoken to her much in the last days. She's been lost in those books…"

"I know. That's my point," remarked Anne. "She barely comes out of that hut, and when she does, it's like she's moving through a dream. Yesterday, Zaine was making one of her little digs at Raif, and Cinda didn't even blink. I don't think it's that she's tired of their banter, which I could understand, it's that she's… removed from it. From us all. If Cinda doesn't have a connection to the rest of us, what will that mean? We're all that she has, now. If she isn't fighting for us, what is she fighting for, if she's fighting at all?"

"Are you suggesting an intervention?" asked Vurcell.

"I'm not sure," responded Anne. "I think… I think she's becoming obsessed with gathering knowledge and power. We've all seen it happen enough to other spellcasters and nobles. Power is more addictive than poppy oil. I worry what that will mean if we're successful and Vaisius Morden is deposed. You've never wanted the throne, Rew, so maybe it's a struggle for you to understand, but seeking power is in her blood, it's what she was raised to do. That is the only life she's known. Have any of you met a noble who would turn from power? If Cinda defeats Vaisius Morden, we might no longer have a king, but a queen."

"I see why you wanted the children gone for this," murmured Ang. The former ranger shifted uncomfortably then admitted, "I haven't spoken to the lass much. She scares me. I haven't seen power like hers before, except from the king himself, and he's absolutely terrifying."

Vurcell fidgeted absentmindedly with the handle of one of the enchanted falchions that had belonged to Vyar Grund. He cleared his throat. "Anne, are you certain about this? She's just a girl, and no matter how powerful or distracted, I haven't noticed any vile intent in her. Are you sure she's not simply distracted by the weight of it all?"

"Of course I'm not sure. I... She's been with us for months. She's a good person, truly, but she's not the same as she was at the beginning. It's all changed her, but after Jabaan... the weight of what she did there, the burden of what's coming... People have broken under far less stress than what Cinda is dealing with. We keep telling her she's the one, the one with the power to face the king. What if she decides she ought to be rewarded for that task? What will we do?"

"We don't need to worry about that," declared Rew.

Anne raised an eyebrow.

Rew stood from the log they'd been sitting on while watching the weapons practice. He brushed his hands off on his trousers and added, "We don't need to worry about Cinda trying to seize the throne once Vaisius Morden is off of it."

"It's something to keep in mind, isn't it?" suggested Ang. "If she makes the attempt, we won't have an easy time stopping her. King's Sake, do we even try to stop her?"

Rew shook his head but did not respond.

"More secrets, Rew, even now?" asked Anne.

"It's, ah, it's not so much a secret as… an uncomfortable truth," mumbled Rew, shaking the cup he held in his hand, sending the roasted and salted nuts spinning against each other. He wondered, briefly, if it was better to let Anne stay worried Cinda was going to try to seize the throne. He coughed, looked around, and then continued, "The tools to defeat the king are not conventional. He's too powerful. A glob of liquid fire, a well-swung blade, these are not the things which will bring him down."

"Aye, it'd be too easy if a blast of death's breath ended the greatest necromancer the world has known," remarked Ang. He frowned. "So how do we go about defeating the king?"

Again, Rew did not respond.

"Rew…" began Anne, "what are you expecting Cinda to do?"

"It's not me… It's complicated, Anne," responded the ranger. He sat back down on the log beside her. "Necromancy is an art of death, and through death, great power can be achieved. There's a way that… Pfah, we're talking about the king. There's only one way I can think of for a lass like Cinda to defeat him, but what wouldn't we sacrifice to remove him from the throne?"

"Wait!" snapped Anne. "Are you saying Cinda has to die?"

Rew met Anne's gaze but couldn't summon the words to explain. He didn't need to. She could see it in his eyes. She blanched and looked sick.

"We don't have to worry about Cinda seizing power," reiterated Rew quietly. "When it's done, she won't be able to."

"Blessed Mother," hissed Vurcell. He paused a moment. Then, quietly, he asked, "Does she know?"

"She does. She has a right to be distracted, distant. It's not fair, what we… what I am asking of her, but what choice is there?"

LATER THAT EVENING, REW SLUNK INTO THE SMALL CABIN CINDA WAS ensconced within. She'd rarely left the place in the two weeks they'd been in the little village. Anne had been bringing the young necromancer food, and Rew knew she only slept two or three hours each night. All of her time was spent poring over the books they'd gotten from Lucia in the Arcanum and Jacob in the temple for the Cursed Father. If she hadn't already, she couldn't be far from memorizing the contents of both books cover to cover.

"The others are worried about you," Rew mentioned, ducking his head as he slipped through the doorway.

"But not you?" Cinda responded, not looking up from her book but appearing unsurprised at his presence.

He shrugged and sat across from her cross-legged.

She marked her place in the book and closed it. She turned her cold green eyes on him. "Have a seat."

"I told the others what fighting the king will cost you."

She ran a hand down the spine of her book and stared at him. When he did not continue, she asked, "And were they worried about me before or after that conversation?"

Rew rubbed his head. He needed a shave, among other things. He cleared his throat, and responded, "Both."

"The burden is heavy. I suppose it'd be disappointing if they weren't worried about me," she replied. "What is it you want, Ranger? Are you asking me to come out and smile? Cheer on Zaine's and my brother's sparring? Pretend this doesn't end the way we both know it will?"

"I want you to tell me about the deaths."

She blinked at him.

He waited.

Shifting, she scowled. "Blessed Mother. Anne's gotten all worked up over it, has she? Well, if it will get you out of here quicker so I can get back to reading... yes, I can feel the deaths."

"And?"

"My guess—and it is only a guess—is that Vaisius Morden is rebuilding the power we took from him in Jabaan and Iyre. Our victories there may have come at a steep cost for someone elsewhere."

Rew grunted. "That's… not good news."

Cinda shrugged. "I agree, and I could be wrong, but Valchon has no reason to be killing anyone, and your other brothers are dead. I suppose some minor nobles might have gone to war with each other, but this feels… sustained. Systematic. What could it be other than the king?"

"Can you tell where it's happening?"

Cinda shook her head.

Rew frowned. "How many?"

"People die all of the time."

"How many?"

"I have no idea," she answered with a sigh. "The impressions I get are vague at best. If I had to speculate, I'd say a lot. If someone were to die in this village, I would feel it. If someone were to die back in Iyre, I wouldn't, fortunately. Scores of people die every day in the larger cities, and I don't want that rattling me every hour. For me to feel the tide of these deaths… it could be thousands."

"Thousands…"

"Thousands each day."

"You didn't think this was relevant?" questioned Rew. "That maybe the rest of us should know thousands of people are dying every day, likely at the hands of the king, all while he guzzles strength from their departure like a drunk at a wineshop?"

"It's all speculation," responded Cinda. "I told you I could be wrong, but even if I'm not, what are we going to do about it?"

"We could leave this place," suggested Rew. "We can go tomorrow to Carff and then on to Mordenhold where we can stop this. Every day we wait, more people die."

"I'm preparing to face the king. The king, Ranger. The man no one has defeated in two hundred years. Blessed Mother, no one has ever defeated him! I am sorry people are dying, but what you ask of me is not some simple task. I'm not ready. Not yet." Cinda held his gaze for a long moment then asked, "Are you so eager for me to die?"

Rew shook his head. "That's unfair."

"No, it's not."

"Is this a task you want to turn from? Are you afraid?"

"Of course not—no, that's not true. I am afraid. Naturally, I'm terrified, but I'm committed. Even if I wasn't, we cannot turn back now. The king knows us. There are only two ways this ends, and one of them… I will do this thing, but I have to be ready."

"You've read both books, Cinda," responded Rew gently. "You've read them several times. You know what information is in those pages. What else do you seek?"

"Patterns. Connections. There is information in here, valuable information, but Jacob told us he ran out of time to write all of it down. It's not as easy as, 'To defeat Vaisius Morden, Step One.' I wish I could read through this and know exactly what to do, but it's not working that way. I have to study, to figure out what Heindaw intended and how that relates to what Jacob recorded. The secrets are there, or maybe they are not, but the only way forward is study and consideration. It's what I have to do."

"Heindaw told me how to defeat the king. We spoke of it. To tip the stool, you knock out the legs. If we destroy all of the king's crypts, we destroy the king."

"Do you know how many crypts he has?"

"Two less after Jabaan and Iyre."

"Forty-three," said Cinda. "There's a list in the book Heindaw was using. There are larger ones in the larger cities, of course, but there are forty-three remaining temples to the Cursed Father. Some are quite small, I suspect. Over half are in places I've never heard of. We could probably overwhelm the priests there and destroy the temples in the rural towns. It might take us years to travel between all of them, and like you say, every day the king could be killing thousands of others and building power faster than we can destroy it. The largest temples are in places like Carff and Mordenhold. One cannot just walk into Mordenhold, into the king's own palace, and destroy his crypt. I believe Heindaw's logic is sound, but acting on it without the ability to open portals is impractical. I have been thinking this over, Ranger."

Rew frowned and did not reply.

"You don't know any invokers who will assist us, do you?"

"None that have the strength to ferry us across the entire kingdom," admitted Rew.

"So I study."

"Do you believe you'll find a more practical way to defeat the king, then?"

"I'm working on it," huffed Cinda. She looked meaningfully at the book in her lap. "I'm trying to, at least."

"It's close to time for us to leave," said Rew. "Ready or not, we cannot stay here forever."

"I'm going as fast as I can," said Cinda. "I know this is my task, that I was bred for it. For generations, my family tended to our bloodline, culminating in me. They must have known we'd have the strength to face the king one day, but why didn't my father teach me? Why didn't… It doesn't matter, I suppose. Not anymore. This is my task. It's my blood, my purpose."

Rew tilted his head. "Let's dine with Eckvar tonight."

Cinda frowned, her hands working across the cover of the book in her lap.

Rew leaned forward. "That is not a question."

Chapter Two

"Commandant Eckvar," said Rew, bending at the waist, offering the older man a bow.

The other ranger snorted at the gesture.

Eckvar wore sensible, thick woolen trousers the same shade as a walnut, an undyed cotton tunic, soft leather boots, and a leather jacket lined with lamb's wool even though the early spring air had lost its bite. There wasn't a bit of fat on the man, just bone and wiry muscle. Not much hair, either. A thin white fringe crowned his head, and his eyebrows stood out like overgrown hedgerows. Eckvar had no beard, which Rew had always thought was strange. When he was an old man and no longer worried about slipping through crowded undergrowth, Rew planned to have a luscious white beard that spilled down past his belt.

"I'm not the commandant, Senior Ranger," Eckvar rasped. "Haven't been since before you were born. I'm too old for that sort of flattery."

"If you're not the commandant, then I'm no senior ranger," responded Rew. He gave the former commandant a wry grin. "Ranger Blythe is the senior in Eastwatch, now."

One of those pure-white hedgerow eyebrows rose on the old

man's wrinkled face. "The king rescind your papers, did he? Or perhaps you turned in your documentation and retired?"

Rew smirked. "Haven't had a chance to speak to the king about it yet."

"Then, to be accurate, you are still a Senior Ranger, aren't you?" chided the old man. "Don't tell me that if you showed your face back in Eastwatch, Blythe wouldn't be falling over herself to do whatever you asked. It's about more than what the papers say."

"As you say, Commandant."

Eckvar snorted.

"Doesn't much matter what the papers show, does it?" added Rew. "That's not the life I lead. Not the life I'll ever lead again."

"All these other old souls may be too deaf or senile to know what's going on, but I'm not," declared Eckvar. "Well, I am old—ancient, I'd guess you'd call me—and I've gotten a little deaf, but you know what I mean. We can dispense with the dance because these old hips don't move like they used to. You're defying the king, which is why you don't call yourself a ranger. Plenty of others have tried to walk in those boots, lad. The king dealt with them harshly, but they were still rangers. I myself said the words over more than one of their graves. Vaisius Morden may have been the one that put them there, but not even he denied they were rangers. Pfah, look at me. It's been ages since I've traipsed through the wilderness or fought a narjag, but you think of me as a ranger, don't you? The commandant, even, which I haven't been since before you drew breath."

"Defying the king. That's a bold statement," muttered Rew. He drew a deep breath and let it go. Bold but true. "You know, then, all of it?"

"Well, I don't know about all of it, but I know enough. Does that make you feel a little foolish, spending all this time dodging me? Didn't want to tell me what you were up to, eh? Like I wouldn't guess what it meant, you arriving from Iyre right after Heindaw ends up dead. Like I wouldn't see who you were traveling with or hear from the scores of other rangers that were involved. Pfah."

"I didn't want to disrupt your… meditations."

"Naps, lad. They're called naps."

"Naps. I didn't want to interrupt them."

"But you are now!"

Rew grinned. It'd been years since he'd seen Ranger Eckvar. The old commandant had served before Vyar Grund's predecessor, and he wasn't exaggerating when he said he'd been retired longer than Rew had been alive. Eckvar had lived somewhere north of one hundred winters, though he had been claiming for decades he couldn't remember how many, and he looked like every one of those winters had been a hard one. His mind was still as sharp as a blade, though, and it wasn't unusual to find rangers in the village seeking his wisdom. The old man might not be able to see and hear well enough to stalk the clumsiest rabbit through an autumn forest, but he had a keen sense for when something was wrong, and occasionally, he would know what to do about it.

"Before, I didn't want to, ah, test your loyalties," said Rew. "It's not just the defiant rangers who can end up in a shallow grave."

"Loyalty to you or to the king?" barked Eckvar.

"Well, either one," murmured Rew.

"What's between you and the king is between you and the king," declared the old commandant, "and don't tell me about those graves. I've seen 'em, lad. I know the consequences. Besides, I'm not a man who steps between family. And who knows, with your blood, mayhaps it's you I'll owe allegiance to, should I be blessed by the Mother with a few more months in this life."

Rew coughed.

"I've known that for years, lad, long before you had the rangers spreading the word from one end of this kingdom to the other. Subtlety is a lost art." The old man peered at him. "Well?"

"Well, what?"

"Well, what are you here for? I'm old, lad, and I don't have time for subtlety. Neither do you, so out with it."

Rolling his eyes, hoping the old man couldn't see it through his clouded gaze, Rew said, "I only wanted to have supper with you, Commandant, and introduce the lass here to a living legend."

"Ah, now we have it," muttered the old man, turning his gaze toward Cinda. "Not here to learn necromancy from me, eh. Not woodcraft either, though someone ought to teach her. The lass lumbers like an elephant with a broken leg."

"… a what?" asked Cinda.

The old man waved a hand. "Animal from the other side of the sea. Be glad of it, too. Gentle souls 'til you anger them. Terrors in battle." The old man rubbed his bare chin. "Rew has more low magic than I, as does your empath friend, so you're not here for that. Not my cooking either, as I don't cook. Nor my company, as it's as sour as my gut these days. Couldn't be my sage wisdom. Rew's had years to listen to that and hasn't ever shown an inclination to follow my advice."

Rew grimaced at the old man. "That's unfair."

"It's forbidden, so I won't teach you… Is that it? That's why you've come? You're wanting me to teach the lass to commune? Blessed Mother, Senior Ranger, you could teach her well enough yourself. Given everything else you're up to, you wouldn't let a decree outlawing it stop you. Aye, I know you don't do it, but I also know you've as much skill with communion as anyone. I remember when you were younger, you know."

"You can tell us how communion came to be," said Rew, "and why it's forbidden. No secrets, nothing practical, but she needs to hear why. I think it best if it comes from you, and your friend."

The old man blinked.

"This is cute, but I haven't the faintest what either of you is talking about," remarked Cinda dryly. "If we're to hold this discussion in riddles, I have more important ones I've been trying to unravel."

Bobbing his head, the old man murmured, "I see. No riddles, lass. Not for you."

He tilted his head to the side, and from the corner of the room, a hulking black bear emerged.

"Blessed Mother!" shrieked Cinda, nearly falling out of the chair she'd been sitting in and scrambling backward. She raised her hands, and the ethereal green glow of funeral fire began to build, dancing up her palms and playing along her fingers.

Rew held a hand out to stop her.

The old man smiled. "I've few pleasures in this world, but surprising people is still one of them."

The bear waddled up to the old man and sat down beside him. It was large, three times the mass of a man, but as they got a closer look, they saw it was quite fat, and its black fur was speckled with white. It was an old bear that had gone several seasons without stirring itself to hunt.

Cinda drew herself up then tapped a lip with a finger. "Communion. You can communicate with it?"

"I can," replied the old man.

"A familiar, like…" she trailed off, evidently deciding not to share any details of their encounter with Prince Calb.

"Not a familiar," clarified the old man, shaking his head. "A companion. I've no more control over her than you'd have over any good friend, though I do make sure she's well fed, which gives me a method to incentivize her."

"Vyar Grund spoke to animals," said Cinda. "He… used them to fight for him."

"He did." The old man shifted uncomfortably. "There is more than one way to train an animal. Vyar Grund was a lot of things, but kind was not one of them. What he did… was horrible. It was before his time when such practices were banned, but when he was named the Commandant, who was there to stop him? The king isn't one to stand in the way of cruelty."

"You trained Grund?"

The old man shook his head. "I did not train him, but Vyar

studied what I did, and he learned. He was a remarkable man, the Commandant, our most talented high magician in the ranger unit in decades. Good blood, as they say. Adequate in the field. A sly hand at politics, though not sly enough. Second best with a sword, I heard."

Rew grunted.

Cinda turned to Rew. "Why are we here? You want me to learn to talk to animals?"

"I want you to learn why more rangers don't do it," replied Rew. He looked to the old man. "She needs to learn more about that good blood you mentioned. Given what courses through my own veins, I didn't feel it'd sit right, coming from me."

The old man reached over and ran a hand over his bear's fur. "Subtle as a hammer behind a curtain."

"We've felt a large number of people dying in recent days," remarked Rew crisply. "It's time we get moving, time we understand there's more to it than an insane ghost forcing his children to kill each other. She needs to see the full picture."

"Understood. Let's see, where to begin," murmured the old man, his hand continuing to stroke the bear's head and neck. "Communion is low magic. All things are connected, and all life can be communed with. Some people have more talent than others, of course, and some life is more receptive. Rew, for example, has the skill to commune. He can do it almost as well as I, but chooses not to. Not with thinking animals, at least. I've heard rumors that some of the trees in the eastern wilderness are particularly fruitful, though."

Rew winked and gave an apologetic shrug.

"Most of the rangers have a little skill with communion, but it's not something we encourage in the younger generation. Aside from Vyar and Rew, there are few who could convince my bear to act. You witnessed how Vyar abused his talent. Rew doesn't use communion because he says he doesn't like the implications of building a bond with animal life. Feels too familiar, I suppose."

"I've noticed he doesn't like animals," remarked Cinda, giving

Rew a look from the corner of her eye. "Never travels by horse. Wait, what do you mean, too familiar?"

The old man smiled and glanced at Rew. The big black bear shifted and moved its head to rest upon the old man's armrest. It eyed the senior ranger as well.

"I like animals," said Rew. "I don't like what frequent communion does to them."

"Given what you hope to accomplish, Senior Ranger, is it wise to ignore a tool at hand?"

"We're not talking about me."

Eckvar shrugged. "You cannot become who you need to be if you ignore who you are."

"Tell me more," requested Cinda, her gaze turning to Eckvar's bear.

"Low magic is about connection. Connection is about two or more sides," responded the old man. "The first rangers, those who communed with wild life regularly, found that some individuals were easier to bond with than others. Those creatures had an open mind, you could say. The rangers, either looking for useful servants or perhaps just companions out in the wilderness, began encouraging those open-minded individuals to breed. The goal was to develop the trait, like farmers and herders have been doing for millennia with their livestock. Over time, it worked. The rangers would find pairs which bonded well with people, they'd instruct them to produce offspring, and soon, this village and ones like it were thick with squirrels, otters, owls, and I'm told primal sloths, though at some point the rangers must have realized that even a tame primal sloth is a dangerous animal to keep close."

"Vyar Grund had simians at his command," mentioned Cinda.

"I've heard," responded the old man, shaking his head. "It's inevitable, I suppose, that some would seek greater and greater power and wouldn't care what damage they caused on the path to it. Simians are strong and dangerous and far more intelligent than your average…" the man's voice dropped to a whisper, "bear. Simians would be vicious in a fight."

Cinda nodded then remarked, "As would a bear."

Ignoring her comment, the old man continued, "Vyar's life was that pursuit of strength and power. Whether with a blade, his animals, or his magic, he was always trying to become more than he was. That was unfortunate."

"So the rangers bred animals that they would talk to, but something happened…" said Cinda, trying to tease out the reason Rew had brought her there.

"They did breed the animals, and by doing so, they created something different," responded the old man. "The practice has fallen away, fortunately. After my own generation, Vyar was the only ranger who practiced communion regularly. Many don't have the talent. Others followed Rew's example and eschewed the ability. Your companions, Ang and Vurcell, would be naturals if they ever applied themselves to it."

"Why did they stop?" asked Cinda, glancing between Rew and Eckvar. "I understand Vyar took it too far, but why ban the practice because of one man's ambition? We wouldn't ban bows and arrows because one person shot someone, would we? I imagine animal companions could be extremely valuable to a ranger in the wilderness."

"Rangers are stewards of that wilderness," responded Rew. "Protectors of both man and the creatures that exist apart from man. Communion changes that. We make them more like us, and in my experience, that has not been a good thing."

Smiling down at his bear, Eckvar explained, "This girl has lived a long life, longer than any bear would survive on its own in the wild. She's been a companion to me for almost all of those years. But Rew is right. She's lost some of what made her… a bear. She no longer forages for food, does not breed, and while she sleeps as much as any good bear should, her activity largely consists of reminding me through our bond that it's time to eat. Do you see? Because of her connection to me, she is less, less than she should be. Without me, she could not survive."

Cinda frowned at the bear, and Rew sat quietly, watching.

"All of the animals we bred were less," continued the old man. "They were healthy. We saw to that. They seemed happy. They were elevated above the wild creatures they were kin to. They looked down on those wild creatures, though. Thought they understood something the rest of their species did not, but that wasn't the case. The animals are limited by their own biology. What they thought and saw was merely a reflection of the ranger who communed with them. They thought they were more, but they were less. It was a new class of animal we'd created. Haughty creatures filled with their own importance, but they were just a tool for the rangers to use, a mirror to ourselves. Do you see?"

Brushing a lock of dark hair behind her ear, Cinda asked, "I'm not sure. What do you mean they were less?"

"This bear cannot survive any longer in the wild. She can't forage. She can't find a mate. If she did, she wouldn't know how to raise her cubs if a ranger companion wasn't walking her through it. I had to do it for her mother. Her natural instincts have been replaced by my own thoughts and biases. She's not what she was—a bear. She looks down on wild bears. She thinks she's better because of her relationship with me, but she cannot survive on her own because of me."

"I still don't understand," admitted Cinda.

"My bear wouldn't understand either," acknowledged the old ranger. He sat back in his chair, rubbing the bear's head with one liver-spotted hand. "It is difficult to see the bars of your own prison."

"The bear is not viable," said Rew. "She's entirely reliant on Eckvar."

Bobbing his head, Eckvar's eyes glistened. "She's been a good companion to me, but she is not a good bear."

Cinda turned to Rew and threw up her hands. "I thought there'd be no more riddles. What are we talking about?"

"What if," said Rew, "the king was Commandant Eckvar, and you were the bear?"

Cinda's mouth fell open.

"The nobles of Vaeldon believe they are more than their fellow man, but they are just a tool bred by the king for his own purposes. That, lass, is why I do not commune with animals. I will not make a wild creature less than it is, like the king made us. I won't make another creature less than it is."

THAT EVENING, AFTER THE VILLAGE HAD QUIETED AND THE OTHERS had gone to bed, Rew visited Cinda again. The necromancer was back in her hut, the ghastly glow of her funeral fire hanging suspended near the low roof of the place. She'd been experimenting with control, and now, six distinct flames burned in the air, flickering like cold candles, supported by nothing.

Both of the books Cinda had been studying were open in front of her, and for the first time, Rew noticed she was not taking notes. She hadn't written down any conclusions she'd managed to scrape from the volumes, hadn't compared passages, hadn't produced any summaries like he was used to seeing scattered about the desks of scholars and arcanists.

"Memorized everything already?" he asked from the door to her hut.

Cinda jerked, this time evidently not having heard him approach. She gave him a look as if to chastise him for surprising her. "The knowledge in here shouldn't be shared beyond me."

Rew walked into the hut and crouched on his haunches, looking over her shoulder.

Cinda pointed at one of the books. "This is the one from Lucia. It must have been what Arcanist Salwart and Heindaw studied to erect their infernal machine. It's a practical guide to raising the dead and commanding them. It would allow anyone with my talent to perform a similar feat to what I did in Jabaan, assuming they could manage the power from within the king's crypt. Anyone who'd been bred like me could do it with this knowledge, and they may not have a ranger nearby to sock them in the face and break the flow of the magic. This book represents a tragedy waiting to happen, dozens of tragedies, each one worse than the last."

"Always happy to help."

"My talent… is not something that needs to be furthered. Like communion with animals, it's twisted me into something I'd rather not be. And like communion, simply banning it will not work. Vyar Grund did awful things, but it's nothing compared to what is possible with talent and the knowledge in these books. If the knowledge exists, and the ability to use it exists, someone will. Once I've learned what I can, I will destroy these volumes."

Rew nodded grimly.

"And then I must be destroyed as well. Even if it wasn't for… what is going to happen, the line needs to stop with me."

Rew put a hand on her shoulder. He understood what she was saying, and why she said it, but he didn't have the courage to voice the fear as she did.

"I'm an abomination, like that bear your friend raised as his pet. I've lost what made me human. The king has bred the nobility for hundreds of years, crafting us into a freakish subset of humanity that serves no purpose except to scramble for his approval and to keep the rest—the real people—in line. He's designed this, designed me. I'm an act in one of those traveling circuses, performing for his amusement, nothing more."

"It's not just you," said Rew.

"All of the nobility," agreed Cinda. "All of us. That's what we are, his dancing bears."

"I mean me, Cinda. The king… There is no one who understands dancing to Vaisius Morden's tune better than I."

Cinda smirked. "Fine. You and I are both dancing bears. It's not all about me, I know, but today… something about how docile that bear was got to me. We are Vaisius Morden's creatures just as surely as the bear is Eckvar's. The commandant is an old man, his time almost up. Do you think the bear will follow him to the grave, or will it find a way to survive?"

"I imagine—for the bear—a different life is hard to fathom, but life has a way of persisting."

Cinda grunted. "Is that why you brought us to this village? So I could meet Eckvar?"

"No," said Rew, squeezing her shoulder and giving a soft chuckle. "I knew it'd be safe here. This is the home of the king's rangers, the retired ones, but the king pays this place no mind. No one does. Old men returning from the wilderness to more wilderness. They're not useful to the king any longer, not like he'd want them to be. No one but the rangers gives this place any thought at all. I believed that's what we needed, a place of calm to catch our breath and for you to read these books, but I think what you saw tonight was valuable. We—both you and I—needed a reminder of what we fight for. Bloodshed and unnecessary deaths are reason enough, but beyond that, the king has enslaved us. He's bred us like simple animals, and we fight, and we squabble, for what crumbs he allows to trickle our way. We're less than we should be, and like Eckvar's bear, most of the time, we don't realize it."

"You do," said Cinda. "You found a different way. You've never begged for his handouts, have you? Not like the nobility has, like my family has."

"I don't know," said Rew, shifting uncomfortably. "I was raised in the creche. I learned to kill there and sharpened that skill in the world. I've killed many people, including my own brothers, which is what the king wanted from me all along. Today, am I acting on my own, or am I still dancing to his tune?"

Cinda frowned, thrown off guard by the comment. "But if—"

"I think," said Rew, "that prepared or not, it's time for us to go. I don't know what sort of invisible strings the king has tied to me, but I know we cannot stay here. We have to fight the best we're able, even if it means we do his wishes. My father would want Valchon and I to face each other, but that doesn't mean we should avoid the fight. It's hard to know what is right, isn't it? The king's shadow clouds everything, but I'm confident after Stanton, after so much other madness, we have to stop Valchon, and then we have to stop Vaisius Morden."

"I think you're right. We go to Carff, then?"

"Yes. Maybe we can't destroy forty-three temples to the Cursed Father, but there's a big one in Carff. That will help weaken the king. And then… what have you learned from the books?"

"I'll tell you in time."

Rew stared at her.

"How does it feel, having the boot on the other foot?" asked Cinda with a forced grin.

"I had good reasons for not sharing everything with you. You can see that now, can't you?"

"I can, and I have good reasons as well."

Grumbling, Rew replied, "Fine. I'll trust you."

"If we can destroy the temple in Carff, it will help," offered Cinda, "and Valchon, of course."

"I'll worry about Valchon, and you worry about the king," said Rew. He scratched his beard. "And ah, I'll worry about the king, too. We all should."

"Vaisius Morden is my task, Ranger."

"Yes, but he is my father."

Cinda looked at him, her green eyes sparkling. Then, she nodded.

Chapter Three

The next morning, Rew was outside looking over the slow-moving river that crawled by the rangers' village. He sipped his coffee and scratched his belly. The air was cool, but in Carff, it would be getting warm. The early spring was tolerable in the seaside city as a steady breeze blew in from the water, but by summer, the breeze would still, the heat would rise, and the spices in the market would struggle to mask the stench that men left in the gutters, alleyways, and the harbor. The humidity in Carff made it feel like that stink stuck to you, clinging to your skin and clothes until you left the place.

The sailors who filled the dockside taverns always looked eager to arrive and eager to leave. Of course, that could have something to do with purses quickly emptied and a new collection of illnesses from the women trolling the seedy ale sinks.

Rew sighed. He enjoyed an ale as much as anyone, but he didn't miss getting one at places like that. He preferred the quiet waystations on the far reaches of the kingdom, where a man could enjoy his ale and the quiet. The ranger sipped his coffee again and wondered if there would be a day he could venture back out to the wilds with no plan beyond seeing what was there. Get away from the detritus of Carff, the cold stone of Mordenhold, and even the apologetic presence of the ranger village. He would give a lot to breathe clean air and hear not a sound except the wind rustling the leaves. Blessed Mother, he would give up ale, if he had to.

Frowning, Rew contemplated whether or not that was true.

When he had almost finished his coffee, he heard soft steps behind him and kept looking out over the river. Whoever it was, they weren't an enemy. Only a ranger walked like that, but whatever they were coming to tell him so early in the morning, he didn't want to hear.

Ang appeared by his side. Without preamble, he informed Rew, "Ranger Petrana is dead. Vallo went to find her when we couldn't make contact, and he learned of it. Vallo got away cleanly, we think, but it's time for Vurcell and I to leave. The king might be content to leave you alone to face your brother, but he hasn't forgotten the rest of us."

Rew nodded grimly. His gaze stayed fixed on the river.

"They knew what they were agreeing to," said Ang. He put a hand on Rew's shoulder. "It's not your fault."

"Isn't it?"

Ang shrugged. "Vurcell and I are the ones who gathered them and led them to Iyre. They could have stayed at their stations. Others did."

"I'm the one who called to you and asked you to come."

"If the guilt is on you, then it's on us as well. Petrana wouldn't have wanted that. Not for any of us."

"She wouldn't have wanted to be killed by the king, either."

"Probably not," agreed Ang. He paused then added, "So we'll both carry the guilt, then?"

"Aye, I think that we will."

"Do you want us in Carff?"

Rew shook his head. "No. The real fight will be in Mordenhold. Start gathering everyone you can and get them in position. We should get word to everyone, even those who didn't join us. They didn't betray our trust to Valchon, and I'm not certain how the king will take that. We may not be the only ones at risk."

Ang rubbed his lips with a finger and asked, "Should I have Blythe coordinate with those still on duty?"

Rew grimaced. "They didn't join us before because it was too dangerous to leave their stations unguarded. That's still the case."

"She wants to be involved, Rew. Maybe she can join us, maybe she cannot, but why don't we let her decide? She's the one best equipped to decide if Eastwatch can suffer her absence. Besides, if the king starts moving against her and the others, Mordenhold won't be any more dangerous than staying home."

Waving a hand in assent, Rew asked, "You recall the glade in the mountains outside Mordenhold, about two days south of the city? There's a small lake there and a good view of the mountain peaks."

Ang shrugged.

"You don't... Ah, I think it was Vurcell who, well, got to know a woman there for the first time. Think he'll remember the place?"

Grinning, Ang nodded. "Perfect. I imagine he will recall that, and hopefully he can figure a better way to explain to the others where it is, or maybe I should hope he cannot. We could use a good laugh, and seeing my brother tell everyone about that will have me laughing for months."

"I'll try to meet you there, but if need be, the forest around the glade has never been touched by man," said Rew. "I can call to you there. If you hear my call, go to Mordenhold. If you hear to run, scatter and live your separate lives. You won't hear from me again if that's the case. I hope it doesn't come to that, but—"

"Rew, we want to do this. Grant us that, will you? Don't pretend we're foolish children who have no idea what we're doing, what we're risking."

Rew winced. "I'll try."

Ang rolled his eyes.

"It will be some time, no matter what happens," continued Rew. "We'll travel to Carff on the river then skirt around the coast and approach the city from the sea. I don't know if I can surprise Valchon, but I'll try. He'll be expecting me over land."

"The only thing more surprising than a ship would be you arriving at his gates on the back of a horse."

Rew finished his coffee and did not reply.

"It will take us time as well," continued Ang. "The rangers are strewn all across Vaeldon, and the hounds are nipping at our heels. I'd trust the others out in the wild indefinitely, but our contact points are in civilized lands. They had to be for the messages to reach them. Bringing everyone together means we're going to have to risk exposure, and we'll lose some more of us when we do."

Rew grimaced.

"It's what they wanted, Rew."

"Aye, you keep saying that, but it's not what I wanted."

"Well," said Ang, gesturing at Rew with his swordstaff. "It's a good thing none of us care what you want, and Rew, we have to talk about the village."

"I know. I'll warn Eckvar. You'll leave today?"

"Aye, Vurcell is packing now. Last I heard, he was fussing about needing new trousers. Like anyone is going to see us who cares if they are properly mended or not. Some days, he's worse than Anne."

"Safe travels," said Rew, stifling a bitter chuckle. "As safe as they can be."

"You as well," replied Ang. "Good luck in Carff, and give Valchon my warmest."

"I'll be sure to."

"Rew, listen to Anne."

Rew glanced at Ang. "You think my trousers—"

"She's not a military strategist," interjected Ang, "and she doesn't know any more of necromancy than Eckvar's bear, but she knows people. She's right about the connection the group has, the bond. You're all in it together, and it's only together you can succeed."

"Did she tell you to say that?"

Ang smirked. "She didn't, but if she had, I'd have repeated it faithfully for her. Rew, the ties between you are there. Both Vurcell and I can feel it. Real love. You're better together than you are apart."

"Watch it."

"Familial love, not… Real family is what I mean, someone you can put your back to and know they've got you covered. Not family like the one you had or the ones she and the children had. I don't need to tell you of the power in connections, the bonds we choose to be shackled with. The connection is there, forging incredible strength, so use it, will you?"

Rew shrugged and asked, "Where will you go first?"

"Back toward Iyre. Some of our brethren didn't flee far, and they'll be the quickest and easiest to reach. We can't find everyone before the king, so we'll try to gather as many as we're able and hope the rest have enough sense to go to ground."

Rew heard more movement in the village and he glanced over his shoulder. Behind them, Eckvar was shuffling from his hut to the communal hall where everyone broke their fast. His big, fat black bear was waddling after him. The old man felt their gaze and stopped, putting his hands into his opposite sleeves to keep them warm in the cool morning air.

"I heard Vurcell gathering provisions earlier this morning. You're leaving us, Ranger Ang?"

The ranger nodded.

"Then you will be gone soon as well, Senior Ranger Rew?"

"I will."

"Good luck."

"Commandant Eckvar," said Rew, approaching the old man, "I'm afraid our presence may have put your community at risk. Ang just shared with me that one of the rangers was killed, by the king or his minions, we believe. If Vaisius Morden finds we stayed here…"

Eckvar and his bear both snorted. "I've been dealing with the king a lot longer than you, lad."

"I don't think you can talk your way out of this. We mean to overthrow him or die trying. He won't forgive you for assisting us. When we came here, I didn't think he would suspect it. He's shown little enough interest in this place previously, but if he found Petrana, and she spoke…"

"I know I cannot talk my way out," assured the old commandant, "and if Petrana spoke, the king could already be here." Rew opened his mouth to comment, but Eckvar held up a hand to stop him. The old man continued, "The moment you arrived, I knew how it might end. Vaisius Morden ignores us because he can, but he will relish an excuse to strike at us. We know too much about him. We're a threat. He's never been able to act before because he'd lose all the other rangers in the bargain, but he'll have no constraints now. You should remember that. Keep those you care about close by."

"So you'll flee?"

Eckvar shook his head. "I'm too old for that nonsense. No, we'll stay. We'll fight if it comes to that. With a little luck, we'll make the bastard come and do the deed himself."

"I don't want your blood on my hands," argued Rew. "You should leave. You all have enough skill left in those ancient bones to disappear, and without the other rangers, he'll never find you."

"The king won't hear from us where you've gone, lad. He ought to know that, which could be what saves us. We're not worth his time, and if he doesn't come himself, whoever he sends will have a fight on their hands. We'll do some damage to his minions, if they come, but none of us have the craft to injure the king. That will be up to you."

Rew shook his head.

Before he could protest, Eckvar added, "There was talk of you becoming the Commandant, you know, instead of Vyar. I voted for him."

Frowning, Rew crossed his arms over his chest. "And why are you telling me that now?"

"I voted for him because he didn't mind getting blood on his hands," explained the former commandant. "It's necessary, sometimes. There was a period when you didn't mind looking into the dark, facing what lurks there. Then you fell in with the empath, became a ranger, and got soft. That's not a bad thing, Rew, but kindness isn't going to defeat the king."

Rew dropped his arms to his side, shifting uncomfortably. "Who I once was—"

"Is who you need to become again," interjected Eckvar. "It's time to get some blood on your hands. Otherwise, we're all going to line up behind your banner and die for nothing."

Rew gaped at the old commandant.

Eckvar clapped Rew on the arm before he and his bear began walking again to the hall. Over his shoulder, he called, "I'll have them pack some of those roasted nuts for you. I made some with honey. Anne and the children will like those."

Rew and Ang watched the old man walk away. Rew complained, "Old people."

"I know," agreed Ang. He shook himself and declared, "We've both got much to do. Let's get to it."

———

THE RANGER'S VILLAGE SAT ON THE BANKS OF A SLUGGISH RIVER, AND Rew thought it only sensible to take advantage of the waterway which led all the way down to the coast. From there, they could barter passage on a vessel, skirt along the southern shore of Vaeldon, and approach Carff from the sea. Valchon must be waiting on them to appear at his door, and it was the one avenue to approach Rew thought the prince might not expect. Not to mention, riding the waterways was faster and easier than walking, and he didn't think they would have much luck locating an invoker to open a portal for them. If Valchon expected them overland, they could arrive weeks or a month before he would anticipate it.

"Let me guess," grumbled Zaine, "horses were too... hungry or something?"

"Exactly. That's a great point," replied Rew. "You don't have to feed a canoe."

Sighing, Zaine looked down at the two narrow boats Eckvar had provided. They were slender crafts made of wood and bark, lightweight, with enough space for three passengers in each and a bit of cargo. That was all there was space for, though. There was no shade, which wasn't a problem in the forest, but might get uncomfortable near the coast. There was also no convenient and private way to relieve oneself while paddling, but that hadn't occurred to any of the women yet, and Rew felt it best to avoid the subject as long as possible.

"Come on. I've got a seat for you," offered Raif, standing calf-deep in the current, holding the boat for Zaine to climb into.

Anne, surreptitiously, had maneuvered herself into Rew's boat. He suspected it was because she planned for him to do all of the paddling, but the entire journey was downstream, and it would keep his arms and shoulders moving, which would pay off when he had to draw his sword again.

Cinda eyed her brother and then Anne. She pressed her lips together and declared, "I'll ride with you, Ranger."

Grinning, Rew gestured for the women to board. "I'll take the rear so I can paddle, unless you want to?"

They did not deign to respond.

Zaine clambered over the supplies to the bow of the gently rocking second canoe with careful grace, but when Raif slung a leg over the gunwale and tried to step in, he tipped the vessel over and pitched Zaine face first into the water.

Rew pushed his canoe off the bank and hopped in. He informed Anne and Cinda. "The provisions were well-wrapped in oilskin by the rangers, so no problem there. Those two… well, hopefully, this is a good lesson."

Zaine came up spitting a mouthful of river water and spluttering. Raif was back on his feet, standing knee deep and trying to right the canoe.

"I think, ah…" stammered the big fighter.

"You get in first," instructed Zaine, shaking water from her hands, her tunic clinging to her like skin. Her hair was plastered to her head, and she was waist-deep in the river. "I'll hold it steady. I can't get much wetter now, can I?"

Mollified, Raif struggled into the canoe. Zaine leaned heavily on the side of it, and Raif cursed and grabbed the gunwales to prevent himself from flopping over the edge into the water again. The thief gave him a predatory smile, then hopped into the boat. She told the fighter, "You're rowing."

Paddling around in front of the others, Rew called, "Right. Perhaps I should give a few pointers?"

LONG, EASY STROKES PROPELLED THEM DOWN THE RIVER, THE current doing half the work for them. The seats weren't exactly comfortable, but they were better than the carriage they'd been stuffed in the last time they'd been on the road toward Carff. While she'd grumbled for an hour or two about horses, once Zaine dried off, the speed and ease of passage on the water quieted her.

"No rapids on this river, are there, Ranger?" she called out suspiciously.

"None at all. This is the narrowest point we'll see, actually. As we get farther south, more tributaries join the flow, and it's quite wide by the time we reach the coast."

"Shavroe?" asked Raif, dipping a paddle and pushing his canoe forward to where it drifted beside Rew's.

"Aye, that's the city at the mouth of this river. I think we'll stop in, resupply, take some rest, and find a berth on one of the coastal-huggers. It's not Carff, but Shavroe is a big enough port we'll have no problem doing so. The entire Western Province ought to be in chaos, which will help cover our approach. There'll be a hundred vessels a day docking in Carff from the west, and they can't search them all. I think it will be an easier entry that way than attempting the gates. Worst case, if Valchon's net is too tight, we can disembark on the beaches west of Carff. That'll still save us weeks of travel."

"Chaos in the Western Province," wondered Cinda, "how do you think that will affect our travel? Will the surviving nobles there not pledge fealty to Valchon? Surely they can't think to continue the fight. I would have thought the madness was over with, except for the part we hope to play."

She was at the bow of Rew's canoe and had spent most of the day with her head tilted back, enjoying the dappled sunlight as it played over her face. She'd tossed her books into the fire the night before they'd left and seemed to have regained some sense of the girl she'd been at the start of their adventure. She wasn't, Rew knew, but skimming along the water must have reminded her of her old self, which reminded Rew of how she'd been as well. It was bittersweet.

He cleared his throat and answered her, "I suspect most of the common folk aren't aware of the Investiture, much less what it means that two of the princes have fallen. As long as armies aren't marching across their fields, trying to recruit their sons, or raising their taxes, they'll pay no more attention than they have to. For a farmer or a brewer, it doesn't make much difference who sits the throne. It only matters that your family is home, that you've coin in your pockets, and the markets have the goods you need."

"All of this chaos you are predicting is just the nobles, then?"

"It's always the nobles," replied Rew. "Outside of them, the spellcasters, and the soldiers, few even know what's going on. There will be rumors, to be sure, but the nobility isn't exactly free with the details of how the king is winnowing down his sons, you know? It may be a relief for the common folk, not having anyone fiddling with the laws or demanding some new tithe. They'll carry on as they always do."

Rew dipped his paddle and churned it through the water, sending them skating down the center of the channel.

"The advantage for us will be the distractions for the nobility and everyone in their service. They will fall in behind Valchon, as you say, but until he's crowned king, they'll use the opportunity to reposition themselves. Earning the surviving prince's favor is only one way to gain power during the Investiture. There will be assassinations, minor clashes, that sort of thing as the remaining nobles try to gobble up more territory from each other. That sort of conflict is the perfect cover for us. It's like pinching the bum of a serving wench who's got her eyes on the performance on stage."

"A vulgar way to put it…" said Cinda.

Rew shrugged, but she didn't see the motion.

Anne turned around and scowled at him. He winked back at her. The empath had run the only inn and tavern back in East-watch, and she knew he wasn't one to pinch a bum, whether or not the lass was distracted, but she would feel remiss if she didn't give him a look over it, and he would feel remiss if he didn't slide in the occasional glib quip with the sole purpose of annoying her.

It was a long journey to Shavroe. They had to entertain themselves somehow.

The day passed mostly in quiet as everyone kept to themselves and considered what was to come. It seemed Anne and the younglings were actually impressed with how smooth the journey had begun, and it helped that in the isolated forest near the ranger village, they saw no one else on the water. That would change as they moved farther south, but for now, it was as if they had the world to themselves. The party was so content that not even the complexity of relieving oneself caused much of a stir.

Raif and Zaine became not exactly coordinated at paddling their canoe, but they managed to only flip over one more time when they both saw a turtle and got excited about it. Their bickering over that spill was friendly and had no edge. Rew offered to let Anne and Cinda have a turn paddling, and Anne crisply informed him she was doing the cooking, so he could move the boat. He grinned at her back, having expected her to claim something along those lines. Cinda accepted the paddle he offered, and even occasionally dipped it in the river, but as often as not, she turned them in the wrong direction.

Rew wondered more than once whether it was intentional, and if it was, he granted her a grudging respect. It was the same way he'd gotten out of washing the pots after supper each evening. Do it poorly enough once or twice, and no one asked you to do it again. Most of the time, Cinda sat with the paddle sideways across her lap, basking in the sun and watching the banks slip past them.

Traveling with the current and paddling leisurely was pleasant, and while they had somewhere to be, they did not strain themselves. There were weeks ahead on the water, and they would face inclement weather, hard times paddling, and other difficulties. In those first days, Rew let them enjoy the trip.

At the end of the first day, as dusk began to dim the light on the water, the ranger kept an eye open and found a clear space near a gentle bank. They steered the canoes over and dragged them free of the water, lest the current take them in the night. Anne handed Raif a small hatchet and asked him to cut some firewood. Then, she began unpacking the pots and utensils for supper. Rew took Zaine deeper into the woods to have a look around and to find some game trails where they could set snares. He found the signs of rabbits and taught the thief how to catch them.

"We'll come back tomorrow and check," he told her, pointing at a snare they'd just set. "I'd wager a couple of silver we'll find this occupied at sunrise."

They didn't see anything within a quarter league of them except forest, so they returned, and Rew gathered his things to toss a fishing line into the river.

"Think you'll have any luck?" asked Anne from near the merry little fire where she was organizing her supplies.

"I do," said Rew. He pointed to where the bank overhung the water. "Perfect spot, right here. See the bugs beginning to fly about? Supper time for the fish as well as for us."

"I got some oil from the rangers," responded Anne. "Catch us a few big ones, and I'll fry them up. We're counting on you, Rew."

He snorted. "Don't spoil my luck."

Rew fished. Before long he hauled in several heavy trout. Raif and Zaine sparred while he fished, though at least from Raif's perspective, it appeared to be mostly about the flirting and not the fighting. Zaine took the opportunity of Raif's complacency to wallop him with the sticks she was using to practice with.

Cinda sauntered by to watch and gave the thief a wink, which spoiled any progress her brother might have been making with Zaine, and then she joined Anne at the fire. She asked the empath, "Teach me?"

Smirking at her, Anne replied, "Of course, but why now, lass? You've been on the road with me for months, and you haven't picked up as much as a paring knife unless I told you to."

"Because… people ought to know how to cook," replied Cinda. "It's the only way to feed yourself, if you don't have servants and others doing your bidding. I… I'm not a noble, anymore. Not really. I've decided that I should know how to feed myself."

Anne looked at the girl then at Rew. The ranger cast his fishing line back in the river and tried to ignore the conversation.

"Well, first…" began Anne, and then she proceeded to teach Cinda how to fry fish.

Chapter Four

The days on the river passed easily. They would drift downstream, paddling periodically when they floated into sluggish eddies and letting the current take them when it picked up. The farther south they got, the more people they saw on the water, though at no point was it crowded. Commerce across Vaeldon would have come to a standstill months before as conflicts erupted amongst the nobles trying to curry favor with the princes, and it would be worse now that two of the princes were dead. Major families would be striving to align behind Prince Valchon, and minor families would be in open battle with each other hoping they had an opportunity to smite rivals and expand their holdings before anyone noticed.

The provincial capitals were far off, but rumors had a way of flying. The details of the rise of the undead in Jabaan and the destruction of the Cursed Father's temple in Iyre might not reach the hinterlands and wouldn't be understood if they did, but people had heard enough that they were nervous. They would stay near their homes until things quieted back down.

But people still had to eat. Even when there were not the barges and merchants' sloops that might normally trawl the river, there were fishing boats, rafts, and local peddlers who had an easier time transporting their goods on water than on the roads. The party steered clear of most of the other boats and the villages they traveled between, though periodically, Rew would paddle his canoe up beside some of the rafts which served as floating taverns for the fishermen and others on the river. They served grilled skewers of meat, whatever fruits and vegetables the nearest village specialized in, and crudely distilled spirits or ale and wine. The stuff was cheap, which was either a positive or a negative, depending on how one looked at it.

The party didn't speak more than necessary when they stopped beside the floating taverns, and they got few questions. Rew imagined that in more peaceful times, it would be common to see travelers along the river, and their group was not so far out of place that it drew curiosity.

Rew and Raif did most of the paddling, but it was easy work, and it kept them fit. Zaine began fishing as they went, and while the center of the channel was a poor place to do it, she had time on her side and most days hauled in enough fish to supplement the supplies they'd brought from the ranger village.

Anne spent her hours mending their clothing, cleaning Zaine's fish, organizing their supplies, and other small tasks she could perform while perched in the middle of a canoe. The empath, while clearly enjoying the time on the water, was never content if she couldn't stay occupied.

Cinda was quiet and rarely busied herself with anything. She'd destroyed the two books she'd been reading, but Rew guessed she was still thinking about them. She would stare at the riverbanks passing beside them but didn't rise to any of the banter amongst the rest of the party unless she was directly asked a question. At night, she would help Anne with the cooking. She always volunteered to clean up the dishes and pots, and then she would lie on her bedroll looking at the stars above them.

With limited physical activity, Cinda's necromancy meant she hardly needed to sleep, but she went through the motions. Rew wasn't sure if it was to convince the others she could live something like a normal life, or to convince herself. He tried speaking to her, digging into those strange thoughts that must be coursing through her head, but she brushed him off. She was not depressed, exactly, but she wasn't happy, either. At night, he watched her lying on her back, her green eyes reflecting the night sky, but she wouldn't turn his way even when he was sure she could feel his presence.

He supposed there was little to be happy about, except for the moments of levity during the long days on the water. Ahead of them was all darkness and danger. That weighed on Cinda more than the other younglings because she understood. Rew wanted to take the burden from her, to help carry it, but he didn't know what to say to cut through the fugue that clouded her mind. He tried, in stuttering, flailing attempts, but she turned him away with brusque responses or she changed the subject.

Asking Anne quietly one evening while Cinda was down at the water, Rew wondered whether there was anything they could do to cheer the young noblewoman, but Anne simply shook her head.

"What would you do, have a party for her?"

Rew shrugged.

"She'll get through it," said Anne, though from her tone, it wasn't clear she believed what she was saying.

Rew wasn't sure any of them were going to get through it, not really. Things weren't going to be like they had been, and maybe Cinda realized that, while Rew still needed to. He cursed at himself. He had realized it, but he wouldn't let himself admit it. Just days ago, when he'd been dreaming about disappearing into the wilderness again, he'd been ignoring the reality of the situation. It was like an ache, what he wanted and what he knew wasn't going to happen. He knew, in his head he knew, but a part of him wouldn't give up hoping for something different. Perhaps Cinda had grappled with that reality already and emerged out the other side.

But while Cinda was quiet and rarely joined the conversation, she did seem to enjoy being around it. She watched her brother and Zaine avidly, whether they were sparring or flirting, or frequently, both. She helped Anne as much as she could when they were on land, and she never moved off to be alone.

The one person she didn't seem to appreciate being around was Rew, and it took him nearly a week, but he eventually decided it was because he, more than the others, understood her burden. He knew what she was thinking, what worried her. He knew the pain that was in her blood, and she didn't want to be reminded of it. Cinda didn't need to talk about what was coming. She needed to forget it, at least for a while. Rew hadn't been helping. Once he realized her need and started having simple innocuous conversations with her, Cinda's attitude toward him warmed.

The trip was a pleasant continuation of the rest they'd gotten in the ranger village, but it came to an end one morning an hour after they'd gotten on the water. They rounded a bend, and in front of them, stretching across the waterway, was a wall of debris. Waterlogged tree branches, refuse, and boats. It took Rew a moment, but he saw behind the first layer of wreckage that a chain net had been strung across the water.

"Bandits," he called to the other canoe, loud enough for Raif and Zaine to hear him, but hopefully not loud enough for the sound to reach the shore.

He backpaddled, slowing the canoe and then letting it drift on the current. Several vessels were wedged against the chain net in front of them, and on the riverbank, Rew could see where others had been beached after they'd presumably been overtaken by river pirates. It was a tactic more common to blockade a city during a siege, but it worked well enough for stopping all of the boats coming downriver. There was no way to sail past the chain net, and by the time victims saw the trap, it was too late to get away.

Rew turned and looked behind them, still holding the paddle but eyeing where his longsword and hunting knife were sticking out beside their gear. The bandits would stop them with the chain then close in from behind preventing any escape, except no one was behind them.

Zaine stood carefully in her canoe while Raif held them steady. She'd grabbed her bow and nocked an arrow and was scanning the shoreline, looking for the enemy.

Rew waited, the two canoes floating slowly closer to the barrier, but nothing happened. No one came out to surprise them, no arrows came whistling their way, no boats appeared to block the passage back upriver.

"You feel anything?" he asked Cinda.

The necromancer was looking around as curious as the rest of them. "Death near those boats on the shore. Ten, fifteen souls. Days old. Might have been more than one incident. More nearby."

"Most of the river traffic we've seen has been local, and the last village was half a day behind us," mused Rew. "It's a good spot to set an ambush, far enough away the locals wouldn't quickly discover it and warn everyone headed this way. They can probably unanchor those chains and move them when things get too hot around here."

"Aye," said Zaine, still standing in her canoe, "but isn't the whole point they should come out and demand all of our jewels and women or something? Or… could they be waiting for us to come ashore?"

"Those boats can float," said Raif, pointing with his paddle toward the shoreline. "I think they'd come after us rather than letting us head back upstream. Surely no unarmed merchant would set foot on the bank right here and let themselves be taken. Unless, do you think, we scared them off?"

No one responded to that.

"Maybe someone killed the bandits but couldn't figure a way to release the net," suggested Anne.

"Perhaps," said Rew, not fully believing the explanation. He waited a moment longer, but when the bank and the river remained silent, he advised, "Let's go look. We're not getting these canoes around the chain unless we portage, and even if we turn around, we've got to come ashore somewhere. I don't know of any highways near this section of river, so if we leave the waterway, we'll delay ourselves by weeks. Maybe the local peddlers can wait for someone to clear the way, but we can't."

"Unless they are hiding in those trees waiting on us," warned Zaine. "We could be walking into a trap."

"It doesn't look like anyone is alive around here," said Raif, leaning over and struggling to pull his armor from where it'd been strapped down in the canoe. "But if they are, they're going to find out we bite a lot harder than a common peddler."

"I think if someone was spying on us right now, I'd see signs of it. Everything looks to me like this area has been abandoned for days," responded Rew. "We'll come ashore quietly, and I'll scout around. If we see anyone, we get back in the boats as quick as we can. Try not to engage. If it comes to that, stay—"

"We know. Stay behind you," finished Raif sardonically. "We've traveled with you before, Ranger."

Rew grinned at him. "Good advice never goes stale."

Raif rolled his eyes dramatically.

They reached the bank and disembarked, pulling their canoes onto shore between two larger vessels. One was a fishing boat, and the other was a slender ketch that could have been used to transport paying passengers up and down river. Rew peeked over the gunwales, but both boats were empty of people and anything of value. It looked like they'd been stripped of equipment and would need to be refitted before they were worthy of a long journey. Raif and Zaine crouched down near the ends of the boats, peering into the forest around the river.

"Stay here," whispered Rew. "Guard the canoes. I'll come back within the hour."

Showing the comfort they'd all gained in each other's skill, Raif simply nodded, and Rew slunk from the shoreline and the boats into the cover of the bushes a dozen paces away. It was still early in spring, but they were far enough south that the air was heady with new growth. For one of his skill, there was more than enough cover to keep him out of sight if anyone was lurking nearby.

First, Rew moved to the end of the chain that held the net across the river and found it looped around a thick tree trunk. A sturdy lock clamped it in place. He thought Zaine could open the device, but he would explore first before coming back to get her. For those without a thief handy, the only other way to clear the river would be to cut down the tree or figure a way to snap a link in the stout chain. Both were possible but wouldn't be easy to accomplish before the river pirates found you.

From what he could see, there'd been no recent attempts to open the way, though the metal on the lock and around it showed old scarring. It wasn't the first time someone had used the technique to block a river, he guessed. These pirates had experience. He listened for a moment but didn't hear anything except for the normal sounds of the forest.

If someone had fought the bandits and killed them, why hadn't they bothered releasing the chain? Presumably they would have wanted to continue their travel on the river, and even if they didn't, it was the right thing to do. He scratched his beard. If someone had fought the bandits, where were the bodies? Pirates would hide their victims, but if anything, pirates killed by vigilantes would be displayed as a warning to others. No one would bother burying the ruffians.

Rew moved farther out and then walked a semi-circle around where they'd come ashore. He found a newly worn path through the forest that must have been from the river pirates, but nothing else. The bodies of the victims could have been dumped in the river, stolen goods might have been carted away, but there were no signs of violence on shore, and the bandits wouldn't have left their chain in place if they were relocating. The net of thick metal links would be more valuable than any cargo they would take off an individual boat this far from the mercantile capitals.

Rew considered broadening his circle but instead decided to

follow the path deeper into the woods. He moved two dozen paces off to the side and stalked parallel to it, giving himself a chance to find cover if someone came along the path, but they didn't.

Instead, he found the remains of the bandits' encampment. From the stink of their latrine, they'd been there a week or two and had gotten comfortable but hadn't been there long enough to erect any permanent structures. There was a dead campfire, hammocks hung between several trees, a large pile of a variety of goods they must have stolen from passing boats, and a smaller pile of mutilated bodies.

It took no time at all to realize they'd been attacked by Dark Kind. The creatures had paid justice to the pirates, rending and tearing their flesh as they'd consumed them. There were several dead narjags in the heap as well, but from the numbers, it appeared the Dark Kind had gotten the better of the fight.

Rew squatted and then crab-walked around the scene, seeing prints from a score of narjags and half a dozen ayres. He scowled. He wasn't familiar with the lonely area they were traveling through and had no idea whether Dark Kind were common in the region. They did find isolated places and gather there, but none of the villages upriver showed any of the defensive structures he'd expect if they had narjags for neighbors. If the Dark Kind were known to haunt the place you lived in, you learned to defend yourself, or else you didn't live for long.

There was a considerable amount of wealth piled around the camp, but most of it was bulk goods or personal items. Rew doubted any of it would be of use to his party, so he didn't bother to search it. They'd been restocked with the finest quality of goods in the kingdom by the rangers, and Eckvar had given them a fat purse as well. Even had Rew wanted the coin he could get from selling the stolen goods in the camp, they were traveling by canoe, which would make transporting bulk items impractical.

Rew stretched his back and looked around the campsite again. There was another path from the camp that led deeper into the forest. The way the bandits had come? It had the look of a hunter's tract, and he suspected that the bandits had followed it when selecting a site for their piracy.

He muttered to himself. The path led deeper into the forest, away from the river, implying whoever used it didn't live in the village they'd seen half a day north. Did those people know they were sharing the forest with narjags and ayres?

Rew turned and went back to find the others.

ZAINE SET TO PICKING THE LOCK THAT HELD THE CHAIN, BUT ONCE IT was released, it would take some time for the current to clear the debris that was stuck in the channel. Rew figured they had an hour or two before the way was open enough for their canoes to slip through, so he headed back to the site of the river pirates' camp and then moved deeper into the forest. The tract went somewhere, and with bandits and Dark Kind moving about in the area, he was curious where.

He'd only made it five hundred paces when he heard voices ahead. Rew melted into the forest and drew his longsword.

A deep voice and a high one resolved into a middle-aged man and a boy. A boy and his father, it looked like. They wore the clothes of foresters, and both carried bows with arrows nocked. On their belts, they had quivers and utilitarian knives, with small travel packs on their backs. Woodsmen who must have some sense of what lay ahead.

"Ho, friends," called Rew, stepping into view. The man immediately drew his arrow back, but Rew called again, "I'm not with the pirates. We were traveling down the river and found their net and then their camp."

The man did not lower his bow, but he didn't release his arrow, either. Rew held his longsword to the side but didn't sheath it. He thought the pair weren't threats, but you never knew.

"You killed them?" asked the gruff man. "Rumor came on the river they were all dead. Thought I'd come and make sure."

Rew glanced at the boy.

"He was supposed to stay behind, but I found him waiting for me an hour outside our village. Far enough I'd waste my day if I had to bring him back. Smart lad."

Rew smiled. "Children."

"Children," agreed the man.

"The bandits are all dead," confirmed Rew. "We got stuck by their net, but when no one appeared to try and rob us, we came ashore to investigate. The remains of their camp are just a quarter league back down this path."

The man lowered his bow and spit to the side. "Good riddance. They've been plaguing us for a week. We've been trying to muster enough strong arms to force them out, but we're not soldiers around here. We sent word to the baron, but he's days away and like as not won't help anyway." The man paused. "If not you, then who killed these men? If we can pass, I'd like to see for myself. I've some skill at reading the signs."

"Dark Kind," replied Rew. "Narjags and ayres."

The boy laughed, disbelief on his grinning face, but the man appeared worried.

"Are they common around here?" questioned Rew.

"Not since my father's time, but I've heard some serious men talking…" mumbled the forester. "We thought at first there was trouble with another noble. I've heard of armies marching in the east. That shouldn't affect us here, I told everyone, but then… The baron has been calling for men. Everyone's been ignoring the call, thinking he's making some play to expand the barony, but two days downriver, there was an… attack. My cousin saw what was left. Awful, nasty stuff. The whole village was killed and…"

"Eaten?"

"Aye," replied the man, glancing at his son with pained eyes.

"The Dark Kind are a lot closer than two days," warned Rew.

"Can I see?" asked the man.

"Of course," responded Rew. He glanced at the boy. "It's not pleasant."

The man shifted on his feet.

Rew told him, "I can take your son around the encampment to my friends. We can offer some protection while you look at the site and a fire tonight if you don't want to travel back alone. We have women with us, if that gives you any assurance."

The man seemed to make a decision and agreed to Rew's offer. They took the boy wide of the bandit camp and left him in Anne's care. As they walked away, the empath was already asking if the boy was hungry, complimenting his bravery, and making the lad feel comfortable.

"You're sure it's the Dark Kind?" asked the forester. "You've seen their work before?"

"I'm sure," responded Rew, and left it there.

The man seemed to take the ranger at his word. When they found the camp, he was messily sick to the side. When he'd finished emptying his belly, the forester stood back from the charnel scene, wiping his mouth with the back of his hand.

"I... apologies," muttered the man. "I'm a hunter, but this... I never seen anything so brutal, even to animals. My thanks, keeping the boy from witnessing it."

Rew nodded.

"I can look, but, ah..."

"Twenty narjags, six ayres," replied Rew. "Are you familiar with these creatures?"

"I've heard the stories, like anyone has."

"The stories are true."

The man cringed.

Rew pointed toward where he'd seen the tracks of the Dark Kind departing. "Headed southeast, though I didn't follow them far."

"Arhold," muttered the forester.

"I haven't heard of it."

"It's a town of about five hundred." The man shifted uncomfortably. "My own village is northeast. I've got to get my boy back, warn the others."

Rew closed his eyes.

Would the Dark Kind attack a town of five hundred? A year ago, he would have said no. A year ago, he would have been shocked to find twenty of them and their ayres traveling together at all. Such fractious creatures would have turned on each other as quickly as they would attack any people they stumbled into, but the evidence was there, and he'd seen stranger things over the last few months.

Did it matter whether or not the creatures would attack a village? They went to face Valchon and then the king. The fate of Vaeldon rested in their hands. Only Cinda could defeat Vaisius Morden. Only their party could end the reign of a two-hundred-year-old necromancer who treated his kingdom and its populace like a feast for his own pleasure and power.

"Ranger," said a quiet voice. Rew turned and saw Cinda at the edge of the bandit camp, her arms crossed over her chest, her face blank. "Zaine picked the lock. My brother hauled some of the chain out of the way. We can get through."

Rew's lips twisted into a sour grimace.

"I heard talk of a town?"

"Arhold," said the forester. "It's a day southeast of here. Same way these creatures went. I suppose it's too late to get word to the town or send them any help. Good strong backs in Arhold, though. I hope… I think, they may be able to hold out. Ah, these narjags, you've had experience with 'em? It's not as bad as… it's not all like this, like what they did here, is it?"

Rew and Cinda held each other's gaze.

"Five hundred people is a pittance compared to what I feel happening out there," whispered Cinda.

"That's what my father would say," murmured Rew.

Cinda closed her eyes, and when they opened, it was almost as if her funeral fire was burning deep within those orbs. "It's a bad idea and a poor strategic decision, but we're not lost yet, are we?"

"I like to think we're still fighting the good fight."

"I'll tell the others we're going to Arhold."

Rew turned to the forester. "I'm afraid we cannot offer you that campsite, Friend."

"Who are you?"

Staring into the forest, southeast toward Arhold, toward the Dark Kind, Rew responded, "The King's Ranger."

Chapter Five

R ew couldn't think of a good reason not to follow the
pathway the forester had described leading to Arhold. The
Dark Kind were near feral. They acted purely on instinct and
would not have set an ambush or left scouts behind to watch for
pursuit. They only thought ahead, to their next meal.

There was no complaint from the group when Rew had told
them the situation. They'd all gathered supplies from the canoes,
hidden the boats within the forest so they could come back, and
then marched into the trees after a hurried midday meal. Arhold
was a distraction, a waste of time, but they had to do it to prove to
themselves they still had a shred of humanity left.

The tens of thousands of deaths in Jabaan trailed Rew and
Cinda like a cloak of sorrow. They couldn't run from it. They
couldn't shed that weight. They had to carry it. Perhaps it would
be an easier burden if they could counter it with some good.

In his own mind, Rew had tried to justify what had
happened in Jabaan. Calb would have killed at least as many
battling with his brothers. That was probably true, but it didn't
matter. It wasn't Calb who'd nearly destroyed the city. Rew had
demanded Cinda raise the dead so that they could escape. When
her magic had spiraled out of control, instead of stopping her,

he'd used it. The bloodshed of innocents was on his hands, and however he tried to rationalize it, whatever reasons he concocted, much of the palace had died in the battle because of what he'd set in motion and because of what he'd waited to stop.

They could make those tradeoffs, sacrifice some lives to win Vaeldon. They had to if they wanted to defeat Valchon and the king. It left him hollow, but he could carry that burden, live with it. The alternative was failure, and that would be worse. They would not give up and leave the kingdom to the king. Rew could shoulder the burden of a mistake. He could second-guess himself and keep moving. But he couldn't choose to turn his back on his responsibility again, not and live with himself. He had to try.

His brothers and his father would have ignored Arhold, and that meant Rew would not. He wrestled with the logic of it and eventually decided maybe that was the point. Going to Arhold was illogical. It wasn't a decision he was making with his head but with his heart. It was foolish and soft-hearted to ignore the importance of their quest, and that was why they had to do that exact thing. They still had to listen to their hearts, or they would be lost.

As they strode down the path, he and Cinda walked close together, and once, she reached out and gripped his hand, squeezing it tightly. He looked at her and saw his thoughts reflected in her eyes. They didn't need words to explain how they both felt. Their sorrow was heavy, but they would manage. This would help.

"Blessed Mother, I wouldn't mind an ale tonight," groaned Rew, leading the party down the forest path, thinking that in addition to his heart, he ought to be listening to his gut, and his gut was saying to get drunk.

"You'd like an ale every night," accused Zaine.

He peeked over his shoulder, forced a smile onto his lips, and winked at her. "Some more than others."

"It's out of our way, but this doesn't have to take long,"

declared Raif from the end of the line. "Twenty narjags, six ayres, we've faced worse odds and finished them quickly."

"You nearly got killed when we faced better odds," reminded Rew.

"Aye," retorted Raif, reaching back to pat the hilt of his greatsword over his shoulder. "That was then. This is now. We can handle this."

The lad made a fair point, and after another hundred paces, Rew told him so. When they'd first departed Eastwatch, Raif knew as much about swinging his greatsword as he did about shaving his chin and wooing the ladies, which was to say he knew nothing worth knowing. The fighter still spent more times feeling for hairs on his face than he did sliding a razor over them, and as far as Rew knew, he'd had no success with the fairer sex, but Raif had learned the use of his blade.

With Rew's tutelage, supplemented by Ang and Vurcell recently, and a burning desire to impress Zaine, Raif had thrown himself into practice, forging himself into the fighter he'd once dreamed he would become. Now, Rew would stake Raif against any soldier in the king's legion, if not against many of the king's rangers. And Zaine had become a fair shot with her bow, when she wasn't thinking about it. When she got an opportunity, she didn't hesitate with her daggers.

Cinda… Rew sighed. Cinda was the most dangerous of them all.

He kept walking silently.

They were unfamiliar with the terrain they traveled, but trusting the forester's estimations, Rew stopped them two hours from Arhold. They had moved quickly, their legs and bodies well-rested after so many days on the water. There was still some daylight left, but when approaching Dark Kind, Rew had learned to go cautiously and to avoid encounters at night whenever possible. If they came much closer and the wind turned against them, the Dark Kind could detect their scents.

Raif had been confident they would be able to face the pack

with little difficulty, and Rew agreed, but that didn't mean they should be reckless.

Rew would take the last watch, and he would wake the others an hour before dawn. They would cover the remaining walk to the town, and with any luck, they would arrive outside of Arhold while the narjags were still circling outside of the place. They would get help from the village if they could, but as Raif claimed, Rew thought their chances against twenty narjags were fair to good.

They'd considered walking on into the night, but the truth was, either Arhold had defended against the Dark Kind, or it was too late. The creatures had too much of a head start, and while they'd decided to come against all logic, Rew wouldn't entirely ignore practical realities.

ANNE WOKE HIM, AND REW ASSUMED HIS WATCH. THE AIR WAS CRISP, the sky cloudless. He stretched then began wandering around the outskirts of their camp. The breeze was calm and hardly stirred the new leaves budding on the trees. He could hear Raif—no, Zaine—snoring. He scowled at her dark form. How could a girl her age snore so loudly? Shaking his head, he kept walking, listening as the first of the morning birds began to stir and to chirp. In an hour, their songs would fill the forest.

There was something else. Rew stopped walking, just listening and extending his senses. He felt nothing near them, but he could hear something. After cracking his neck and removing his cloak, he climbed a tree. There was enough light from the early dawn to make it easy, and he ascended thirty paces then stopped and listened.

Yips like that a small dog would make, or an ayre.

He waited, hanging in the branches of the tree. The sounds were far off, and with the gentle wind, he suspected they were too far away from the ayres for the beasts to pick up the party's scent.

The barks were coming from the southeast, and they were moving but not very far. Had the ayres surrounded Arhold and were circling it? It matched what he was hearing, but that was beyond the thinking of the narjags and their mounts, unless…

He kept listening and began to wonder, were the sounds he was hearing caused by just half a dozen ayres? Could this pack be coordinated somehow, like others they'd encountered? Uncomfortable thoughts scratching at him, Rew descended and woke the others half an hour before they'd planned.

———

THEY CREPT CAUTIOUSLY DOWN THE PATH. THE WOOD WAS SHOWING more signs of human occupation as they got closer to the town— stumps where trees had been felled, tracks on the path, but so far no Dark Kind. They could hear them, though. High-pitched yips echoed through the forest, coming from several directions. Rew concluded there were more ayres ahead than the signs they'd found back at the river pirates' campsite. It was a sound assumption there would be more narjags ahead as well.

He had drawn his longsword, and the others had their weapons out also. They moved as quietly as Raif could, his steel armor clanking and scratching with every step. Holding up a hand, Rew paused them. He crouched, his weapon at the ready.

There was a crash of broken branches. Heavy bodies were smashing through the undergrowth.

A blue-skinned ayre burst into view fifty paces in front of them on the path. It barked a quick, eager call. There was a narjag on its back, and the foul creature kicked its heels into the mount, pointing a filthy shortsword at Rew. The ayre charged, and two more of its brethren came pelting out from the woods behind the party.

"Those are yours!" cried Rew.

Zaine released an arrow, which smacked into a narjag rider. The Dark Kind flipped over backward, falling off its ayre, but the canine creature kept coming, its jaws spread wide, spittle flying as it ran.

Raif jumped in front of the others, thrusting forward with his greatsword like it was a pike and he was taking a cavalry charge. The ayre in its eagerness plunged directly onto the blade. The enchanted steel slammed through its body and plunged deep until the beast crashed into Raif. The fighter took the blow on his shoulder and held his ground as the dead ayre slumped in front of him.

Cinda stepped to the side and whipped her hand like she was throwing a knife in a tavern. A billowing cloud of cold fog rushed from her and engulfed the second ayre and its rider, enveloping them in death's breath. The ayre took two more steps and then collapsed, both it and the narjag stone dead.

It all happened in a blink, and then the first ayre, which had appeared farthest away, was bounding at Rew.

The ranger stepped into the attack, slashing around with his longsword and taking the ayre in the throat. His enchanted longsword cleaved through the blue skin, decapitating the big dog-like creature and carrying through to smash into the narjag, flinging the Dark Kind back, a trail of foul, sticky blood flying behind it in a fan. The narjag landed in a crumpled heap, and the ayre skidded to a stop, two paces behind its severed head.

The party listened for more of the creatures, but all they heard were excited yelps in the distance.

"They're coming toward us," warned Rew.

Zaine gestured down the path to Arhold. "After you."

They started moving, and Cinda called out, "Why were there three of them? You said six attacked the river pirates, right? I can hear... more than three remaining out there. There have to be a dozen."

"It could be more than one group converging on Arhold," speculated Rew, and before the others asked, he added, "If that's the case, something must be coordinating them. It's rare to see so many together, and why haven't they attacked? In my experience, Dark Kind fight, or they run, nothing else."

"Can we talk about this after we get to Arhold?" asked Anne, jogging behind Rew down the path.

"Sure, but I don't know if it will be any safer there."

The sounds of the ayres were growing closer, and there was a cacophonous burst of howls behind them when the creatures must have stumbled across the bodies of their brethren, but by then, Rew and the others were emerging into a clearing that surrounded the small town of Arhold.

The settlement was surrounded by temporary fortifications. Debris piled between several of the buildings—tipped-over tables wedged in gaps, lattices of thatch that must have been pulled down from rooftops, and wagons wedged in between fieldstone houses. It wasn't much, just enough to slow the rush of attackers and maybe give the defenders time to pick them off.

They couldn't tell, on the run as they were, but it appeared between one hundred and two hundred modest buildings were in the community, and they could see several score of people. Men with a motley assortment of weapons and farming implements stood behind the crude barriers. Young boys and women were perched on rooftops with bows.

Those boys and women were standing and pointing, and Rew guessed that behind them, ayres were racing in pursuit. He and the others ran toward the town, where several of the men were pulling back a section of the barrier.

"Hurry!" called the men.

They made it half a dozen steps from the town. Then, Rew and Zaine turned while the others hustled inside behind the makeshift walls. Zaine raised her bow, sighting at a narjag and ayre that were galloping in front of four other pairs.

"Shoot the ayre, lass," instructed Rew.

She adjusted her aim and let fly. From above, a dozen villagers released their shafts, and arrows rained on the Dark Kind in a hail, leaving two of the ayres and three of the narjags dead on the grass. The others, some wounded, fled back into the forest. Calmly, Rew stepped through the barrier after Zaine, and the men there hauled it closed.

"I'm afraid y'all have made a terrible mistake," drawled a man. "The town might look safer than out there, but they got us surrounded. You're stuck."

The speaker was huge, with broad shoulders, arms as thick as a normal man's legs, a prodigious belly that protruded over his belt, and a black beard streaked with white that hung down to that belly. In a meaty fist, he balanced an impressive wood axe resting on his shoulder.

"You're the leader of this town?" inquired Rew.

"We've a town council, but ah, I've been assigned to heading the defense, such as it is," answered the man. Intelligent eyes studied them from his weather-beaten face. "Did some soldiering back when I was the lad's age. Y'all aren't from around here. Adventurers? If you're part of that group we heard about near the river…"

Rew shook his head. "The bandits are dead. Killed by the Dark Kind."

"Dark Kind," said the man, his gaze flicking out of the town toward the edge of the forest where even now they could see flashes of motion as blue-skinned ayres and sickly gray narjags moved in and out of the trees.

"Narjags and ayres," said Rew. "I'm guessing they're not common around here?"

"Not since I've been living in the region," muttered the man. "Twenty-five years, that."

Rew looked around the town, seeing curious, frightened faces peering back at him. Children, less than ten winters on them, clutched bows and knives. Farmers and foresters carried the tools of their trade. Mothers tended to the younger children in front of a big building off the village green. Even from two blocks away, Rew could see each of the women had a weapon on her side or propped nearby. It was a siege, and these people had settled down to fight or die.

"How long?" asked Rew.

"Three days since we saw the first one," replied the man. "We didn't know what it was. Killed a few folks out in the woods, and when we went to figure out what was going on, we quickly realized we needed to pull in. Council had everyone arm themselves, and we started securing the place as best we could. There are more of 'em now. Lots more today. They've made a few attempts at the town, but the arrows have been keepin' 'em back. Unfortunately, we only got so many arrows. I've been thinking about sending out a party to collect those we've used, but those dog things—ayres, you said?—are fast. Not sure we can snatch up many arrows without losing a few of us."

Rew nodded grimly.

"I know you don't got nothin' to do with this town, but you look like you know the use of your weapons, and we can use your help defendin' if you're willin'," said the woodsman. "And if you're not, I don't mean to play it like this, but you don't got much choice. We tried to get folks outta here to find help, and none of 'em made it more than a dozen steps into the trees. You don't wanna know what happened to 'em when they fell."

"I've got some idea," remarked Rew.

"It's like Stanton," murmured Cinda.

"Aye," said Rew. "A bit like that."

"We left there, and we know how that ended. I don't know if I can stomach that again."

"I know, lass," repeated Rew, his gaze roving from the townspeople back to the trees where the Dark Kind were swarming. Gaining numbers, he guessed, preparing for an attack big enough to overwhelm the paltry defense around Arhold. If there were enough of them, they would come later that night.

"You don't look surprised to find yourself in these circumstances," remarked the woodsman.

Rew snorted. "Not the first time something like this has happened to us."

"So you are adventurers?"

"Not of the sort you mean," answered Rew. "Mind if I climb up on one of these buildings to get a look around?"

"You'll help us?"

Looking at Cinda and seeing her slight nod, Rew responded, "We'll try."

Chapter Six

Balancing atop the thatched roof of the highest building in the town, Rew and Zaine turned, him using his spyglass, her with her hand held above her eyes to block the morning sun. Below them, the woodsman called up, "Mind if I stay on the ground?"

"Of course," said Rew. "We're just trying to get a feel of the terrain and a rough count of how many we're facing."

"Too many," muttered Zaine beneath her breath.

"How many you have?"

"I've seen a score of ayre, a hundred narjags, but that's just an estimate on the ones we can see," replied the thief. "Could be ten times that many hiding back in the trees."

"That's about what I've spotted, but for what it's worth, I don't think they'll be hiding," said Rew. "They're showing themselves to intimidate the villagers, to pin them down. If there were a thousand narjags out there, they would have attacked already. No, they're showing what they have to keep everyone bottled up. Maybe they'll gather more forces, or maybe they're just waiting until night. The woodsman said there were more today than yesterday. How many do they need?"

"Showing themselves to pin the townspeople down is a grand

strategy for a narjag, don't you think," remarked Zaine. "Could there be a valaan out there?"

"I hope not." They kept looking until Rew found what he was searching for. "There." He handed the spyglass to Zaine.

The thief followed where he was pointing. "Three of those shamans."

Rew nodded. "They don't look scared, so I don't think there's a valaan nearby, but I still don't know what to think of them. Do they command any sort of magic, or are they some mockery of leadership the Dark Kind have developed after encountering enough of us? Even in the rangers' stories, and from everything I've seen with my own eyes, narjags don't work like this."

"You'd know," said Zaine. She waited a moment then added, "Back in Falvar, Alsayer was controlling them, right? And in Stanton, it was Calb. Could someone be…"

"Maybe," said Rew, "but that doesn't make much sense, does it? Why would Alsayer—or anyone—direct a pack of narjags to attack a random town in the middle of nowhere? Before, in Stanton and the Eastern Territory, Calb sent his minions to destabilize the place, throw Valchon off guard. Calb and Heindaw are dead, so neither of them are directing it, and Valchon couldn't care less what happens out here. I don't think this is directed, not by a spellcaster, at least."

"It's something new then," concluded the thief.

"Yes and no," muttered Rew. "I don't think Calb meant this to happen, but that doesn't mean he's innocent."

"What? He's commanding Dark Kind blindly from within the crypt?"

"No, he's dead. I'm sure of that, but what if Prince Calb created something… different. Think about it. Prince Valchon was breeding an army of his own spellcasting children. Heindaw was trying to figure a way to raise the dead. Calb wasn't as savvy as his brothers, but he wasn't stupid. He had to have some inkling of what was going on. King's Sake, he'd be dead long before we got to him if he was that big a fool. He would have had spies near his brothers, and he would know what was coming. What if he twisted the narjags somehow and created these shamans? Could be he's not directing them any longer, but the shamans survived his fall."

"Could be," said Zaine noncommittally. "How does that help us?"

"It doesn't," replied Rew sourly, "but if there are Dark Kind roaming Vaeldon, and they've got these narjag shamans to organize them, the creatures are going to be a graver threat than anything this kingdom has faced in the last fifty years since the valaan last gathered them into an army. Look at this group, one hundred strong, big enough to take on a decent-sized town. With two of the three princes dead, the king focused on... whatever he is doing, there's hardly anyone to defend the common people. Take the Eastern Territory. When we left, there wasn't a noble alive within two hundred leagues, and half the soldiers and spellcasters had killed each other. We haven't seen a soldier or a patrol since we left Iyre. Blessed Mother, it was the Dark Kind who took care of those river pirates, not the local nobility."

"So what do we do?"

"We can't do anything about groups of Dark Kind scattered all over, but we can do something about this one."

Zaine lowered the spyglass and eyed him skeptically. "You're going to fight one hundred narjags by yourself? Bold even for you, Ranger."

"Not by myself. You're going to help."

She handed him the spyglass and climbed down from the roof. He heard her muttering, "I don't know why I asked."

———

THEY GATHERED EARLY THAT AFTERNOON WITH THE WOODSMAN AND the other town leaders involved in Arhold's defense. The townsmen were nervous, as they should be. Only the woodsman had any proper military training, and while several dozen of the townspeople were skilled archers, they never would have faced anything as sturdy as an ayre. A poor shot, and a wolf or cougar would run away. A poor shot against an ayre, and the creature would rip your throat out.

"Once they begin, a fever will come over them, and they won't stop until we kill them all or they kill each other," advised Rew. "We might be able to scatter them if we take down the shamans, but if they're already engaged, I don't know if it'll do us any good. They must be stopped before they get within the boundaries of the town."

"What do you suggest, then?" questioned the woodsman. "I recall enough of my old life to know we're best off behind cover, but that seems a risk in this situation. If they get amongst us… What about fighting our way out, instead?"

Rew shook his head. "We can't fight our way out, not with so many children under our protection, and you're right, trying to hold the walls you've put up would be almost as bad. In a castle, it works because the only way for your foes to get to you is with ladders or complicated siege machines. Here, the ayres can simply leap your walls, or the narjags could pull them down in moments. It's not a wasted effort, but it won't stop them if they come en masse, and once they get into the town, they won't seek out combatants like human opponents would. They'll seek the easiest meat they can find."

Silently, the townsmen turned their eyes toward the center of the settlement, where the youngest of the children had been collected.

"Exactly," remarked Rew. He rubbed his head. "We can't let them make a coordinated attack. No matter what we do to defend, if they all come streaming out of those woods, we're going to take more losses than any of us can stomach. We've got to take the fight to them, but we've got to be smart about it." He glanced around the group. "I'll go after the shamans. Cut the head off the snake, so to speak. Once that's done, this many narjags will fight each other as hard as they do us, but for me to get to the shamans, someone's got to distract their minions."

"I can," said Cinda.

"Your strength is too volatile, lass. If our plan works, you won't be able to gather enough of it, you understand?"

She nodded.

Rew cleared his throat and added, "If our plan doesn't work, stay ready. You're the last line of defense."

"I can be part of the distraction," offered Raif.

"And I as well," declared Zaine.

"We'll help," said the woodsman, eyeing Cinda curiously. He raised his voice, and it sounded like timber falling. "The lads and I can swing as hard as anyone, though we could use some pointers on how best to do it against these things."

Rew nodded. "This could work. We draw the Dark Kind out of the forest. The archers train all of their fire on the ayres, and then, everyone leads the narjags on a merry chase until I can get to the shamans. Once those are gone, the narjags will tangle each other up. You can retreat safely, and we'll let them slug it out outside of the walls. Cleaning up the survivors is a much easier problem to deal with than taking all one hundred of them at once. I think that's about as low risk as we can make it, given the circumstances."

"To draw them to us," mentioned Raif, "we're going to have to engage."

Rew winced. "Don't get lost in it, lad. Do you think you can do that? Keep it under control."

Raif grinned. "I can try."

"I'll connect with the women," declared Anne. "I'll find a suitable place for the wounded and gather the supplies we'll need."

"Have some faith," suggested Rew. "Maybe we won't have any wounded."

Anne raised an eyebrow at him. "I know how your plans work."

"You have a better one?"

Anne crossed her arms over her chest and did not respond.

Gesturing to Raif and Zaine, Rew began to instruct the townspeople to split into groups that could fight and those that were best with a bow. The younglings took over and began organizing their respective groups and assessing what else they might need and how they could work together.

Rew turned to the woodsman and lowered his voice. "You have any ale in this town?"

"Really, Rew?" chided Anne.

"Not for me," said Rew. "Well, not until later. These men look like good, stout souls, but it's hard to face a narjag when you've no experience. A mug or two might bolster their courage enough we can pull this off. Anne, if they lose faith at the wrong moment and try to flee…"

The empath opened her mouth to protest, closed it, scowled at Rew, and then finally allowed, "A mug or two for courage, no more. Don't make me heal someone because they were too drunk and fell on a narjag's spear."

Fighting to keep a grin off his face, Rew nodded solemnly.

THEIR ASSUMPTION WAS THAT SHORTLY AFTER NIGHTFALL, THE DARK Kind would attack. With over one hundred of them in the woods, and only five hundred souls in the town of Arhold, half of those children and most of the adults unarmed, there was no reason to wait. Under the cover of night, the Dark Kind had the strength to overrun the town, and even if they were showing evidence of strategy, Rew couldn't bring himself to believe whatever was commanding them would care about their losses.

That gave Rew and the others only a few hours to prepare.

Anne's work was the most involved, as she had specific needs and instructions. The women of the town seemed happy to have someone who sounded experienced to guide them, and already, they had wounded they were struggling to care for. Anne granted some small empathy, though not enough for any of the towns-people to know what she was doing, and then issued instructions on how to best care for the injuries.

Zaine had collected the archers, though she found there wasn't much she could tell them they didn't already know. By and large, the foresters of Arhold were better shots with a bow than the thief, but the simple fact that she didn't appear afraid of the Dark Kind was enough they listened to the young woman.

Raif was surrounded by twenty men who were all nearly as large as he was. They were people of the soil, hardened by a life of heavy labor. They looked as strong as oxen, and the mallets, axes, and scythes they hoisted were as brutal as any weapons of war, but Rew called Raif aside once he saw them assembled.

"Lad, that's a mean-looking bunch, but you can't let them engage too closely. They've no armor like you do, and while I don't doubt they'll put those axes through the narjags easier than they can a tree trunk, they'll know nothing of defense and have no feel for the madness of an actual battle. You've got to get them away before they become entangled. If they're fully engaged, they won't have the cover of the archers, and they won't have protec-tion if they turn their backs on the Dark Kind."

"We'll hit the Dark Kind hard enough to knock them back on their heels. Then, we'll retreat," assured Raif. "We won't stay close, but we've got to give you time, Ranger."

Shaking his head, Rew insisted, "Don't worry about me. I'm mobile enough I'll be fine out there. These men, ah, they look slow."

Raif frowned.

"Big men are like that," explained Rew. "Strong, but they can't run. Can barely turn themselves around, you know?"

Flexing his gauntleted fist, Raif replied, "Ranger, some people call me a big man."

Rew held the boy's gaze.

"Are you saying I can't run?"

"Not very fast," mumbled Rew under his breath. "Look, lad,

just give yourself and the others time to get away before the narjags can grapple with you, and don't forget, they have ayres as well. There's not a man alive who can outrun one of those."

Raif threw up his hands and stomped away.

"Tact, Ranger," said Zaine from behind him. "Next time, try a little tact."

"Someone has to tell him," replied Rew. "You can do it next time if you like."

"Gladly," said Zaine with a wink.

Fighting a smile, Rew instructed, "It's a real concern about the ayres. I want all your arrows at them at the beginning of the fight, but make sure your archers don't get out of position and can't hit the narjags when Raif's squad starts to come back. I suspect they'll need the cover."

"And you, do you want a few foresters watching your back?"

Rew shook his head. "Just watch what I can do when I'm in the woods by myself."

RAIF AND THE TWENTY TOWNSMEN WALKED OUT ONE SIDE OF THE village. They were as armed and armored as could be managed, which meant Raif was fully-armored and the rest of them were wearing heavy leather aprons from the blacksmith's forge, cloaks wrapped and tied around their arms as makeshift bracers, and all of their thickest jackets and scarves. It wouldn't stop a direct strike from a weapon, and the ayres' jaws were powerful enough to bite through the sturdiest leather, but it was better than nothing.

Rew had thought so, at least, until he spied one man wearing a pot atop his head. Rew took the pot from the man and told him no.

Above Raif and the woodsman, Zaine had deployed two score of the town's archers across the thatch rooftops. Most of them were skilled, and they were used to hitting moving game when hunting, but it would be different when lives were at stake, and their friends and neighbors were dying in the field. Zaine had let an arrow fly, sending it soaring halfway across the open land between the town and the trees. She instructed Raif not to move beyond it.

"We can't cover you past there, and even at that distance, our aim will be shaky."

"If you don't hit them, the threat of arrows should still keep the Dark Kind back," assured Raif.

"I meant I might accidentally hit you, you fool."

Raif drew a deep breath, his greatsword resting in one hand, his armor rustling. He pushed back his dark, lanky hair with his free hand and looked around. He leaned close to Zaine and asked, "A kiss for good luck?"

"Maybe if you were your sister," replied the thief. Then, as easily as a squirrel, she scampered up the side of a hut and onto its roof.

Raif turned to Rew. Quietly, he asked, "Do you think she was jesting?"

Rew grunted and did not respond. The ranger knew better than to wade into that mess.

He left the young fighter and the others and moved quickly through the town. He waited a moment until he heard a call signaling Raif and his squad had passed the barricades. He stayed for a count of thirty breaths, his eyes fixed on the forest, and then Rew hopped the short wall the townspeople had erected and started jogging toward the woods.

He assumed he would be spotted, as not all the Dark Kind would have moved to intercept Raif yet, but as long as the fighter and the men from the town drew enough eyes, Rew would have a chance.

Ayres yipped and barked, signaling to their fellows there was easy meat. Rew could see the dark blue streaks as they charged through the forest coming around toward where Raif and the woodsmen were marching out. Ahead, he heard a low growl from somewhere within the foliage. At least some of the creatures had not been distracted.

Rew sped up, hurtling toward the wall of forest. It would be harder for any straggling Dark Kind to spot him once he was in the woods. He entered the brush and moved to where they'd last seen the three shamans several dozen paces deep into the trees, but he couldn't see them now. Would they follow the rest of the Dark Kind to face Raif? If so, this was going to be a very bad, very short-lived plan. Rew needed to find the exact spot they'd seen the creatures and then track them. He would need to do it under attack.

As he reached the trees, a narjag came hurtling at him, its face all teeth and awful breath, a hatchet clutched in one clawed hand. The narjag seemed like it couldn't decide if it should bite him or swing the hatchet, so Rew lunged at it, grabbed it around the neck, and smashed it forehead-first into a tree, cracking the creature's skull.

He moved deeper into the brush, and an ayre with no rider sprang off a stump and came soaring at him. Rew thrust up with his longsword, taking the beast in the chest then dodging to the side and letting it sail past him.

Two narjags scrambled up behind it, and he kicked one in the stomach, sending it flying backward off the stump, then caught a strike from the second on his bracer. He shunted it aside, drew his longsword across the narjag's neck, and then ran forward and stabbed the first one before it could rise.

The ayres were barking ferociously from the opposite side of the town, and Rew guessed they were drawing most of the other blue-skinned beasts toward their calls, but the section of forest he'd entered was still thick with slower-moving narjags. He killed several and began to worry there were more of the creatures than the one hundred he and Zaine had seen from the rooftops.

Rew paused and looked through the branches and the leaves back at the village. He was in the place where they'd seen the three shamans. The earth was disturbed. There were small broken branches and scuffs. There was a curious assortment of smooth stones arranged in a pattern around a stick stuck into the earth. He didn't have time to examine it, but he quickly saw impressions where narjags' clawed feet had moved away. He began to follow the trail.

Screeching howls, high-pitched yips, and snarling growls echoed through the woods. Narjags began to converge on Rew, bursting from the bushes, careening around tree trunks with hunger and rage twisting their faces.

Rew fought his way through them, always trying to keep an eye on the trail of the shamans. It occurred to him the signs could have been left by any of the narjags. The shamans dressed differently, and they might be slightly larger, but without close observation, their footprints would be indistinguishable from the others.

The ayres, mercifully, seemed to have been drawn to the commotion Raif and the villagers were raising, and individual narjags were a small threat to Rew. They didn't bother to hide the sounds of their approach or to come in a pack, so each time, he had notice to set himself and then dispatched the individuals quickly.

For several hundred paces, he moved deeper into the wood, losing sight of the town behind him, wondering where the shamans were going. Were they not commanding the other creatures as he'd thought?

As he went farther, the attacks from the narjags slowed and then stopped. Ahead, there were two wooded hills, and the signs of the shamans wound between them. Rew slowed, frowning. Something was not right. They were almost a quarter league from Arhold now, and if the shamans were meant to be directing the battle, they wouldn't have been doing it from so far away.

Cautiously, Rew looked around, and even though he half-expected it, he was still surprised when they sprang the ambush. A score of narjags screeched and exploded out of hiding, but they did not attack. Instead, they surrounded him. One of the shamans stepped from hiding and gave him a sickening grin, its fat, pasty lips spreading to expose its rotten teeth. It was like the shaman was eyeing him to make sure it knew who they'd caught.

Rew groaned. Ambushed by narjags? If he died, his name would live forever amongst the rangers in infamy. It was the first time he'd ever heard of the narjags attempting to ambush someone, and he'd been in a constant running battle up until this point, but at the moment, that wasn't making him feel any better.

The shaman raised a hand and whistled a sharp call. The rest of the narjags attacked. They came in a screaming, thrashing pile, all pretense at organization lost when the shaman released them to battle.

Rew ran to the left, drawing his hunting knife and smashing into a wave of claws and teeth. He swept his longsword ahead of him, chopping a path, but there were too many, and he felt a spear dig into his leg, a knife draw across his ribs, and a jaw clamp on his ankle, sharp teeth piercing the soft leather of his boots.

He kicked, knocking the narjag loose, the teeth tearing his flesh as they were jerked away. He slashed his knife into the face of another, sending it stumbling back, then bashed his sword against the head of a narjag in front of him.

Erasmus Morden seemed to be calling to him from within his tomb, begging to be released from the steel prison. Rew could feel his ancestor's rage, throbbing like a heartbeat, howling like an autumn storm.

Rew smashed his way out of the narjag pack, earning a deep cut on his elbow and lacerations all down his legs and sides as clawed hands scrabbled at him. His clothing and skin were ripped into ragged strips, but the wounds were superficial. The narjags hadn't gotten a blade deep into him, and he was moving fast enough all their teeth and claws could do was tear his skin.

He spun, stabbing and hacking, retreating up the slope of one of the hills. A narjag jumped on him, knocking him onto his back. He buried his hunting knife in the thing's belly and shoved, losing his grip on the bone hilt of his weapon. Standing, Rew backed farther up the hillside.

The shaman was following closely behind the pack of attacking narjags. It kept giving low, hooting calls, as if encouraging them on.

Rew swung ferociously, trying to keep the narjags away so he had room to fight. His backswing caught a narjag across the skull that had been sneaking up behind him, and it gave a startled squeak, as surprised to be struck by the blade as Rew was to have hit something. The narjag fell, and the ranger stumbled over it as he avoided the main strength of the pack. He flopped onto the side of the hill and thrashed his longsword to keep the Dark Kind off him before switching his grip to the other hand.

He yanked a dagger from his boot and flung it between the approaching narjags. Steel flashed in the sunlight. The dagger thunked into the shaman's chest. It fell back, wheeling its arms wildly. A narjag rushed at Rew, and one beside it hacked at its fellow with a sword, fighting to get to Rew first.

Rew staggered to his feet, his jaw dropping as the narjags turned on each other, the fervor of battle consuming them as they fought each other just as hard as they tried to fight him.

He stepped away, killing the narjags that approached him, but half a dozen and then a dozen fell to their fellows. Then, there was one, and Rew easily finished it. He stood, panting, blood dripping from more wounds than he cared to count.

When he'd caught his breath, he started shuffling deeper into the forest. There were two more shamans out there. The one he'd killed had been commanding the narjags with more control than he would've thought possible. What were the others doing?

He found them huddled over a large, cloudy crystal rod the length of his forearm. Both of their hands were on it, and it seemed to be pulsing arrhythmically and producing a piercing, humming noise. Watching the crystal, listening to it, it was like an impression was being stitched upon his thoughts, an impression of a valaan. In his mind, the valaan turned, and suddenly, the narjag shamans scrambled back from the crystal, rising to fight.

"King's Sake, they can do magic," coughed Rew, staring aghast at the two shamans.

Unfortunately for the narjags, their magic did not seem to include any combat spells, and while the shamans were larger than their brethren, they were no match for a ranger when he was angry. Rew chopped them down in short order and squatted before the crystal rod.

He kicked it with his toe then touched it hesitantly with a finger. Nothing happened. He held it up, but the light barely eeked through the cloudy rod. It was heavy and of poor-quality crystal. He shook it then stuck it beneath his belt. However the thing operated, he didn't have time to find out now.

Blood dripping, barely able to walk, Rew stumbled the quarter league back to Arhold.

Chapter Seven

Rew made it to the town and hopped over a heavy piece of furniture that had been wedged between two houses. Once in the safety of the town, he leaned back against the wall of a hut and slid down. None of his injuries were serious, but there were a lot of them, and they stung fiercely. He pulled aside a bit of torn trouser and looked at where a jagged hole had been bit into his calf.

Blood oozed down his leg, and he squeezed his muscle, pushing more of the precious liquid from his body. Narjags were filthy creatures, and if he didn't get a poultice and some herbs on there quickly, he would be afire with fever. Sighing, he made to stand and go find his pack.

Anne called to him, striding purposefully down the dirt street. "Stay there, Rew. Let me see what you've done to yourself."

"Done to myself?" he grumbled. Looking up at her, he asked, "Were you watching for me?"

"No," she answered, kneeling down in front of him. When she saw his suspicious look, she added, "I asked several of the children to do it. They came and found me when they saw you staggering out of the forest. You killed the shamans?"

"I did," he replied.

"And you want healing?"

"No, I—"

"I already know your secrets, and I shouldn't have asked because I don't care what you answer," interrupted Anne. She raised her hands and put them on the sides of his head. Her eyes tightened, and she sucked in her breath.

"That bad?"

"No… it's just…"

"Erasmus. You can feel him?"

Anne nodded.

Rew let his head fall back and closed his eyes. He could feel the curious tingle of Anne's healing trickling through his body. None of the cuts that marred his flesh were deep, but there were a score of them, and it felt like ants were crawling over his skin as the shallow lacerations began to knit themselves together unnaturally fast.

After several minutes, Anne clicked her tongue and told him, "You should be back to normal by tomorrow, but if it wasn't for me, you'd be getting a nasty infection from these wounds. I suppose we ought to expect narjags aren't cleaning their weapons often or—the thought sickens me—scrubbing their teeth. Try to avoid getting cut and bit by so many of them next time, will you?"

Rew snorted. She was trying to make it a jest, but he could hear the tension in her voice. She'd felt what was in his soul now, and it hurt.

He asked her, "The others?"

"Back behind the barriers," said Anne. "Raif got scuffed up a bit, as he does, but he managed to disentangle the townsmen and escape when the narjags all fell upon each other. Ah, Rew, did the three shamans do this to you? This looks like it was a bit more than that…"

"They set an ambush."

"Narjags set an ambush that surprised the King's Ranger?"

Rew winced. "Don't tell anyone."

"I won't, but Rew, how did they do that? You've been hunting these things for years, and I don't think I've ever seen you get hacked up like this just from some narjags."

"Well, there were a lot of them, and they've never set an ambush for me before, either. There's more, Anne. They were communicating with a valaan. I think that's what was coordinating this entire attack. Something is going on that I don't understand, and that worries me."

He closed his eyes again. Much of his pain was gone, but the exhaustion of the day and the worry about what he'd found still clung to him.

Sighing, Anne poured more empathy into him, and Rew could feel the warmth radiating through his body. It'd been years since he'd felt her healing, and she hadn't been as skilled then, not as sensitive. She'd already stopped the bleeding and now began more extensive repairs. Her empathy reached deeper than the last time he'd been awake when she healed him. She touched more than just the physical hurt. He thought he could sense her absorbing the torment of Erasmus Morden's rage, though that wasn't her intent.

Rew wanted her to stop, but she wouldn't unless he used physical force. She cared about him too much to stop. She would soothe the pain Erasmus left in Rew, but the taint of that ancient magician would stick with her like an oily film. Rew wondered if she could also feel the anguish that caused him.

Erasmus Morden, the king's father, rode in Rew's thoughts like a trespasser clinging to the back of a carriage, not always obvious, but always there. Unlike those unwanted passengers who sometimes managed a free ride in the cities on the backs of the nobles' transports, Erasmus wanted to take over. He was always waiting, biding his time until he could spring up to the front, take the reins, and what remained of Rew would be nothing more than forgotten cargo.

One more time? Two more times? How many chances could Rew give him, opening up the ancient magician's tomb, letting his soul free even for a moment? Those moments were all that

Erasmus needed, all that it would take to wedge himself in the opening, gaining his freedom. Back in the woods, thinking he would die to a pack of narjags, Rew had almost drawn on the power in the sword. Would that have been it? What would Erasmus do once he took control of Rew? Where would he direct his rage?

Anne sat back, a frown on her lips.

"What?" asked Rew, nervous the empath had sensed the direction of his thoughts somehow, worried she knew he'd been thinking about her.

"That went quickly," she responded. "Too quickly."

Rew sat up and looked down at himself. He was sore, but through the tears in his clothing, all he could see was smooth skin. Not even a scar.

"I should have asked for your healing earlier," he muttered, testing his arm where a narjag had chopped into it earlier. It'd been nearly useless by the time he'd made it back to Arhold. Rew added, "You've gotten better, Anne, but this? I don't recall you being so, ah, efficient with the children or the others."

"We're closer to each other than I am to anyone else," murmured the empath. "Empathy is about connection, and…"

"And we're connected."

"Closer than I've ever been connected with anyone," she replied, a stiff smile on her lips. She shifted. "Rew, that connection does more than improve my healing. I can feel Erasmus. It's like he's… eating your anger, except that's not it. He's not consuming it. He's… wallowing in it. I think he grows stronger with it."

Rew blinked at her. "Is that… What does that mean? Are you telling me not to get angry?"

"I think it means you shouldn't let him out anymore," suggested Anne, "and yes, I suppose you shouldn't get angry, either. It will make him stronger."

"Right," said Rew. "I'll, ah, give it a try."

She patted him on the knee, as if knowing how ridiculous such a command was, then tried to rise but stumbled as she stood.

Scrambling to his feet, Rew caught Anne's shoulders. "I'm sorry…"

"You wouldn't accept my healing, Rew," replied the empath. "I didn't listen, and I healed you when you were unconscious. I shouldn't… I shouldn't do that. This isn't on you. It's on me. This time… It doesn't matter. I felt it before, and I felt it again. It's Erasmus, not you."

"But if it wasn't for me—"

"If it wasn't for you, I would have never left the women's colony, and I would have been hung the moment the king's black legion arrived to pay revenge for the rebellion. How many other times have you saved my life or rescued me from something even worse than death? We have too much between us to keep score, Rew. This is unexpected, but it's not your fault. Not my fault, either. It just is."

He grunted. "Should we check on the others?"

Anne shook her head. "There were no injuries to our companions, but a number of townspeople were wounded. I did what I could, and they're stable now. I didn't want to expend too much energy in case… Two of them died. They didn't even make it back to the town. I was able to grant empathy to those who survived long enough to receive it, and it was enough."

"Oh."

"Arhold was under attack when we got here, Rew. We did not bring this on these people. These Dark Kind had nothing to do with us or anything we've been working on. Carry the guilt you've earned, but not this."

They began walking through the village, and as they did, Rew considered that. The town was under attack, and Anne was right. It had nothing to do with them. But those narjag shaman had set an ambush for him. Surely they wouldn't have done that for anyone with a sword who'd been running into the woods. They couldn't have known he would come slinking out of the town to hunt them, could they? And they'd been… communicating with a valaan.

They'd been using a crystal, a mystical-looking trinket like old women would sell on the fringes of any major market gathering, but it had worked. He'd felt the valaan on the other end, and it had seen him. He'd fiddled with the crystal before returning to the town, but in his hands, it was dead stone. He was sure of what he'd felt, though. Somehow, the shaman or the valaan had activated the thing and used it to communicate.

The attack on Arhold had involved over one hundred narjags and a score of ayres. It'd been planned and directed. The plans had been adjusted when they'd realized Rew was there. The implications tumbled slowly, and by the time they'd reached the opposite end of the village, Rew realized they had some very large problems.

His personal problem was that either the shamans or the valaan had recognized him and had modified their plans to catch him. Beyond that, valaan were directing companies of narjags from afar. Somehow, they had lieutenants capable of handling the orders, but why? What goals would the Dark Kind have for a campaign against Vaeldon? Rew couldn't begin to guess, but he was certain he wouldn't like the answer if he found out.

At the wall surrounding the town, Raif was standing, surrounded by a gaggle of townspeople. His greatsword was unsheathed, and while he'd wiped away some of the dark blood of the narjags from the gleaming steel, there were still dark, sticky streaks dirtying the huge, enchanted weapon. His armor had a few extra dents and scratches, and there was a shallow cut near his hairline, but he was in good health and better spirits.

The big woodsman was standing beside him, but while that man had been assigned by Arhold's council to lead the defense, he was silent as his neighbors breathlessly made reports to Raif. The big fighter, the Baron of Falvar, listened patiently and issued instructions calmly and concisely.

Raif knew nothing about siege warfare or defending a town, but Rew supposed the lad knew far more about facing narjags than any of the townspeople did. They sensed his confidence, and it gave him the authority to lead, at least in that moment.

Rew moved past the cluster of people and gazed out over the barrier to the field surrounding Arhold. It was littered with the bodies of Dark Kind and those of two fallen men. Some of the Dark Kind were studded with arrows. Some were hacked apart brutally, either from Raif's greatsword or the axes and scythes of the townspeople. Many of the Dark Kind appeared to have been savaged by their own. In the distance, Rew could see motion within the trees, but there was no immediate threat.

The ranger counted quickly and estimated fifty or sixty of the Dark Kind had fallen on the field, the majority due to arrows or their own fellows. With the thirty he'd faced on the other side in the woods, they must have felled four out of five of the creatures which had been harassing the town. There would be another score lurking in the forest, if they hadn't turned against each other.

With the knowledge they'd earned through experience and a little more preparation, the town should be able to defend against such a threat, and in time, the Dark Kind would seek easier meat or each other. Not such a good thing for neighboring settlements, but with coordination, the townspeople could make contact with other villages, form a regional militia, and hunt the creatures down. Rew thought it safe to assume most of the creatures in the area had been at Arhold. They'd been building their forces there, which meant other Dark Kind would have been called if they'd been nearby.

Even if there were others close, there were skilled foresters in Arhold, and now that they knew what they were looking for, they could track the narjags and warn the other towns if more came into the region. They could also follow the ones that were already there and finish them. The people would be safe. Their work was done.

"Well, Ranger, I see you were successful," said Raif when he noticed Rew and Anne standing there. The fighter frowned when he got a closer look at Rew's ruined clothing. "Bit rougher than expected?"

"Aye," said Rew. He glanced around, seeing the townspeople listening in on the conversation. He decided they needed to hear what he had to say. "Narjags were waiting for me. They planned an ambush."

"The shamans?"

"The shamans and a valaan directing them from afar. I saw them using a crystal to do it. I felt the connection, but when I killed them, I couldn't get it to work again."

Raif rubbed his chin, ignoring the gasps of those around them. "Strange, eh?"

"Very strange," agreed Rew. "I can't imagine something like that has happened for some fifty years, since the last war with the Dark Kind."

"Directing them from afar…" murmured Raif. "At least the valaan wasn't here to… Well, now that I think about it, perhaps this is worse. If it could direct this group, then how many other companies of Dark Kind are roaming Vaeldon and coordinating their efforts? Something like this happened fifty years ago, you said?"

"Yes, the valaan raised an army. I don't know if they used the same methods I just saw to coordinate, but they had to have had some system. That rising happened around the coronation of a new king as well," continued Rew, absentmindedly fingering the tears in his tunic. "My guess, a conjurer—you know who—built an army of these things thinking to use them against his rivals. Perhaps he assisted them with capabilities like communication and modified some of them to be shamans, I don't know. Maybe there have always been shamans, but I just never encountered them in the eastern wilderness. There's no need for coordinated efforts out there. Point being, the Dark Kind don't have a human leader any longer. Their plans and goals will be their own."

"That, ah, that's not good, is it?"

"It's not," agreed Rew. He glanced back out over the field. "I'm not sure what there is for us to do about it right now. To face an army of Dark Kind, you need an army."

"The rangers?" asked Anne.

Rew shrugged. "They could help, but they're scattered. When Ang and Vurcell have had time, we could try to get a message to them, but it's going to be a lot more complicated than what I can send through the trees. Besides, it could be a month or two before they've all gathered."

"We have to do something," remarked Raif.

"I can't disagree with the sentiment, but what do you think we can do?"

The big fighter grasped the hilt of his greatsword with both hands. Around them, the townspeople were quiet, obviously not understanding the bulk of the conversation, but even in remote Arhold, they would have heard stories about the war against the Dark Kind fifty years before. They might not have believed those tales, but the last few days had likely changed what they thought was real and what was myth. How could they doubt any of it when one hundred of the foul beasts had just assaulted their town?

"We need to go," concluded Raif. "We have to… continue our quest. That has to come first. Cinda?"

The lad's sister nodded.

Rew had already decided the same, and he suspected Cinda was a step ahead of him, but Raif needed to see on his own, to understand what they faced. If they were successful against Valchon, against the king, they would need Raif to understand, to be able to sort through difficult choices. More and more, Rew was accepting that killing the king was going to be the end of the journey for some, and the start of something else for others. The survivors of the war between men would have to raise the banner again and march to face the Dark Kind.

THEY PLANNED TO REST THAT NIGHT THEN DEPART IN THE MORNING. After a hearty stew at the town's one guesthouse, Rew and Anne told the others they would take a walk to settle their meal. The children likely assumed it was a pretense to get away, but they were used to that sort of thing by now.

Anne and Rew strolled arm in arm, walking aimlessly in the small town, nodding to the residents that were still out at dusk, looking up at the rooftops where even now children and some of the younger adults kept watch. They would be up there for some hours yet, and then the adults would take over. The foresters would be placed in a rotation with at least half a dozen of them on duty at all times. Women and some of the older men were on the streets, walking steady patrols.

The townspeople acknowledged Anne and Rew, and a few offered thanks, but they said little else. It was too odd, the Dark Kind attacking and strangers appearing out of nowhere, fighting the evil creatures and then planning to disappear the next day with no explanation. It was too great a change in the world for the people of Arhold to accept it so quickly, but at some level, they understood their circumstances would have been much worse without the party showing up. They were grateful but still frightened. That fear would serve them well.

"Do you think they'll be able to track the Dark Kind and finish them?" wondered Anne.

In the distance, they could hear the occasional yip of an ayre. Some of the blue-skinned canine-like creatures had fled, but a few of them had stayed in the surrounding woods. A few of them or more? They sounded to the south now, but earlier in the night, they'd been north. Still trying to complete the shaman's last instructions, or just hoping the villagers would venture out and they could pick off an easy meal?

"I don't think they'll have difficulties finding the ayres if they keep making that ruckus," said Rew, scratching his beard, wondering if there was a barber in the town, "and Arhold's foresters ought to have little trouble tracking the remaining narjags. Could be a tussle once they find them, but the towns-people should be up to it. Might be worse if the fleeing Dark Kind find another, smaller community."

Anne was quiet.

"You think we should help?" he asked her.

"I do."

"Anne," said Rew, leaning close to her as they walked. "We could track the Dark Kind, finish them, and maybe save a few lives. But if the ayres get moving, you and the children aren't going to catch them. Even for me, it could take weeks to hunt all of these things down. It might be impossible if they fled in different directions. Every moment we delay is time that Prince Valchon will continue to lash out. It's time that Vaisius Morden will stay upon the throne. It's time that this sort of thing will continue with no one in power to stop it."

"Vaisius Morden has been there for two hundred years," mentioned Anne. "What's another week?"

"More than a handful of lives, I'd guess…" he told her. "Do you still feel the deaths? Cinda said it could be thousands a day."

"I hate to turn my back on people we can see and touch," said Anne. She hugged his arm. "It feels wrong to not do whatever we can to help, but I agree, we can't ignore what is happening elsewhere."

"We are doing what we can," insisted Rew. "This will all continue until the Mordens no longer rule. Completing our quest against the king will allow whoever takes over to marshal forces to track down the Dark Kind. All of them. Once and for all."

"And who will be taking over, then?"

Rew didn't respond.

Anne waved her hand around, indicating the town. "What happens to these people when Vaisius Morden is dead, if it's just another noble who sits upon the throne? Nothing will change for these people until something changes for everyone, Rew. Whether it be a Morden, or Baron Barnaus, or a… Fedgley, what will change for these people?"

"Well, without the king and his children spending Vaeldon's gold and lives on the Investiture every generation, towns like this will be free to form their own defenses…"

"Will they be?" asked Anne. "You're expecting a new, benevolent king who won't require tribute in wealth and blood? I doubt that. I think it's more likely, the kingdom will splinter, and warlords will carve out bloody hunks, all fighting for their own piece of land. The nobles will try to subdue more territory, and they'll raise levies and force the commoners to join them when they do it. It's what nobles always do, except now there will be no one to stay their hands, to prevent open warfare that spans the continent in hundreds of small conflicts. The ambitious nobles like Baron Barnaus may attempt to take the throne, but I doubt he could hold it. How many like him will march on their neighbors instead? Vaisius Morden has spent centuries breaking the backs of every noble and commoner alike in this kingdom. Without that iron fist holding everyone at peace, what can we expect, except war?

Rew grimaced. "What would you have me do, Anne? Sit the throne myself?"

"It's worth considering."

Rew disentangled himself from Anne and threw up his hands. "You want me to raise a banner and march on all of those recalcitrant nobles? That's war, too, you know."

Anne caught his arm again. "They've been trained for two hundred years to kneel to a Morden, Rew. All their lives, that's all they've ever done. It's all they'll ever do, as long as there is someone to kneel to. Don't be the king your father is, but you can use his legacy of terror to take command and forge something new, something better."

Rew snorted but didn't trust himself to respond.

They made it to the edge of the town and peered out at the darkening forest. Already, beneath the branches, night had fallen thick and deep. The field was still lit with the last wink of dusk, but as they watched, even that began to go. Sparks of light, sporadic and faint, blinked in and out of view.

Rew struggled to control his breathing, struggled to absorb what Anne had said. She didn't think… She wouldn't suggest… But she had. Not for him. Not his own sake. She knew he wouldn't want the throne, and that it would cause him nothing but anguish. But for the sakes of towns like Arhold, all of the places from the women's colony in the west to Eastwatch in the east… For that, for all of them, what was too much to sacrifice?

"Fireflies," murmured Anne.

"Yes. Thousands of them. Tens of thousands."

"Beautiful, isn't it?"

Rew squeezed her arm tight.

After a long moment, they heard behind them, "Little specks of light in a vast sea of darkness. Like us, don't you think?"

Anne glanced back. "Zaine, getting philosophical this evening? Rew, did you know she was following us? You're getting lazy in your old age."

"Or maybe I'm getting better," suggested Zaine.

Rew laughed. "Maybe you are, but you didn't follow us. A moment ago, I heard you three houses back asking one of the townspeople which way we went. I can see your eyes, too, Cinda, especially at night, and Raif, half the town can hear you walking about."

The necromancer stepped beside them. "What were you discussing so late this evening?"

"Nothing."

"Wondering who will face these Dark Kind when all of this is over?" inquired Cinda.

Rew winced and glanced at her suspiciously. Her tone had been flat, but he thought he detected a hint of amusement in her voice. He'd heard them approaching, and he was sure the younglings hadn't overheard his conversation with Anne, but as her powers expanded, Cinda was becoming distressingly insightful. She was spending too much time thinking.

"Ah," murmured Cinda, glancing between Rew and Anne, "that is what you were talking about. Someone will have to take command, to muster the armies. If we're successful, there will only be one rightful heir to the throne, only one person everyone in Vaeldon would be willing to follow."

"I'm just a ranger," grumbled Rew, "and I don't expect anyone would want to follow me."

"A ranger and a son of the king," mentioned Raif. "By law of succession, it'd be your right. Not to mention, if you were the one who killed the king and all the princes, who's going to argue? It's your seat by both the spoken and unspoken laws of this kingdom. I don't have a head for politics and strategy, but even I can see that."

"I don't think the kingdom needs another Morden to raise his banner and occupy that role," responded Rew. "We do this so Vaeldon can move on, not stay mired in the past, anchored by the weight of my family's legacy."

"The kingdom will split then," argued Cinda. "The provinces, and likely the duchies and baronies, will all march against each other. Those fireflies out there, instead of sparks of hope, will be like the flames of war stretching from one side of the kingdom to the other."

Rew watched the fireflies and did not respond. Cinda harrumphed, and she and Anne shared a look.

"What do we do, then?" asked Raif. "After, I mean. Not just us, but Vaeldon? What happens when the king is dead?"

"I can't tell you," said Rew. "I don't have an answer for everything."

The children fell silent, and Rew felt Anne clutching him tightly. He didn't think she liked the idea of him on the throne any better than he did. But... he didn't know what to tell the others. They were right. He'd already known, though he refused to admit it, even to himself. Who else could rule without dragging the kingdom into a war worse than the Investiture? No one.

Zaine leaned forward, elbows on a wagon that had been

parked sideways to help defend the town. She stared out into the dark, listening to the racket of the night insects and the occasional howl of the ayres.

"You said they're coordinating," she mentioned, "and that it might be like the war against the Dark Kind fifty years ago."

"Maybe there aren't as many of them this time."

"But maybe there are. Maybe there are more."

Rew was silent. What could they do about it? Fighting the Dark Kind would require an army, and he didn't have one. He grimaced and hoped no one saw in the dark. He didn't have an army, but he knew where to find one.

Chapter Eight

The next morning, when faced with the younglings' requests to track the Dark Kind that had fled and the prospect of hiking a day in the wrong direction to recover their canoes, the party resupplied, and Rew agreed to follow the Dark Kind into the forest, as long as they were headed downstream, parallel to the river.

He thought they would spend a day or two tracking the creatures then cut south to one of the towns on the water where they could find another boat. They had plenty of coin to hire passage, if they could find a vessel taking passengers. The travel in the canoes on the narrow upper fingers of the river had been peaceful, but as more streams joined the main flow, traffic would increase, and travel in the canoes could be dangerous and slow compared to a ship they could raise sail on. And after the encounter with the trap the pirates had set, Rew wouldn't mind a few more people in their party.

The townspeople of Arhold were more than happy to provide what provisions the group needed, and the gruff woodsman walked them to the edge of the forest as dawn was cresting the tops of the trees.

"Y'all folks saved us, you know," he said when they got there. "So many of those things... we never would have survived."

"I'm glad we happened by," responded Rew.

"Is the council reaching out to neighboring settlements?" asked Anne. "We'll take care of the creatures we find, but they probably split up when they fled. You should be prepared for more of them."

"Aye, we've thought of that," replied the woodsman. He shifted and looked down at his boots. "This morning, the council retired, I guess you could say. Elected me mayor to take their place. I didn't want the job, but they told me that's why I'd be good at it. What can I say to that? They thought that with the risk of more'o these critters, it made sense to have one man in charge. No time for discussion if we're attacked again, you know. One man in charge keeps down the squabbles."

Rew grunted and looked toward the forest. The comment was true, and it hit close to home. His companions carefully looked everywhere but at him.

The woodsman continued, "But your suggestion is a good one. I'll send runners today to the villages and towns around here. Some sort of militia'll make sense until things settle down. Maybe by then, they'll let me out of politics, and I can get back to mindin' me own business."

"They're lucky to have you," murmured Anne, her shoulder brushing against Rew's.

Grinning, the woodsman shook his head. "I've got experience that's older than any of these younglings here, but I've forgotten most of it. I put down a couple'o those monsters, but I don't think they much noticed. Were plenty more behind 'em. Ain't me Arhold was lucky to have. I'd offer you payment again, but we know what you'll say. Wish I was able to do somethin' more for you. You've got my prayers to the Mother, for what good it'll do you. Every night, I'll have the women do a vigil, and we'll speed you on your journey with all the Grace we can call upon."

"We appreciate that," responded Anne, "and Grace of the Mother on you as well."

The woodsman nodded, looking like he wanted to say more.

Wordlessly, Rew turned and led the party into the forest. He could feel the man's eyes on him, feel the question that he didn't want to answer. The man wanted to know who they were, and Rew wasn't sure what to tell him.

THE DARK KIND WEREN'T UNDER THE INFLUENCE OF THE SHAMAN any longer, and they had no inclination to travel together. They'd been caught up in a frenzy, and the town had proven too tough a nut to crack. The easiest sustenance for the creatures was each other.

So, while there was no clear, discernible tract that all of the Dark Kind were taking, there was a harried flight through the forest with numerous of the beasts all headed in the same direction, which was proven when they stumbled across the mutilated bodies of the Dark Kind that had become the hunted instead of the hunters.

There was no love between the Dark Kind, and it was sickening seeing what they'd done to each other. It made Rew's stomach sour, imagining a large force of these beasts rampaging across Vaeldon. The havoc and terror they would bring to the people of the kingdom were too awful to dwell on.

Even if they were outnumbered and outclassed, the Dark Kind would still cause untold horror. The valaan cared nothing about how many of their charges died. They cared only for the blood and chaos they could sew. They were driven by hunger, like the lesser Dark Kind, but also by anger. They thirsted for revenge even more powerfully than for blood.

If they were led capably, they would avoid the major cities at first and might not bother with the stray hermit or traveler. It was the small settlements like Arhold that would bear the brunt of the Dark Kind's fury. Those places were large enough to sate even a big war party but not so large as to have walls and professional soldiers defending it. In the interior of Vaeldon, few settlements would have rangers. Towns like that were fattened lambs left alone in the field, oblivious to the danger they were in.

But Rew knew he'd been right earlier. They could not face an army of the Dark Kind without an army of their own.

An army.

He growled a curse beneath his breath, drawing a look from the others, but he didn't explain, and they did not ask.

It took them half a day, but finally, they stumbled across three living narjags. The creatures were thin and didn't carry any of the crude weaponry that narjags typically scavenged from their victims. These were the runts, the weakest of the pack. They must have survived by hiding when the rest of the Dark Kind were running and fighting.

Rew heard them ahead and slowed the company. He went on alone, and by the time the narjags had scented him, he was already amongst them. He skewered one with his longsword then drew the weapon out in a wheeling attack and swept the head off another. The third attempted to run, but Rew knelt and pulled a throwing dagger from his boot. He flung it at the back of the narjag, and the creature went tumbling head over heels. Rew stalked after it and finished it as the others arrived.

"Disgusting," said Zaine, pretending to lose her lunch.

The three narjags had been gnawing on the corpse of an ayre. Given the state of the beast, Rew guessed they weren't the first to it. They were simply scavenging what other Dark Kind had left behind.

"If the narjags took down an ayre, there will be a large pack ahead somewhere," said Rew, making a quick circuit of the scene. "Eight to ten of them, looks like."

"Ten narjags," boasted Raif, "that should be no problem for us."

"Overconfidence has killed more soldiers than the cunning tactics of an enemy," remarked Rew.

"You didn't see me outside of Arhold," snapped Raif. "We went against a hundred of the Dark Kind and only lost two men! That's the stuff of legend, and we didn't even have you at our side. Ten narjags isn't a problem."

Rew walked over to the big fighter and grasped his armored shoulder. "You're right. Arhold was the stuff of legend. Experienced veterans may not have handled it nearly as well as you did. It was good—no—great work, lad, but two is more than zero, you understand me?" Rew looked around the group pointedly then back to Raif. "We can't afford to lose anyone, and we can't afford to rely on Anne's healing after every fight."

"She healed you yesterday!"

"She did," responded Rew. "I should have been more careful going after those shamans. I was overconfident, and it nearly cost me a great deal. My folly is a good lesson for all of us."

Raif brushed back his hair from his eyes, looking like he wanted to argue, but then he nodded and allowed, "Understood."

Rew turned, met Anne's gaze, and then followed the trail the pack of narjags had left. The lad wasn't a child anymore, but he still had much to learn about leadership and the true cost of battle.

The narjags they were following had done nothing to hide their passage. Other tracks crossed the way, some before the larger group, some after. They could spend weeks hunting each individual Dark Kind and still not know if they got them all. If they caught up to the group of ten and finished them, then Rew hoped the younglings would be satisfied, and they could turn back to the river and the faster travel toward the coast.

By nightfall the first day, they still hadn't come across the narjags, so Rew decided they would camp and restart the search in the morning. It was odd that the narjags hadn't rested. That was their typical behavior following a feast, but he was coming to accept there was nothing typical about the creatures they were chasing. Before the younglings had arrived in Eastwatch, he'd never seen anything like this.

They skipped the fire, but in the early spring, the weather was pleasant without it, and they had a cold, roasted chicken from the townspeople in Arhold. Had the Dark Kind managed to form a crude organization? A brutal version of government? It was almost laughable, except they had coordinated the attack against the town. Even with guidance from a valaan, that was difficult for low beasts to accomplish, and the valaan hadn't been there.

What did the crystal mean? Did the Dark Kind fashion it somehow, or had Calb given it to his summonings to form his army? Chewing on a leg of the chicken, Rew wondered how Calb had even communicated with the Dark Kind. From the ranger stories, no conjurers had been able to do such a thing in decades, not since—

He coughed and nearly choked. The others looked at him, but he waved them off and pointed to his throat with the half-eaten drumstick. He sat it down and scowled.

The story was that conjurers hadn't been able to command Dark Kind for years, but that wasn't true. Outside Falvar, Alsayer had commanded the creatures. He'd called to the narjags and set them on the city. They'd been Calb's summonings, Rew thought, but Alsayer had given the orders. How, and why?

Sighing, Rew decided he wasn't going to untangle the mess of questions that were swirling through his thoughts, but he realized there was one man who could clear it all up. That bastard, Alsayer.

The spellcaster had commanded the Dark Kind outside Falvar. The more he thought it over, the more certain Rew became. Could Alsayer disrupt them somehow, keep them from people? Did he have anything to do with what was happening now? Could he have turned the creatures from Stanton instead of letting Valchon destroy the city?

Rew stood, no longer hungry. He told the others he was going to wander around for a bit, check out the nearby terrain, and he did.

An army of Dark Kind. It would take an army to stop them, unless Alsayer could, but if the spellcaster could, why hadn't he? Alsayer was a calculating, ruthless man, but Rew believed that even he would hesitate at the destruction Valchon caused in Stanton. That was a level of depravity unseen outside of the Investiture, and what could Alsayer have possibly gained by such a calamity?

Perhaps he could only command so many of the creatures, or maybe he hadn't been willing to risk Valchon's wrath. Or maybe Rew was wrong about him.

Ghosting silently amongst the trees, Rew wondered. Was that the spellcaster's plan? Let the princes and Rew all fight it out, then Alsayer would take their place? Become king?

But Alsayer knew the outcome for the winner of the Investiture. He couldn't want that, could he? He'd always been content to be near the seat of power but had never shown an interest in occupying it. He was fond of the shadows and working anonymously. He certainly wouldn't be fond of the king stealing his body and using him like a meat puppet. No, Rew eventually decided, even if the spellcaster thought he could outsmart Vaisius Morden, which was doubtful, he still wouldn't want the headaches of rule.

So what, then?

Walking aimlessly, his instincts guiding him in the dark forest, Rew moved silently, causing no more stir than the insects and the night birds. The ranger had wandered several hundred paces from their camp when behind him, cutting the night like a wound, he heard a startled scream and a bestial roar.

Rew spun and ran.

There was a clash of steel and Raif's bellowed retort to the narjags' anger.

Light flared amongst the tree trunks, pale and sickly. Then it winked out.

A snarled cry and a shout of warning.

Rew came crashing out of the trees and into the midst of a vicious fight. The only light was a trickle from the moon and stars, but he could see well enough to understand what was happening.

Narjags darted about the camp, using their better senses to try and spring at the humans from behind. Anne and Cinda tumbled past, the empath wrestling one of the foul creatures, Cinda trying to stab it with her belt knife without hitting Anne.

Zaine leapt in front of Rew, one dagger gleaming, the other bloody. She ripped a blade across the face of a narjag then plunged her second dagger into its side. She moved, and a snarling narjag fell where she'd been, scrambling after her, tripping over its fellow, and getting a nasty bite on the leg for its trouble. Rew stabbed both of the fallen narjags and moved into the camp.

Raif, roaring like a hurricane, was drawing most of the creatures toward him. He spun like a child's top, his greatsword smashing and crashing through Dark Kind with every powerful rotation. The Dark Kind were holding back, like they were afraid of the fighter, which showed more wisdom than Rew would have granted them, but a few slipped behind Raif's strikes, and the lad was forced back. When his spinning stopped, he stumbled, dizzy and off balance from the momentum, and the narjags swarmed.

Rew leapt at their backs, his longsword cleaving rancid meat and dark blood, his hunting knife rising and plunging as he waded into the thick of the awful beasts.

Raif saw Rew coming and shoved his way free, pausing for a breath. Then, he darted to the side and pounded toward the edge of their encampment. Raif's arms and legs churned. Then, he was on a large narjag. A shaman. It wheeled a heavy club at the big fighter, but Raif took a stutter step on his approach, letting the club whistle by harmlessly. He stepped forward and hammered his greatsword down on top of the shaman's head, killing it instantly.

The other narjags in the camp screeched and fought, suddenly clawing into each other as ferociously as the humans. In the madness, Rew killed the things as quickly as he could, and Zaine joined him, working along the edges of the pack, cutting them away whenever one stumbled out of the chaos. Raif arrived back, and it was over shortly after.

Spitting, the big fighter complained, "I got some of their blood in my mouth. It tastes like… Pfah, I can't even describe it. It's awful."

"Aye." Rew laughed. "But did any of your blood get in their mouths? That's what you should worry about."

Looking down at himself in the dark, Raif admitted, "I'm not sure. They nicked me in a few spots, I think, but it doesn't hurt any worse than usual. It, ah, sometimes it takes me a bit to feel it…"

A berserker. Through and through, though the lad had shown a little sense during the fight. He'd dodged a blow, which he didn't always.

Rew turned to Zaine, and in the moonlight, he saw her grin. "I'm fine. I just pointed them all toward Raif."

"Thanks for that," quipped the fighter.

"Finally pulling your weight around here," declared the thief with a giggle.

Raif groaned theatrically.

Rew turned toward where Anne and Cinda had stumbled earlier and found the empath standing and adjusting her blouse, tugging it over her shoulder where it'd been torn away.

Anne assured him, "I wasn't injured, but next time we find a town of decent size, we're going shopping. If that thing had held onto my shirt another breath, I'd be rather immodest right now, and there's no amount of washing and mending that is going to get the stink of narjag blood out of this cotton."

"You're sure none of them hurt you?"

"Not me or her," responded Anne, looking down to where Cinda knelt on the forest floor.

The necromancer looked up, her green eyes sparkling. "I… I

couldn't draw any more power. I cast a blast of funeral fire, but when I tried to pull the strength from the departing soul, there was nothing. Even when Raif started killing more of them... I felt like I was drinking from an empty cup. I tried, but it—"

"Lass," said Rew, kneeling in front of her, "the Dark Kind have no souls. Not like you and me, at least. Not like Anne would tell you is watched over by the Blessed Mother."

"T-They don't... then how..." stammered Cinda. "How did Vaisius Morden push them back when he founded the kingdom? If he couldn't draw power from the Dark Kind, then..."

"It wasn't just the Dark Kind who died when he consolidated power two centuries ago," said Rew. "He... The stories are, he would join every battle halfway through."

Cinda's eyes closed, hiding the green glow that had been growing there for months.

Rew raised a hand to comfort her but then lowered it. What could he say?

"Come on, lass," he attempted, standing and looking around to the others. "We're going to want to relocate camp tonight. These things may already smell like Raif after a few days on the road"—

Zaine cackled at that.

—"but by morning, they'll be worse than Zaine," finished Rew.

"Hey!" barked the thief, sounding strangled as she forced out the word between unladylike snorts. She coughed and wheezed then finally managed, "You should smell yourself, Ranger."

"Oh, good come back." Raif laughed.

Zaine punched him, her fist thudding dully against his steel armor. She screeched again and grasped her knuckles. Anne stepped in front of her, taking Zaine's injured hand. Rew and Raif shared a wink before retreating to pack up their gear.

As they knelt over their kits, Raif whispered, "I appreciate that, Ranger. That girl has the sharpest tongue I've ever heard.

Thought the way she was looking, we might feel how sharp her daggers were, too."

Rew smirked, smacked the lad on the shoulder, and said, "I keep telling you, you've got to know when to retreat."

The fighter, still chuckling softly, began tucking away Anne's cooking supplies.

"Good work these last few days, Raif."

Chapter Nine

They'd followed the pack of narjags deep into the forest, far from the paths worn by human travelers. The wood was not as wild, as old, as the wilderness east of Eastwatch, which meant there was thick growth along the forest floor and travel was more difficult.

Rew was used to slipping easily between lowered branches and grasping bushes, but even for him, the constant work of ducking and twisting was tiring. It was spring, and while the temperature was still moderate, beneath the trees and behind walls of vegetation, there was little wind, so the air was close and thick with pollen.

They'd all removed their cloaks and tied them to their packs, which either stuck up and added another hand-length to how far they had to duck beneath a branch or hung low and tended to bounce against the backs of their legs when they squatted. Raif and Zaine fiercely debated which was more annoying.

The terrain was filled with low ridges and narrow valleys that more often than not hid slender streams that tumbled down and away. Those streams would lead them to the river, but along the banks, thick rhododendron grew like a vegetal wall, and Rew knew from experience trying to force their way through the tangled branches would be more work than it was worth, so he led them at an angle, crossing the streams, keeping the water in sight for a while, and always moving south on a tortuous path over and around the rocky outcroppings that sprouted in steep spines.

Down near the streams, biting insects rose like arrows from a defending army when they approached, but Rew found several plants they could use as natural repellants. He slathered the oils from the leaves on thickly, and after the first two hours, no one complained about the stickiness or the unusual scent.

"Gather everything you can," instructed Anne, and Rew collected and put away sheafs of herbs for the empath, some to ward against the insects, some for cooking.

As they hiked, Zaine kept her bow strung, ready to take down a deer or any other game they spied, but their travel through the forest was too loud and whatever was out there was frightened away. The waterways up in the hills were too narrow to be home to many fish, but they still had ample supplies from Arhold.

They stopped for the night on a relatively flat stretch several dozen paces from the water and high enough they could get a breeze. Anne made a pot of rice and beans. The empath pulled out a string of fat sausages and began carving them up, dropping the hunks of meat into the pot and seasoning it with dried peppers the townspeople had given them. Rew provided several herbs he'd collected, and Anne picked out a few, plucking the leaves with dexterous fingers then dropping them into the pot.

Savory smells began wafting up, but Anne shooed them all away. "The more time it has to cook, the better it will taste. Go on now. Find something to do."

Inhaling a heady whiff from the pot, Rew wondered if waiting was worth it. Then, Anne stood and made as if to kick him in the rear. Scuttling away, Rew told the younglings to bring their weapons and to come with him. Yawning loudly, Raif and Zaine followed him, with Cinda trailing behind.

The necromancer had been quiet all day following her failure to help against the Dark Kind. She'd known where her power was drawn from, but Rew suspected she'd gotten comfortable drawing that strength from the king's own wells, the crypts in Jabaan and Iyre. It wasn't as personal when the power she wielded had been taken from a stranger one hundred years before. When you were relying on people you knew to die so you had strength, it was a difficult bite to swallow.

He'd instructed her to practice drawing the ambient power from the forest as they moved, but she complained there was little of it to draw. He knew that, they were leagues from any permanent settlements, but sometimes hard things still had to be done. Rew hoped he had a way to shake her out of her stupor, and then she could get focused again.

"Ranger," complained Raif, eyeing Zaine out of the corner of his eye, "we've been sparring for months now. I know we need to stay sharp, but is this really necessary? I fight with a greatsword, and she fights with daggers. I think we've learned all there is to know about facing each other, and after a trek like today and the fight with the narjags yesterday, we could use some rest."

"Anne always tells us," added Zaine, stretching her back and then covering a yawn with a fist in an exaggerated show, "that rest is important."

"You both know the use of your own weapons," agreed Rew. "I've been impressed, really. Arhold, the narjags we faced yesterday, it was all well done, but, Raif, what happens if you lose your greatsword in the middle of a fight? Will you use your fists or try to scavenge a blade just like the one you lost? Have you seen a narjag toting a greatsword? A complete fighter is not one who only knows the use of one weapon. Or, Zaine, what will you do if we're up against a heavily armored opponent?"

"I'll let Raif handle them," mumbled the thief, though she didn't put any weight behind the comment. She knew where Rew was going.

"Hold on," said Raif, guessing what Zaine must have

suspected. "You want us to switch weapons? Zaine can't even lift my sword."

"Yes I can!"

Rew shook his head, smiling. "At the next town, we're going to buy you some different weaponry, and if we have the space, you're going to practice with them. It'll be good for you, but we don't have access to an armory out here, so that's not what we'll practice today."

Raif frowned, and Zaine crossed her arms over her chest. She asked Rew, "You want us to spar with your longsword?"

Shaking his head, Rew drew his sword and said, "It's too dangerous for you to wield this blade. If you accidentally released its power... No, Zaine, it's not dangerous for me. It'd be dangerous to you. Instead, I want you to spar against my longsword."

"W-Wait…" stammered Raif, taking an inadvertent step back. "You don't practice."

"I will today."

"This is going to be fun to watch," quipped Cinda, giving her brother and the thief a wicked smile.

Rew grinned at her. "You too, lass."

The necromancer blinked at him.

"What?" asked Zaine. "You want… We take turns against you? Is Cinda supposed to borrow a fork from Anne and stab you with it?"

Rew began pacing the clearing, spinning his longsword and stretching his arms, shoulders, and waist. "No, I want all three of you to try me at once. Come hard. You won't hurt me, but watch for each other. We have Anne, but I don't think she'll appreciate having to patch you up if you're injuring your friends. Give it a real try, but the most important lesson today is about learning to work together, to use your talents in conjunction. There's more to it than swinging a sword hard or sneaking up behind someone. There's more to it than unleashing whatever stored power you can get your hands on. I need you to understand what each other are capable of, to be creative, and to work as a cohesive team."

Cinda scowled at him, but Zaine looked interested. Raif looked uncertain.

"You have five minutes to strategize," Rew told them, "then come at me. I'll be counting. If I have to come to you, I'm going to leave some welts."

HE WAS WORRIED CINDA WOULD FIND THE EXERCISE FOOLISH AND would sit it out, but he knew she was involved when after four minutes, a brilliant clap of thunder and burst of startling white and green light erupted in front of his face. A cold, bitter wind slapped his skin but did little else except force him to take a step back. He'd been waiting for something to happen and was well anchored in the wilderness around them.

He'd claimed that they wouldn't hurt him, but with power to draw upon, there were few people Cinda couldn't hurt. As he felt her magic ripple around him, unable to break his protection, his lips curled in relief. They were in the wild, far from the places of man. The ranger had strength in the woods, and the necromancer did not.

Before the magic petered out, Raif charged, wheeling his greatsword above his head and unleashing a powerful blow, though Rew sensed the fighter hadn't put his entire weight behind it.

Rew ducked easily, but Raif careened toward him, evidently trying to bowl over the ranger with an armored shoulder. Rew hooked a foot against Raif's ankle and kicked, sending the fighter sprawling.

Calmly, Rew turned and found Zaine stalking up behind him.

The thief's lips twisted. Her eyes flicked toward Raif, who was slowly pushing himself up from the turf, and then toward Cinda.

Grinning, Rew held his longsword to one side and his open hand to the other side, inviting her attack.

Zaine sighed and ran forward. She tried misdirection, feinting a blow toward his head but coming at his torso. Rew simply stepped into her attack, behind her guard, and bonked her gently on the head with the hilt of his longsword.

"Ouch!" complained Zaine.

Rew grabbed her and spun, putting the thief between himself and Cinda, pushing her backward so Zaine had to stumble awkwardly to avoid a fall. On the way, Rew touched the edge of his longsword to Raif's neck as the boy rose off his knees.

Cinda was building a small cloud of death's breath in her hand, but it lacked enough strength to do more than irritate an opponent, and she hesitated, not wanting to fling it where it'd do just as much damage to her allies as to Rew.

"You all hesitated," chided Rew, reaching Cinda and sticking his longsword around Zaine to tap the necromancer on the arm. "Maybe next time, we should use sticks, so you'll actually swing them. Cinda, that was good work not unleashing your power against Zaine, but you shouldn't have held back on your first strike. Against a single opponent you might not be able to handle, give them your all."

"We can't fight you!" complained Zaine, shaking her bicep where Rew had grabbed her and then rubbing the growing lump on her forehead where the hilt of his longsword had tapped her. "You've been training at this longer than I've been alive, you know."

"And if you're facing Prince Valchon, will you use the same excuse?"

The thief muttered a curse.

"We're in the middle of nowhere," said Cinda. "There aren't any people within leagues of here, much less anyone who happens to be dying at the moment. My powers are weak in a place like this."

"Ah, well hopefully we can trick Valchon into following us

into a crypt, just like we did his two brothers, and surely at no point the prince thinks that maybe, just maybe, fighting us in a crypt is a bad idea," responded Rew dryly. "He'll know by now exactly how his brothers failed, but I'm sure we can come up with some believable ploy to bring him to the one place you can over-power him. And of course the king is a gentleman. He'll let you draw on whatever necromantic power is around before he partakes."

Cinda's brow bunched, and she opened her mouth but then closed it.

Rew turned to Raif, wondering what excuse the big fighter would have, but the lad admitted, "I held back. It's hard to swing this blade at a friend, particularly because I, ah, have a habit of going a bit berserk. With a big thick branch, have no fear. I won't hesitate to bash you over the head with it."

"Fair enough," said Rew with a laugh. He paused then looked at the three younglings. "Your plan didn't work, but you're thinking in the right direction. You know your strengths, and you tried to take advantage of them. It failed partly because I know you so well, and maybe you want to account for that, but leaning into those strengths is your best bet. Most opponents won't know you at all, so layered distractions, an attack from behind, are all elements of a good plan. Now, help me find a branch big enough for Raif, and let's do it again."

THE NEXT DAY, THEY FOUGHT THROUGH THE FOREST UNTIL THEY stumbled across a slender dirt path. Rew could smell the moisture in the air, and when he crossed the road and looked, he found they were two hundred paces from the river. The bank was heavy with growth, and so far from anywhere, they weren't hiding from anyone, so they took the road and headed south.

Along the way, they spotted a plodding wagon carrying a heaping mound of beans. They asked the driver how far to the next town, and he told them half a day. The man offered them a ride on his wagon, but they declined.

The sad-eyed mule pulling the wagon looked like it was already teetering on the edge of death, and Rew didn't want their added weight to end the poor creature. Resting their legs wasn't worth bearing that on his conscience. The driver pleaded, and quickly, they realized the man was lonely, and had they rode with him, the driver wouldn't have shut his mouth for a minute. They walked on, easily pacing out of earshot of the wagon driver, and nodding at the other occasional travelers on the rough road.

Rew savored the silence.

Most of the commerce going in or out of the region would be moved along the waterway, so the people they saw on the road were locals—farmers or crofters going to town to barter their wares, locals taking the road to reach a neighbor or relative, and few others.

Rew suspected their party was the only one to walk that road who came from outside the region, and they drew the stares commiserate with their status as strangers. Raif, in particular, would be remarked upon. They'd seen no one else armed like he was and certainly no one wearing armor. Cinda would have drawn her share of gossip as well, except these people likely had no idea what her crimson robes signified, and after so long on the river, then in the forest, it was becoming rather difficult to see what color those robes were.

"I know you'll just call me a pampered noble for saying it," declared Cinda, "but I'd give nearly anything for a proper bath and laundry."

Zaine grinned and plucked at the cotton tunic she wore beneath her vest. "Give? Pfah! I'd kill a man to join you in that bath." The thief flushed. Then, she stammered, "I-I mean, I wouldn't, ah, join you. I didn't mean, unless… no. I wouldn't… actually kill someone, to bathe, that is."

"I think I know what you meant," said Cinda, her green eyes twinkling.

Zaine's face turned beet red, and Cinda smiled at her. Rew wasn't sure if the smile was meant to make Zaine feel better or whether it was at her expense. Later, he wondered if it'd been meant to be an invitation, and he suspected Zaine was wondering the same.

Anne, as watchful as a hawk, interjected and began asking what sort of mending their clothing might need and how many items they would want laundered, so Rew stopped paying attention. Whatever he told her, Anne would do as she pleased with his clothing, even if it meant mending things that were just going to get torn and dirty again as soon as they left. Over the years, he'd found it was easier for all involved to just let her do as she wished.

Tate had been the only one who could reason with Anne when she set her mind to something, but Rew had never figured how the old ranger had managed it. Maybe it was because Tate had been old and was beyond caring about Anne's stern looks. Or maybe it was because Tate rarely drank, so he never feared Anne cutting his supply of ale. Rew rubbed his head and decided that had been it, though the realization didn't help him much. He had a hankering for an ale later that evening.

The river road was easy walking, and Rew would have considered taking it farther toward the coast, but through the sporadic gaps in the vegetation on the bank, he saw a variety of crafts moving up and down the waterway. It wasn't crowded out there, but there was enough traffic he suspected the town they were approaching was a decent sized one. It meant they might be able to hire a faster boat than the dinghies and barges that were common.

With a vessel equipped for sailing and the current carrying them downriver, they would make it to the coast four or five times faster than they would on foot, faster than with horses, which he made pains to mention several times before the others began bothering him about it.

When they reached the town later that day, Rew was pleased

to see that it was larger than Arhold, and he spied the tips of docks jutting out into the river. There were boats tied there, and a few short masts they could see over the low-slung buildings of the town. There were no walls around the place, and it looked peaceful.

"They'd be in a heap of trouble if anyone ever attacked them," complained Raif, holding a hand over his eyes and studying the place. "Even the temporary fortifications Arhold erected would be impossible here. Look how wide those streets are. They're spread out like they never even considered how to defend the place. Pfah. Who designed this settlement?"

"Someone not worried about attack," remarked Zaine. "I envy them. No concerns for Dark Kind, irritating nobles…"

Raif put his gauntleted fists on his hips. "Nobility aren't the cause of all of life's conflict, you know."

Zaine tilted her head to the side and grinned at the nobleman. "Oh, which conflicts are they responsible for, then?"

"Never mind."

They trudged into the town and were pleased to find it had a proper inn. Most of the other patrons looked to be bargemen and those stopping over from a longer journey on the river. Rew realized they'd been lucky to stumble into a large settlement, as the smaller villages would be passed over by the bulk of the travelers.

The place wasn't up to Anne's standards, but the innkeeper was able to refer them to a washerwoman who could launder their clothing by evening. Once he got to describing the baths situated behind the inn, Anne relented. Rew was suspicious the water was simply river water, which they could have had for free and a lot cleaner away from the town, but it was warmed by braziers beneath the tubs, and there was soap. The ale the innkeeper drew was poor quality, but the wine was better than they had a right to expect.

Rew watched Anne take a hesitant sip. Then, he nodded to himself when her lips curved into a satisfied grin. If she was enjoying the wine, he figured he would get used to the taste of the ale after two or three more mugs of the stuff.

Anne saw Rew's look and warned, "Don't you smile."

He tried to keep his face blank then quaffed another mouthful of the sour ale.

It was still a few hours until dusk when they had arrived, so before the drinks, they'd busied themselves cleaning up, seeing the washerwoman, and visiting the general goods store to see what supplies were available that hadn't been in the more isolated town of Arhold.

Anne had purchased a new outfit for Rew and several for herself. Cinda had declined any new attire, as she preferred her necromancer's robes. Zaine looked interested but wouldn't try anything on, which made Anne exasperated, and they all stalked out without buying anything for the thief. They made some other small purchases, and Raif meandered down the street and bought some steel links to make repairs on his armor. Rew paid for it all. When they'd settled back at the inn, Anne went to adjust the hems of her new garments, Raif saw to his armor in his room, and Cinda disappeared into the baths. After giving several nervous looks toward the back of the inn, shifting from foot to foot, and adjusting her hair, Zaine had joined Rew for an ale.

"Drink up before Anne sees," he'd advised.

"What makes you think I want to get drunk?" questioned Zaine.

Rew glanced at the back of the inn where Cinda had gone to bathe. He shrugged.

Scowling at him, Zaine tilted up her ale mug and poured another. She wiped the foam from her mouth and said, "You know, it's been months since I've thought about stealing something."

Rew blinked and scratched his beard. "Uh huh. That's good, I guess. Real good. I suppose we've been positive influences on you. Making an honest woman out of you, finally."

"I never used to go an hour without sizing up those around

me, wondering who had a fat purse or wasn't paying attention," continued the thief, ignoring Rew's comment. "It was a lifestyle. Always, it was on my mind, and usually, I was practicing. Even when I knew they wouldn't have the coin to be worth the risk, I'd go and cut a purse just to see if I could get away with it, and if I couldn't, it'd give me a chance to prove how nimble I was on the escape. I picked locks to bakers to boost a muffin and locks to armorers when I knew damn well they'd taken their coin from the shop and the last thing a thief needs is noisy armor. It was… a lifestyle. That's the word for it."

Rew waited for her to say more.

"I did need the coin. It was the only way I could survive without spreading my legs. Not many choices for a young girl on her own and with no trade, eh, but it was more than that. It was something I was good at, and I won't lie, I got a thrill every time I did it. Maybe had I wanted to, I could have found myself a proper job. I don't know. Looking back, maybe I was born a thief. I never dreamed of another life. Not for long, at least."

"A hard life makes for hard choices," replied Rew, raising his mug in a toast.

"I didn't think much about my victims, then," said Zaine, her look undirected, perhaps from that mug of ale or perhaps just lost in her thoughts. "Of course, whoever they were, they almost certainly had more than I did. Still, doesn't make it right, stealing from them."

"You did what you had to do. It was the only way to survive. Now that you're with—"

"I think I need to start stealing again."

Rew coughed, nearly spitting a mouthful of ale on the table. "What?"

Zaine lowered her voice and leaned over conspiratorially. "Shh. There's folks in here that don't need to hear this, but I said, I think I should start stealing again."

Sitting back, Rew picked up his ale mug and then put it back down. "I didn't think that's where you were going with this. You're saying you want to… steal?"

"You heard me."

"That's not necessary," replied the ranger. He shook himself. "We've got plenty of coin, lass. You're traveling with nobles now. In fact, if I had to gamble on it, I'd wager my purse that it's got more coin in it than anyone else's in this place. You don't need to… We've plenty of coin. More than enough. You don't need to make those hard choices you used to."

Zaine wiggled her fingers under his nose. "It's not about the riches, Ranger. It's about staying in practice. I was thinking about that the other night, after you drubbed us. Raif's a fighter. That's plain enough. Cinda is our necromancer, as was mightily confirmed in Jabaan and Iyre. Anne is the empath. You're the ranger, and I'm the thief. We play to our individual strengths, which makes us stronger as a team. We work together, like you said. It's been months since I've cut a purse, and I worry I'm getting rusty. If I don't practice, I can't play my role."

Rew rubbed his head. "Zaine, it's not right. Your victims, remember? Maybe they had more coin than you back then, but no one in here has more coin than you do now."

"What if I just steal from the rich? Nobles, merchants, those folk. You can't tell me you care if I steal from a noble."

"Stealing is stealing."

"You think Anne would object," mused Zaine, tapping a finger against her lips. "You're probably right. I don't think she'd like it. Course, I wasn't planning to tell her, so it's only a worry if I get caught."

"It's not Anne. Well, not only Anne that I'm worried about. It's… Stealing is wrong, Zaine."

She waved a hand to dismiss him. "You'll come around. I won't take anything from anyone who needs the coin to eat. First noble we see, just you watch, you'll be cheering me on."

Rew drank deeply of his ale.

"What if I stole from you?"

Rew coughed again and, for the second time, nearly spit out his ale all over the table. He sat the mug down and gave the eager thief a harsh glare.

Zaine sat back, her ale mug held jauntily in her hand. "That's what we'll do. I'll steal from you. No victim, no cause for Anne to be concerned, right?"

"I'd be the victim!" burst Rew.

"You pay for everything anyway."

He stared at her. "So if you're successful, you'll start to pay?"

"Of course not."

Rew was furiously thinking of objections to this plan when Anne and Raif returned. The empath began haranguing Zaine about going out and getting more clothes. It seemed the washer-woman wasn't able to save many of their old garments. As Anne had worried, narjag blood didn't come out easily.

"Zaine looks pleased," whispered Raif hoarsely, settling down next to Rew and helping himself to the ale pitcher, "even with Anne bending her ear like that. Looks like she got away with something. She didn't… She hasn't taken her bath yet, has she?"

"She has not," croaked Rew, surreptitiously checking to make sure his coin purse was still full.

"Good. Good."

Raif settled himself into complimenting Anne on her new clothing and telling Zaine how fine he thought she would look if she ever decided to wear a dress. The empath beamed at Raif's praise and gave Rew challenging looks, as if he'd ever said she looked anything other than good. Zaine studied Rew with a mischievous twinkle in her eyes. The ranger drank his ale and brooded.

Until he saw Zaine's grin blooming. Then, he drank his ale, and he sweated.

Chapter Ten

L ater that evening, an hour after nightfall and while his stockpile of coin was still mercifully untouched by Zaine, Rew saw what they needed.

"That's the man."

"He looks…" began Raif.

"Like a noble?" finished Rew.

"Not one well accustomed to travel," retorted the fighter. "When I was a child, my parents made me wear similar dress during special events. Pfah, look at all that lace around his neck and the hose! Imagine climbing a mountainside wearing that."

"You wore tights?" questioned Zaine.

"Years ago," admitted Raif, staring at the man Rew had pointed out. "The velvet of his doublet would be ruined in half an hour of stalking through the forest. And… surely those gems on his fingers aren't real? I think that man may be pretending to be more than he is. No noble, not even a duke or a baron, would wear so much adornment on a journey. Look around. There are no soldiers here. He's practically asking to be accosted by ruffians."

"Aye," said Rew, "he's perfect."

Raif frowned.

"You mean he couldn't have gotten far on his own, dressed

like that?" questioned Cinda. "Way out here, he must have arrived on a boat."

"Exactly," replied Rew.

"A merchant?" wondered Raif. "I've never seen one dressed like such a fop, but..."

"Merchants dress like beggars," replied Rew. He studied the man a moment longer then added, "They don't want you to know they have coin to afford whatever price you're asking. So, not a real noble, not a merchant, but as Cinda said, he got here somehow, didn't he? He has to be a passenger on a ship that he doesn't own."

"That could be true," admitted Raif, "but we're doing an awful lot of guessing here."

Rew shrugged. "We could ask every person in this building if they happen to be sailing on a fast ship that is available for hire, but it seems quicker to guess, and odds are, there isn't an empty ship sitting at the docks looking for passengers from this town. We need to find a vessel already enroute and do some fast talking to get ourselves onboard."

"Guessing might save some time, but only if you're right," retorted Raif dryly.

Rew winked at him.

"If he's not the owner, then how are we going to hire the ship?" questioned Cinda. "A captain won't deviate from their route on the word of a passenger, no matter how finely tailored that ridiculous half cape he's wearing is. You've got a full purse, Ranger, but we're competing with permanent employment, and if the captain leaves the service of his master to ferry us down river, he might be facing more consequences than just losing his job. He could be hung if they accuse him of stealing the vessel."

"Maybe they're already headed south?" responded Rew. "Only way we'll find out is to ask, and if they're not... we offer some gentle persuasion."

Raif cracked his knuckles.

"Gentle, I said," chided Rew. "Remember, we've got to sail on the ship for a week. If we force them to carry us, they'll spend the entire time looking for a way to betray us, and once we get to Shavroe, it's certain they'll call the authorities the moment the lines are tossed to the dock."

"Tip him overboard when we're underway…"

Sighing, Rew shook his head. "It takes a crew to sail a ship, Raif. You children have so much to learn. We begin with diplomacy, and I won't hear of another plan until we've tried it."

"Share your wisdom with us, then, Wise One. How do we talk a ship's captain into taking us to Shavroe?"

Rew lifted his ale mug. "Look at the man's nose. It's purple with swollen and broken blood vessels. It's a sure indication the man enjoys a drink."

"You'd know," quipped Anne.

Pretending he didn't hear her, Rew continued, "All we have to do is get him drunk and let his secrets pour forth. We sort through them, find the one which gives us leverage, and off we'll be."

"Blessed Mother, Rew," barked Anne, "are you sure this isn't just an excuse to get yourself drunk?"

Grinning, Rew bowed toward Zaine. "Not I, but our intrepid thief. She's going to go have a few drinks with this man, and when she's done, he'll be begging to accompany us all of the way to the coast."

"And how am I supposed to convince him to do that?"

Wiggling his eyebrows, Rew suggested, "You're the thief."

"I'm not going to sleep with the man, if that's what you're suggesting," huffed Zaine.

"Of course not," mollified Rew. "If you did, it wouldn't be a theft. It'd be a deal, value for value. No, we need a ride on this man's ship, and as our team thief, I don't expect you to give him fair compensation for it."

"Fair compen—Pfah. If I slept with him it'd be more than fair value. It'd be the night of the man's life. We ought to own the ship after that," retorted Zaine. Then, she blushed and glanced at Cinda. "I don't… I'm just talking, you know."

Rew produced two silver coins, spun them on the table, and said, "Not that I think you'll need these, but just in case, since you're a little rusty."

Zaine sat still for a moment, thinking. Then, she stood and snatched the two coins. "Very well. Get packed, everyone. We'll leave at dawn."

As Zaine moved toward her mark, Anne looked on disapprovingly, but she must have felt everyone could guess exactly what she would say in such circumstances, so she didn't bother.

Rew thought it would have been better if she had. Then, he could stop imagining what she was thinking and just hear it and be done with it. She was like that. A scold, but she let people make their own choices and live with the consequences. With any luck, though, there would be little in the way of consequences tonight.

They all sat watching Zaine curiously as she seemed to have little trouble ingratiating herself with the fop. They couldn't hear a word of what was said, but they could see her expressions, how she acted in response to the man's comments. They were hoping that soon, they would see the moment he acquiesced to ferrying them down to Shavroe, though Rew had his doubts.

Raif, ever the protector, watched with hard eyes, prepared to stand and charge in between Zaine and the overly attired man at the blink of an eye. Rew didn't think it would come to that, but if it did, they might be able to use it. The ranger didn't want to encourage Raif to use his fists in that manner, but every now and then, a slug to the chin got results. If they could embarrass this man into thinking he'd propositioned a proper lady, then maybe that was the leverage they would need to earn a ride. Nobles didn't think twice about stepping on the backs of the commoners, but when it came to the honor of their own women, sometimes, they were funny about it.

Hopefully, Raif's fists wouldn't come into it, but it was worth considering as a backup plan. Rew had been honest when he said that if the ship was headed north, coin wasn't going to turn it around. Cinda had been correct when she'd surmised that if a captain deviated from his route, he would be facing time behind bars or worse.

Most likely, worse. Theft of a decent quality sailing ship would mean a team of private investigators—mercenaries, really—who would be willing to follow the perpetrator to the end of the kingdom to bring back his head. In Rew's experience, owners of ships viewed their vessels as both property and as a mistress. That made it dangerous, taking another man's ship without permission.

So, Rew hoped Zaine would succeed. If she didn't, they could be waiting for days, or they could be following Raif's more violent instincts. Either way was better than walking to Shavroe, but neither option left Rew with a good feeling.

They couldn't wait, he tried to rationalize. They had an important quest, and their mission was more critical than whatever a nobleman might be doing flitting about the kingdom. Pfah. Nobles were probably causing trouble, and it might do everyone some good, taking their ship and slowing them down.

Through the course of the night, it dawned on Rew that Zaine had been right. When it came to thieving, as long as the victim was a nobleman, Rew found he really didn't mind it so much. A merchant, well, he would have another ale and think about that.

"This might work," said Cinda, sounding surprised.

Rew nodded. "Aye, it might. It always goes against my better instinct, letting Zaine have some rope to do what she does, but in this case—"

Anne shifted in her seat, and Rew quieted. Best not to push it until he was sure the plan had actually worked. The thief had started well enough, getting the man to purchase her a drink, and it seemed it was still going smoothly. The man had open eyes and appeared interested in what the thief had to say, and as any well-versed temptress knows, Zaine was letting the man himself do most of the talking, which from afar, it seemed he was doing a lot of.

Zaine's tinkling laughter reached them from half a dozen tables away.

"She's doing a superb job pretending to laugh," said Raif, his fist clenching and unclenching on his ale mug.

Cinda patted him on the shoulder, though out of his sight, she was rolling her eyes.

Soon, the tartly-dressed dandy and the thief were both glancing toward the party's table, and Zaine looked to be pointing them out and telling the man about them.

"Describing the berths we require, presumably?" asked Anne. She tried to sound critical, but Rew could hear the curiosity in her tone.

"She's got to learn," remarked Rew. "We're all right here watching her, so this is good practice."

"Learn?" asked Anne, frowning at him.

Rew shrugged and did not respond. It wasn't the time to tell Anne he and Zaine had discussed practicing her thieving. It was the sort of activity Anne would feel obliged to disapprove of, no matter how many times Zaine's skills had been of use.

"And they're watching us," mentioned Cinda, turning slightly as if to pretend she hadn't been watching them.

"And laughing still," added Raif.

Zaine and the dandy ordered another round, and the man's face was rosy with mirth by the end of it. He'd stopped glancing at the party and was outright staring at them now. Finally, he leaned over, grasped Zaine's hands in both of his, and seemed to be offering effusive thanks.

Raif scooted his chair back to stand, but Cinda caught his sleeve. "He's just holding her hand."

"And that's all he'd better be thinking about doing," growled Raif.

Zaine and the man stood, and she sauntered back to the party's table, leading the man behind her. Rew could hardly believe it.

"We have our ride," declared Zaine. "This is Raponne. He's a passenger on a sloop, which he tells me is the fastest and most tastefully appointed vessel on the river. Wine, fine cheeses, and speed. What else could we ask for?"

"And how does one become a passenger on such an impressive vessel?" wondered Rew, looking Raponne up and down.

Up close, the man didn't have the face of nobility. They'd been bred for magical talent for centuries, and it gave them all the similar look of distant cousins. This man was common, but his clothes were expensive enough, and his hands didn't appear to have ever engaged in serious labor. A merchant, but then wouldn't he own his own ship?

"He's an artist in the employ of Duke Vincent of Shavroe," declared Zaine, a grin splitting her face. "Such a fortunate coincidence. I've always wanted to visit the coast and see the grand city of Shavroe, and to do so with one of Vaeldon's most famous artistic talents? Thanks to the Mother's Grace."

"Well, I'm headed north…" reminded the artist.

""Such a fortunate coincidence," drawled Rew, catching onto Zaine's game. "Raponne? Wait, the Raponne, is it? Why, I'm honored to have met you. Your name is spoken from one end of this kingdom to the other, is it not?"

"Soon. It will be soon," crooned Raponne. His eyes twinkled, obviously enjoying the praise. "The lass is overly generous, as are you, my good man. Why, the odds of encountering someone who's seen and appreciated my work…"

"Your work?" choked Raif. "What, ah, what sort of art do you do?"

"Raif, this is *the* Raponne," gushed Zaine. "Don't you recall, in Iyre, we heard stories of his prodigious skill, and of course, the prince himself had one of Raponne's paintings hanging in his study. I couldn't believe it myself when he told me who he was. I've heard so much about his art that I demanded he show us. Unfortunately, he's told me he only has supplies for his charcoals at the moment. His paints don't travel well, you understand? It's a boon, though, that he does have his charcoals. He uses them for his more adventurous works."

"Adventurous?"

"Yes," replied Zaine, her eyes burning with excitement that Rew found highly disconcerting. "Raponne specializes in nudes…"

"Zaine, you don't have to!" cried Raif, starting to rise again.

"…of men," finished the thief.

"What?"

"I know," purred Zaine, mischief practically blazing from her beaming face, "I was so excited when he told me. He looked you over and says he's inspired. The physique, the scars… I told Raponne how much it'd mean to me to have you immortalized in, ah, parchment and charcoal, and he told me how much pleasure it'd give him doing the work. It's a win for us all!"

"Nudes?" whispered Raif.

"Well, we didn't discuss it being plural," said Zaine, putting an arm through Raponne's and beaming down at Raif, "but I suppose, why not?"

AFTER GIVING PROPER DEFERENCE TO ZAINE'S RISQUÉ PLAN, AND WITH regards to the rising storm cloud of Raif's demeanor, and that Raponne kept insisting he was traveling north to Iyre, Rew implemented his own version of the idea and proceeded to get Raponne wildly, filthily, savagely drunk.

Not even Anne complained as Rew ordered pitcher after pitcher. Raponne haughtily voiced disdain for ale and expressed a preference for heady wines, but Rew convinced him that artists had to live life along a spectrum, and sometimes, getting muddy with the low was the fire that forged high art.

It helped that Zaine lavished praise on Raif as thickly as she had Raponne, discussing the fighter's bravery, his charm, the way he looked without a shirt, and his skill with a giant blade. Raif didn't quite know what to do with the barrage of compliments, but he didn't protest, and Raponne remained interested.

The artist, it seemed, had actually become somewhat popular in Duke Vincent of Shavroe's court, but Rew guessed the man was unknown outside of it. Raponne clearly sought the sort of recognition all men of the arts seek for their genius. It was easy enough to convince him they'd heard his name all across the kingdom, and breezy descriptions of far-off capital cities stirred the man's imagination.

"Well, of course, Prince Valchon has one of your works hanging in his breakfast room," declared Rew. "I'm surprised you did not know, but I suppose no artist can truly appreciate their own influence, can they? So tightly focused on creation, I daresay, you don't have time to consider your own, rapidly growing, fame!"

Raponne expanded like a roll in an oven. "Why, naturally. All that matters is the art."

"Indubitably."

Zaine leaned toward Rew and hissed, "Is that even a word? He's an educated man, Ranger. He's going to see through—"

"It's a real word," Rew informed her.

Zaine looked skeptical, but she leaned into the flattery, and as the night wore on and the tide of ale rose, their praise began to grow so outrageous that Rew had to grip the thief's knee beneath the table to stall her from continuing one particularly ludicrous account. She also misused the word indubitably several times, but by then, Raponne was in high enough spirits he didn't notice.

The artist had a willful disregard of the coming dawn as many a creative type had and was content to fill the dark hours with drink and listening to his own accolades. Though surely, the man must have been suspicious that they'd witnessed so many of his works and heard so many comments from esteemed nobles throughout the kingdom.

Rew wondered how many paintings Raponne could have possibly produced, but he plied the artist with more and more ale, and before long, the other man was teetering and singing songs that he certainly had not learned in any proper nobleman's court. Most of their party was too exhausted and too drunk in their own right to listen, but Zaine looked interested at some of the sauciest lyrics, and Rew imagined the thief was squirreling away the phrases to burst out at some inappropriate moment.

Rew waited until he judged it was time, balancing on the verge of Raponne's gleeful intoxication and his impending unconsciousness. It was three hours before dawn. Rew sent Anne and Raif to gather their things then slung Raponne's arm over his shoulder. Weaving and stumbling, more dragging the man than walking him, the ranger took the artist to the docks. The others caught up half a block from the river, and they meandered to the vessel that Raponne, through squinted eyes and a great deal of uncertainty, identified as his.

It was, as the artist had described earlier in the evening, a sleek-looking sloop that was well-cared for. It was manned by a nightwatchman, and evidently, the rest of the crew was berthed on the vessel, as the young watchman called down a hatch at their approach.

"He's back, and he's proper drunk again, Captain."

A put-upon-looking man ascended from a small hatch after a minute. His hair stuck up wildly, and his jaw cracked with a terrific yawn. He rubbed his face, as if pressure on his weathered skin was going to wake him up.

"Aye, put him in his cabin, will you?" instructed the captain, shaking his head at Raponne's sodden state. He called to Rew and the others, "A silver for your trouble of returnin' him to us."

"A silver?" huffed Rew. "The man was on the verge of causing real trouble for himself back at the tavern."

"A silver each," grumbled the captain, and he gestured for a sailor who appeared behind him to disperse the funds.

"We don't need your coin, but, ah, you should know, he agreed to take us to Shavroe," claimed Rew.

"Shavroe?" questioned the captain. "Nah, Friend, we're

headed north. He's going to serve in Prince Heindaw's court, and while I've a slight doubt that this sod agreed to ferry you anywhere, I'm certain he didn't agree to turn around and go south. It's right fat commission he'll earn in Iyre."

"Been taking your time on this journey, have you?"

"What's that mean?"

"Prince Heindaw was killed several weeks ago," explained Rew, dropping Raponne to the wooden wharf so the sailors could drag the man up the gangplank. "There is no court, or at least, not the sort Raponne would fancy joining."

The captain scratched his head. "We left Shavroe two weeks back."

Rew held his hands up. "The prince is dead. Last I heard, it's unclear who even commands in Iyre. Word has to be all over town by now, if you want to check."

"You're sure that Prince Heindaw…" mumbled the captain, "because Prince Calb—"

"Was killed almost two months ago in Jabaan," finished Rew. "I know. Makes one think it must be related, right? The river pirates are certainly taking advantage. We found a net across the channel just a few days north of here. Boat like this would be a mighty rich catch for men like that. How well are your sailors armed?"

Raponne raised his hand, as if signaling to the sailors to come collect him. The arm wobbled then pointed toward Raif. Slurring like a man who'd had more than a score of ales, because he had, Raponne demanded, "I've a new muse! Take him to my cabin!"

"Duke Vincent won't like this," retorted the captain, eyeing Rew and the others suspiciously.

"I'm in charge here," bellowed Raponne, the effect slightly less impressive as he was rolling around on his back, too drunk to sit upright.

A dog began barking somewhere back in the town, and the captain scowled at all of them. "I don't have time for this fool-ishness."

"Captain," assured Rew, "Prince Heindaw is dead. The temple of the Cursed Father was burned to the ground, and much of the palace was destroyed. There's no law there, now, and if I was you, I wouldn't risk my ship going anywhere near the place. I understand we're strangers, and I don't expect you to believe it on my word alone." He glanced at Raponne. "Or his word, I suppose. So why don't you go into the town and ask anyone you meet? Iyre has fallen, and your mission is impossible. You can't be faulted for going home when there is clearly no point in continuing."

The captain looked uncertainly from his drunken charge to the town beyond them.

A sailor cleared his throat. "Ah, Captain, at our last berth, when I went to the market for produce, I did hear there'd been a conflict up north. I didn't realize the prince... I thought maybe they'd gotten confused with Prince Calb, but thinking about it now, these folk might be telling the truth."

Zaine toed Raponne gently in the back with her boot.

"Of course they're telling the truth," Raponne shouted from their feet. "We leave now!"

The captain and the mate shared a look, and without knowing the men, Rew was able to interpret it easily enough. They were ready to be done with the artist, and downriver was quicker than upriver.

The captain shook himself then instructed the crewman, "Go find someone awake and make certain we're hearing the right rumor. The rest of you, make ready to sail."

Acting like it pained him, the captain allowed Rew and the others onboard, and in minutes when the crewman returned and confirmed Heindaw was dead, the captain cast off the lines, and they turned the vessel around, headed back south. Raponne, once they started moving, was messily sick over the side of the gunwale until the sun rose.

Chapter Eleven

When the artist Raponne awoke sometime near midday, he was irritable and confused. Then, he realized they were traveling south, and he was outraged. It seemed he'd been promised great rewards in Iyre, both for him and for Duke Vincent. Even aside from the size of his commission, working in a prince's court was the sort of opportunity that might elevate an artist's fame to the level Raponne believed he was due.

But outraged as he was, he was also exceptionally hungover and had difficulty continuing the argument between bouts of leaning over the side of the sloop and heaving, though hours before, he'd already evacuated the contents of his stomach. He was also not enjoying the bright sunlight and was particularly sensitive to loud noises.

When Rew moved to stand in front of the sun and began speaking in an exaggerated tone, as if trying to get a distracted child's attention, Raponne retreated back into his cabin with a bottle of expensive-looking wine. The captain noticed Rew's antics, but it seemed he'd come to terms with the change in mission and was bemused rather than annoyed.

Raponne reemerged near supper and managed to hold a conversation that time, though he strenuously refused to eat. He was still outraged, but somewhere in the throes of his stupor, it had finally sunk in that Prince Heindaw was dead. He'd protested that the prince couldn't be, but the hard assurances from Rew and the others convinced him of the truth. It was such an outrageous lie, if it was one, that no one would attempt it. If Rew and the others were lying, it would be discovered when they arrived in Shavroe, if not before when they stopped to gather provisions. And if a lie, they would have a terrible time explaining to the duke why they'd commandeered his vessel and his artist. A long stay in the duke's prisons was the best they could hope for.

With the prince dead and his commission and dreams ruined, Raponne returned to his cabin to refresh himself, he said, or sulk, as Cinda described it.

The captain, following the unpleasant confusion, cheered up. It seemed he was quite happy to be returning to his home and family instead of venturing north into the thick of uncertainty. He, and the rest of the crew, had heard about the destruction in Jabaan, and some part of them must have known that one prince falling in such horrific circumstances meant danger for the entire kingdom. A second prince getting killed in his own capital was no coincidence. Beyond that, the captain and crew were experienced men of the world, and they knew that without anyone in authority, river pirates and other bandits would fall over themselves trying to take a sloop like Duke Vincent's.

With matters settled, the captain found them an out of the way corner at the prow of the vessel where they could lay out their bedrolls and string a tarp overhead to block the sun and the rain. For a party used to sleeping outdoors, it was comfortable enough, and the sun felt good on their skin. The lap of water against the keel of the sloop, the soft conversation of the sailors, and the crack and thump of the sail as the breeze carried them downstream were comforting sounds to fall asleep to.

The sailors gambled, drank grog, and performed their duties all while ignoring the party as best they could. Cinda and Zaine would have drawn the men like bears to honey normally, but Raif had donned his steel armor and propped his greatsword nearby, which was enough to drive them away. After a day on the water, Rew realized, these were men of the city as well as the greater world. They were men in the employ of a duke. They understood the importance of Cinda's crimson robes. Raif need not have scowled at the sailors to keep them from her.

Some of those men might have even guessed there was a reason this odd group of travelers knew so much about Prince Heindaw's demise. Sailors were generally regarded as a frolicsome lot, willing to berth in any port whether or not there was a storm, but they were also superstitious and careful when at work. One didn't survive long on the open sea by steering directly into thunderclouds and rocky shorelines. It would be impossible for them to know the details or how deeply involved Rew and the others were, but the sailors knew a forbidding coast when they saw one.

But while the girls were left alone, after three days on the river, Raponne seemed to recover his vigor and his zest for drawing young men with charcoal. He started loitering near Raif, showering the lad with compliments, which only served to make Raif nervous. The artist then began showing Raif pieces from his portfolio, which only served to make Raif blush. By the time the artist recalled a befuddled promise in exchange for passage on the vessel, Raif was stone-faced and ignoring the man.

Rew tried to get a wager going on whether Raif would toss the artist over the gunwale or jump over himself, but Anne put a stop to that. Raponne turned to the captain for relief and enforcement of what he viewed as a verbal contract, but the captain very obviously wanted nothing to do with it. The artist then turned to Zaine.

She perused his portfolio, making sly comments to Cinda, questioning why anyone would have any interest in such odd-shaped appendages. The necromancer smiled tolerantly then finally leaned close and whispered into Zaine's ear. The girl blushed and dropped the portfolio back into Raponne's lap like it had burned her. The artist offered his portfolio to anyone else who wanted to look, but no one did.

Later, Rew asked Cinda what she'd told Zaine.

"I told her that I wasn't interested in men or in women," responded the necromancer. "We have too much ahead of us for those considerations."

"Really, that's what you told her? She looked—"

"No, Ranger, that's not what I told her. What I said was between her and I."

"Giving her false hope, then?"

"Who said it was false?" responded Cinda with a lascivious wink. She grinned at his response, then said, "Don't worry, Ranger, that's not what I told her, but what's it matter? We do have too much ahead of us, and hope, false or true, is all that we can cling to."

BY THE TIME SHAVROE CREPT INTO VIEW, THE RIVER HAD GOTTEN WIDE and slow. Small clumps of vegetation poked through the crawling brown waters, and the stream spread into an expansive delta, framed by marshy land and scores of islands and narrow channels. Low mangrove trees and scrub hid little, but there wasn't much to see beyond them. The land was flat, and only Shavroe managed to stick out above it.

They lined the gunwale, elbows on the wood, watching as the city seemed to emerge like a pig waddling out of mud. The air was thick with the tang of the sea and the curdled reek of rotting vegetation.

"This rated a duchy?" complained Raif, looking with distaste at a long, green reptile that slithered off the muddy shore at their approach. It floated in the water, egg-yolk eyes watching them as they drifted past.

"Quite the mouth on that thing," remarked Zaine.

"Not a good place for a swim," agreed Rew.

"Not a good place for anything," concluded Raif.

"There's a robust sea trade," mentioned Rew. "Goods flow from the Northern and Western Provinces down this river to Shavroe, and they trade them there with the western half of Vaeldon and visitors from across the sea. Carff does more trade. It's closer to foreign lands, but Shavroe collects its share of coin. Richest city in the west outside of Jabaan and Iyre. A third of the kingdom's exports flow down this river."

"And two thirds the kingdom's stench?" questioned Zaine, dramatically pinching her nose.

Grinning, Rew told her, "Wait until we get there. It's still got the stink of swamp mud, but you can add in the refuse in the harbor and the filth of two hundred thousand people."

"Wonderful."

"We won't be here long," said Anne, eyeing Rew from the corner of her eye. "Just long enough to find a coaster to get us to Carff."

"Aye," agreed the ranger. "I hope not long at all."

"Do you need me to get someone else drunk?" quipped Zaine.

"I think we'll try paying coin, this time," replied Rew. "There's regular traffic between Shavroe and Carff. There's certain to be a merchant headed east who has a little extra room in the hold. It'd be ideal, actually, if we can find someone shipping legitimate goods. We can arrive unsuspected and then disappear amongst the chaos of the port. I warn you, though, the berth on the coastal runs won't be as comfortable as we've had here. This sloop is a pleasure craft meant to carry the duke and his favored servants comfortably. The coastal runners are meant to wedge every bit of merchandise aboard with little regard for passenger or crew. It's going to be tight, but it's the best cover we'll find for sneaking in beneath Valchon's watch."

"There are few things less pleasant than a long voyage on the sea," added Anne. She stood upright and stared at Shavroe. "I'd rather be in a prison than be a sailor."

"It can't be that bad," protested Zaine. "I've seen some pretty foul places on land, you know."

"We'll see, won't we?"

Looking discomfited, Zaine turned and eyed the cabin where Raponne was allegedly packing up his clothing and art supplies. "Think we'll be able to lose him at the docks?"

"At the rate that man performs physical labor, I think we'll be on our second bowl of stew and third ale by the time he gets out of there," assured Rew.

"What if we didn't lose him?" asked Cinda. "It's worth considering if the man can help us further."

Rew rubbed his head. "You want to see the duke?"

She shrugged. "If we talk fast enough, maybe he'll get us passage on a ship."

"Or hang us from a rope outside his walls…" worried Zaine.

"After the Arcanum, we spread the truth to convince the nobles to support us—or I should say, to convince them to not support the princes," reminded the necromancer. "That began before Iyre. This man, Duke Vincent, will know Calb and Heindaw are dead. If he accepts that we were responsible, I don't think he'll stand in our way. He won't be allied with Valchon, will he? Not as a duke in the Western Province. He has as much to lose as us. He was the exact target for the truths we've been spreading."

"Who can guess the loyalties of a duke?" murmured Rew. "It's a risk, lass. For all we know, he's looking for a way to curry favor with Valchon right now, and the moment we walk into his door…"

"There's an army of Dark Kind forming, didn't you say?" continued Cinda. "When this is all over, you're going to have to raise the banners. You need help to face those creatures, and you may as well start with Duke Vincent."

"Me? I'll need help?"

Cinda's eyes glittered like emeralds. "Who else is there?"

"We'll do our part when the time comes," boomed Raif. "My

sister has a good point, though. The five of us can't defeat an army of narjags. It's going to take the might of the nobles, and well, why not start here?"

Rew nodded, but he didn't turn from Cinda. The five of them. That wasn't what Cinda had said.

She brushed her crimson robes. "If Valchon or the king have decent spies in the city, they'll know we're there anyway. We might as well make ourselves known."

"The entire point of this was to slip around Valchon's back," challenged Rew. "Perhaps there are spies, and maybe they'll see us, but unless they can portal, they won't have a quicker way to Carff than the sea. At worst, a spy could arrive in Carff when we do. At best, no one sees us at all. Either side of that wager, we win. If there are spellcasters watching, they'll be watching Vincent's fortress, and those are the ones we need worry about. Pfah. Let's get you changed out of those robes, and—"

"I'm not hiding anymore, Ranger, and neither should you," declared Cinda. "Valchon knows we're coming."

"If he knows we're coming on the open water, it's going to be an abbreviated trip, lass," warned Rew. "You saw what he did to Stanton. Out on the water, we'll have nowhere to run, nowhere to hide." He held up a hand. "I know you said you're done hiding, but wouldn't you rather hide than feel a maelstrom raining down on your head?"

Cinda brushed a lock of dark hair behind her ear and offered, "We've all got as big a stake in this as you do, so how about this? I'll change my clothes if you agree to see Duke Vincent."

Rew crossed his arms over his chest, thought about it, and then agreed to visit the duke.

———

WHEN THEY DISEMBARKED ON THE WHARF AT SHAVROE, REW HAD TO almost physically drag the children along. Salt and big white sea birds had been floating on the breeze for hours, sure signs the ocean was beyond, but before they'd reached it, they'd taken a man-made channel away from the mouth of the river. It brought them into a large basin on the side of Shavroe that was protected by stout sea-walls. The passage had obscured the sight of the water beyond, and it wasn't until they'd put boots on stone that the younglings had turned, looking down the length of the wharf and out at the open water.

They stood transfixed, watching as endless rolling waves approached, crashing on the walls surrounding the harbor. Boats ten times the size of the one they'd arrived on were towed out of the harbor or flew along beyond it under the power of the rushing wind. The air reverberated with the roar of that wind and the waves, and the particular calls and rhythms of a major harbor.

Voices, speaking languages familiar and strange, all sounded equally odd, as the sailors chanted and cried in their own patois, each one cobbled together from wherever they were from, the dialects of the men they shared berths with, and the lands that they had visited. It was a stew that was exotic and delightful.

Raponne tsked and fretted, apparently worried how the duke would handle his unexpected return. He pressed them, "You are sure the prince is dead?"

Rew nodded and did not respond. The artist had asked him a score of times that morning, and the ranger didn't have anything else to add on the matter. He frowned, looking at the beads of sweat forming on Raponne's brow.

"You left in the duke's good graces, didn't you? What are you worried about? It wasn't you who killed the prince."

"If only it was," tittered the artist. He cleared his throat. "Vincent is, ah, was Calb's man, you understand? With Calb dead, the thought was that Heindaw may offer protection. I was, ah, going to convince him to accept the duke's fealty. It's not my fault, I know, but nobles… The duke's going to be angry and frightened, and he's going to take it out on someone. It won't be me. Of course it won't be me, but ah, this was meant to be… I was trying to win the duke's attention back, and—"

Rew grunted, waving for the man to be quiet. "We're here. Let's just go and see what the duke says."

"You'll speak on my behalf and tell him there was nothing I could do?"

Rew started down the gangplank and did not respond.

The artist came shuffling after with two sailors lumbering behind, hauling a mountain of stuff, which made Rew wonder how temporary the artist's commission had been in Iyre. Raponne was traveling like a nobleman on the move rather than an up-and-coming painter hoping for an audience at court. Get the duke's attention back? What had the artist done?

Evidently, whatever Raponne's troubles with the duke, his reputation was sound enough in Shavroe that when they reached the fortress, they were quickly allowed inside and ushered to a study to wait for the duke.

The fortress was a blocky, ugly structure that had been erected in an earlier age. It faced south, watching over the sea, guarding the mouth of the river to prevent invading armies from plunging deeply into the kingdom before meeting resistance. Rew hadn't heard of any invading armies wanting to do such a thing, but when Shavroe had been constructed, evidently it had been a worry.

The building was sturdy enough that it had withstood centuries of autumn storms that battered the coast with shrieking wind and torrential rain. That wind had the strength to tear down a house, which was why most of the finer homes in Shavroe all huddled in the fortress's lee, protected by its bulk.

Catapults lined the battlement like vultures along the roof of an abattoir, and idly, Rew wondered if any of the giant machines worked. It would be a chore, keeping the things well-maintained in the heavy weather and salt air. Whether for show or actual defense, he supposed they had worked, or perhaps, the people from across the sea were content to enrich themselves through trade and had no interest in tussling with Vaeldon's interminable line of powerful necromancers.

The duke's sitting room was the tactile opposite of the exterior of the fortress. It was draped with lush fabrics. Luxurious velvet curtains, the same purple as fine wine, framed the windows. Teal couches were covered in the finest silk and piled with viciously stuffed down pillows. The rugs were practical dark hues, but when Rew stepped on them, his boots sank, and it was like walking across sand.

There was no gold or silver sparkling on the mantle and tables like one might see in the richest of mercantile houses or the princes' private quarters. Instead, Duke Vincent displayed his wealth in hedonistic comfort. There were far more sumptuous blankets and plush pillows than any man might practically need. The only hard surfaces were a wooden desk, polished to the point they could see themselves reflected on its glossy front, and glittering crystal decanters of wine. Rew had no doubt the contents of the decanters were squeezed from grapes grown on vines as old as the kingdom itself then stored in casks for a lifetime. The wine probably tasted spectacular, but the pleasure was about drinking something so difficult to produce and expensive to procure. With a glance, Rew could tell that was what drove Duke Vincent. He craved the luxuries no one else was able to enjoy.

Where drapes and pillows did not cover the walls and surfaces, there was a profusion of canvasses with charcoal sketches. They were like mushrooms popping up after weeks of rain. Rew's gaze had flicked over the drawings, looking for other hints of threat or some clue as to the duke's temperament, but it was the artwork which gave it away.

Raponne's eyes slid over the room like a snake over grass then narrowed when he came to a wide triptych hanging above the fireplace. It was a naked man, his head and shoulders on the leftmost of the canvas panels, his feet and legs on the rightmost. Rew looked away from the panel in the middle. The ranger was a grown man, and he'd seen some things, but he hadn't seen something like that displayed so prominently above someone's fireplace.

Zaine whistled appreciatively, and Raif glared at her.

"I thought you liked girls?"

"I do," replied the thief. "I like cozy country cottages as well, but I'm still impressed when I see a big castle."

"Cozy country cottages?" asked Cinda. "Have you ever been in a country cottage?"

The thief winked. "Not yet, but I'd give one a try if I got the opportunity."

"That is not my work," said Raponne, his voice cracking like ice.

"It's like we walked into the sausage case at a butcher's shop," complained Raif, waving his hands in disgust at the charcoal drawings which seemed to grow in number the more one noticed them.

"Duke Vincent appreciates my work capturing the human body," scoffed Raponne, though immediately after he said it, he shot a nauseated look at the triptych.

"I do, my friend," purred a silken voice, and a man who could be no other than Duke Vincent sauntered into the room and perched on the arm of a high-backed chair behind the desk.

He wore a flowing, white silk blouse and dark, snug trousers that were obviously styled after Prince Valchon's regular attire. That wasn't a good sign.

Raponne pointed at the triptych hanging above the fire. His pursed lips and his hurt eyes did the talking.

"The kingdom is changing," murmured Duke Vincent. "My decorations change as well."

"You sent me north to get rid of me," accused Raponne.

Duke Vincent's mouth opened in mock surprise, and he held up his hands as if to ward off the accusation. His fingers glittered with the precious metal that was absent in the rest of the room, and the motion opened his shirt, displaying a smooth, tightly muscled chest. His head was bald, gleaming in the light which fought through the thick drapes around the windows, and he looked disturbingly a lot like the late necromancer Ambrose, except Duke Vincent had eyebrows.

Placing his fists on his hips, Raponne took a step forward and declared, "Prince Heindaw is dead."

"So I heard."

"When did you hear?"

Duke Vincent reached to his desk and picked up a small bell. He rang it.

"I don't know you, do I?" he asked, looking over the rest of the party. His gaze paused on Rew then lingered on Raif before cutting back to Rew and away again. "Not artists, I see. Perhaps you will tell me of yourselves over refreshments?"

"Not a bad idea," replied Rew, looking pointedly at the crystal decanters of wine.

Behind them, the door opened, and Rew turned. He cursed and backed away.

The man who entered had arms like a blacksmith and a face like a brick. There wasn't a hint of emotion in his hard glare. That wasn't what had startled Rew, though. In the man's hands, he clasped a slender wire. An assassin's garrote.

Rew grasped his longsword and his hunting knife.

"He's not here for you," assured Duke Vincent.

"Who?" asked Raponne, starting to turn.

The newcomer was at the artist's back in a blink, and he wrapped the garrote around Raponne's throat.

Rew began to draw his longsword.

"Senior Ranger," said Duke Vincent, "this has nothing to do with you."

He didn't let go of his longsword, but Rew glanced at the duke in surprise. Senior Ranger. Blessed Mother, he was going to put his boot into Cinda's backside for talking him into seeing this man.

They waited uncomfortably while Duke Vincent's assassin killed the artist Raponne. Zaine, in particularly, looked sickened by the casual attack.

As Raponne kicked at the plush rugs and clawed helplessly at his murderer's wrists, Rew cleared his throat and asked, "I assume this man is guilty of some crime?"

"Do the rangers investigate murders, now? I believed that was the role of the magistrates. Either way, aren't we rather far from your territory?"

"I'm an agent of the king, and the king rules all of Vaeldon," replied Rew. He grimaced at Raponne. "I grew fond of the man on the journey down here. Well, not fond. I don't like him at all, really, but I'd like to know the reason for this."

"Yes yes, not too fond, I hope?" Vincent laughed. He waved a hand as Rew again began to draw his longsword. "Raponne was passing secrets. My secrets, Prince Calb's secrets, many dangerous murmurings, and unfortunately, I could no longer allow him to stay within my court. He was a traitor to his liege, Senior Ranger. Under the king's law, this is justified."

"Why'd you send him to Heindaw, then?"

"Raponne comes from a wealthy Iyrean merchant family, and the tariffs I earn from their business refurbished our seawall two seasons back. No matter his crimes, it'd be rather… complicated if they learned his blood was on my hands. I figured, why not let Prince Heindaw deal with him? Heindaw had used him to spy on myself and Calb, but with Calb dead, Raponne was more liability than asset. Better he explain matters to the rest of the family. Unfortunately, I heard the news about the prince's untimely demise shortly after they headed north. It leaves me no choice but to deal with this matter myself." Vincent looked down at his manicured fingernails then to his assassin. "Almost done?"

The big man nodded, muscles bulging as he yanked the garrote tighter. He offered, "I can finish in the hallway."

"Yes, please do."

The assassin dragged Raponne out, though most of the fight had already left the artist. His heels twitched and slid across the plush carpet. His face had turned the same color as Duke Vincent's drapes.

"What was the point of that display?" Rew asked Duke Vincent. "You could have done that before we got here or any time after we left. Did you think to intimidate me?"

The man gave an oily smile and replied, "I needed to show I'm a man who does what he must."

Rew studied the duke, from his fine clothing to the depraved decorations he surrounded himself with.

"Prince Valchon has gifted my court with a new spellcaster," said Duke Vincent, breaking the silence. "It's, ah, a new breed of spell casting, though I shudder at the term in this case."

Rew cringed.

"You've heard of them, then? You know of what I speak?"

"I heard they were called hunters," said Rew. He stamped his boots. "The ones we encountered had a resemblance to…"

"To Valchon himself," finished Vincent. "It's quite unnerving. Hunters… Yes, I can see that. They are predators, and us normal men are their prey."

"You want to discuss this… simulacra of the prince with us?"

"That and other matters," confided Vincent. "Wine?"

"Absolutely."

At the same time, Zaine quipped, "Indubitably."

Rew scowled at her. She flushed. Then, her eyes fell to the carpet which still showed clear drag marks where Raponne had been taken away. She looked sick, and Rew wanted to reach over and hug her shoulder, but it was not the time.

The duke strode across the room and poured the glasses of wine himself, filling one for each of his guests then one for himself. He swirled the glass, watching the vibrant liquid bleed languidly back down the crystal. He stuck his nose in the goblet, inhaled, and then took a sip. He returned to his desk, sitting again on the arm of his chair.

He raised his glass. "To small pleasures."

Rew drank his wine but didn't respond to the toast.

"I know we are not friends, but let us pretend that we are," began Vincent. "I wasn't a particularly loyal man to Prince Calb, but I wasn't disloyal, either. I never betrayed him outright, but I could have. Calb and I tolerated each other because it was in both of our interests. He was my liege, and the threat of his might kept others from bothering me. My port supplied half of his tax revenue, so he ignored my peccadilloes. Both Valchon and Heindaw had agents visiting me weekly, but I never did more than listen. Everyone knew Calb wasn't going to win the Investiture, but I hoped staying loyal would prove my value to whichever of the brothers triumphed."

"You bided your time to try and select a winning side."

"Yes, I did," admitted the duke. "I hope you don't think that was crass. Once Calb fell, Valchon began making more strenuous advances, along with a number of thinly veiled threats. I do control the second most important port in the kingdom, after his own city, of course, and I've spent decades ensuring that my family's tentacles are embedded deeply in this place. Without us, my children, our cousins, the administration of the port will be a shambles, and it will be terrifically expensive for whatever noble thinks to take my seat. It's the way we've always worked. That being said, when Prince Valchon issues a warning, you take him at his word."

"I understand."

"When Heindaw fell, within a week, this—simulacra, you called it?—of Valchon arrived in my court. A spellcaster with unique talents, we were told, and it's true. Valchon was the only surviving prince, so what was I to do? I'd heard the rumors I am sure you started, but the king hasn't acknowledged you, has he? I rather thought Valchon would become king any day, so I let this new spellcaster into our councils, and he's stuck there like a tick. It disgusts me, Ranger. My family is pure, our blood crafted with as much care as this wine but for centuries longer. The Vincents are works of art."

Rew blinked and looked slowly around the room and the canvasses hanging there, trying not to show his disgust.

Vincent laughed. "Don't worry. These are not of my relatives, and most of the drawings are not of me. I meant the magic in our blood, not, well, I suppose there are several ways one could appreciate our breeding."

Rew drank his wine.

"What Valchon has done is a travesty," continued Vincent. "It sickens me, as it would anyone of noble blood, but I'm a practical man, and I've been disgusted by other things that I've found a way to live with. My wife, for one, but I'm getting lost from my point. I could live with this… false offspring, except as the spell-caster entrenched himself, it became clear how deeply Valchon trusts his spawn, and I realized that if Valchon becomes king, what need does he have of us, the nobility? If he can spread his seed and whelp scores of these… things, then could he not place them on thrones all across the kingdom? I assume they'd be more loyal to him than I, which is not saying much. All parents want more for their children, don't they? Why wouldn't he assign them territories? Do you understand my concern?"

"Yes, I believe so."

"It's not just a threat to me, but the entire ruling class outside of Valchon himself," continued Vincent, a sour pout on his lips. "What can I gain if Valchon ascends to the throne? In time, his bastards will learn enough of my business they can replace me, or maybe he'll just decide I'm not worth the hassle, and he'll eat the losses in tax revenue for some years before they can reestablish the trade. With a long enough horizon, it'd be possible for them to run our port, no matter what sabotage I'm able to enact before I'm replaced."

"You're supporting me, then? Is that what this is about?"

"I suppose so," said the duke, his voice bleeding like wine down the glass. "It's true, then, the rumors? You are a son of the king? And you mean to defy him?"

"I've already defied him. It's all I've ever done."

Duke Vincent laughed and raised his glass in another toast. "True enough, Ranger. True enough."

Turning his wineglass in his hands, Rew admitted, "I did not expect this conversation."

Vincent replied, "And I never thought I'd be throwing my weight behind some country ranger who doesn't have the manners to change his muddy boots before being shown into my chambers."

Rew looked down. "Sorry about that."

"You are not, but what does it matter? You're the only hope for Vaeldon's noble class, so you have my support in the fight against your brother. That is where you are going next, correct? Good. You have my support against the prince, though I'll readily admit, I will not openly join you in contesting Vaisius Morden. I can live with the king, and he's… the king. It's beneath the Morden's rule that my family has grown to be what we are. What happens between you and your father is between you and he, but to face your brother, what do you need?"

"First, what do you want in exchange?" questioned Rew.

Smirking, the duke told him, "Nothing I do not already have. I want to remain the Duke of Shavroe. I want my children to enjoy the spoils our title brings and my eldest to sit the throne when I tire of it. That is all. I don't want Jabaan, and I'll thank the Mother if I never have to put foot in Mordenhold again. The Vincents are happy with what we have. For generations, we've secured good marriages and strengthened our magic. Shavroe's trade has grown bountiful under our watch, and we only want to keep it."

"Nothing? You expect me to believe you want nothing?"

"A holiday from paying the king's levies for a decade? The new king's favor when it comes to matching my daughters with extremely wealthy, magically gifted suitors?"

Snorting, Rew responded, "I'm not the king."

Duke Vincent raised his wineglass and his eyebrows. "Not yet."

"Not ever."

"Perhaps I misinterpreted your defiance. If you successfully dispatch your brother and overthrow your father… what, exactly, do you expect to happen next?"

Rew grunted and did not respond.

"It must be uncomfortable, going from the wilderness off the boundaries of any map to such a prominent role in the kingdom," continued Vincent. "I won't press you, but I will offer my advice if there comes a day you want it. For now, you will do your best to defeat Valchon? Promise me that, and I am yours."

"Fair enough. In exchange for… my good word, we need passage to Carff in a vessel that Valchon will never suspect is carrying me."

"Approaching the kingdom's most powerful invoker trapped on a boat? Risky, but I suppose no risk and no reward. I can do this. What else?"

"Basic provisions."

"Obviously. And?"

"That's it."

"Truly?"

Rew patted the wooden hilt of his longsword. "I have what I need."

"Very well. It seems neither of us is a greedy man. Not yet, at least. I agree to your terms, and I will see to the ship."

"We'd like to leave as soon as possible."

"Of course, but ah, there is one other matter."

Rew snorted. Of course there was one other matter.

"The spellcaster I mentioned… I'd prefer if he was no longer a member of my court."

"You have your own assassins, Duke Vincent."

"None like you."

"I'm a ranger."

"Now, you are," responded the duke. He stood. "Look, you seem familiar with these offspring of the prince. You must have some idea of what they are capable of. I can't use my people against the thing because I'm terrified they'd fail. Already, others have tried. Minor nobles, jealous spellcasters, and they've all ended up brutally murdered. And that's when... You know what these creatures are capable of? Getting murdered by one is a mercy."

"They drain the soul from a person. They consume its power."

Vincent nodded, his eyes serious. "I worry for myself. I worry for my family. I cannot move against this thing unless I'm certain it would work, and the truth is, my people do not have the skill to succeed. But you... Pfah, we need not have secrets. I'm familiar with your past, before you became a ranger. You can do this, but even if you fail, I can make sure it doesn't tie back to me. Help me in this, Senior Ranger, and it's one less of these foul creations that can stalk you from behind. Help me, and we both benefit."

Rew glanced at the rest of the party then shrugged. "All right. I'll kill it for you. Then we sail."

Chapter Twelve

Rew stood back in the doorway, looking out over a balcony, down at a colonnade, and across a manicured garden. Hidden in turns by the flowering trees and shrubs of the garden and the fluted marble pillars of the colonnade was Valchon's simulacrum. Purple robes flapped behind the thing as it walked purposefully, its face blank, its hair styled to mimic the prince's.

It clutched a folder filled with sheafs of papers, though if the creature was anything like Valchon, it would give those papers to an aide to read. Behind it, two soldiers marched briskly, wearing the gleaming copper breastplates of Valchon's men.

Rew scratched his beard. Calb and Heindaw were dead. Did Valchon still fear his men getting attacked by invokers, or had no one gotten around to changing the army's attire? The copper breastplates were next to useless in any encounter that didn't involve spells being cast, and outfitting so many troops with them must have cost a fortune.

The simulacrum entered a doorway and disappeared, the two guards following on its heels. Rew stayed concealed, thinking.

The guards were always present. He estimated there were two score of them in the city, all tasked with watching over the simulacrum. Would Valchon also assign his whelps spies dressed in common clothing? When traveling, the princes would normally layer protections around themselves, both obvious and hidden, but did that caution extend to... whatever that thing was? Was it the hunter's own senses that had alerted it to previous attackers, or was it guards lurking unseen?

Rew shuddered. However the simulacrum had detected the attacks against it, it looked identical to a younger Valchon. Rew could clearly recall the prince when he'd been a young man. They'd both lived in Mordenhold, and they'd both enjoyed the privilege and the risks of being the king's sons. Once Rew had abdicated his role, making Valchon the eldest prince eligible to inherit the throne, they'd gotten close. As close as sons of Vaisius Morden could be, that was. They'd watched each other's backs against the others. They'd caroused together whenever they slipped out from under the noses of the weapons masters, tutors, and arcanists who constantly dogged them to study. Not friends, but companions who had much in common.

Rew hadn't hated his brother, then. He'd been sad for him and for their other brothers. Valchon had not yet unleashed a maelstrom that had killed fifty thousand people in Stanton. Now, Rew had no moral qualms about facing Valchon or his spawn. They'd made their choices and proven the danger they posed. The kingdom would be a better place without them.

But Rew did feel some hesitation about simply walking up and attempting to stab the simulacrum. Not for moral concerns but practical ones. The day before, Duke Vincent had shared what he knew of the monstrosities.

"They're much like the prince," Vincent had explained, cradling his expensive wine, his tone somber. "They think like him, and from what I can tell, they've been trained by him and those around him. It's rumor only, and perhaps you'd know better than I, but I'm told Vyar Grund himself oversaw their practice with a sword. Another rumor is that Grund is dead now, for what that's worth. It seems Valchon himself taught the whelps to cast spells."

"He did?" asked Rew, startled.

"They have unique capabilities, but at least this one is also an invoker," shared Vincent. "I—fortunately—don't know how talented it is, but you should be prepared for the standard assortment of spells. I witnessed one of the other attempts at the creature's life. Out of nowhere, it called two whips that looked to be made of pure lightning. It was terrifying."

Rew grunted. "Yes, that's Valchon's spell."

"In addition, the thing seems to have unusually sharp senses. Smell, hearing, or something else, I don't know, but I can tell you, anytime I approach, it knows I am there. The other assassins who have attempted to slay the thing have all failed because it was ready the moment they showed themselves. I can only guess at the nature of its senses, but you should approach with caution."

"Wonderful."

"And you know they can suck strength from others?"

Wincing, Rew nodded.

"There are reports of people missing in the city," continued Duke Vincent. "I suspect it is this thing feeding on my subjects, but so far, the victims are missing and are not the listless lumps of flesh that are left over after a person is drained. I cannot prove it's the simulacrum. Regardless, expect it to be powerful. It's been gathering strength in Shavroe for a month, with little need to use it. What that means... I don't know, except it's dangerous."

Rew sat back and closed his eyes.

"I want to remind you, Senior Ranger, this cannot come back on me," warned Duke Vincent. "If it finds out I worked with you, it will kill me and my entire family. Perhaps you wouldn't lose sleep over my death, but my children... Their blood would be on your hands."

"It won't come back to you."

"I don't even know if Valchon's creations can be killed," worried the duke. "I—"

"I've killed three of them so far," interrupted Rew. He opened his eyes and met the duke's gaze. "I've killed three so far, and I'm just getting started. Don't worry. It won't come back to you, and soon enough, you'll be rid of this thing. That's not to say it will be easy, though."

"I see," said the duke, a smile curling his lips. "I knew I was right to support your claim to the throne. What do you need?"

"The throne? No, I—Never mind. A little time is all that I need."

THE EASIEST THING TO DO WOULD HAVE BEEN TO HAVE SOMEONE ELSE spring the ambush. There were several hundred people in Duke Vincent's fortress at any given time, and the simulacrum couldn't be prepared for all of them at all times. It would be prepared for Rew, though. He knew it deep down. The ones in Olsoth had recognized him when they'd seen him. This one would be even more prepared, as word would have reached Valchon about the deaths of his other spawn by now. It made it dangerous for Rew to approach, but he wouldn't risk any of his companions against such a deadly opponent. Even if the creature wasn't waiting for the attacker, the things were blazingly fast. Duke Vincent's news that this one could invoke made it all that much worse.

An alternative would have been to try and sneak up on the simulacrum while it slept. Surely it did. As far as Rew knew, only necromancers did not, but he worried what wards the thing could set with its spellcasting and how quickly its senses would wake it if someone came into its room. Rew was stealthy, but it'd been years since he'd had to put that skill to the test outside of the forest. In the cold stone of the fortress, he would wager on the simulacrum's magical defenses and preternatural abilities.

He didn't think a ranged weapon, like an arrow, would be much good, either. When he'd first faced the things in Olsoth, they'd easily dodged spells and even a swing from his longsword. If it could do that, then the whistle that heralded an incoming missile would be plenty of notice for the creature to avoid being struck, and if the first attempt missed, they'd lose any advantage of surprise.

After several failed assassination attempts, the simulacrum would be expecting more at all times. Alone in its chambers, when moving about the keep, it would be ready. The one place Rew considered it might not be on the defensive was when it was hunting. Predators thought of prey when they were on the hunt. They never thought of other predators. Rew had been one, once. He knew.

But setting a trap for the thing in the city of Shavroe would be nearly impossible. Rew didn't know how the simulacrum exited the fortress. He didn't know where it searched in the city for bodies to drain. It was like trying to set a snare on a game trail in the forest when you couldn't identify the game trail. It would be completely random guesswork, but if the thing had been hunting, it was putting the bodies somewhere, and he could make a better guess at that, at least.

The easiest place in Shavroe to get rid of a corpse with no one knowing about it was behind the city, opposite the sea. Surrounding the delta that Shavroe guarded were leagues of narrow canals, swamp, and thick tangles of mangrove trees. There were reptiles back in there which could consume a man in a single bite, Rew had been told. He'd never bothered to go looking for the things, but he didn't doubt it. On the plains south of Olsoth, there were the great land wyrms. In the depths of the wilderness in the east, there were primal sloths and wyverns. Shavroe had its monsters as well.

Duke Vincent listened to Rew's plan then shook his head. "I think you need to approach from within a crowd. Confuse it with the scents and sounds of other people. You could get close that way then stab it in the back."

"Killing it is the goal, but I'd rather do it without Valchon learning what happened. In a crowd, we can't hide what occurred, and chances are, I'd be spotted by Valchon's soldiers before I could get away, unless I killed all of them too, which the prince would definitely hear about. My way, there's no body and no evidence. I want Valchon confused and off balance. I also don't want to leave obvious signs that I'm coming to Carff from Shavroe. No matter how good our cover on the boat, if he knows we're in your city, he'll expect us by sea, and Duke Vincent, I promised this wouldn't come back on you. How can you plead innocence if it happens in your city in front of everyone?"

The duke grunted. "Good point."

———

REW CROUCHED AMIDST THE CLOSE BRANCHES AND ROOTS, WATCHING Shavroe's mud harbor. It was a series of derelict docks that jutted out from the warehouse district of the city like rotten teeth. The docks were decrepit, fragile things, unmaintained by the duke or any private citizens, mostly used by impoverished fishermen who could no longer afford seaworthy vessels to ply their craft on the open water.

Instead, those fishermen slipped out the back of the city, heading into the narrow, dank channels that hugged the dry land like a dying relative. There were fish in those waterways, though they were the kind thrown into over-spiced stews in the meanest, dingiest taverns in the city. Frogs, too, which were served to drunks who couldn't tell the difference between them and greasy chicken or sometimes at more respectable tables if the novelty was in fashion that season. Aside from the lower quality of the catch, the real reason it was only the poorest fishermen trawling the swamp was the danger from the giant reptiles who shared the muddy water. Those reptiles would eat a man as readily as a fish.

Rew had been told that the giant, toothy monsters didn't typically assault a boat, but leaning over the edge or setting foot on the muddy shore where it wasn't blocked by mangrove roots was an occupational hazard, and when the alligators got into a frenzy, then it was best to make all speed away in any direction that you could. Just because they didn't typically assault a rowboat didn't mean they couldn't.

At night, the waterways through the swamp were filled with pale eyes floating just above the dark surface, watching and waiting.

Rew had been given stern advice. Before you reach over the gunwale, make sure none of those eyes were nearby. Nervously, the ranger glanced around, but like before, he didn't see any of the creatures near him. He went back to watching the mud harbor.

So far that night, several boats had shoved off and been rowed silently into the maze of open channels that wove through the swap, but Rew didn't think any of them carried Prince Valchon's offspring. He wasn't even sure the man would come this way. It made sense, as a possibility, that the swamps were where the simulacrum would dispose of its victims, but it could be stacking them in a warehouse until someone found them for all Rew knew.

He did know, now, that there was an awful lot of criminal activity occurring after midnight from the mud harbor. There'd been several impoverished but honest-looking fishermen, and a dozen nefarious-seeming characters who were up to no conceivable good. They hauled away innocuous packages that might have been stolen merchandise, big barrels of likely illegal spirits, or unloaded nondescript crates coming in, presumably smuggled to avoid the duke's tariffs, and at least one pair of thuggish goons dragged an uncovered body into their rowboat before setting off.

It confirmed Rew's suspicion that the swamps were a great place to hide such incriminating evidence, but the frequency of traffic to and from the mud harbor made him doubt his instincts. When he'd strolled by those derelict docks during daylight, they'd been vacant, only a few stray cats scavenging bits of cleaned fish or hunting the rats.

The rats, it seemed, had grown into men and were now hard at work scurrying about beneath the cover of night. Duke Vincent's soldiers must have known these activities were going on within their city, but maybe they felt it best to keep the business at the mud harbor, so the rest of Shavroe could remain clean.

Rew sat for several hours. He was perched on a rotten log dragged a dozen paces above the shore and in the middle of a thicket of mangrove roots that stood like prison bars in front of him. He'd selected a speck of island with no easily accessible shore, hoping it would keep the alligators away. He'd slathered himself with the thickest, rankest mud he could find, which on the edge of the swamp, was pretty rank. By the time he'd begun to lose hope that he'd ever smell again, he began to wonder if he wanted to smell again given the state of himself. He'd also started to think he was wasting his time.

It'd been a wild guess, based on nothing other than the theory that the simulacrum must be doing something with the bodies of its victims. Rew was coming to the conclusion that Valchon's minion wasn't rowing itself out of the mud harbor each night. The creature had found somewhere else to stash the bodies, or maybe there weren't bodies. Duke Vincent was convinced because people were missing, but people always went missing in port towns like Shavroe. They could have been press-ganged into service on a long sea journey, or they could have been killed by some other lawless faction. They might have been recruited into a plot around the Investiture or fled after news of the princes' downfalls. People went missing for dozens of reasons, and the chaos of the Investiture fueled rumors that might make it seem more than it was.

Two hours before down, while Rew was wrestling with calling it a night, another boat shoved off the docks of the mud harbor. This one looked much the same as the others, except one person rowed it. The figure was heavily cowled, nothing visible except a lumpy silhouette. The boat was full of something, though, judging by how low it rode. As the figure propelled the vessel across the water, Rew grinned ferociously.

Powerful strokes sent the boat skittering forward like a water bug. It moved with twice the speed of the others Rew had seen that night. Maybe not noticeable to anyone who hadn't been sitting, covered in foul swamp mud for hours with nothing to do but watch, but it was obvious to the ranger. The person wielding those oars was no normal man.

The hunt began.

Rew slipped across the top of the low island he'd been waiting on and clambered into the tiny boat on the other side. He knew Valchon's whelp had sharper senses than he did, so he didn't trust his ability to follow the other boat across the water without being caught, and if it came to a race, the simulacrum appeared to be quite capable of moving its boat quickly. If it came to a fight, Rew didn't want to think of the complexities of battling the thing while they were both balancing in small boats, particularly when the simulacrum could fling fireballs, and Rew could not.

He had to get ahead of it.

The channels were a warren of twisting, slow-moving water, bordered by humps of land and vegetation that had somehow sunk roots deep enough not to be washed away in the seasonal floods. It was a convoluted maze, but immediately from the mud harbor, there were only a few options. For its dark work, the simulacrum wouldn't be choosing one of the main waterways, and the creature just needed to go deep enough into the swamp it could dump some bodies and then return before dawn. That gave Rew a decent chance of guessing which way it would go.

The ranger hauled on his oars, his boat shooting across the water toward the mouth of the closest channel. It was hidden from view from the mud harbor by the island Rew had waited on, but the way the simulacrum was rowing, its boat would round the island quickly.

Rew got into the channel and breathed a sigh of relief while still pulling hard on his oars. Along the wending way, he would be hidden by bends and turns for a little while longer. His boat glided soundlessly deeper into the swamp, and after five hundred paces, he came to an open junction where several of the channels collided. The water was still, as the lazy currents gently churned into each other. Rew crossed the open space and stopped rowing. He coasted several dozen more paces.

He let his thoughts float, drifting like the heavy clouds of silt that roiled along the murky waterways. He reached, seeking what he could feel was out there all around him. He made contact, sent his message, and waited.

In moments, the simulacrum appeared, speeding out into the open. Its back was turned toward Rew, but as it entered the tiny lake, it also stopped rowing, stood, and turned.

"You are waiting for me?" it asked, in a slightly higher pitch than Valchon's voice.

"I am," said Rew, his words barely cutting through the heavy air of the swamp.

The simulacrum was quiet for a long moment, its boat moving slowly, insects chirping and buzzing around them, hidden frogs croaking loudly, and all else still. Rew breathed in and out, the thick stench of swamp like mud in his lungs. The water around them was soundless, their boats hardly rocking from tiny waves that lapped against the sides.

"I'm told you killed three of my brothers in Olsoth," said the simulacrum. "Father warned us about you, said you'd be coming for us. I'm surprised you knew to find me here, but I'm glad it is me you found."

"Brothers?"

The thing didn't respond.

"So you are children of Valchon."

"Of course we are," replied the creature. It reached up and pushed back its hood. "Do you not remember this face?"

"From long ago."

"Pfah. Twenty short years ago. I was born while you were still in Mordenhold, though some years after you turned your back on your responsibilities. Did you know that?"

"I didn't," replied Rew, shifting as the two boats drifted toward each other, each carried on a separate current from the different channels converging in the lake. "Valchon was running a separate creche all of that time? I had no idea."

"Yes, something like that," replied the simulacrum. "He was vigorous, my father. He sired—ah, I should not tell you that, should I? He sired me, and my brothers, and raised us."

Rew snorted, the sound odd in the stifled air of the swamp. "Raised you? That's not the whole truth, is it? What did he do to you?"

The simulacrum's head tilted, and it replied, "He improved us."

They were both quiet, the boats pushed on a lethargic course to meet near the center of the lake.

"Why are you talking to me?" asked Rew.

"Father wouldn't be pleased," responded the simulacrum with a short laugh. "He told us to kill you quickly, if we could, but I am curious. You killed my uncles in battle, which not even Father had accomplished yet. You killed three of my own brothers. No one outside the family has killed any of us. We're too fast, too strong. How did you do it? Some trick, some power Father does not know of? He described your capabilities, and it seemed to me you were the weakest of our blood. It had to be deceit, but to fool them all? It made us curious. What have you planned for me, out here in the middle of nowhere?"

"No one outside the family has killed any of you… Valchon killed some of you, then, or you killed each other?" questioned Rew, sickened at the idea.

He could hear the mirth in the thing's response. "Only the strongest are fit to wear this face. Only the strongest are able to do what is necessary. Surely you, of all people, can understand that. You've killed brothers for the same reason as I. You and I share that."

"Not for long," murmured Rew quietly.

The simulacrum seemed to have heard him, and it raised one hand. An orange and red glow bathed its face as liquid flame began to build around its hand. "Confronting me on a boat was a stupid idea. Perhaps you could have defeated me with a sword but not if you can't reach me with it. Pfah. What were you going to do, throw one of your daggers at me? Did you not know I can cast spells?"

Rew tilted his head. "Your brothers in Olsoth fought with swords. They were stronger and faster than a normal man, thanks to your sick ability, but... no spells. Can you all invoke or just you? Were they foolish to not use all of their powers or were they weak?"

"So you did know I could cast? How did you—Ah, the duke," replied the simulacrum, the fire consuming its hand, reaching higher in writhing tendrils. "He's more cunning than we gave him credit for. I knew he wanted my blood, but I thought he was too cowardly to spill it. I'll have to do something about him when I return."

"It is just you who can invoke, then?"

The simulacrum let the flame around its hand grow, casting its face and maniacal grin in a violent light. "It's only my invoking you need worry about. The only thing you'll ever need to worry about again."

"Interesting," said Rew, studying Valchon's whelp. "It's just you. By blood or—You take that ability from your victims, don't you? It's not just their vigor you drain but their talent."

"What will I draw from you, Ranger?" asked the simulacrum, a sharp laugh cutting through the turgid air of the swamp. "My brothers will hate me for this coup. Die knowing that I'm absorbing your magical talent. What other tasty skills do you have, Ranger? I can't wait to find out."

"You should have paid more attention to your father's warnings," mentioned Rew. "He knows what I can do. He should have prepared you."

"Prepared me?"

Rew nodded. "For this."

There was a rush as a giant body heaved out of the water. The simulacrum's boat rocked hard. Faster than a blink, the creature spun, but the wood of its craft was already splintering, and murky swamp water spilled in. The simulacrum chopped its hand down, and a glob of fire flew half a pace into the yawning maw of an alligator.

The reptile choked on the flame, thrashing for a second and bellowing a shockingly high-pitched cry before sliding back, its insides cooked by the unnatural heat, but behind it, more came. Dark, leathery skin scraped against the wood of the simulacrum's boat. Jaws clacked, and a throaty roar reverberated through the mangrove trees. Scores of eyes, floating just above the water, reflected the light of the simulacrum's flame.

Frantically, Valchon's whelp attempted to build more fire. It drew a sword with its other hand, but its boat was sinking, and it was already past its knees in the dark water. It was a hundred paces from the nearest shore, and around it, the muddy water boiled as more leathery bodies swam closer.

The simulacrum flung its fire, and those yellow eyes glimmered, sparkling around the sinking boat like a field of fireflies. A powerful jaw closed on one of the simulacrum's knees, and Valchon's spawn stabbed with its sword, the bright steel piercing thick hide, but another of the animals churned through the water, chomping at the simulacrum's arm.

The hunter punched with a flaming hand, its legs splashing in the swamp water that filled its boat. It seemed to jump, and Rew's jaw fell open. The simulacrum was stepping across the backs of the alligators, headed toward land. Then in front of it, a slow twist rent the air. Purple and gold—the spinning vortex of an opening portal. Rew thought for a second the simulacrum was going to escape and slip through the tear in the air it had opened, but one of the alligators rolled, and the hunter stumbled, a boot plunging into the tepid water. Then, its flaming hand splashed down as it tried to steady itself.

The alligators were a churning mass, and one must have closed its jaws on that burning hand. It turned, dragging

Valchon's spawn beneath the water, spinning him, the water glowing as the simulacrum disappeared beneath the surface.

The beginnings of the portal winked out.

It was difficult to see in the froth, but light flared as the spell-caster attempted to fight off the alligators. The smell of burning flesh joined rotting mud, but there were scores of alligators in the lake, and when one was injured or killed, another crawled over the body. More than once, the simulacrum broke back above the surface of the swamp, but its flame had died, and it was struggling to call more. In the darkness, it was difficult to tell which of the flailing bodies was man and which was reptile. For minutes, the violent battle continued, but Rew knew well before the thrashing stopped that it was over. For a long time, the alligators fought for the scraps of the dead man.

Eventually, they realized there was more flesh that had been in the boat—the simulacrum's victims. Those people weren't dead, but the life had left them, and there was no resistance when the alligators found them.

Disgusted, Rew watched the roiling mass of leathery bodies until the water stilled, and then he watched for some moments longer. The simulacrum had almost escaped his trap by running across the backs of the alligators toward a portal it opened on the move. It was stunning that it'd kept its balance, that it had the intelligence and the speed to even try something like that. The presence of mind to force open a portal while the reptiles were biting at it... If the alligators hadn't dragged it beneath the surface of the water, things might have turned out differently. The simulacra were tougher to kill than Rew had realized, but he'd proved again that they could be killed.

After several minutes, when he was certain the simulacrum was safely torn to bits and residing in dozens of different alligators' stomachs. Rew released his thoughts from the reptiles, giving them a push to move away from the open lake.

His mind echoed with the primal urges of the monsters, their simplistic notions rooted in tens of thousands of years of instinct.

It was the depth of those thoughts, their consistent nature, that had allowed the ranger to connect with them while crouched and waiting on the island outside the mud harbor. He was lucky they'd stopped in the ranger village, that he'd had the chance to feel the bond between Eckvar and his bear again. Rew had been reminded of the communion that his low magic could bring, the connection he could build between himself and the life of the world. He'd found a thread he could understand in the dull minds of the alligators, something he could touch and encourage.

He'd told them, "Come. Feed."

Chapter Thirteen

"Are you sure that was worth it?" questioned Zaine when Rew returned from Duke Vincent's baths. "You smelled like…I don't even know. Do you know how rare that is, when I don't know what to say?"

"Yes, I have some idea of how rare that is," grumbled Rew. "Look, the simulacrum is dead, and no one will ever know what happened to it. Him. Whatever. The point is, yes, that was worth getting a little muddy for."

"Maybe to you," muttered Zaine, eying him and rubbing her nose with the back of her hand.

Rew sighed and looked around. They were housed in a rarely used basement that was designed to store provisions in case of a siege. It must have been constructed ages ago, and it looked to have been as long since it had been used. In modern warfare, sieges didn't last long, so such rooms weren't necessary. Valchon had destroyed Stanton in half an hour. They'd overrun Jabaan with undead in just a little longer. Against such deadly force, you were better off investing in good wine and figuring a way to drink it quickly than you were stockpiling months' worth of dried beans.

But the room suited their purposes. They'd been hiding from

the simulacrum and its attendants, and now they were killing time until their ship left. A stay at an inn would have been more comfortable, but it wasn't worth the risk of being seen by Valchon's spies when they were so close to leaving for his city. Duke Vincent had stalled departure of any westward-sailing vessels from his harbor, just in case someone had already seen them, but such measures could only be sustained for so long, and there was no reason to make it easy for the spies. Any sighting of them now, combined with the missing simulacrum, wouldn't be difficult to interpret.

"We leave with the morning tide?" asked the thief.

"We do."

"And that murderer is going to be on the boat?"

"He is," confirmed Rew.

Zaine looked upset, but Rew didn't know what to tell her. The story Duke Vincent had concocted for their cover was that the assassin who'd killed Raponne was fleeing for his life. In Vincent's telling, Raponne had remained his court favorite, and he'd been overjoyed when the artist was unable to serve in Prince Heindaw's court. In a fit of jealous rage, the assassin had killed the artist and fled for his life to escape the vengeful duke. In Carff, he would make a show of arriving in the port and begging the prince's mercy in exchange for sharing information he'd overheard his former master saying about Prince Calb. Duke Vincent had divulged legitimate secrets about his liege to give the story credibility. It cost nothing to share them now that Calb was dead.

It was certainly a dramatic story. Rew wished it wasn't, but Vincent had claimed the surest way to avoid suspicion was to hide beneath such a ludicrous guise that no one would suspect them.

The ranger had been hesitant, but the more he thought about it, the more it made sense. Prince Valchon would have people searching merchant cogs and passenger vessels that were docking in his harbor. They would have suspicious eyes and suspect something of everyone. To slip through that net, Rew and his friends had to give the watchers an answer. When Valchon's people prodded at the unusual circumstances around the arrival of the ship and found something, they could stop looking. Hide in the open. It was what Vincent had been doing his entire life.

Still, they'd witnessed the assassin strangle Raponne to death, and Zaine had become attached to the extravagant artist. Raponne had been hard to take seriously, but the thief rarely took anything seriously. It was going to be difficult for her to spend a week at sea with the assassin, and Rew was half-worried she'd stick one of her knives in the man or get caught trying to.

Anne assured him Zaine wasn't a killer.

She wasn't yet, agreed Rew, but things change.

When they arrived at the dock shortly after dawn, they saw the same captain who had been hauling Raponne north up the river. He laughed when he caught sight of them approaching and asked, "So it wasn't all a lie?"

"Not all of it," responded Rew with a wink.

The captain tossed up his hands then grumbled even more when he realized part of the plan involved providing cover for Rew and the party as part of his crew. Rew and Raif had the build of men used to labor, but Anne and the girls did not.

"What, you think they're going to believe a lass like that is being used to clean the bilge? They could pass for nobility easier than they could sailors."

"Put a wool cap on them, the right clothes, get a little sun and salt on their faces…"

"We've got three deck swabs, then?"

"She can be your wife," said Rew, pointing to Anne. He turned to Cinda, "And she can be your mistress."

"Wait, only I have to work?" complained Zaine. "That isn't fair."

"You have a better idea?"

"I'm the mistress, and Cinda swabs the deck."

"I'm jesting, Zaine. No one is actually going to be pushing a mop, though I do think we need to learn enough about operating the ship we can look as if we know what we're doing when Carff's pilot boards us to take us into the harbor."

He glanced at Cinda and frowned. The young necromancer was changing, slowly, but changing all the same. Her eyes were a brighter green than just months ago, and her skin was pale. Would Valchon's men be trained to identify those signs? Anne could dress Cinda up, put paint on her face to modify her look, but more and more often, it was obvious that Cinda dealt with powers beyond their world. It left an aura about her that could not be disguised if one knew what they were looking at.

Rew asked the captain. "Anne can be your wife, Zaine a deckhand, and I'm guessing you've got a hidden place or two you can stow valuable cargo?"

The captain stuck his thumbs into his rope belt and frowned.

"I've never met a captain who doesn't," pressed Rew. "I'm a ranger, not a customs officer."

"I can hide the girls if they don't mind a squeeze."

Zaine perked up, but Rew shook his head. "Sorry, lass, but we can't all be hiding, and it's Cinda they'll recognize."

"Cinda and you," retorted Zaine.

Rew shrugged. "That still leaves you learning to trim a sail."

"I don't even know what trim means," protested Zaine, chasing after Rew as he went to stow his gear.

"It'll be good for you to have an honest profession," remarked Rew dryly. "And maybe once all this is done, we'll put you on a ship headed south."

"South?" asked Zaine, glancing out the mouth of the harbor in confusion. To the south, there was nothing but water. "Is that the lands beyond the sea? I thought they were east?"

"I guess you'll find out, won't you?"

Later that night, Rew found his coin purse had gone missing again.

Rew sat at the prow of the ship, the tin mug with his grog ration dangling in his hands. His fingers and his palms were raw from handling ropes all day, but the grog was helping. He'd insisted that, even though none of them were sailors, they do what they could to assist the crew. Any goodwill they bought with their labor might pay off later. They knew nothing of managing a ship at sea, though, so in addition to coiling ropes, he'd been given the night watch. He wasn't really sure what he was supposed to be looking for. All he could see was the water reflecting the sparkling silver light of the sky and the sky itself. If there were storms or pirates sharing the open water with them, they were nowhere to be seen.

Five leagues off the port side was the coast of Vaeldon. During the day, it stretched out like a line drawn with a thick brush between sea and sky. The barely visible land was the only thing that separated the two yawning chasms of blue. Where they were sailing, the land looked like nothing more than an afterthought. It gave one perspective.

At night, the land was invisible, though occasionally he thought he detected a glow that would signify a decent-sized settlement. Individual lights, lanterns or fires, were too far to see, but he'd been told the sailors marked the settlements when following the coast because at night, it was the easiest way to measure distance traveled. Rew supposed it was also a good way to make sure you didn't run aground.

"This grog is awful," complained Zaine, coming to join him, plopping her elbows beside his on the gunwale.

Rew grinned. "Quiet feet, just like a sailor."

"Like a thief," corrected Zaine. "Or did you forget your missing coin?"

"I'm going to need it back."

"Don't worry. I haven't spent it all, yet."

He glanced around the nearly empty deck behind them then sipped his drink. His lips twisted into a grimace.

"See!" snapped Zaine. "You think it's awful, too."

"It's the cheapest rum the captain can buy, mixed with a squeeze of lime juice, a bucket of water, and supposedly a bit of sugar, but I can't taste that. It is awful stuff unless you're at the sea, looking out on the open water. Then it hits just right."

"If you say so."

"You'll pour me yours, then?"

Zaine didn't respond, but she stayed beside him, and together, they looked out at the dark water.

"I've been meaning to ask you. What will happen when this is all over?" wondered the thief. "Not just this voyage, but Valchon, the king, all of it. I don't think we'll be going back to our old lives, will we?"

Rew shrugged. "Do you want to?"

She shook her head then added, "That's assuming we survive the next couple of months. I'm not sure how good a wager that is. The world'll be different if we do, won't it?"

He sipped his grog again. "I hope so."

"What do you think we'll do?"

"Anne'll be the easiest. However this turns out, people are going to get hurt. She'll do her part, save who she can, whichever side they were on before. Once they know what she's capable of, whoever has the throne will want to keep her close. There's nothing a ruler fears more than their own mortality, so there's nothing more valuable to them than an empath with Anne's skill. Even Vaisius Morden would make ample use of her talents. He's only switching bodies every generation, and while to an extent he's invulnerable to attack, his bodies age just like the rest of us. Good thing, for our purposes, but even outside the extremes, there are a thousand ailments that plague nobility and commoner alike, and you can't put a price on health. The king's probably got a dozen empaths in his service, but nobody has one like Anne."

"If we defeat the king, won't be you on the throne?" asked

Zaine. "I imagined Anne would stay by your side and keep you sober, or do you think she's got better things to do?"

"Blessed Mother, I hope she's got better things to do," said Rew with a wink and a sip of his grog, "almost as much as I hope I'm not on the throne."

"Who will take command, then?"

"I don't know," answered Rew. "I worry about it, but I can't think of that now. Survival first. One step at a time. If we live, there will be time to figure out the next moves."

"It could be you on the throne, couldn't it? You are the son of the king. It'd be your right, Raif told me. I mean, we're the only ones who know it's been the same man—soul—this entire time. Everyone would expect that if you're the surviving brother, you've earned the seat. Could be another relative, I suppose. You got any others? Are they all like the ones I've met?"

"It's… something to consider. The one thing I know, this kingdom doesn't need another Morden in control."

"Alsayer might do it."

Rew snorted and didn't respond.

Zaine grinned. "Raif? Is that why you've been spending so much time alone with him recently?"

"He's grown a lot since I first met him. He's turning into a leader," said Rew. "Could be a good leader, in time. Not sure he should be ruling all of Vaeldon…"

"Definitely not."

Rew smiled and looked back at the sky reflected on the water.

After several silent minutes, Zaine said, "I don't think he'd want to be king any more than you. Don't think he'll be content to retire to Falvar, either. Not that I think he'll want adventure. When it's all said and done, he could be looking to settle down, but I don't know what that will mean. Don't think he does, either. Course, he's thick enough it might not have occurred to him yet to worry about it."

Rew nodded. "Aye, might be hard to return to Falvar after all of this is done. Should be some prospects open, though, for an eager nobleman looking to make his way in the world. The Blessed Mother knows, we've run into more dead nobles than ones who still live. Who knows? If we're successful, maybe Raif will find himself running a duchy somewhere. Lad like him, that'll stoke his pride for a few years, and then he'll realize a quieter place like Falvar would have been better all along."

"He'd like a duchy," said Zaine. She drummed her fingers on the railing then quaffed another swig of rum. "Or maybe not. I think he's losing his taste for fighting. Not that he's lost his nerve or that he'll back down from what we face, but now that he's seen a bit of war… Victory isn't so glorious when you're standing in a puddle of your own blood and piss."

"He's grown. Dreams and the real thing are sometimes only passing acquaintances. I was the same when I was young. Big dreams."

"Are all boys like that?"

"Most of us when we're young and some when we're old," Rew admitted with a laugh. He knocked his mug against Zaine's. "You've grown, too. No more thieving when this is done, am I right? Could be a gentler world, with no Mordens on the throne. Lots of ways a lass like you with a bit of wit could make a name for herself."

"You offered to make me a ranger, once. Rangers will still be needed, don't you think? Someone's gotta keep an eye on the wilderness. Whoever is on the throne, farmers won't want wyverns and primal sloths taking up residence in their barns."

"I stand by that offer, if I'm in a position to grant it," said Rew. "King's Sake, even if I'm not, I'll put my word in for you. You're right. No matter what else happens, there'll be a need for those who can watch the boundaries of this kingdom, to stand between man and monster. Monsters of the wild or the monsters we've made. You'd make a great ranger, Zaine."

"It's a promise, then?"

"Consider it one."

"And Cinda? What will become of her?"

Rew stared out at the sea and did not respond.

DAYS FROM CARFF, THE TRAFFIC ON THE SEA LANE BEGAN TO increase. At first, it just seemed they'd happened across a congested stretch of water, but as they came closer to the capital, it was obvious there was an unusually large number of ships sailing there.

"What do you think it means?" wondered the captain, standing beside Rew, looking ahead where tall galleons and their sails crowded like shoulders in front of a street theatre performance.

Rew ran a hand over his head, wishing he'd bought a razor in Shavroe. "I think it's folks coming to swear fealty to Prince Valchon. His brothers are dead, and they think he's going to be crowned king. There's value, I imagine, in being the first one to show deference and bend the knee, particularly if you've recently been associated with one of the losers."

Duke Vincent's assassin sauntered up beside them and gave Rew a toothy grin. "I guess they don't have much faith in your chances, eh?"

Rew shrugged and did not respond.

The assassin looked over Rew at the captain and winked. "Look at the two of us, sittin' here talking to the future king and all. Think he'll remember us when he's got that crown atop his brow? Maybe he'll make you a baron and me a duke."

"A duke?" asked Rew. "Learned all you need to know from Vincent?"

After spitting a thick stream of murky brown over the side of the vessel, the assassin barked, "I learned the important parts. I'll figure out the rest as I go. You doing it, then, taking the throne if you're successful? Duke Vincent said you'd decline it, but I said no one turns from that kinda wealth and power."

Rew didn't reply.

The assassin shrugged. "Be that way. I'm just playing about being a duke. Too much tallying and dinners with nobles stuffed tighter than the turkey for me. That's not for this old chap. I figure I'll have plenty of work, though, no matter what happens. Men in my profession are going to have our pick of contracts. The way I see it, I'd rather be the one sneaking up behind the throne than sitting on it, you know?"

Rew rubbed his face with both hands.

"Aye, you know as well as I," remarked the big assassin, nodding authoritatively. "Bet that's why you told Vincent you wanted no part of it. Smart, that, but Blessed Mother, it'd be a bit of fun being king, wouldn't it? Have everyone jumping at your call, get to punish all your enemies and no one says a word. The girls… Pfah. Not ever going to be my seat, but if you take it, I'll be there."

Rew glanced at the man.

The assassin gestured for the captain to leave, and once the other man was out of earshot, the big assassin continued, "I know who you are and what you did between the creche and the rangering. My pa worked for the king, too. Told me the pay wasn't as good as private commissions, but that the work was steady and interesting. Dangerous, too. Best of the best did that sort of work, my pa said. Those that were in it for more than the gold."

"What are you getting at?"

"One professional offering his respects to another, that's all," said the assassin. "And… if you do need someone down the road, I'm loyal to Duke Vincent as long as he's paying the most, if you know what I mean. Man sittin' on the throne can't be doing his own dirty work, can he?"

Rew sighed and looked back out to sea at the boats in front of them. The assassin gave a final nod then padded away.

The captain returned and asked, "What was that all about? He didn't offend you, did he? That man likes to push his nose in where it doesn't belong…"

"No, he didn't say anything... Just, things used to be simpler, didn't they?"

The captain laughed. "Ain't never been simple working for Duke Vincent, but I think I know what you mean."

Behind them, reclining beneath the tarp they'd strung over the prow to serve as their sleeping quarters, Zaine frowned and fiddled with the hilts of her daggers.

Chapter Fourteen

Carff's port was overcrowded. Ships were scattered outside of the secure walls of its harbor, at anchor or floating listlessly, waiting to get in. Some of the more creative captains appeared to have beached their vessels on the leagues of sandy shore that spread out around the sprawling city.

It would be a dangerous maneuver for a ship laden with cargo, but when the only freight was a pretentious nobleman who refused to wait, the captains on the smaller vessels could get away with it. Of course, as he sat looking balefully at the harried activity near the harbor mouth, Rew admitted that calling a noble pretentious for not wanting to wait was unfair. This one time, it was unfair.

The captain of their vessel hoisted Duke Vincent's colors and skillfully maneuvered his ship closer, weaving through the congestion like an urchin skipping a bread line. They received plenty of hard glares from other crews as they cut in front of them, but two princes were dead, so there were only two men left in the kingdom who outranked a duke. Evidently, none of the waiting ships carried another duke who might have standing to argue.

Though, that didn't mean the other vessels were clearing the way. Duke Vincent had been Prince Calb's bannerman, which wouldn't get you far in Carff during the Investiture. There were three hours of tense sailing as the captain skirted amongst the larger ships and shouldered around the smaller ones. The duke wasn't actually a passenger, so they weren't due even the small deference the other captains were reluctantly granting, but that was part of the plan.

When they finally made it within a quarter league of the harbor mouth, a small ketch appeared with a frustrated-looking official, two sailors, and two others staring glumly out at all of the waiting traffic. Pilots, guessed Rew, and the official was meant to ensure the pair only steered the right boats.

The official stood up on the prow of his ketch and called, "Is Duke Vincent truly aboard? Most dukes are arriving by portal."

The captain shuffled his feet and replied, "Ah…"

"King's Sake, turn this thing around!" barked the official. "And whenever I see you on my shift, I'm going to send you to the back of the line again. I don't have time for this."

The captain produced a coin purse and jingled it. The official wouldn't be able to hear the sound over the water, but the message was clear enough.

"Pfah, man, every one of these captains is trying to bribe me. Unless you're offering the deed to your boat, I'm not interested."

The two pilots seemed interested, but no one asked them.

"There are special circumstances," cried the captain. "I would like to discuss the matter in private, to explain our situation."

"Everyone has special circumstances," snapped the official. He turned as if to instruct the sailors manning his ketch to move on to the next hopeful.

"I'll give you the coins just to come up and talk," pleaded the captain. "Two minutes in my cabin, that's all I ask. If I can't convince you, then I won't hinder you moving on, and we'll dutifully take our place at the end of the line if someone can point out where that is."

The official looked annoyed, but he expertly evaluated the coin purse. "Gold in there?"

"Silver."

"Make it gold, and I'll come aboard." The official hesitated and then added, "And keep the purse of silver for my crew to share."

"Rather rich," complained the captain. "Used to be a handful of copper bought good service in these waters."

"How special are your circumstances? Are they more special than the scores of other hopefuls I've spoken to today?" questioned the official, gesturing at the mass of ships clustering around them. "Look around. There are hundreds of them. It's a matter of supply and demand, Captain."

"Come aboard. I'll get the gold." The captain turned to where Rew was standing shirtless and barefoot, a woolen cap pulled down close to his eyes and a coil of damp rope slung over his shoulder. "I didn't expect to be held outside the harbor. It's up to you to talk our way in."

"I've got an idea," assured Rew.

The official was hauled on deck by several of the sailors, and he brushed his hands against a heavy doublet, looking around the ship disdainfully. It was clear he didn't think their circumstances were going to rate special entry into the harbor, but when the captain dangled the coin purse again, the official grimaced and followed him into his quarters.

Rew came closely behind, and the startled official turned when the ranger closed the door.

"This is a private conversation," scoffed the bureaucrat.

Rew said nothing. He simply raised a heavy, wooden belaying pin and smashed it across the side of the official's head. The man slumped to the floor bonelessly. Rew assured the worried-looking captain, "He'll be fine."

Rew hoped so, at least. As long as he hadn't shattered the man's skull, Anne ought to be able to fix him up. Rew frowned. Anne could have put him to sleep without the violence being necessary, but hindsight and all. A lesson for the next time.

"What now?" questioned the captain, looking extremely

nervous to have an official from Prince Valchon's court lying unconscious in his cabin.

"Go tell the pilots and those sailors that he's inside the cabin reviewing some secret documents then give them the coin purse."

"It's just got copper in it. We told them it was silver."

"You'd better find some silver, then," suggested Rew.

The captain sighed but did as instructed. Evidently, tricking the crew and paying them seemed a more appealing notion than admitting to them they'd assaulted the prince's man. Rew scratched his beard. He figured the ruse would get them into the harbor easy enough, but there would need to be some quick talking when they tied to the wharf.

Anne entered the cabin, scowling. "Really, Rew? They're going to search the ship, aren't they? I can heal the man, but we have to leave him unconscious, or he's going to warn them. How are we supposed to explain this? No one is going to believe he knocked his head on the doorframe."

"Make sure he lives, and then let's drag him down below, strip his clothes, put him in a hammock, and splash a couple of mugs of rum on him. Can't be the first time the harbormaster has searched a ship for contraband and found a hungover sailor in the hold. We don't have to fool them long, just long enough we can slip off this boat and into the crowd."

Muttering what were either prayers to the Blessed Mother or entreaties for her to curse the ranger, Anne knelt beside the official, and shortly before the pilots boarded, they dragged the man below.

With some sailors tending to the official's disguise—they knew what it ought to look like—Rew climbed back up the stairwell to the deck to reassume his role as a surly crewman.

The hulking assassin found him. "You know if you let that man live, he's going to talk. Whether it's a few hours, or a few days, he's going to talk. Did he get a good look at you? If he's able to describe you and that description is passed around, how long do you think before the palace hears of it? King's Sake. Even if he can't describe you, we arrived on Duke Vincent's personal craft. That's noteworthy, Ranger. Word will get around, and Valchon's spymasters will piece it together in moments. Hope you don't need more than a day or so to do your work."

Rew grimaced.

"You've gotten soft," accused the assassin. "Should have tied a spare anchor around the man's neck and put him over the side."

"Maybe."

The pilot passed by them and began issuing instructions which Rew pretended to understand. When the pilot was back out of earshot, the assassin continued, "It's the woman, isn't it? She doesn't know who you are."

"She knows who I was."

The assassin was silent a moment. Then, he said, "I'll take care of it for you when she's not looking. Call it a favor on behalf of my pa. He had a lot of respect for you and what you've done. Said you were the best there was. A favor with nothing asked in return, but you're the type to remember favors, aren't you?"

Rew turned away without responding.

"Come on, man. Don't tell me you're still upset about that fop, Raponne. It was on the duke's orders. What was I supposed to do? Run away?"

Rew grunted. "You could have."

The assassin glared at him.

Sighing, Rew admitted, "Aye, I understand it's not your fault, but I hope you understand, I don't like that the world works the way it works. It doesn't have to be like that. We don't have to be like that."

Shrugging, the assassin replied, "It is what it is. Nothing's going to change that, so men like us may as well get paid."

"I've got to tie some ropes or something," muttered Rew. *Men like us.* He closed his eyes and said, "I appreciate you dealing with the problem below."

The assassin offered a small bow, touched his forehead, and then disappeared below deck. The pilots were stalking about the vessel, half-smiles on their faces, which might have to do with the half pouch of silver each of them got, issuing instructions for the crew to take the ship into the harbor.

Rew had no idea what to do to prepare a sailing vessel for dock, and even after a week at sea, he didn't understand half of what the pilots were saying, but he knew how to look busy without doing any real work, so he set to it.

Zaine joined Rew, glaring at the assassin's back when he vanished down the hatch. She shook herself and asked, "Need some help?"

Her wool cap was pulled low like his own, hiding her hair, and she wore filthy, salt-stained clothing borrowed from the youngest, smallest member of the crew. Upon close inspection, she didn't look much like a cabin boy to Rew, but if all went according to plan, they wouldn't rate more than a cursory inspection. Just in case they did get some close looks, Rew bent and checked where his longsword was hidden beneath a pile of spare sail.

When he stood back up, he whispered, "You have any idea of what we're supposed to be doing over here?"

"No," responded Zaine, her voice muffled through barely moving lips. "I can't understand anything these sailors say. For the last week, any time someone looked at me, I just tied two ropes together. I probably knotted half the cords they've got on this boat, but so far none of them have complained. Or, maybe they did, but I couldn't understand it."

Rew rolled his eyes but then picked up two pieces of rope.

THE HARBOR MASTER LOOKED LIKE HE COULD HAVE BEEN THE OLDER brother of the official unconscious in the hold of the ship. He was overdressed, likely underpaid, and clearly hankering for a bribe the moment he realized Duke Vincent wasn't on board.

"You shouldn't have been allowed to dock, you know," he

mentioned, speaking quickly as if he wanted to settle the matter before the other official appeared from within the captain's cabin and tried to share in the next round of payments, "but now that you're here, it'd be an awful chore to turn around, wouldn't it?"

The captain dithered, pretending he didn't know exactly what the harbormaster wanted. The two soldiers who'd accompanied the harbormaster shifted, looking bored and letting their gazes rove over the deck. If the ship were to stay on dock, Rew imagined that those soldiers would be tasked with searching it. Just the two of them. It could take all day.

The soldiers were bored, but Carff was on high alert, and they were doing their jobs, if not very quickly. The pair of soldiers saw when the bulky assassin crept up from below, casually walked to the gunwale with a pack on his shoulder, then tried to climb overboard as if no one was looking.

"Hold!" barked one of the soldiers, his hand falling to the sword at his side.

"Who are you?" demanded the other. "What are you doing?"

The harbormaster looked on confused, and down on the dock, Rew heard calls from other men in Valchon's service inquiring what the commotion was.

"Just, ah…" began the assassin, then he bellowed, "Leaving!"

He charged the two soldiers, bowling them over before they had a chance to draw their weapons. He leapt up on the gunwale, gave Rew a wink and a nod, and then hurled himself overboard, crashing down into the cloudy water of the harbor with an enormous splash.

"He's an assassin!" cried the captain. "Take him. Take him! He killed a man in Shavroe and has been holding us captive all the way here."

It wasn't clear if the other soldiers on the docks believed the captain or not, but when your job was protecting those docks and someone arriving there was accused of being an assassin, you captured him.

Dozens of armed men swarmed the sides of the wharf, trying

to look around the ship to see the man swimming and splashing about on the other side. They were calling for a boat, but so far, none of the armored men looked eager to jump into the filthy water.

The captain grabbed the harbormaster's shoulder and dragged him to the edge of the ship to look down at the fleeing assassin. He was babbling loudly in the official's ear.

Rew and the others sauntered down the gangplank, calling and pointing any time a soldier glanced their way. A few looked as if they would have stopped the ranger and his party, but they couldn't ignore a man who'd assaulted the prince's men and was in the process of fleeing toward the city.

Snatching a heavy bundle of goods that were unattended on the wharf and gesturing for the others to pick up something as well or to take a cart, they made their way into Carff.

THE STREETS WERE A CURIOUS MIXTURE OF FULL AND EMPTY.

Near the harbor, the byways and taverns were overflowing with sailors who had made it to the docks and were busy losing the coin from their voyage. The finer establishments were packed as well. Nobles of all sorts, from all over the kingdom, strode about pompously, making loud declarations in favor of the prince, and eyeing each other suspiciously.

Rew guessed not a one of those nobles had gained entry into the palace yet, and likely never would. The prince had known who his allies were when the Investiture began, and Rew knew Valchon well enough to guess that these latecomers were unlikely to be rewarded for professions of loyalty a month after all of Valchon's rivals were dead.

Those who didn't seem to be there to kiss Valchon's ring, or in the city on commerce, were staying off the streets. Either they'd been frightened off by the influx of visitors, or they'd surmised something about the fall of Stanton and what that meant for anyone residing in a crowded city. The locals they did see hurried about on specific errands and didn't linger in the streets to talk with their neighbors or the shopkeepers.

They saw plenty of soldiers moving about but no spellcasters. Those must have all been sequestered near the palace for Valchon's personal defense. It was only Rew, now, that the prince had to worry about. Valchon would keep his more powerful servants close. All except for one.

There was a flash of purple ahead. It could have been a visitor from Iyre adorned in the city's most vibrant dye, or a traveler from across the sea, or a performer at the theatre, or any number of other reasons someone might wear the color, but it wasn't. In Carff, word would have spread that a new class of spellcasters were wearing purple robes, and that meant no one else would dress themselves in the same shade.

The garb of a spellcaster carried privilege, but it also brought danger. Even in peaceful times, spellcasters were targets of rivals, and if one didn't have the necessary talent, it was an easy way to end up dead. No, if someone was wearing those purple robes, there was only one explanation.

Rew gathered the others and hurried them down a side street, emerging into a wide boulevard that had few of the open shops and street vendors they'd seen on the main avenue. Instead, this corridor was congested with heavily laden wagons carting spices from the harbor to the market.

The walls of the buildings bracing the boulevard were high, and there were few windows. It gave the street a tunnel-like feel, and as the sea wind blew in from the harbor, the street was a funnel for the pungent scent of the spice wagons and the salty tang of the water.

"We're going to get run over," complained Zaine, stepping quick to dodge around one of the lumbering wagons.

Rew pulled the others close and said, "I think I saw a hunter back on the pedestrian streets. It was a man with dark hair wearing a purple robe."

That shut Zaine up.

"Valchon knows we're coming, and what use are these things he's created if he doesn't set them looking for us? They'll be in the streets at the major intersections. They might be ahead of us, but at least on this route, we've got the cover of the spices to hide our scent."

"Can they smell us, truly?" wondered Zaine. She gestured around them. "The city is full of strong odors, and while I agree Raif has a particular aroma after a week at sea, it can't be worse than any sailor who recently docked."

Rew shrugged. "The fact is, we don't know what senses the hunters have."

"Aye, but if they're hunting for us, would they be wearing those robes?" questioned Zaine. Then she frowned. "I suppose it doesn't matter if it's looking for us or not, does it? We can't risk one of those things finding us before we've even properly gotten here."

"They'll recognize us if they see us, but we should be wary of other senses as well," agreed Cinda. She glanced at Rew. "You're thinking of finding lodging near the market?"

He nodded.

"You're not getting anywhere near the palace with these things out hunting for you. We're going to have to take care of them before we confront the prince."

"I think you're right," agreed Rew, "so we'll find a place to stay, and then we'll go about getting rid of them."

"You'll kill them?"

"Better than facing them all standing beside the prince."

"We'll help you, Ranger," said Raif. "You can't do this alone."

"That might be true."

Anne, rubbing her nose with the back of her hand, muttered, "I hope I get used to this."

Chapter Fifteen

"I thought we were going to be staying somewhere like a brothel," remarked Raif, glancing around the broad, comfortable room tucked neatly beneath the eaves of a stately ceiling. Thick, ancient wooden beams spanned the space. They were hung with sparkling lamps filled with clear oil. They'd lit several, and they burned with orange, yellow, and blue flame, lighting the room with a shower of gem tones.

Shabby couches, once fine, were sprawled across the wooden floor in loosely organized formations, and thin screens had been placed between several of them, giving the open room a more intimate feel. The room and everything in it were infused with a curious odor, partly the earthy aroma of roasted coffee grounds, some from oils that burned in the lights, and mostly the heady mix of spices that suffused the streets and open areas of Carff.

The room had the air of ignored luxury.

Zaine plopped down on one of the couches, and a thin cloud of dust billowed out around her. She rubbed a hand over the silk armrest of the couch. "I always imagined brothels would have big plush couches like this. Do they?"

Raif blinked back at her. "How would I know?"

They both turned to Rew. Shaking his head, the ranger held up his hands and said, "Don't you dare."

Grinning, Zaine replied, "I wouldn't mind going to find out, one day. It'd be a bit more fun than staying in a museum, eh?"

"No one's going to recognize our faces when we're staying in a museum," reminded Rew.

"That's because no one is here," retorted Zaine.

"Exactly," agreed Rew. He gestured around them grandly as if giving a tour, "The Carff Spice Museum was founded… hundreds of years ago, probably. It's filled with exotic spices, seeds, and almanacs depicting every bit of minutia about every bit of spice and herb that's known in Vaeldon, and some that aren't, despite the prodigious efforts of the museum's scholars. It's an ideal place for anyone looking to learn about spices but not actually use them, as nearly everything catalogued here in the museum is available for sale two blocks away in the actual market. Of course, it's also an ideal place for those looking to cover their scent and hide somewhere no one will come looking for them."

Zaine fell back on the couch and laughed. "I appreciate the insight, Ranger."

"You really want to go to a brothel?" Raif asked her.

She winked at the fighter.

"No one is going to any brothels," declared Anne. She glared around the group then pinned Rew with her look.

"What?" he protested, "I'm not the one who said it. I brought us to a museum."

Not paying attention to the rest of them and their banter, Cinda had walked to one end of the expansive room where she was rubbing the sleeve of her robe on a large, circular window so that she could peer down at the street three stories below them.

Anne began giving instructions to Raif and Zaine to clean up the room and make it livable, and Rew strategically slipped away.

He joined Cinda and looked down at the teeming throng below. There was frequent traffic in and out of the building where people visited the coffee house which occupied the entire first floor. It was a well-known spot, regularly patronized by foreign merchants looking to do serious business for entire cargos without having to brave the madness of the spice market itself. They could conduct their business, have a cup of coffee, and then be on their way to the more entertaining parts of Carff without having to rub shoulders with the sweating, swearing masses in the crowded market.

The second and third floors of the building housed Carff's extensive spice museum and seed library. It was funded by the king, or maybe the prince, Rew supposed it had to be one of them, and had a mission to collect and archive all manner of flora that crossed Carff's docks or was brought down from the interior of the kingdom.

He wondered if Vaisius Morden or Prince Valchon had any idea they were financing a place like this. Few others seemed to realize it existed, but as a ranger, Rew occasionally came across unknown species of plants, and he and his team would ship the materials to the spice museum for whatever academic purpose it served to document the material and then store the information where no one would ever go looking for it.

Ranger Tate had done the same for decades before Rew's arrival, and he'd impressed the habit on Rew, though Rew had always done it more for Tate's benefit than anything else. He was glad he had. There were former rangers working at the spice museum, helping the arcanists identify and store the plant matter and communicating with those in the field. Rew was relying on those rangers for assistance, now. The arcanists, unlike most of their profession, seemed to care nothing at all for what was happening outside of their ledgers and their musty tomes. They'd barely looked up when the old rangers had led Rew and the others to the empty loft above the museum.

It made one wonder how many such places existed, where learned and accomplished men and women retreated from the world into one of their own design. They could have been important people had they wanted to be.

Rew sighed. On the verge of facing Prince Valchon, he could have used Tate's wisdom. The rangers at the spice museum were well aware of what had occurred in Iyre, and they'd offered their help and advice with eyes open, but it wasn't the same. Tate had always been able to find the heart of a matter, and Rew had put great store in the man's opinions.

If Rew died, it wouldn't much matter what Tate would think of things, but if they were victorious, it was the sort of knotty problem the old ranger excelled at untangling. Go on to face the king, of course, but what then? Should Rew try to play king-maker? Raise the banner for some noble and put them on the throne before anyone realized what was happening? If he didn't, would Vaeldon splinter into dozens of warring kingdoms?

It might be better that way. No single, all-powerful monarch to rule them, but Vaisius Morden's ominous presence had kept the peace, outside of the generational bloodbath of the Investiture. A broken kingdom wouldn't be better than that, not at first. That was a foolish lie Rew told himself because he didn't want to consider the alternatives.

He scratched his beard. There was an easy way to stem the initial chaos, but it meant another ruler with another iron fist. Did one way or the other mean more death and suffering in the long run? Was it man's nature to war, or was there a path to a better way? Was he just wasting his time, because when he considered it, if he were to name a king, he didn't have the faintest idea who that might be. Certainly not any of the sycophants that cluttered the halls in Mordenhold. None of the dukes or barons that clung to regional power were much better, though Barnaus had seemed a reasonable chap. Would men like Duke Vincent bend the knee to a baron from a remote city that he would view vastly inferior to his own realm?

"I'm glad they're with us," said Cinda quietly, nodding back behind them and interrupting his thoughts.

Rew looked at her then at the others.

Her face blank, Cinda continued, "I find my tongue isn't as

sharp as it used to be, and the quips don't come to me anymore. I've lost my sense of humor. It's comforting to hear Zaine and my brother tease each other. It reminds me of spending time with the other girls in Worgon's court or even back in Falvar, though half the things Zaine talks about I hadn't heard of, then. We talked about dancing, getting swept off our feet for a midnight ride with a handsome duke, or maybe kissing when we were feeling bold. I was innocent. It wasn't as fun. Not as terrifying, either."

Rew nodded and didn't respond. She had the truth of it.

"Zaine and my brother couldn't have had more different backgrounds, but they jest just the same. In a different life, Raif would have been getting deflated just as skillfully by a lady of the court, if he was lucky. I imagine in the thieves' guild Zaine's quick tongue would have served her well, or do you think it would have gotten her in trouble?"

"First the one, then the other," said Rew with a chuckle. "I imagine she'd find herself in a good bit of trouble, poking fun at the foibles of those who ran the guild. Doubt they have the same sense of humor that your brother does."

"Good trouble," muttered Cinda. She leaned her face against the window, looking out at an angle down the street toward Prince Valchon's palace. "Is that the sort of trouble we're trying to make? It doesn't always feel like it."

"I don't know if it's what we're doing, but yes, good trouble is what we're attempting. Disruption, bringing down the powers that rule this place… It's trouble, but I think it will be good, eventually." He was quiet for a moment then added, "Jabaan wasn't your fault, Cinda."

"Whose fault was it?" she asked. "Prince Calb for defying us? If he'd just laid down and died, I wouldn't have done it, but that's not an argument we can make, is it? Because Valchon could turn it right back against us. If all his brothers—you included—laid down and died, he wouldn't have had to destroy Stanton. It was Calb's Dark Kind he was destroying. At least, that's what he blamed it on. It is the truth in a twisted sort of way. Without his brothers challenging him, Valchon would have had no reason to attack Stanton. What's next? What else has to fall for us to finish this?"

"Jabaan wasn't your fault," he reiterated.

"I could feel those souls, Ranger," whispered Cinda. "I dragged them back from death, and I commanded them. They killed at my bidding." She turned and shook her head, stopping him from responding. "I lost control, yes. I didn't mean for all of that to happen, for so many to die, but that is what happened. So many did die. That is on me."

"Cinda…" began Rew, unsure what to say to the girl. "You're a good person. It wasn't—"

"No, Ranger, I am not." She held his gaze, her green eyes flaring. "I think… I need to embrace that. I'm not the hero of this story. I'm not the one to bring peace and prosperity to this kingdom. I can only bring suffering and pain, but maybe we need that. There has to be fire to burn away the filth of Vaisius Morden's rule. I am that cold fire, and I will burn his presence away. That doesn't mean I'm a hero. Far from it."

She turned and looked back into the room where Anne was standing, fists on her hips, instructing Raif and Zaine on how to clean a couch cushion. It seemed that neither of them had ever done such a thing before.

"You know," said Cinda, her voice barely audible even to Rew who was standing beside her. "You know, but I don't want them to know. As long as I can be, I'd like to be his sister, her friend. I won't be, when it's done… but for now, I will hold onto that."

"You don't know how this will end, Cinda. You shouldn't lose hope."

"It's my hope, Ranger, that I'm not the hero," retorted the necromancer, "because we cannot win if I am."

"THE SEED MAN GAVE YOU THIS?" ASKED ZAINE.

"He's a seed librarian, I think," corrected Raif.

"Curator," remarked Cinda. "The manager of a museum is known as a curator."

Zaine looked skeptical. "Are you making that up?"

"Eldon is an arcanist," said Rew. He smiled at their startled looks. "Yes, like Salwart, Reynald, or Ralcrist. His realm of study is different, but just as they did, he has dedicated his life to the pursuit of knowledge."

"Power," interjected Cinda.

"Most of them, yes, but Eldon… he's not like most of them." Rew gestured around the dusty loft they'd made their home. "Does this look like a seat of power to you?"

"And you think these herbs will make us undetectable by the hunters?" asked Zaine, peering at the dried sprigs in Rew's hand. "Looks like the tip of a pine bough, to me."

"It's not," assured Rew, twirling the dried bit of twig and nettles between his fingers. He frowned. It did look kind of like a pine bough. When had Zaine learned to identify a plant? He cleared his throat and said, "Cabsinthia. It's from the lands beyond the sea. Sailors wear them around their necks for luck, though Eldon tells me there are legitimate properties when the nettles are boiled in a tea or soaked in a rum barrel. Even a little bit of the resulting liquid can make one invisible to the kraken. Presumably, that's what started the superstition about wearing them."

"The kraken?" choked Raif.

"They live in the sea," explained Rew.

"And this herb protects against them?" questioned Raif. "Why didn't we know about it when, you know, we were just on a boat traveling across the sea?"

"I knew you'd be able to deal with anything we saw."

Raif gaped at him.

"Kraken populate deep sea trenches that go down farther than the tallest mountain rises," said Anne, giving Rew a look. "We were never in any danger of seeing a kraken while within sight of the coast."

Rew grinned and told them, "Arcanist Eldon speculates, and I think he's correct, that this treatment may work equally as well against the preternatural senses of the hunters. They'll still be able to see us, smell us, or hear us, but if they can't use their magic to track us, we've got a chance."

"We can make some tea then go stab the hunters all in the back?" Zaine's eyes were wide. "How certain is this arcanist? We don't have a good record with those fellows, you know."

"I don't think it will be quite so easy as walking up to the hunters from behind, but I'm confident this will help. The hunters in the plain south of Olsoth followed us even in the night when they shouldn't have been able to detect us with normal senses, and that got me thinking. I'm speculating that the land wyrms have some primal sense like the kraken, and they're able to detect life at a distance. What if the hunters were able to absorb that ability? That's why the Olsoth hunters could track us across a featureless plain at night, but the hunter in Shavroe didn't spot me until it was too late. It might be why we haven't been discovered in Carff, yet, or maybe their senses are confused in the city. Either way, the safe thing to do is ingest some of this herb, and we'll have a chance at stealth."

Cinda brushed her hair back then shrugged. "I suppose that makes sense. Where do we get more sprigs of the stuff? I'm assuming that piece is in no condition to provide us any value."

"It certainly wouldn't make a good tea," declared Anne. She shot Rew a look. "And we're not going to try it in rum."

"We need to find a newly arrived sailor with a fresh sprig or two," said Rew, grinning at Anne. "Unfortunately, sailors are a rather superstitious lot, and they may not just hand it over. We've also got to consider Valchon's security coming and going from the harbor quarter where all of the sailors are quarantined. We'll figure that out. Then, Anne, it's up to you."

The empath snorted. "You want me to make the tea?"

Rew grinned at her. "Would you rather I make it?"

"You're sure we need to sneak back down to the docks?" questioned Zaine. "The way was guarded when we arrived, remember? If we hadn't lucked into picking up some merchandise, we would have had to do some fast talking at that checkpoint. That's a lot of risk for some leaves."

"Nettles," replied Rew.

"Whatever," said Zaine. "How are you getting in there?"

"I'm not."

"Then who is?"

Everyone in the party turned and looked at her.

"What?"

"Well," said Raif slowly, "you are a thief."

Rew and Zaine sat in a brightly lit, noisy tavern. Lanterns, hung high on the walls, spilled golden light down on the revelers, and a dozen men in various parts of the room danced their fingers along the lengths of simple wooden flutes or plucked the strings on zithers. For the last several minutes, Rew had been trying to determine what song they were playing and was slowly coming to the conclusion that none of them were actually playing the same song. Given the skill of several of the musicians, that didn't necessarily hurt the performance.

Zaine looked around balefully, her expression as sour as spoiled milk. She complained, "It'd be easier to take their coins."

Rew laughed. "Of course that's easier. When sailors arrive in port, it's expected they spend every copper of their pay. That's what keeps them going back out to sea. Those men live in short, frantic bursts. Didn't you see how cramped their quarters were below deck? A smile from a pretty lass sustains them while they're trapped out on the water. They'd rather think the smile was offered freely than to distract them while their purse was being sliced open along the bottom, but either way, they know when they return to the water their purse will be empty. I imagine the missing coins go down a little easier if they can trick themselves into thinking they almost found the love of their life."

"Pretty?"

Rew rolled his eyes.

Perking up slightly, Zaine began studying the room again.

They'd been there for two hours now, after sneaking through the blockade Prince Valchon's soldiers had set around the harbor district. It seemed that a handful of docks were designated for nobility and other prominent arrivals, and from there, entry into the city was easy. They'd been lucky on their initial arrival in Carff, but now they were seeking foreign sailors, who weren't granted such parole. Crews from merchants and vessels from across the sea were directed into a ten-square block district and contained there, though few of them were complaining.

There were taverns, brothels, wine shops, herbalists, gambling dens, and even a few places to eat and sleep. It was all that a visiting sailor could hope for, and it seemed Valchon's administrators had made sure the venues were well-stocked and prices were kept low. The prince wanted to make it difficult for strangers to gain entry into the city proper, but he didn't want to cut off the commerce that was the life-blood of Carff.

But while it was easy to keep the sailors contained with pleasant company and drink, it wasn't so easy to keep the merchants themselves locked away in the small area. The ship owners and captains were used to nicer, quieter quarters than the common sailors, and they had business to conduct within the city. They needed to sell cargos, negotiate commissions, arrange repairs, pay tariffs, take out loans, and even visit the palace to conduct business with Valchon's people.

Rew and Zaine had seen that while those merchants were given great scrutiny when they left the quarantined district, no one seemed to care much when they returned.

Zaine had scouted out several of the check points where people came and went and told the others her plan was to attach herself to a returning captain, as it seemed all the soldiers gave them was a polite wave when they reentered the quarantined zone. Rew had approved the plan then had been instructed by Anne to accompany the young thief.

She'd told him crisply, "You cannot allow a girl her age to roam unaccompanied in places like that."

Zaine had protested that she would be fine, but in the end, it seemed she was happy to have Rew's company. Finding a captain had been easy enough, as the first man they approached had assumed they planned to be stowaways, and a single silver coin was all he needed when they promised it wasn't his ship they would hide on.

Locating a tavern packed full of foreign sailors was easy enough as well, but when it turned out few of them spoke the king's tongue, and all of them were interested in finding a quiet corner with Zaine to do something other than talk, she'd relied on Rew to ward off the most ardent of the potential suitors, and they'd settled down to formulate a plan.

"I'm not going to… do that to get some tiny clipping of an herb."

Grinning at her, Rew had responded, "I don't expect you to, but you've got to get one somehow. What's your plan?"

She'd been pondering that for hours now, looking around, trying to pick the easiest of the marks. She'd fiddled with the laces of her tunic but then stopped. She'd begun to stroke the hilts of her daggers until she saw Rew's stern look in response. After that, she'd drunk several ales, perhaps hoping for inspiration at the bottom of each mug.

Rew had waited patiently, happily ordering more ales for himself and reluctantly for Zaine, glad to be away from Anne's scrutiny for the night. He'd considered mentioning to Zaine that if she paid attention, she would pick up a handful of sailors in the room speaking the king's tongue, and she could simply ask them for some of the herb. If they were reluctant to hand it over, it shouldn't take more than a few coins to convince them. The stuff wasn't expensive. It was just rare in Vaeldon, and not all of the sailors could be bound by old superstitions. It was drinking tinctures from the herb that actually gave them the protection, after all. As he poured himself another ale, Rew decided the experience of coming up with a plan on her own would be good for Zaine.

Not to mention, he'd found his coin purse missing that afternoon again, and after cajoling her to return it and finding it suspiciously lighter than when he'd lost it, he wasn't in the mood to be helpful. Let her make it more complicated than it needed to be. He'd decided he would advise her when he got an apology and his coins back.

Scowling at the drunken sailors crowding around them, Zaine whispered to Rew, "How do male thieves do it?"

Rew laughed, the ale slowly working wonders to improve his mood. "You know more about that than I do."

She shrugged and admitted, "From what I saw, they'd lurk outside in an alleyway and bash someone over the head as they moved from tavern to tavern. We didn't have sailors in Falvar, but we had wagon men, and they aren't so different. Inside a tavern, the danger was women getting close and putting their fingers in your purse. Outside, it was straying into dark shadows when the city watch wasn't nearby."

Rew nodded. "So you don't want to flirt, and I'm guessing you don't want to assault any of these poor men."

"I'm not entirely closed to the idea," declared Zaine, sniffing as a particularly rancid sailor stumbled behind them, sloshing his ale and belting out what sounded like a sea shanty in a language no one else in the room spoke. Sighing, the thief crossed her arms over her chest. "Well, since you're here, what would you do?"

Forgetting about his light purse, Rew winked then pointed to a man two tables down from them. He was blinking dazedly at another man standing atop the table furiously stomping to a beat almost in time with one of the musicians. Around the first man's neck was a thin cord. They could barely see the top of a sprig of herbs tucked into his shirt.

"My guess," said Rew, "that man's going to be passed out from drink within the next quarter hour, if not sooner. Give it a full hour, and there will be dozens of them with faces down on the table and snoring. It's frowned upon in establishments like these to steal from anyone passed out from drink, as it's not seen as sporting, but soon enough, we'll have our opportunity. As long as you're subtle and light-fingered, it ought to be rather easy. There isn't a clear eye in this room to watch you work."

"And we're sure we have to drink that tea?" asked Zaine, perhaps considering how long the unwashed sailor had been storing the herb down the front of his shirt.

"We'll rinse it first, and don't tell Anne the details of where he was keeping it, eh?"

Zaine pretended to vomit.

Rew clapped her on the back. "Cheer up. We've been in the city less than a day, and already, we're making progress."

Chapter Sixteen

"You're sure this is going to work?" asked Zaine, looking disdainfully into a murky brew that swirled ominously in her cup as she rocked it back and forth.

"Pretty sure," replied Rew. "I mean, the theory makes sense, at least."

"That doesn't sound very sure."

The ranger shrugged. "Those hunters south of Olsoth tracked us somehow, and they seemed more skilled at it than the one I faced in Shavroe or the ones here. If they're consuming the souls of people, then couldn't they absorb some of the magic along with strength and speed? And what reason would they have for roaming the plains south of Olsoth if not to drain the land wyrms? It'd be easier than finding a kraken, and there's nothing else out there. We don't know if there were more of them we didn't face, so to stay hidden, we've got to drink it."

Zaine looked skeptical.

"Makes sense to me," declared Raif, and he tossed back his tea, his throat bobbing as he swallowed it in big gulps. He finished, sat down his mug, and wiped his mouth.

"How was that?" asked Zaine. "It didn't taste… bad?"

"I've had worse. Could have used some sugar. It was a little…

I don't know, musty?" replied Raif with a shrug. His eyes narrowed suddenly at Zaine's expression. "Why?"

Zaine coughed and looked at Rew. Sighing, the ranger picked up his mug and downed it like Raif had. He figured that no matter what the stuff tasted like, there was no sense drawing it out, and he was confident his assessment was correct. The hunters had been on the plains south of Olsoth for the wyrms. They'd been draining the giant monsters and absorbing not just the strength of their souls but some capacity for the monsters' magic. If more of the hunters had that ability, their party needed the protection the herbs would provide.

The thought made Rew dreadfully uncomfortable. If the hunters could suck the magic from the wyrms, then what other powers had they gained from the monsters in the far-off parts of the world? The one in Shavroe had absorbed the talent for invoking. What other spellcasting were the simulacra capable of? There would be no telling what skills and hidden talents each one would have until they faced them. Rew shuddered.

Zaine noticed, and her lips twisted. She pushed her mug away.

"No, that's not what…" muttered Rew. He pushed the mug back to the thief. "I was thinking about the hunters."

Looking unsure, Zaine finally picked up her mug and drank her tea.

"You're worrying about what else these hunters might have taken?" questioned Cinda. She tapped her empty mug with a finger. "We can protect ourselves from being sensed by the powers of the wyrms and the kraken, but… what else are these things capable of? If we saw three of them in Olsoth, it's fair to assume Valchon is sending them far and wide to collect whatever skills he deems worthy. The strength of primal sloths, land wyrms … What of wyverns?"

"I don't think we have to worry about that. Not even these things would survive an encounter with a wyvern," responded Rew. "I hope."

"Well, we can assume Valchon is sending his spawn all over, seeking the powers he admires most."

"He was sending," corrected Rew. He ran a hand over his head, feeling the short hair sticking up in a rough stubble. "Now that Heindaw is dead, Valchon will have called back his dogs. They'll have gained whatever powers they could, and now, they'll be in the city waiting for us."

"Maybe," said Raif, "but like in Shavroe, he could be using these… things as emissaries."

"No," argued Cinda, "I think Rew is right. What could be more important for the prince than stopping us—stopping Rew?"

"It is a good point, though," said Rew. "The hunter in Shavroe was, well, still in Shavroe. Valchon could have opened portals and pulled back his simulacra within a day or two if he wanted. Why leave that one there?"

"As a sort of warning?" wondered Cinda. "When we killed it, we let Valchon know where we were coming from. He could have placed them at other major cities on likely routes and checked in with them through portals regularly. Now that one is dead, so the others aren't necessary."

Rew nodded. "Aye, but he didn't make any extraordinary efforts to search our vessel, and if he knew we were coming from Shavroe, then Duke Vincent's own ship would be the first one to look at. King's Sake, we know what Valchon is capable of. He wouldn't have hesitated to sink every boat that came from there. What would have stayed his hand?"

The party sat silently, thinking, but none came up with an answer.

Finally, Cinda brought up the obvious. "He wanted us here."

"Like Heindaw wanted us in Iyre," agreed Raif.

"Not exactly," said Cinda. "Heindaw wanted me. Valchon… maybe he needed to kill us in person? Casting a maelstrom and sinking our ship wouldn't bring the closure he needs for the king and the rest of Vaeldon. If our truth has spread widely, then he'll want a visible end to you, Ranger. Splashes of meteors into the sea aren't going to do it. He'll want the body."

Rew stood and began to pace. "It's not a bad thought, but if that's all it was, he could have caught us at the dock. We weren't that stealthy sneaking in through the harbor district. I'd been thinking we were subtle, but… were we?"

"The plan worked," mentioned Zaine. "We're here, and if he knows where we are, he hasn't moved on us yet. He's not going to be like Heindaw, is he, waiting for us to attack the palace? A better plan would have been to show up in the middle of the night last night when we were all sleeping."

"Waiting for us is not his way," confirmed Rew. "Valchon is powerful, but he's also inclined to rely on his allies—Pfah. That's it. His allies."

"What?" asked Zaine and Raif at the same time. They gave each other shy grins then turned back to Rew. Again, they spoke at the same time, "What?"

"Alsayer," guessed Cinda.

"Exactly," replied Rew, punching a fist into an open palm. "That slippery bastard has been dogging us since the beginning, but he's been curiously absent since we went through the portal to Jabaan. He's not going to stop his plotting until he's dead, so unless that's the case, he's out there somewhere maneuvering against us. King's Sake, I wish I knew what he intended. It fits, though. He's been putting us in place as neatly as if we were pieces on a Kings and Queens board, but why does he want us here, if not to feed us to Valchon?"

"Is he plotting against us?" questioned Anne.

Rew blinked at the empath. "Well, of course he is."

She began picking up everyone's empty tea mugs and setting them beside the basin they used to wash their dishes. She studiously avoided Rew's gaze.

"Hold on," barked the ranger. "What are you saying?"

Anne turned back around to face the party, wiping her hands on a rag. "I'm asking, are we sure Alsayer is plotting against us?

He keeps saying we don't need to be enemies, right? Maybe he means it."

"Anne…"

"He threw us through a portal which deposited us in a room with our sister who tried to kill me. If you hadn't been there, she would have killed Cinda," remarked Raif, "and that was before Calb's imps came storming up the stairs. We had to run from his entire army then were chained against a wall awaiting execution."

"He plucked us from beneath Valchon's thumb and put us in position to surprise Prince Calb, who if you recall, we were trying to assassinate," argued Anne.

"Alsayer captured my father's wraiths—and my father!" snapped Cinda.

"He captured the wraiths, but to our knowledge, he didn't use them," retorted Anne. "He didn't give them to the king or to the princes. Remember, he lost that box of his, and it was only then Vaisius Morden got his hands on the things. And your father… It was Kallie who killed him. I won't say Alsayer was treating the baron well, but he kept him imprisoned in Spinesend instead of turning him over to Arcanist Salwart or Prince Heindaw. Why didn't Alsayer hand over the baron? It was a lot of work to capture the man, and he was doing no one any good in Spinesend."

"Perhaps you forgot that Alsayer killed our mother," concluded Cinda, her voice as cold as her funeral fire. "He murdered her then commanded the Dark Kind to attack Falvar, and while you're right, Kallie wielded the knife, Alsayer is just as guilty for the death of our father. That man is our enemy. There's no doubt about it."

Anne's lips tightened into a grimace. "I… did forget about your mother. I'm sorry. You're right. The spellcaster has done awful things to you and your family."

"He's done awful things, but maybe Anne has a point," said Rew quietly. He clenched his fist on the table, "I hate to admit it, but while he's been a thorn in our side—worse than that, I know

—he hasn't been hindering our mission as much as he could have."

"Thorn in our side," exclaimed Cinda, jumping to her feet. "He's killed most of my family!"

Rew glanced at Anne, but he didn't speak. Cinda was glaring at them both, her green eyes sparking dangerously, her nostrils flaring as breath exploded in and out of her.

No one spoke for a long while. Then, Raif cleared his throat and asked, "Are you suggesting Alsayer helped us get back into Carff? That the spellcaster is the reason Prince Valchon hasn't moved against us?"

The empath shrugged. "I don't know. I can't fathom that man's motivation, but like Rew said, he hasn't hindered us as much as he could. He sent us to Jabaan and didn't interfere with us going to Iyre. Is it that big a stretch to think he helped cover our arrival here? I'm not saying we forgive him. I'd never suggest that. He's a terrible, evil man, and he doesn't deserve our trust, but what if his goals align with our own? I think we'd all agree he wanted us to kill Calb, right?"

Rew let his head fall back so that he was staring at the ceiling. "He asked me to wait to kill Valchon until after the prince dealt with the Dark Kind in the Eastern Province. Until after Stanton, it turned out, but yes, I think he sent us to Jabaan to face Calb. If he'd wanted us dead, there were easier ways to achieve it. Heindaw believed I called to Alsayer when we were in Iyre, do you remember? He was waiting for the spellcaster when the rangers arrived. Why did my brother think Alsayer and I were in league?"

"Exactly. Alsayer waited until after Valchon destroyed Stanton, killing tens of thousands, and then working together, the two of them deposited us in Jabaan," drawled Cinda. "I agree he wanted us to kill Calb, and I'll grant you Heindaw as well, but it seems pretty obvious if that's the case, Alsayer was working for Valchon this entire time. Valchon wanted his brothers dead as much as we did. Why would we assume anything other than that Alsayer is still working with Valchon?"

"But why would he be doing it? He has nothing to gain."

"So he can be second in command when Valchon burns us to cinders and ascends the throne," growled Cinda. "Is there an official position, right hand of the king? Or maybe he'll get a province to run until Valchon's children come of age. Surely handing our heads to the prince will earn him a duchy, which is plenty of incentive for anyone."

Rew crossed his arms over his chest. "Valchon has a small army of children, and they've already come of age! The ones I killed were older than you! Pfah. Alsayer was the one who captured your father. You're right. He was also the one who tricked Valchon and the king into believing it was Kallie who had the power to oppose them, which is what kept the king off our backs, and think about what you're saying. Alsayer knows what will happen if Valchon ascends to the throne. He knows the king will inhabit the prince. More than anyone, Alsayer will understand he can't earn loyalty from the future king. I'm beginning to see, I think. Alsayer knows what you can do, and he's passed on chances to kill you. He wants our mission to be successful."

"So he wants me to… kill the king? This is getting convoluted, Ranger. The man killed my father, who had my blood and a lot more experience. If our talent is required to face Vaisius Morden, why destroy it? It's easier for me to believe he's our enemy because that's exactly what he seems to be."

"Alsayer is a lot of things, but he's never what he seems to be."

Cinda threw up her arms and flopped back down into her chair. Muttering under her breath to Zaine, she asked, "Fetch me some of that wine you stole from Curator Eldon, will you?"

"Librarian, I think," murmured Raif. "It's a seed library, so he's a librarian, isn't he?"

"Arcanist," corrected Rew absentmindedly. He began to pace. Zaine, looking slyly at Anne, skittered away and ducked behind a partition in the far corner. When she emerged, she held two wine bottles by the necks.

"Pour me one too," instructed Anne with a heavy sigh, "and for Rew, I guess. You know he's going to ask for it."

Ignoring them, Rew kept walking back and forth, his thoughts muddled. He wanted the connections to fall in place, for some final section of the puzzle to be illuminated, but it wasn't. Alsayer had helped them, in his callous way, but he'd put them in danger time and time again as well. He and Rew had fought. The spell-caster had fled each time. But he hadn't... No, he had pulled his punches. More than once, Alsayer had held back. Whatever he wanted, it wasn't their deaths.

But that didn't make the rest of it any clearer. What did Alsayer have to gain if they killed Valchon? Conversely, what did he have to gain if Valchon killed them?

The king knew Cinda was the dangerous one, now, and that her sister had been a decoy. Would that lead the king to Alsayer? The spellcaster had to be worried it might. No matter how carefully he thought he'd buried his involvement, Vaisius Morden was a difficult man to fool. Was that why Alsayer seemed to have vanished, or had the king already found him? Maybe Rew was hiking in circles, wasting his time, and the spellcaster was already dead.

Cursing to himself, he decided they needed information, but there was no one in Carff he could trust. Anyone who wasn't a supporter of Valchon would have fled the city. Even the former spies that might have infiltrated Valchon's circle to curry favor with Calb or Heindaw would be gone by now, so who would know the inner working of the prince's plans? Who would know the mind of the prince himself, who could understand—

Rew stopped pacing and smiled. He turned and told the others, "I have a plan."

"King's Sake," muttered Zaine, and she reached to refill her mug with more wine.

Rew crouched behind a stack of half-completed barrels. The sounds of Carff rose and fell around him like waves in the sea, but in the courtyard of the cooper's shop, it was quiet. The stave makers, binders, and other workers had all gone home hours before, and the streets in the commercial district were quiet.

They were close, though, to the madness and excitement of a patch of gambling halls and wine sinks. It was a street away, so no one would stumble across them, but close enough it wouldn't be unusual to hear a sharp-pitched scream in the night as some unfortunate took a wrong turn.

Rew hefted a barrel stave and touched the hilt of his longsword with his other hand. He would have rather held his longsword, but tonight, their aim was to capture, not to kill.

A night bird called out, a poor imitation of the gulls which feasted on the leavings of Carff's waterfront. A flood of relief washed over Rew followed by a tide of nerves. The plan was working.

He'd been confident it would until Anne had insisted she play a role. Rew hadn't considered how that would affect his patience, waiting for hours in the dark, hoping Anne managed to bring their quarry and that she didn't end up locked in some dungeon in the city awaiting torture. Or worse, that he might find her later drained for the power in her soul and her abilities as an empath.

He hadn't considered that until he'd been in position and it was too late to call it off. The skills of an empath were rare, and even poor practitioners of the art found themselves in high demand as nobles and wealthy merchants begged for their services. In a city like Carff, Anne could have lived like a queen serving the needs of the elite, or she could have attached herself to Valchon's court or any other that she chose.

The princes, even the dukes and the barons, had coin to buy anything. They had armies of staff to attend their every whim, but you couldn't buy your health unless you could afford an empath, and there were few empaths with the experience and talent of Anne—fewer still that were willing to sell that talent for nothing more than gold.

But the hunter wouldn't know of her skill. Rew told himself the hunter would have no idea what Anne was capable of. She would be like any common woman in Carff. There was no reason to give her special attention, no need to attack her until she'd shown the simulacrum what she claimed.

Rew had thought Zaine might play the role of guide, continuing her education in subterfuge, or Raif as the most likely to volunteer to put himself at risk. Cinda was the bait, so it couldn't be her. Rew was the jaws of the trap, and the hunter might recognize him, besides. But Anne had refused to allow either Raif or Zaine approach the hunter and had insisted that she be the one to fetch the simulacrum and trick him into thinking she knew where a necromancer was hiding.

Aside from dealing with a hunter who might have her description or could decide to take her not even knowing who she was, the greatest danger was that the hunter would bring others. If there was more than one of Valchon's simulacra, their plan wouldn't work. If there was a company of soldiers or spellcasters with the creature, they would have to abort. Rew and the others had routes to safety. If the ambush was called off, they would be in little danger with enough warning, but it would be nearly impossible for Anne to slip away once she was with the hunter.

Each moment he'd waited, terrible thoughts had raced through his imagination. Anne lying vacant-eyed and drained in some alleyway. Anne dead. Anne being brought in front of Valchon. Anne…

Rew shook himself and dismissed the barrage of concerns. He'd heard Zaine's call. Anne and the hunter were coming, and the hunter had come alone. If not, the cry would have continued several more times.

He felt relief he'd guessed correctly, the hunter would seek the glory of recovering Cinda himself and wouldn't have alerted anyone else. The hunter might not think it was Cinda, but he had to wonder. Surely the creatures were aware of the girl and how interested Valchon would be in her. It would be a boon to any of the simulacra to bring Cinda to Valchon, and if they didn't, absorbing her powers for themselves would be plenty tempting.

How else was one of the identical whelps going to set themselves above their brothers? Even if they didn't know it was Cinda, necromancy was a rare talent, and Rew doubted any of the simulacra had found a living practitioner they could suck the talent from. A spellcaster that was outside the employ of their father or the king would be fair game. Whether they suspected it was Cinda or not, Rew had gambled that the hunter would come and that it would come alone. So far, it seemed to be working.

Anne stepped into the gateway of the courtyard.

Rew watched from between the thin gaps in the unfinished barrel he hid behind. Stacks of lumber, bands of steel, and buckets of nails sat around the open area like body parts in a butcher's shop. The coopers' supplies were left in the open, safe from rain in Carff's dry season. The raw materials were not worth stealing had thieves snuck into the yard.

Anne walked several steps into the courtyard and stopped, waiting. She moved from foot to foot, clearly nervous, but she wasn't giving any signs to Rew or the others. She wasn't indicating they should flee. The hunter was a predator. Her fear wouldn't be unusual around the creature. Rew had told her she didn't have to hide it, that she could allow the hunter to feel her panic. If anything, it would make the hunter overconfident.

Long moments passed. Then, behind Anne, a shape detached itself from the shadows. Like a snake wending through the grass, the hunter fell in behind her. The empath started walking again, and Rew shifted. He hated seeing her out there with that thing behind her.

The hunter moved, purple robes flowing like a dancer on the stage. Two broad-bladed shortswords hung from its hips, and leather bracers encased its arms. Rew couldn't see its expression in the dark courtyard, but its head turned slowly and purposefully, taking in the shapes scattered around the courtyard left by the coopers and watching for an ambush. Maybe it commanded high magic like some of its brethren. Maybe it'd absorbed other abilities before being recalled to Carff, but Rew was sure this thing knew how to fight. Every step it took screamed danger.

The hunter carried itself with the confidence of one of Mordenhold's most experienced weapons masters, and it took in its surroundings with the care of a ranger or a thief.

Turning his head slowly so as to not show any motion the hunter could detect, Rew glanced up to the walls around the cooper's workspace and hoped to the Blessed Mother that Zaine stayed in hiding and didn't try to reposition for a better shot.

The thief was serving as their eyes, making sure the hunter came alone before they acted, and she'd demanded to have her bow with her in case she needed to take the thing down if it went sideways on them.

Watching the way the hunter moved, Rew knew she would have no chance of slaying it even with the best aimed arrow. The hunter buzzed with potential kinetic energy. It seemed to breathe vigor.

Shifting his grip on the barrel stave in his hand, Rew pretended he couldn't feel the moisture left by his palm. What was he, a green recruit on his first foray into the wilderness? He'd killed four of these things already. This hunter should be scared of him.

Of course, this time, he had a long hunk of wood, and the hunter was carrying two swords. This time, he had the chance to see the predatory grace it moved with. He saw it was older than the others he'd faced. It would be stronger, faster. Anne was beside it, exposed. This time, Rew wasn't trying to kill it. He was trying to capture it.

Chapter Seventeen

I n front of a door to the interior of the cooper's workshop was a thin wire strung through a series of metal loops and tied to the trigger of a crossbow. The crossbow was hidden, except for a narrow space it was aimed through. If a foot or leg moved the wire more than a finger-width, the crossbow would fire, hopefully.

They hadn't bothered to test it. Rew had thought it unlikely the hunter would overlook the crude trap, and as he watched the simulacrum approach, he was certain it'd see what they'd done. The creature had the lithe grace of a natural predator, and it was looking for surprises.

Anne and the hunter came near the door, and the empath gestured ahead. Too loud for the empty courtyard, she said, "She's in there, but the door is locked. I can't get it open."

The hunter slid around Anne, its feet barely seeming to touch the hard-packed dirt. Rew could see the gleam of its eyes as they moved restlessly, observing everything. It came closer, and the ranger held his breath.

Around him, he wore a cloak of shadow pulled tight. He'd drawn in and trapped his scent. He didn't move. He didn't breathe. He was as invisible as his craft could make him. In the dark, in hiding, he would be completely undetectable to a normal man, but the hunter was no normal man, and Rew's heart thundered as the creature approached. Could the thing hear well enough to detect his heartbeat? Rew hadn't thought of that. What else hadn't he thought of?

But the hunter slowed, and its attention did not turn to Rew. Instead, it studied the thin wire stretched across its path. It seemed to pause, as if to ask Anne a question, but instead, it stepped forward, its gaze shifting to follow the wire as it disappeared into the pile of debris.

A heartbeat before he thought the hunter would see the crossbow pointed at it, Rew launched himself from hiding, swinging the barrel stave with all his might at the back of the hunter's head. His cloak of shadow fell away, and there was nothing he could do to hide the sound of the swinging stave.

The hunter tensed. Then, it moved, but while it was faster than any normal man, Rew was no normal man, either. His barrel stave fell on the hunter, but instead of its head, he smashed the wood down on its shoulder. He connected with all of his strength behind the blow, and the barrel stave snapped.

The hunter was knocked forward, and as it fell, it slapped the wire, tugging the trigger of the crossbow. There was a thump as the crossbow fired, launching the bolt point blank at Rew. Yelping, the ranger dodged the moment he heard the click.

The bolt flashed toward him, slashing across his arm then thudding into the half-finished barrel he'd been hiding behind. The hunter rolled away, kicking out with a lightning-fast foot, but Rew was already out of the way. He reached back and snatched another barrel stave from a pile of them. The hunter rose to its feet, one shoulder held lower than the other, and it drew its shortswords.

"You. I should have known."

"Me," agreed Rew.

The hunter tilted its head, looking at the hunk of wood in Rew's hands, then asked, "You meant to capture me?"

Nodding, Rew conceded, "I'd hoped to."

"I suppose I ought to do the same with you," mused the hunter. "Father would appreciate having you alive, but that's not as fun for me."

The hunter attacked with the speed of a streaking hawk. One shortsword thrust at Rew's neck, and the other chopped down trying to take him in the knee.

The ranger backed away, not trusting the wooden stave against the hunter's shortswords. They gleamed in the night. Razor-sharp steel, well-wrought, or even enchanted? Rew scowled. He had considered that he might not land his initial blow on the hunter's skull, but he'd figured he would cripple the thing even if he missed. The way it moved, though... it was like watching a swollen stream pour over rocks and around branches. Fluid, powerful. The shortswords danced like a serpent's tongue. Even on the injured side which Rew had struck with the stave, the hunter was only slightly slower.

The hunter feinted and probed, and Rew guessed the creature had spoken the truth. It would take Rew alive if it could, but the hunter would enjoy the kill if it couldn't.

Rew kept backing away, occasionally meeting the hunter's swings with the stave, grimacing as pieces of it were carved away. His longsword hung at his side, but if he drew it, the fight wasn't going to be about capture any longer.

They fenced, but the hunter was quickly growing tired of the farce and began to press Rew harder. The ranger retreated then moved to hold his ground. He let the hunter swing at him, and when the blow missed, he whipped his barrel stave at the hunter's wrist.

The hunter caught the strike with its other sword, the edge of steel embedding into the wood. The hunter slashed upward with its second blade and smacked into the stave with the flat of the sword, knocking the wooden club from Rew's grip.

"King's Sake," growled the ranger, shaking his empty hand. He'd gotten a splinter from that. He was sure of it.

The hunter grinned at him then spun just in time to see a barrel filled with nails, hanging on a rope, swing out of the darkness.

The barrel smashed into the hunter, sending it flying backward, its shortswords spinning from its hands as it was crushed by twenty stone of weight at speed.

From above, Raif cackled madly. The fighter had been in charge of unleashing the barrel when Rew maneuvered the hunter into position. They'd hoped Rew's initial strike would fell the thing, but it always paid to have a backup or two.

"Well done!" cried Anne, scurrying forward.

Raif began to clamber down from the pulley assembly the coopers used to move materials across the yard. Rew approached the hunter, pulling a set of steel restraints from behind his back. He had cuffs for the hunter's wrists and ankles, all connected by a stout series of links. The hunter, when it woke, would be incredibly strong, but Rew was fairly confident the steel would hold it. If not, they were going to have to kill the thing.

He was more worried it'd be able to invoke, but they needed information, and anything they tried to get it would be risky.

"It's alive," called Cinda from the doorway she'd emerged from. She had been hiding in the building, in case somehow the hunter could sense her high magic.

Rew opened the first manacle and bent to attach it to the hunter's wrist.

The thing's eyes flicked open. It spit a mouthful of blood and teeth to the side then kicked Rew in his chest, flinging him backward. As he was thrown into the air, he felt a tug at his belt, and his eyes widened. The hunter had gripped his longsword before it kicked him, and the enchanted blade was drawn smoothly.

Rew slammed against a pile of loose lumber, his chest throbbing. He stared open-mouthed as the hunter rose to its feet. Blood dripped from its chin, and it moved awkwardly like several of its bones had been broken. There was a muffled crunch with each step it took, but somehow, it came closer. What sort of monster had this thing found and drained? Its resilience was impossible, yet there it stood in front of him. Its eyes gleamed with pain and glee. Rew's longsword was held confidently in its hands, and now, he was unarmed.

The creature cackled, "Father warned me about this blade. I can't wait to see his face when he finds I killed you with—"

Rew released the magic within the sword.

Soft white light flared along the blade, and the hunter gasped.

"This is… amazing." Awe dripped from its voice. "With this, I could—"

"You're right," said Rew. "I'm helpless against you while you're holding that blade. I give up. Take me to see the prince."

The hunter's eyes were fixed on the longsword, and its arms began to tremble. Beneath its breath, it murmured, "The power…"

Rew knelt and held up the steel manacles. With a smile, he said, "Why don't you put these on me? And go ahead and sheath the sword. No need for it to taste blood tonight. My blood, your blood, we're all family. We all come from the same lineage. Why spill what we share?"

The hunter's eyes rose, and its lips curled with mad glee. The tip of the longsword wavered, but the hunter didn't seem to notice. It mumbled, "What are you talking about? I feel the strength—"

Raising his hands, Rew shook the manacles.

Young eyes, Valchon's eyes, looked down at him with greed, bloodlust, confusion. The soul of Erasmus Morden raged from within its prison of steel. It hungered. It sought its own blood. Rew felt it like a twinge from an old, familiar wound. His ancestor called, Erasmus Morden's imprisoned soul screaming for release, for violence. Steel quivered in the hunter's grip as the ancient spellcaster clawed for control. The hunter had no idea what it held. It didn't even know it was in a fight.

"Do you want me to put these on myself?" asked Rew calmly. "Valchon will want me alive, you said? I surrender. Take me to Valchon."

Opening and closing its mouth several times, as if having trouble speaking, the hunter finally quaked. "Yes."

The point of the longsword twitched.

Rew closed one steel link around his wrist. Then, he closed the other. "I can't reach my legs. Sheath the sword and you do them? Look, I am no threat. I'm unarmed, and my hands are bound. Valchon will want me alive, won't he? He's going to offer you rich rewards when you bring me to him."

The simulacrum raised the longsword, its arms wobbling, its expression growing more and more confused. "What is... what is happening to me?"

"Valchon will want me alive," repeated Rew, holding his shackled wrists in front of him. "There's no need for bloodshed."

The hunter attempted to slide the longsword through its belt, but the blade instead punched into the creature's abdomen, piercing the skin and stabbing through to slide out the back of it like the hunter's flesh had no more resistance than vapor.

The hunter gasped and fell to its knees, blood pouring down its side, soaking the longsword. Blood leaked from its lips and splattered as it gasped and tried to speak. "What..."

Rew lurched off his knees, his hands still clapped in the manacles. He closed his eyes and whispered a prayer to the Blessed Mother. He called, "Anne, be ready when I draw the blade."

He reached forward, grabbed the wooden hilt of the longsword, and wrestled with the will of Erasmus Morden.

HOURS LATER, REW'S TEETH STILL HURT FROM GRITTING THEM. HIS jaw ached, and his hands were covered in blisters where the wooden hilt had spun. Erasmus had tasted blood, but he hadn't been sated. It'd been a long struggle to force the old spellcaster back into his steel tomb, to seal the ancient magician's soul inside. Rew had resisted the urge to draw more blood, to finish the hunter, or his companions, but it'd been close.

Anne had rushed to the hunter's side while Rew battled the spirit of his ancestor. She'd put the hunter to sleep then tended to his wounds. She left him injured, so he would be weakened once he woke, but she'd made sure the man wasn't going to die on them. It would be a shame after so much effort.

Their plan hadn't worked, exactly, but they'd executed it well. Rew was proud of the younglings for playing their parts, and he'd told them so. He was proud of Anne as well, but he'd been unable to bring himself to speak to her since they'd captured the hunter. He'd faced Erasmus again, and Anne had felt that dark stain upon his soul. She knew, now, what it did to him when the power of the sword was unleashed. She hadn't offered to heal his small wounds, and he hadn't asked.

When they'd bound the hunter with enough chain to secure a dozen men, they dragged his unconscious body to a wagon and, with all of their help, hoisted him into it. They'd returned to the seed museum and secreted the man amongst the dark, unused storerooms in the basement.

When Anne left to wash her hands of the hunter's blood, Rew asked Zaine and Cinda to stitch up the cuts he'd taken.

"Won't Anne… Are you two fighting?" wondered Zaine, gathering the supplies from Rew's pack and sorting through them.

"No," replied Rew. "It's complicated."

"What does that sword do to you when it's activated?" questioned Cinda.

"That's the complicated part."

"I thought we weren't keeping secrets from each other any longer."

"What'd you read in those two books you studied so hard in the ranger village?"

Cinda didn't flush. He wasn't sure she could anymore, but her eyes flared, burning bright green before she calmed.

"You two…" grumbled Zaine, peering at a needle in her hand as if trying to remember what it was used for. She had thread in the other hand but hadn't yet managed to connect the two. Sighing, she glanced between Rew and Cinda. She told them, "Before we split to set the ambush, I let Raif kiss me."

"What?" barked Cinda,

Zaine shrugged. "I've had better. Softer, you know? Figured I had to give it a shot, at least once. Told him he'd have to shave before the next time and scrub his teeth with powder. I don't think there'll be a next time, but if it keeps his breath fresh, that's better for all of us, don't you think?"

"You kissed my brother?"

Zaine leaned closer to the other girl. "Would you rather I have kissed you?"

"No, I... I just didn't think you liked..."

"I don't," assured Zaine. "Women all the way for me. Still, try new things, right? Also, I stole his coin purse when we did it. I don't think he's noticed yet."

Cinda laughed and shook her head. "You're incorrigible."

"I'm incor—What?"

Rew, crimson liquid leaking down his arm where his open cut still bled, gestured to the needle and thread in the thief's hands. "Either of you care to get to work before I bleed to death?"

"I've never really been much for sewing," admitted Zaine.

"I'm the daughter of a baron," said Cinda. "We had a dozen maids to do our mending. It doesn't look like a deep cut, Ranger. It ought to clot, sooner or later."

"King's Sake," growled Rew. He turned and called across the room. "Raif, you busy?"

The fighter stomped over. He smiled at Zaine then frowned when he saw her holding the thread. "Haven't gotten very far, have you?"

"I'll buy you an ale if you stitch me up," offered Rew.

Raif shrugged then took the needle and thread from the thief, his hands lingering as he touched hers. The thief winked at him. Then, she and Cinda scampered away. He watched them go, a yearning look in his eyes.

"Blessed Mother, lad, she likes girls!" cried Rew. "She's told you that. She just let you kiss her so she could steal your coin purse."

Raif's hand dropped to his belt, to where two thin leather thongs hung with no purse attached to them. The fighter frowned.

"I'm bleeding, here," reminded Rew.

Turning to eye Rew's shoulder, his frown turning to a scowl, Raif held up the gleaming steel needle. "This might hurt a bit."

The ranger sighed and closed his eyes without responding.

———

REW LIFTED THE HOOD OFF A LANTERN AND SHINED IT DIRECTLY INTO the face of the hunter. The rest of the room was pitch black. It was like he was shining a spear of light into the other man's face. The hunter shifted, then raised its arms, rattling the manacles against the stone column at its back. It smirked at Rew.

The hunter was sitting, splayed-legged, his arms to the sides, snug against the stone column they'd bound it to. The creature had cloth wrapped around its hands like mittens, secured with cord as tight as they could tie it. The hunter's clothing was torn where it'd lost control of the longsword and stabbed itself, but the injury was just a puckered pink scar after Anne's healing. Yellow and purple spread from it because Anne hadn't bothered to heal all of the internal damage. The hunter was dirty with soil, blood, and sawdust after being dragged from the cooper's workshop, stuffed in a wagon, and then unloaded in the basement. They hadn't fed it or given it water since its capture.

"You know I can see you," drawled the hunter. It smiled. "My eyesight is far better than yours."

"How much better?" wondered Rew. He made a rude gesture and asked, "Can you see this?"

The hunter shook its head and glared at Rew. The creature pulled on its chains, as if wanting to return the motion, but couldn't with its hands bound to the sides.

"Sometimes, it's easier to conduct these things with the cover of darkness," acknowledged Rew. "It's thin cover, but every little bit helps the conscience."

"You'll torture me, then?"

"If we have to."

The hunter tugged on the chains harder but with no different results. it wiggled its fingers, pressing them against the fabric they'd tied around its hands. Rew watched. How close did one have to be for the hunter to drain your soul? Did it have to be its hands? Was contact with skin necessary? Did the hunters function the same way Heindaw had when he'd done it to Rew? The ranger waited, but he felt nothing. That was only a little comforting.

In Olsoth, they'd seen a hunter work, and Rew had guessed Heindaw had used a similar technique, but they didn't know anything at all for sure, so they'd wrenched the hunter's arms back and as far away from its body as they could. They'd put the makeshift mittens on its hands and hoped it was enough. There was still great danger keeping any spellcaster alive, particularly one who had the capability of pulling your soul from your body and feeding on it. The hunter was an abomination. It had to be stopped, regardless of Rew's quest against Valchon and the king. The hunter's evil couldn't be allowed to continue.

Rew studied the other man's face. A young Valchon. Twenty-two, twenty-three winters? It appeared older than the others Rew had faced but identical in all other respects. The extra few years might explain why this one was stronger. What other talents had it picked up? Rew grimaced. There were so many of them. There must have been numerous mothers, but how come none of the mothers' features showed in the faces of these creatures?

Anne had examined the hunter extensively while it was unconscious. It was decidedly human, biologically normal, except it was unusually healthy. Its heart and lungs, muscles and ligaments, all were in superb condition. They assumed that was a side effect of retaining the souls of others. The life of its victims filled the hunter.

Cinda had studied the hunter as well.

Rew had asked her, "Do you feel… fulfilled when manipulating lost souls you're able to bind? Does it, ah, nurture you?"

Shaking her head, Cinda brushed a lock of hair behind her ear. "I don't… take the souls. A necromancer borrows the power of a soul's departure, or we tie it back to the body. It's different, I think. We are channeling, where it appears these creatures are consuming. The soul is a sort of food to them. Maybe they don't need it to survive, but it allows them to thrive. That is uncomfortable to think about, even for me. Their magic is… permanent."

With that grim thought, they'd set up the room for the interrogation. They'd secured the hunter, killed all of the lights, and placed the lamp in front of it. In the corners, they'd positioned a few surprises waiting for Cinda's commands.

The hunter looked at Rew, blank-faced. The ranger wondered just how much the thing could see with the light shining in its face. Could it see what was standing in the corners of the room?

The hunter asked him, "Shall we begin?"

"How does he do it?" asked Rew.

"Who?"

Sighing, Rew answered, "You're going to make this difficult? How did Valchon create you and your… brothers?"

"Well," said the hunter, "First, there is a man and a woman. If they like each other, and perhaps after a few drinks, they find a quiet place, and—"

"Yes, I'm aware of that part."

Shrugging, his chains rattling, the hunter responded, "You seem like someone who hasn't experienced it. Thought I'd clue you in."

Rew squatted right behind the lantern, ignoring the hunter's jab.

"Shouldn't you be threatening me?" asked the hunter. It yawned. "I have places to be, so let's get on with it."

"Valchon was full of bluster, too, when he was your age," said Rew. "You look just like him, maybe five years after he left the creche. Did he tell you about it? Has he told you anything other than how to fight? I was curious, when I killed your brothers, if he was like a father to you or like a king. Our family forgets, sometimes that those are not the same things. Does Valchon love you?"

The simulacrum laughed uncomfortably.

"All brothers," continued Rew. "You look just like him. Modeled after him. Evidence he loves himself, I suppose, but little else. Is there a you, or are you just a shadow of Valchon? No one has ever accused the king of being a good father, but at least Vaisius Morden allowed us to be ourselves. He encouraged it. I became a ranger instead of competing with Valchon for the throne. Valchon took his own path, with our father's blessing. That's a sort of love, don't you think, allowing someone to be themselves? I imagine you've never felt that."

"Is this meant to be torture?" snarled the hunter. It pretended to yawn again. "It's working. I'm just about ready to talk if only to shut you up."

"I wonder if I knew your mother," mused Rew. "I met many of Valchon's flames. I did more than just meet a few of them, if you want to know. What was your mother's name? What did she— Ah, you never met her, did you? You were raised by weapons masters, spellcasters, and arcanists. Only had your brothers for company? Tell me if I'm wrong."

The hunter glared at Rew.

"No love there," murmured the ranger. "Are you going to kill each other one day, like Valchon and I? Must have been difficult, growing up with only enemies around you. We had friends, our cousins, and all of the pleasures of Mordenhold around us. Young members of the royal line with the coin and attention that comes with the position, we lived fast and freely. You've never experienced anything like that, have you? Grown up in seclusion, and now that you're in the world, people are disgusted by you."

"My father is not the foul beast that… the king is," muttered the hunter. "He cares for us deeply and saw we had all we needed."

"What do you think will happen if Valchon ascends to the throne?" wondered Rew. "You believe there won't be a ninth Investiture? Ah, but it won't be you competing for the throne, will it? If Valchon intended you to be his heir, he would have had you at the creche in Mordenhold, with the others, learning the ways of this kingdom. Those are the children he's willing to acknowledge. You… He kept you a secret."

"That's not true."

"It's not?" replied Rew. He let the comment hang there. He leaned forward and drove the wedge deeper. "He taught you how to fight, but has he taught you how to rule?"

The simulacrum blinked back at Rew, uncertain.

"What do you know of Vaeldon's trade agreements with other nations? Taxation? Which department in the king's administration handles public works, and what are their priorities? How are decrees communicated throughout the kingdom? Are Mordenhold's defenses paid for with levies on the territories or tariffs on trade?" Rew shook his head. "Do you even know what happens when the Investiture ends? I bet Valchon told you he'd be crowned when his brothers were dead, and that was it. Calb and Heindaw are dead, but Valchon isn't king yet, is he? Do you know why?"

A low growl emanated from the hunter's throat.

Rew stood, his hands on his hips. "He's trained you like a dog but hasn't given you the love even the mangiest mutt deserves. It's sad. I'm sorry I'm the one to bear the tidings, but Valchon has other children in Mordenhold, ones he acknowledges, his real children. They know the answers to everything I just asked."

Rew leaned down and closed the hood of the lantern, casting the room in dark then turned and began to walk toward the door.

"Wait," barked the hunter. "Do you not have any real questions for me?"

Speaking over his shoulder, Rew responded, "I doubt you have any answers."

He left the room and walked down a long hallway, through

several layers of hanging sheets of wool, and then into a brightly lit room where his companions waited.

"What's he doing?" he asked Cinda.

"Just sitting there," she responded, her eyes half-closed.

"No magic, nothing?"

"No sign he has the skills of an invoker so far," responded the necromancer, brushing a lock of hair behind her ear. "I think that's confirmation these things only have the talents they're able to absorb, and Valchon hasn't sacrificed any of his invokers to feed this beast, so to speak. Enchantment is no risk to us while he's chained up. If he could conjure, I think he would have by now, or perhaps he's struggling to call his imps to him. If he doesn't know his own location…"

"Keep an eye on him," instructed Rew. "Invoker or not, he's far too dangerous to leave unattended."

"My minions are watching and waiting."

"We're sure he can't see them?" asked Zaine.

Rew scratched his beard. "I don't believe he can, though I was startled at how easily he spotted me behind the lantern. Still, my illusions held during the initial ambush, and I think they'll hold now. The advantage of Cinda's… friends, is that they don't draw breath and have no heartbeat or other signatures that the hunter could hear even in absolute silence. Unless he can see through the pall of darkness I cast, I don't think he knows who is in there with him."

"Friends," muttered Raif, giving an inadvertent shiver. "I don't think I'll ever get used to that."

Cinda eyed her brother unblinking.

Raif questioned, "How long will those strings on the crossbows stay taut?"

"A few hours," responded Rew. "We can't risk any longer than that. The strings may loosen. I could lose my grip on the shroud, or the hunter might get creative. Cinda, how long can you hold the bindings?"

"I can hold them longer than we need," assured Cinda.

"There's plenty of death in this city to draw upon, and so far, I'm not having to issue new instructions, just to maintain contact. Eventually, my control will break when I must sleep, but I believe I could hold this for several days, or even a week, with little concern."

"You wouldn't sleep for a week?" asked Zaine.

Cinda didn't respond.

"What do we do when our time is up?" asked Anne quietly.

"These things are an abomination," replied Rew. "There's only one thing we can do."

"It doesn't feel very sporting to execute a prisoner in captivity," murmured Raif.

"I can let him go, and you can fight him," offered Rew.

The fighter held up his hands. "Oh, no. I saw what he could do when we were taking him down. You're right. We can't let him go. I don't like it, but there's only one way this can end."

"Don't worry, lad," assured Rew. "I'll do it."

"Before the next round, let's take some time, get some rest, and something to eat," said Anne. She glanced at Cinda. "Do you need anything?"

The necromancer shook her head.

Anne bustled off to find food for the rest of them, and Rew met Cinda's gaze.

Quietly, so the others couldn't hear her, Cinda said, "I'll do it when it's time. I have something I want to try."

Rew raised an eyebrow.

"If he won't answer our questions in life, maybe he will in death."

Chapter Eighteen

Held captive with no hope of relief, anyone would break under duress. It was just a matter of time and pressure. Unfortunately, they had no time. The hunter was stronger and faster than anyone Rew had seen. It was endowed with unique abilities, including the talent of pulling the soul from a victim and absorbing their skill. They didn't know what sorts of spells the hunter might be able to cast or if it'd taken any other abilities from victims. Rew knew almost nothing about the hunter, but what he knew was enough. They couldn't find out more the hard way. The simulacrum was too dangerous to leave alive for long. That was the mistake Calb and Heindaw had made, and Rew wouldn't repeat it. It gave him one more crack at the hunter. Then, he'd turn the creature over to Cinda to send to the beyond.

During the period they gave the hunter to stew in the dark, Rew grappled with what to say. How could he rip open the crack that he'd made earlier? How could he get inside of the hunter's head? He knew his brother. He'd been close to Valchon and had studied the prince like prey, but as he pondered, he decided there wasn't as much of the prince in these hunters as first appeared. They had Valchon's face and some of his skill, but that wasn't what made the prince dangerous.

Valchon was a manipulator. He collected allies like a noble-woman collected trinkets. Then, he used and discarded them uncaringly. The hunters themselves were evidence enough of the trait, but Rew didn't think they would exhibit it. The hunters had been hidden, kept in seclusion. The congenial but predatory nature of their father never would have found ground to bloom in whatever corner of the world Valchon had raised them.

But the hunter was human. It had been put off by Rew's accusations and claims. It felt the sting of rejection. Rew could use that, work to gain its trust, turn it against Valchon, but building that relationship would take time that he didn't have. Hurting the hunter would take time too, if it even worked. The spawn of Valchon would be used to pain. It would relish the opportunity to battle against Rew, challenging him to break its will.

No, if nothing else, the thing was a fighter. It'd been bred and raised for battle. Pain wouldn't work. Kindness would be the quickest way to break it. That was not quick enough, though, so Rew decided to try honesty.

He entered the room, shining the lantern into the simulacrum's face again. It bared its teeth at him, as if preparing to fight. Rew stayed back from it, both to avoid touching it and to maintain the lane of fire for Cinda's corpses. There were four of those standing along the walls. They had crossbows, and he imagined they weren't particularly good shots with them.

He set the lantern down and crouched behind it. "You know I killed three of your brothers in Olsoth and one in Shavroe, right?"

"And for that, we shall kill you," snapped the simulacrum.

"If you were in contention to compete for the throne when your father vacates it, that should please you," suggested Rew. "Fewer rivals, and all of that."

"Fewer chances to prove myself," retorted the hunter.

"You were confused when you drew my longsword, and I released the power within it. You could feel that power, yes, but you didn't understand it."

The hunter stared back at him, blank-faced.

"That incredible strength you felt surge through you was Erasmus Morden, the father of Vaisius Morden the First. He's your ancestor."

"No—"

"You felt him thirsting for your blood. That's why you stabbed yourself. Erasmus steered the blade into you when you decided you wouldn't take my life. It's the nature of the Mordens. You haven't met any others, have you? Just Valchon and I and your brothers. Where did he keep you?"

"I'm not answering any of your questions."

"Understandable," said Rew gently. "You're scared."

"I'm not scared!"

"You think I brought you here to gain some insight, some knowledge I can use against Valchon? No, that's not it," said Rew. He struggled to keep his face still. He didn't know how much of him the simulacrum could see. He didn't know if it would be able to detect that while he'd started out telling the truth, that wasn't all he was going to tell. "I brought you here to see if I could help you, to release you from his thrall. I want to make you a free man."

The simulacrum coughed. "What?"

"I tasted that freedom myself," said Rew. "For a decade, nearly, I roamed with little thought and no cares for our family. The pain, the hate, it didn't touch me. Valchon must have told you how I was a ranger in the Eastern Territory?"

The hunter didn't answer, but Rew could see the answer in its face.

"My plan is to kill Valchon and then kill the king," continued Rew. "If I'm successful, then you and your brothers are free. You need not fight and kill any longer, or you could, if that's what you want. It would be up to you. Can you imagine freedom?"

"I'm getting bored with your mind games," declared the hunter. "I won't answer what you want."

Rew frowned. He knew nothing of this creature and how Valchon motivated the thing. He had no idea how to twist its emotions to get it where he wanted. With time, he could show it kindness, but it wasn't going to suddenly trust him after two conversations. The hunter had been supped on distrust and suspicion since it had been born, Rew suspected. It knew the truth of what he'd said about Valchon, and Rew thought that truth stung, but he could see in the simulacrum's face it wasn't enough.

Physical pain, emotional pain, it was all the creature had known. Rew couldn't inflict enough damage to wound it beyond what had already been done. No amount of hurt was going to break the simulacrum quickly, so he gestured, and from behind him, Cinda's four corpses shuffled forward. Maybe raw terror would work, and if not...

"You will answer me," said Rew, "in this life or the next. I'd prefer you keep your life, but... what do you think?"

The door opened, and Cinda stepped inside.

"You know what she did in Jabaan, don't you?" asked Rew. "She raised thousands of corpses. She instructed them, and they obeyed. She's a necromancer, as good as any that exists outside of the king himself. You may take your secrets to the grave, but you can't keep them there."

The hunter gaped at the corpses then at Cinda.

"If we had time, I'd try this a different way, but there is no time, so what will it be? Tell us what we need to know, and you can walk free, or we'll kill you and learn your secrets anyway."

Shaking his head, the hunter blinked. "No. Only the king has that type of power. She's... she's nothing more than a girl."

Rew grunted. "You're wrong about that."

"I won't tell you anything," insisted the hunter.

"Very well," responded the ranger. He stood and brushed his hands off. "Cinda, your turn."

Cinda stepped beside Rew, just behind the lantern. She held her hands up and closed her eyes. Several breaths later, she said, "Ah, Rew, I need you to kill him. Sorry. I want to release my binding on these others so that I can focus on him."

"Of course. Good idea," said the ranger. He turned to one of the corpses behind him, took the crossbow from its hands, and raised the weapon to his shoulder. Behind him, the four corpses collapsed into heaps on the stone floor.

"Ready?" he asked her.

"Ready."

"Hold on!" said the hunter. "You're not going to ask me any other questions? Is this meant to scare—"

Rew pulled the trigger, and the crossbow discharged its bolt. The hunter was fast, but it was also chained to a stone column. It tried to jerk to the side, but the bolt smacked into its head, punching through its left eye and deep into its brain. The man slumped forward. Rew tossed the crossbow onto the corpse he'd taken it from.

Cinda's hands remained up, trembling, as if she were struggling mightily with something, but nothing happened. Finally, she turned and shrugged.

"I thought I could harness the soul and learn from it. It was in the book, the one Lucia gave us. It… didn't work. It's like the hunter was fighting it. I think we made an error. Had it not known what I would do when it died, it might not have been able to hold me off. Pfah. It's so hard. The book had technical instructions, but without a mentor to guide me…"

Rew, looking down at the dead hunter, shrugged. "It didn't work the way we planned, but it's one more dead hunter. That's a victory, as far as I'm concerned."

"I could animate it," continued Cinda, "but I don't think it will have retained any useful information in that form. Just vague impressions, which I don't think will offer the answers we seek. It also carries a risk. The hunter didn't know where it was when it died. If we bring it back, it'll know more, and Vaisius Morden may be able to glean information from the soul if he were to capture it, but if you want to try…"

"Whatever was in that book didn't work for Arcanist Salwart or Prince Heindaw, either," said Rew, discomfited by the idea of

Cinda catching the departing hunter's soul and wringing it for information. The thing was an awful creation of Valchon's, and they could use what it knew, but still… "Perhaps whoever wrote that book was just wrong. It doesn't matter. Because it's a risk, because it may not work, because… It doesn't matter. I think we've done what we can. It was a bad plan to begin with. We never stood a chance of breaking this thing's resolve so quickly. There's nothing we were going to do to it that's worse than what Valchon has already done."

Cinda shook her head then tucked her hands within the sleeves of her robes. "I don't think the book was wrong. Remember Vyar Grund? The king is capable of that level of necromancy. I just need to practice. Sorry. I hoped it would work. The next time, I will do better."

Rew turned back to the dead hunter and did not respond.

REW SORELY REGRETTED SENDING THE RANGERS ON THEIR WAY. IT'D been true that not all of them could travel together without drawing too much attention, and it'd been true that Ang and Vurcell were the logical leaders in his absence, but having a few of those skilled trackers now would have paid in gold. He hated to admit it because it wasn't his way, but they could have used the help.

There were others he might have been able to gather quickly, Blythe and her recruits in Eastwatch, a handful of other rangers scattered around the Eastern Province, the retired, white-haired men and women who assisted at the museum, but they were either too old or had been forced to stay in their roles during the attack on Iyre because their presence was vital for the safety of their communities. By the same logic, Rew couldn't call upon them now, and worse, he worried they would answer. By and large, Rew knew the rangers in the east, and he didn't want to draw in more of his friends than he had to. He didn't want to call them away from protecting the places and people he loved.

They knew there were at least two or three more of the hunters lurking in Carff, and they knew they would be on patrols throughout the city, looking for Rew, particularly now that one of their brethren had gone missing in town. The others would be on alert.

To make matters more complicated, they'd just learned from one of the older rangers at the seed museum that Alsayer had been seen recently at Prince Valchon's palace. The spellcaster, whatever his intentions, was alive and in play. They needed to keep an eye on him, and on the simulacra, but they were only five, and most of them didn't have the skills necessary to shadow someone through a crowded city.

"Could we recruit the thieves?" asked Raif when they were discussing their options several hours after they'd disposed of the hunter's body and after several rounds of drinks at a tiny, nondescript tavern where Rew judged they had little risk of being identified. After the hunter, they needed a drink nearly as badly as they needed the comforting presence of other people around them.

Zaine, toying absentmindedly with the sleeves of her blouse, replied, "I could probably find the guildhall, but approaching it will be dangerous. Normally, commissions would move through layers of intermediaries to protect both a client and the thieves. Obviously, we can't trust our information to a network like that. Even for people used to discretion, we'd risk too much. Valchon would pay the thieves a bounty for our heads several times what the entire guild could bring in during the year. Even if we found a senior thief, somehow convinced them to trust us, and were willing to trust them, the amount they'd charge to act against Prince Valchon, the potential future king of Vaeldon... We don't have that kind of coin. King's Sake, I'm not sure Valchon himself has that kind of coin. Thieves don't live long by taking long odds, and to an outsider, our chances probably don't look very good."

"There's no… exchange of favors?" questioned Raif. "Our odds may be long, but if we made them a big enough promise, maybe they'd come around."

"Favors? We're not talking about nobles marrying each other's sisters," said Zaine with a snort

Raif looked offended, but he didn't object.

"I'm afraid anything I raise will be quite obvious out on the streets," said Cinda. "There are some spells hinted at within my books that might help, looking through the eyes of a ghost, you might say, but they're complicated, and ah, they'd require us having a ghost in the first place."

"A ghost?" asked Zaine.

"A wraith," clarified Cinda. "Like my father called. They can be commanded to do more than feast, though that rubs against their natural desires and requires a stronger control. I can try to summon one. I think that part, at least, I can figure out. From there, manipulating it will require experimentation."

"Well," said Rew dryly, "we're not doing that. Maybe if we were out in the country, away from people, but there are a million souls in Carff. We can't allow a wraith here unless you're certain you can command it."

Cinda shrugged. "There's risk in all that we do. If we have a tool at hand, we have to consider using it. Valchon himself was trying to gain wraiths to face your brothers, wasn't he? I believe I can call to them, the ancient souls of the barrowlands, though it would take time."

Rew eyed her. Was it such a terrible idea? A wraith like her father had summoned from the barrowlands would be a powerful ally. Could she call to one from so far away? Could they use it for something other than simply spying on their enemies?

He shook himself. It didn't matter. Maybe she could summon one, but the center of one of Vaeldon's most populated cities wasn't the place for experimentation. If she lost control of even one wraith in Carff, the carnage would be unthinkable.

"We could hire someone else to look out for Valchon's spawn," suggested Raif. "It doesn't have to be a thief. Those simulacra look just like him, so I imagine they're remarkable when they move about the city. I mean, even I could spot someone wearing those purple robes, and it's not like we're asking anyone to take one down, just to keep an eye out and tell us where they are, what they're doing."

"Urchins," said Anne. "No one thinks twice seeing them scampering about and looking guilty."

Rew shook his head. "The urchins are in the pockets of the thieves' guild, if they're any good, and they'll want to be in those pockets if they're not. We can't take the thieves' guild's resources without asking, and Zaine's right. If we asked someone with authority to make the decision, they'll want more coin than we have, or they'll just take the easier profit and sell us to Valchon."

"Know any herbalists in Carff?" Zaine asked Anne.

Anne shrugged. "Of course, but I don't think they'll be much use tracking down hunters for us."

They sat and drank, nursing their ales and wines, nibbling on a platter of sausages, cheeses, and pickles. Anne ducked out and returned with a long, thin loaf of bread from a bakery across the street. It was a little stale, but they tore into it with relish.

The streets outside were noisy, even as the sun set. The two other princes were dead, and the assumption was that Valchon would be ascending to the throne. Everyone believed that when he took his place in Mordenhold, Carff would benefit from his largesse. It seemed that the rumors they'd started in the Western and Northern Provinces hadn't made it east, or if they had, no one believed them. That, or the nobles did believe the rumors, but those in Carff would need to make a loud, visible show of supporting Valchon. They would hang from a rope if they didn't.

But despite the general celebratory air, the citizens of Carff had to know something was afoot. The quarantine by the harbor wasn't normal. There'd been talk of how many copper-breast-plated soldiers were marching through the streets, and the fact was, even with his brothers purportedly dead, Valchon had not been crowned.

Rew wasn't sure where that left them, or if they could somehow use it to their advantage. So far, if there was an angle, he hadn't seen it.

He crunched a pickle and thought. Valchon wasn't like Heindaw, content to wait behind his walls patiently minding the traps he would have set. Valchon believed he was the strongest, the most cunning. He played Kings and Queens against the best in the kingdom. He cast spells that no one except his father could control. He'd had half the kingdom behind him even before his brothers had been killed. He would want to attack. Anything else would make him look and feel weak, and weakness was one thing a son of Vaisius Morden couldn't stand.

Rew tore off a chunk of bread and filled it with the sausage, cheese, and another pickle then bit and chewed. Valchon would want to attack. They could set a trap for him, but where and how? As far as Rew had heard so far in the city, Valchon never appeared outside of the palace. If he traveled anywhere, he did so by portal. That would make him impossible to intercept, and the idea of somehow staging a trap for the prince within his own palace was ludicrous.

They'd managed to capture a hunter and question the thing, but it'd gotten them nowhere. It'd been dangerous, and trying it again would be even more so. Perhaps Cinda could capture the soul the next time, but… Rew finished his food then picked up his ale and drank. Whether or not the lass could perform her necromancy, attempting to capture another hunter was too dangerous. They needed information, though. They had to figure a way to get some advantage. They had to find someone who would know the inner workings at the palace.

A plainly dressed townswoman entered and ordered a jug of ale at the bar, evidently planning to bring it back to her home. Other citizens sat in loose groups, talking, laughing, enjoying themselves. Plainly dressed…

Valchon's spymaster had been attired much like the woman who was leaving with her full jug of ale. The spymaster had been dreadfully injured when Rew had landed on her after falling into the portal room, but she hadn't died, he didn't think. He'd felt her bones break, but he'd also felt her breath on his cheek when he stood off of her. Without an empath of Anne's skill, the woman might never recover. But if she had...

Rew frowned, "Anne, you said you know healers in Carff? Are they good? I mean really good, like Valchon might trust his closest associates to their care?"

Anne pointed a sliver of pickle at him. "I don't know of any healers who would associate themselves with Valchon, but I know the best one in Carff. Does that help?"

"It gives us a place to start."

AN ANCIENT WOMAN, WHO LOOKED AS IF SHE COULD HAVE PREDATED the kingdom itself, gave them a wide, toothless grin. She toddled about her kitchen, boiling water in a tea kettle over her hearth. Heat blazed out from the crackling fire, making the woman's kitchen feel like an oven. Beads of sweat had formed on Rew's forehead, but the woman was such a dear he couldn't bring himself to complain.

She'd placed teacups in front of him and Anne, along with sugar, cream, and a few spices that he recognized smelling in the market but couldn't recall the name of. There were little cakes as well, frosted with colorful confections of sugar.

Anne popped one of the little cakes into her mouth and groaned. She ate another then said, "Don't tell the children about this."

Grinning, Rew helped himself to the treats and was shocked at how good they were. The frosting and the cake on the outside had enough texture to give it shape, but the inside was moist and filled with a sweet cream. Each of the cakes had different icings and fillings, and the pairings complemented each other in ways he didn't expect. There were fruit flavors, honey, cream, and nuts, all in a delightful assortment of different bites.

When the old woman poured his tea, steam roiled off it, and he inhaled deeply, feeling like his toes were tingling. The woman said something, but Rew did not hear. "What was that?"

"She says the leaves for the tea are imported from across the sea," explained Anne. She watched the old woman move about her kitchen. "I imagine that's expensive."

The woman poured herself a tea, scooped a mound of sugar into it, and sipped the liquid without waiting for it to cool. She cleared her throat and said, "Yes, quite expensive. I make good coin here in Carff, when I want to, though I have few occasions to spend it. A visit from a woman like you? That's cause to celebrate."

Anne flushed.

"A woman like her?" asked Rew, nodding toward Anne.

"I've been following her story for years," said the old woman, her voice a dry rasp that Rew had to lean forward to hear. "Some complained when she went to Eastwatch, not fulfilling her potential, but I understood. One only achieves Anne's skills with considerable practice, meaning considerable pain. Few can survive that, and I know of only one who's done so at such a young age. We can ease the suffering in others, but salving our own wounds is difficult. It takes time and support. I told the others it was good Anne found peace. I told them she will be needed."

The old woman bobbed her head, as if confirming her own story, and Rew thought perhaps she was. Did she know what they'd been doing?

"Mother Solomon has been talking?" asked Anne, blowing on her own tea.

"She and others. Many have provided small details, little

pieces of the puzzle for those of us trying to put it together," confirmed the crone. "I myself followed your progress months ago when you passed through here. It caused quite a stir. Such pain…"

"Yes…" murmured Anne.

"And the King's Ranger," said the woman, turning to Rew, "tales of your exploits have spread. You should take care to cover your face when in the city. You've admirers and enemies, boy. Not just the prince and his lackeys. There are many, even people outside the tug of the Investiture, who would make a name for themselves by bringing the prince news of your whereabouts. Why, I could pay for enough of these cakes and sacks of this tea to last me the rest of my life, though I worry some mornings about how long that might be. Maybe it's not such a good bargain, then."

Rew laughed, and the old woman grinned.

"Why have you come?" the crone asked Anne. "Not my healing. It hurts my pride to say it, but I've no more skill than you do. Not my company, though I hope you enjoy it. I cannot get you into the palace, if that's what you're hoping. I've made my stance toward the prince quite clear. I think the only reason he puts up with my presence in the city is that I've helped him in the past. Maybe he thinks I'll help him again, or it could be he knows the others will object if he does anything to harm me. Regardless, particularly during the Investiture, the prince isn't going to let me into his home."

"We don't want to get close to the prince, but what of his associates?" asked Rew. "Do you know who the prince would go to with great need? A woman close to him was badly injured when we were last here. I think he'd spare no expense to save her."

"It's rarely money that buys the talent of one such as myself or Anne," murmured the old woman. She was frowning. "What was the nature of the injuries this associate of the prince suffered?"

"Several broken ribs, to be sure," said Rew, "and likely serious internal damage. Injuries like, ah, a large man about my size fell on top of her from a height." He coughed and sipped his tea. "She'd be of age with Anne, attractive, though dressed as a commoner rather than a noblewoman. The injures happened on the day Valchon's palace was attacked by imps. Was that known within the city?"

"It was known by me," said the crone, her head bobbing gently. "There was a woman like the one you describe, though I did not know she had anything to do with the palace. A former apprentice tried to heal her and could not. I worried what would happen to the girl if she failed, so I helped."

"You know where to find this woman?"

"I don't know where to find her, but I know who she is. She's dangerous, even to one like you."

Rew grunted. "Yes, we know that much about her."

"She won't be happy to see you?"

Shaking his head, Rew responded, "Quite unhappy, if I had to guess."

"The one you seek is Rebecca, the headmistress of the thieves' guild."

"King's Sake!" barked Rew, nearly spilling his tea. "You're sure?"

"Well, it's a good thing we didn't reach out to them…" murmured Anne, scowling at Rew as if he had been the one who'd suggested it. She asked the old woman, "Your apprentice, is she close to Rebecca?"

Shaking her head, the crone replied, "No. She owes a debt to the thieves, the kind not paid in coin. They come to her, and she helps as she's able. I don't think she'd be able to direct you to the guildhall—certainly not to Rebecca herself. She might be able to share a message, but if she did, you'd be putting her in great danger. Even going to speak to her will put her life at risk."

"We'll find a way without compromising you or your apprentice," assured Anne. "Won't we, Rew?"

"We will. We may not know where she is, but we know who she is, and that's even better. Yes, I think we can use that."

"Wait until Zaine finds out," said Anne, shaking her head then taking another of the sweet cakes.

Chapter Nineteen

"The headmistress of the biggest thieves' guild in the Western Province?" babbled Zaine, wild-eyed, her voice an octave higher than normal. "No, I don't know how to find her. King's Sake, I know we want to find someone close to Valchon, but could we perhaps find literally anyone else? Anyone at all? What about his valet, a cook in the palace kitchens, or his barber? Anyone?"

Rew rubbed the top of his head. "The barber isn't a bad idea."

"I didn't mean so you could get your hair cut."

Lowering his hand, Rew responded, "Ah, neither did I. I didn't mean—Pfah. I was just thinking, the barber must get close to the prince. That's worth considering, someone like that, I mean, except they won't know anything about the simulacra. I don't like our chances with two or three of those things coming up behind us."

"They might all use the same barber," mentioned Raif. "They do have the same haircut. We could wait outside the shop…"

"Valchon is a prince. The barber comes to him," said Rew. He smirked and added, "But we'll keep it in mind."

"Do you think Valchon knows this woman is part of the thieves' guild?" wondered Anne.

"I don't know," replied Rew, "but I'm certain that the merchants and nobles in the city don't know. They'll be the largest targets of the thieves. Having the leader of the guild whispering into Valchon's ear would be intolerable. If she's exposed, Valchon will have to do something about her."

"We could hire criers to stroll through Carff sharing the news," suggested Cinda. "We'd flush her out of the palace but also force her into hiding. Which now that I think about it, won't make her any easier to locate, and it's not going to do us any good getting to Alsayer, either. I like the idea of disrupting Valchon's ranks, though."

"Agreed," replied Rew, "but maybe there's another way we can use the information? Instead of rocking the boat, we can set a snare. The woman is the spymaster, right, and she's in a precarious position by his side, so she has to be watching every piece of information that gets to him. What if we write him a letter and tell him who she is?"

"You think she'll intercept it," said Cinda, "but how does that —Ah, you'll sign it yourself. When she realizes we know her secret, she'll have to come to us, but won't she just try to kill us?"

"I imagine that'd be her first instinct, but I don't think she's by Valchon's side because of loyalty to the prince," mused the ranger. "If he ascends the throne, she can't go to Mordenhold very easily because of her position in the thieves' guild. The thieves must be terrified of her turning against them. She knows all of their secrets, after all. Having someone in her position so close to the man who's responsible for stamping them out... It's one thing to embed yourself with the prince, but with the king? They must have taken precautions, gained assurance she wouldn't betray them to improve her own standing."

"Why do you think she's doing this, then?" wondered Raif. "I don't think the deception would be worth stealing a few artifacts from the palace."

"No, you're right. She's playing a deeper game, which is even more incentive for her to come to us. It's a risk, I agree, but we don't need much. I want to know how to get to Alsayer, and I want her to leave us alone when we face Valchon. That's it. Alsayer is as much a thorn in Valchon's side as my own. She'd benefit from giving him to us."

"Unless Valchon needs Alsayer for something," challenged Cinda. "If he's central to their plans, she's not going to give him up. If we meet with her, we'll let her know we're in the city and that we're coming. We lose our advantage."

"I worry we lost that when we killed the simulacrum."

"We could kill her, too, I guess, if the conversation doesn't go the way we like."

"We're getting all too comfortable with killing people," declared Anne.

"She's Valchon's spymaster in addition to being the leader of the thieves' guild…" mentioned Rew. He held up his hands at Anne's look. "All I'm saying, if we're going to pick a point to go soft, I'm not sure this is the right moment."

"She ought to go in front of a magistrate for her crimes, the ones that are illegal, I mean, not that she should skate for helping Valchon with Stanton, but ah, you know what I mean. There's a reason the court system exists, Rew. It's not right to have any one person deciding who lives and who dies."

"We won't kill her," said Rew then glanced at Cinda and added under his breath, "before we question her."

Anne heard him and shook her head.

"What are you going to say in your letter?" asked Cinda.

"I'll address it to Valchon and offer a trade. I won't hire criers to reveal the profession of his spymaster, and he gives me Alsayer."

Cinda's green eyes sparkled. "That might actually work. Valchon doesn't trust Alsayer, and didn't he tell you he'd kill the man the moment he ascended the throne? If I am Valchon, why not let you and Alsayer fight it out now? It's little loss to him, and he gets what he wants, just a little early. I'd guess he thinks you're crazy enough to actually go through with your threat if he doesn't comply, just to disrupt his defenses and deprive him of his spymaster. We're forcing him to choose between the two of them, and he hates Alsayer. If he accepts, he doesn't weaken his position against you by much, and he might gain something. If, as you suspect, Valchon doesn't know her history, and this Rebecca intercepts the note, she'll realize the bargain works even better if she makes it herself."

"Exactly."

"Let's get some parchment, then," said Cinda.

REW WAITED PATIENTLY, STANDING IN THE MIDDLE OF THE SQUARE, the sound of a fountain tinkling on the far side. During the day, the square was filled with vendors selling skewers of meat, grilled onions and potatoes, and hunks of bread stuffed full of heavily spiced meats and vegetables of questionable provenance. In Rew's experience, the more spice a street vendor put in the food, the longer it'd been since they could have served it anywhere else.

In daylight, people would come in a steady stream to the fountain, filling buckets and jugs, and children would be screaming and laughing, running around the square as their parents conducted their business. There were a score of shops surrounding the open cobbles, but they were all closed now. There were no lights in the apartments above them, and all was quiet.

It was a residential quarter. The people who lived in the place were not wealthy, but they were comfortable. The area would see patrols by the city watch but not many. The thieves would operate in wealthier districts of the city, and they would live in poorer ones. The square Rew had chosen was neutral ground.

He had his hand on his longsword. Despite what he'd told the others, he did worry Rebecca might try to kill him. They'd claimed in the note that if he was killed, his companions would share her identity to all. She wouldn't want that, but if Rew was dead, Valchon would become king. If she was actually loyal to the man, revealing her identity could be worth it. Valchon would reward her for Rew's death with a title, land, and mountains of coin. She wouldn't need to work ever again, or as spymaster to the king, she'd have the resources to root out Carff's thieves' guild root and stem.

And if the nobles complained? Valchon might not care if it earned him the crown. None of those nobles had done much to help him in the Investiture. Not that they would complain to the king, no matter how offended they were that one of his advisors was a thief. The period following a coronation was always a time of turmoil in Vaeldon, and that meant fortunes could fall as easily as they could rise. The only comments to the new king any sane noble would be offering would be praise and support.

But the spymaster probably didn't need to work to begin with. Rew figured she was in it for the thrill, not the coin. She might want the thrill of a fight with him or the pleasure of revenge for him falling on her and shattering her ribs, but he hoped she would be interested in the intrigue of contacting him. Rising to headmistress of the guild and as Valchon's spymaster... she must enjoy stalking the shadows, knowing what others did not. Right now, the most interesting piece of information in Carff would be Rew himself. She would want to hear what he said.

Then, of course, she might try to kill him.

What worried Rew more, though, was if the note actually made it into Valchon's hands. They'd realized if Valchon did get the note and did decide to turn over Alsayer, they would have no way of ensuring it wasn't a trap. Valchon could benefit from Rew and Alsayer battling it out, but the moment that battle was over, he would swoop in, or perhaps he wouldn't even wait. He might set them up right away. He wanted both of them dead.

So, instead of putting trust in the prince, they'd put eyes on him. He was at a feast, marking the seasonal change in tides, which evidently was quite important to Carff's wealthy merchants. Cinda had managed to animate a corpse within the palace and had put it in place overlooking the hall. If Valchon disappeared for a moment, then she'd tell Zaine, who would set alight a fire, which Rew would see.

If Valchon portaled to him, it would give Rew almost no notice, but they were going to have to take some risk. Against Valchon, Alsayer, Rebecca, and the simulacra, they had to try and whittle them down. They had to try to crack someone to figure out Valchon's weaknesses. It was a dangerous gamble, but you couldn't win big without betting big.

Like any wager, there was no certainty.

After Rew arrived in the square, he wondered if Valchon would come himself even if he knew Rew was there. The prince had two or three simulacra at his disposal. Would he send them against the ranger? Rew gripped his longsword. He couldn't fight three of them alone without help. He'd promised Anne he wouldn't use it, but with the power of the sword…

Rew's senses were extended, but in the city, he had little sensitivity to feel what was coming, so he watched, and he listened. He was alerted to Rebecca's arrival by her tuneless whistling. She came walking out of the night, hands held behind her back, strolling as calmly as if she were a housewife on her way to the market in the middle of the afternoon. She was dressed plainly, in a style similar to Anne's. When she got closer, Rew could see a smile on her red lips. Her eyes twinkled, though he didn't buy that it was with mirth. If she hadn't become a thief and a spy, she would have been a generational talent as an actress.

"You knew it'd be me?" she asked, stopping a dozen paces from Rew.

"I thought it might be."

"Then your offer was in good faith, despite sending the letter to the prince?"

"I didn't know where to send it to reach you."

"No? You must have had some idea. Not all messages pass through my hands, but this one had to. Why didn't you come straight away? If it was a trap, this seems an odd place for an ambush."

"It's not one."

"Why didn't you come straight to me, then?"

Rew tilted his head and studied the woman. "If I had, would you have listened to me, or would you have attacked immediately? I hoped by giving you some time to consider options, you'd decide listening to what I have to say was the best one."

"Fair enough, but what if the prince had seen your letter? What if I'd told him? I know you want to face him, but weren't you worried he'd bring… friends."

"Friends or family? I've already killed five of them."

The woman laughed, and it sounded genuine. "He has scores of spellcasters and thousands of soldiers as well, you know. I won't give you advice on how to fight my boss, but you must remember the maelstrom he cast over Stanton…"

Rew shrugged.

"I wonder who would win if you and I were to fight?" mused the woman. She took a step closer. "I don't appreciate being blackmailed, and I haven't forgiven you for shattering my ribcage last time we saw each other. Valchon fears you, which means I ought to fear you as well, but you seem to survive as much on luck as on skill. Do you think your luck would hold against me?"

"All I want from you is Alsayer," said Rew. "You have no reason to protect him."

"He works for Valchon, just as I. How can you argue I don't have reason to protect our allies?"

"Are you sure he is your ally? He was working with Heindaw and Calb just like he was with Valchon. Rebecca, he's been working with me as well, but I'm not so foolish as to trust him. Tell me where he is, and we can be done with this."

"You nearly killed me," said the woman. "That isn't something easy to forget."

"You were trying to stab me at the time, if I recall," responded Rew. "I had no plans to attack you until you came at me."

She laughed again. "One doesn't last long in my profession leaving enemies at your back. I thought with the opportunity, perhaps it'd be best to make sure you never appeared behind me. It looks like my intuition was correct."

"Was it?" asked Rew. "Valchon had plans for my companions and me, and you would have ruined them had you managed to kill me. Calb would have lived, and who can say what sort of trouble he'd cause for your boss. That I survived your attack and finished Calb, like Valchon planned, might be the only reason the prince still employs you."

The woman's smile remained fixed on her face, but Rew could see her shoulders tense.

"You didn't know that was his plan, did you? If he kept that from you, what else has he hidden?"

"The nature of my profession is secrecy," scoffed the woman. "Sometimes, that means I keep secrets. Sometimes, it means they are kept from me. There's no one Valchon trusts completely, and that's as it should be. If that's your angle, Ranger, you're going to have to try harder."

"Which profession are you referring to? Spymaster or guild-mistress?"

The woman sighed, her smile slipping. "How did you find out that particular secret?"

"Valchon won't learn of it the same way I did," said Rew. He saw her expression didn't change. "He knows?"

"He... suspects, I think," said the woman. "You were smart to threaten us with it. It'd be untenable to the powerful interests in the city if they knew I was so close to the prince. Valchon rules with a strong hand, but he has to allow them some dignity. Obviously, you knew that. You were trained just as he was, after all. Let us cut to the chase. You must have some offer for me other than your threat of exposure. Protecting my identity isn't enough to betray one of the prince's most powerful friends."

"Alsayer was behind the Dark Kind's attack on Falvar. He can communicate with the creatures and called them to the city. He was there when Baroness Fedgley died. He took Baron Fedgley to Spinesend beneath Valchon's nose and watched the baron die there. He helped Duke Eeron betray Valchon and ambush Worgon. All this time, while Alsayer has professed loyalty to Valchon, he's been working against the prince at nearly every turn."

"You have proof?" questioned the woman.

"I saw it with my own eyes."

The woman snorted. "Meaning you were there as well, but I'm to believe it was Alsayer who did it all, and you are innocent?"

Rew scowled at her. She wouldn't want coin. She wouldn't want promises. She wanted intrigue. That was the only thing interesting enough for the woman to work behind the prince's back.

"Very well," said Rew. "I'm assuming you know Alsayer is hiding from the king, but do you know why? It's because he lied to Vaisius Morden. Not about the Investiture or anything the princes were doing, but something else, something he thought worth risking the wrath of the king for."

The spymaster shifted on her feet and crossed her arms over her chest. "I'm listening."

"Alsayer was involved in a plot against the king himself. He fooled Vaisius Morden and Vyar Grund into thinking—Well, I won't share all of the details. Know he tricked them, and the king did not learn of it until he killed his own Ranger Commandant. When he did, my father scoured Vyar's memories, and he learned of Alsayer's deception. That's why the spellcaster would have suddenly begun avoiding the king. I'll admit I know little of what Alsayer has been doing since, or what his relationship with Valchon is like, but surely you must have noticed something different after Vyar Grund's death?"

The woman stared at Rew for a long moment, unblinking.

"Why did Alsayer tell Valchon the king sought him?"

"He did not tell Valchon anything that we believed, which, knowing the spellcaster, could have been the point. I need to hear more for me to believe you."

"Baron Fedgley was central to Alsayer's plans. He secreted the baron in Spinesend, where Vyar Grund found them both, and we all fought. You heard about that?"

The woman nodded. Then, her eyes widened. "Ah, the girl. If Baron Fedgley was important, then she must be as well. That is why Calb and Heindaw were so interested in her. She's here now, in Carff?"

Rew spread his hands and did not respond.

"Interesting."

"You'll have to go through me to get to her, of course," said Rew, "but first, we still have the problem of Alsayer. He's betrayed both the prince and myself. He's a problem for whoever emerges victorious between us. Allow me to solve the problem."

"You can't find him yourself? I thought you were working together."

"I don't trust him. He doesn't trust me. The bastard knows I'll kill him the moment I can track him down. Valchon has said similar things, which I believe he meant. You know he'll need to kill Alsayer eventually. This isn't a betrayal. We're just taking care of your master's business a little earlier than planned."

The woman's foot was tapping quickly on the cobblestones at her feet. An unconscious tic, or was she trying to look nervous?

"A spymaster is only as good as the secrets she holds. You know things about myself and the Fedgley girl that your master does not. But Alsayer knows far more. He's not just a threat to Valchon, he's a threat to your position at Valchon's side."

"I'd always heard you were the straightforward one," murmured the spymaster. "I was told you liked things simple. I wonder what the prince would think about all of this deceit at your hands? What would he say if he found out we are meeting?"

"I'm not going to be talking to him about it," replied Rew with a tight grin. "In a world of uncertainty, you can trust my brother will hear nothing from me. The next time we see each other... You've threats all over, but me spilling secrets is not one of them. For example, if the king finds Alsayer under Valchon's wing... I don't need to tell you how he'd react. The king, Valchon, you, me, everyone wants the spellcaster dead, so help me do it. Tell me where he is, unless… Do you trust Alsayer? You'd be the only one, I think."

The spymaster coughed and gave a small smile. "That's a fair point, Ranger."

Rew waited patiently.

"You took a big risk meeting me."

Rew nodded. He gave her a thin smile. "Guildmistress, spymaster, you like to play both sides. A woman like you knows how to protect her flank, hedge her bets. You must have considered that I've killed two of my brothers, and Valchon none. How confident are you that he can defeat me? Tell me where Alsayer is, then you and I have no quarrel, however this ends."

"That man attracts enemies like offal collects flies," admitted the woman. She stared at Rew a long moment, then said, "You're right, I do know how to hedge my bets. Remember that. Alsayer comes and goes from a series of portal stones hidden within a manor house. I'm not sure if he knows we're aware of the location, but he might be. He's as hard to grab a hold of as smoke. I'll give you the address and a warning to approach carefully. Before you killed Calb and Heindaw, I would have guessed Alsayer was the more dangerous of the two of you. I was certain Valchon would slay you all. Now, I'm not sure."

Rew nodded in acknowledgement.

"Ranger, if you're really going to kill Alsayer, do it quickly."

Chapter Twenty

A pale, blue-white light flickered, and Rew heard the sound of soft shoes on the stone floor. Two iron lamps sprang alight, their wicks suddenly burning with warm, orange flame, casting a dim glow on a long wooden table beneath them, barely illuminating the half dozen tall stone arches arranged in a semi-circle on the opposite side of the room. Long, black robes billowed as Alsayer strode toward the table.

Rew slipped from behind one of the stone arches, moving after the spellcaster silently. Alsayer reached the table, and a moment later, Rew grabbed his shoulder and spun his cousin around. He had his fist raised to crash it into Alsayer's face, but he paused. Blood dripped from Alsayer's nose, and the hair of his beard was singed. The stench of that burned hair clung to him, and his clothing was torn and dirty.

Fear, relief, and then trepidation flickered across Alsayer's face. He kept his arms by his side and muttered, "You. Do we have to do this now?"

"Yes, Cousin, we do."

"Can we go upstairs, then? I have a particularly fine vintage we can enjoy while we talk. I… need something to drink. It's been a day."

"What makes you think we're going to talk?"

"Because you would have stabbed me in the back if you wanted to kill me."

Alsayer wasn't a fool, and he had a point.

Rew gripped the spellcaster's shoulder tight. "You're right. I do want to talk. I have some questions for you."

"Any reason you want to do it down here instead of with a glass of wine in hand?" complained Alsayer. "Surely before you surprised me, you searched my home looking for traps. I'm no more dangerous to you upstairs than I am down here." The spell-caster glanced around. "Where are the others? You haven't left the girl unattended, have you? Rew, if the king or Valchon find her…"

"I'm well aware of the danger she's in."

"Good. Good," said Alsayer. "We're going to need her. Does she… How much does she know?"

"I'm the one asking the questions," snapped Rew.

"Go ahead and ask, then."

Rew studied the spellcaster, looking into the man's eyes. Alsayer still appeared uncertain, but he didn't seem afraid. He hadn't fought back. The ranger guessed that the spellcaster wasn't done with him, yet, but what sorts of plans hid behind those hard eyes?

Alsayer licked his lips, smearing the blood that had dripped there from his nose. He repeated his previous claim, "We don't have to be enemies."

Rew let him go and replied, "We'll go upstairs to talk, and we'll see about that. You lead the way. I'll be right behind you."

Minutes later, they sat in Alsayer's comfortable study. The spellcaster held a crystal goblet of wine in one hand and a linen cloth in the other which he used to dab the blood from his nose. Rew sat in a chair facing him, his longsword drawn and sitting across his lap. He eyed Alsayer like he would a snake coiled to strike.

"Really, Cousin, if I wanted to attack you, I would have

already, just as you would have struck me. Have a drink and relax a moment. We're both wanting to talk. We are safe here."

"Are we?" questioned Rew. "I found this place, didn't I? Valchon knows you come here and that you have portal stones in the basement."

"Of course he knows," replied Alsayer. "He's always known I'm playing more than one game, so periodically, I have to allow him to see my cards. He knew I was coming and going without tripping the wards he's layered around the city and the palace, so once most of my business was done, I let him figure out how I do it. He has the place watched, though I've layered wards to trip if anyone comes inside. If they'd seen you, I suspect Valchon would already be here."

"I saw the watchers, but they did not sense me."

"Like I told you, we're safe."

"Did you sense my arrival?"

Alsayer dabbed at his nose again, his eyes fixed on Rew. He didn't respond, which was answer enough.

Finally, Alsayer lowered the blood-stained linen from his face and said, "Prince Valchon doesn't have the subtlety that you do. If he broke in, he wouldn't wait calmly for us to finish this discussion. Since he hasn't attacked, we can assume he isn't here and that none of his minions know we're in here talking. How did you find this place, by the way, and how did you avoid my wards? I'll admit that surprises me. I didn't think you were capable of evading the traps I set. What have you been doing since you left the wilderness, Rew?"

"You're too confident, Cousin. You're smart and capable, but that doesn't mean you're the only one who is."

Alsayer gestured with the bloody linen napkin, as if to concede the point.

"What happened to your nose?"

"Dark Kind. That fool Calb unleashed more than he understood. Once the king is dead, we're going to have an awful time facing the things."

"We?"

"You'll let the Dark Kind overrun Vaeldon? Not much of a ranger, if that's the case."

Rew frowned.

Alsayer sipped his wine then asked, "You've traveled far since we last spoke. Haven't you noticed the Dark Kind are acting unusual? You should know better than anyone what is happening."

"I have noticed... odd things," admitted Rew.

"Calb conjured a fraemoth," stated Alsayer. The spellcaster shook his head ruefully. "I'll admit I failed to anticipate that. Pfah. As you said, he was more capable than I imagined, though not half as smart. Had I known he would attempt it, I would have stopped him. I can't fathom why he believed he could control the thing. Now it's out there, building and organizing. It'll be worse than it was fifty years ago, Rew. Such a disaster."

Rew blinked at him. "A fra—What?"

"If the valaan are the Dark Kind's captains, then the fraemoth is the general," explained the spellcaster, dabbing at his nose again. He looked at his blood on the napkin. "They have extensive magical capabilities, which I very recently ran afoul of. I would advise you to avoid the thing, but if you do, who's going to face it? Your father certainly hasn't bestirred himself to address it."

Rew looked up at Alsayer. "I encountered some narjag shamans communicating with a valaan through a crystal. I picked the crystal up, but it appeared simple stone to me. Was that the work of this... fraemoth?"

"Likely," said Alsayer with a shrug. "There hasn't been a frae-moth in our world since before either of us was born. Their magic is... strange. It doesn't work according to the rules of our own talent, and I've witnessed several odd outcomes. Could it be powering crystals other Dark Kind can use to communicate? I haven't seen it myself, but sure, it could be."

"The last time a fraemoth was in Vaeldon was fifty years ago?"

"That was the last time anyone conjured any new Dark Kind.

How Calb did it…" muttered the spellcaster. "I was certain he didn't have the skill, but it's here."

"Could someone else have conjured it?"

Alsayer snorted, then shook his head. "Who? Your brother was a fool, but he was the most powerful conjurer in the kingdom. He's dead now, so how he did it doesn't matter. The important point, the last fraemoth I can find reference of was killed by the king fifty years ago, and he didn't make the effort to write down what he did, or what it did. I personally have no interest in going to ask him. He's… more closed than he used to be. He's traveled a dark path, and I don't think he is happy with what he's discovered. Even if we weren't plotting against him, I'd be staying far from Mordenhold."

"He found out you lied to him," mentioned Rew. "If you go to Mordenhold, he's going to take your soul."

Alsayer gave Rew a pained smile. "He did, and you're right. He would."

Rew waved his hand around the room they were in. "Isn't it a bit dangerous to be hanging around Valchon's court? The king knows you were working with Valchon. I'd guess Carff is the first place he'd come looking for you."

"The prince needs me," said Alsayer. "He'll protect me as best he's able. Of course, that only goes as far as claiming to his father that I'm not here and sheltering me under the wards he's layered around the city to obscure his own machinations. I suspect if Vaisius Morden finds me, Valchon won't lift a finger to intervene. The king is distracted, though. It wounds my pride, but the truth is, tracking me down is not one of his priorities right now. That's not a good thing, Rew."

"Valchon needs you… Why?"

"To help kill you, of course."

Rew gripped the hilt of his longsword.

Alsayer waved at him impatiently. "I thought we were beyond that. We're not enemies, and I have no intention of trying to kill you. I lied to Valchon about it, obviously."

"You lie to everyone."

"True," admitted Alsayer with a wink, then he sipped his wine.

"How do you figure we are not enemies?" pressed Rew. "You don't recall the last several months?"

"We both want to overthrow the king, and I hope we'll both want to fight the Dark Kind after. We approach it differently, but both of us want what is best for Vaeldon and her people. What else needs be said? The closest allies can still have disagreements, Cousin."

"You killed Baron Fedgley and his wife. You've undermined my efforts and thrown me into the face of danger. You've cast dozens of spells at me, any one of which may have killed me. Those aren't the actions of an ally."

"His own daughter killed Baron Fedgley," retorted Alsayer, "and if my spells had killed you, then you're not the man I thought you were—or the man that the kingdom needs."

"Kallie killed the baron, but not the baroness."

"Yes, there is that," murmured Alsayer. He shrugged. "This is war. Things happen. Casualties are unavoidable. You look healthy enough to me. Come on, Rew. I'll be offended if you believe I fought you as hard as I could."

"Did you direct the Dark Kind to attack Falvar?"

The spellcaster winced. "I admit that looks bad. It was before I knew of the fraemoth. I thought… I learned from Calb how to command them. It was expedient."

"Expedient?"

"I had to convince you to join the fight. If the tug of the Investiture wasn't going to do it, I knew it'd take something more, ah, extreme."

Rew blinked at his cousin.

"You were on the verge of returning to the wilderness after depositing the children in their parents' laps," said Alsayer. "You wanted nothing to do with the Fedgleys. As long as Falvar seemed safe for them, you'd have no reason to stay. I struggled between the attack by the Dark Kind or kidnapping the empath. Maybe I choose poorly, I don't know, but it worked. You are a part of this, now. Besides, I was already kidnapping Fedgley himself, and how many kidnappings can one conduct in a day?"

"Hundreds of people died in Falvar," said Rew coldly. "All to… put the children in danger? To force me to save their lives?"

"You want to compare numbers? How many did you kill in Jabaan? I heard twenty thousand."

Rew scowled at Alsayer and raised his glass to his lips. It was empty. He stood to refill the goblet. While pouring the wine, he asked, "This isn't poisoned, is it?"

"No, it's not. Fill mine up, will you? That should reassure you."

Rew collected Alsayer's glass, and while he was taking it from his cousin, he asked, "What about Stanton? Could you have instructed the Dark Kind to move on from the city so Valchon did not call the maelstrom down upon it?"

Alsayer grimaced.

"If we're comparing numbers…" drawled Rew.

"I meddle in the shadows," murmured the spellcaster, looking honestly distraught. "Perhaps I could take on Valchon, but not while the other princes still lived. If I set myself against all of them, I'd fail. Stanton was… an oversight, a mistake. A grave one. It was… a test. Not of the magic. I knew he could conjure the maelstrom, but to actually use it in such a way? Against so many of his own people? Stanton proved how necessary it is to do the work that we do. That sort of thing cannot be allowed to happen. You think ill of me, I know, but surely you can't think I wanted that?"

Settling back down, Rew leaned his longsword on the side of the stuffed chair and drank the wine. Alsayer watched him quietly. Rew asked him, "Tell me, Cousin, what is all of this about? You're burning every bridge you come across, putting yourself on an island. No matter how this ends, I don't see it ending well for you. That's… not like you. Why are you doing this?"

"Do you remember when we were young in the creche during the previous Investiture? It was like watching sport, cheering on our local team, but it was our fathers we cheered, and they were maneuvering to kill each other. I think often about the day word came that your father killed mine. You, Valchon, the others, were happy about it. It was like… you'd won something, but my father was dead. I never cared for the man, but I lost something all the same. From then on, I was an outsider, a bastard."

Rew swallowed. "I'm sorry. I didn't… We were cruel. We were young."

Alsayer waved a hand dismissively. "No, you're not sorry, but that's no matter. In the blink of an eye, I went from a future prince of the realm, a potential king, to a bother at best, a threat more likely. You and the others were untouchable, but my siblings and I were subject to the intrigue the creche was training us for. How many from our generation still survive? Aside from you, me, and Valchon, it cannot be more than one or two. One of our cousins fled across the sea, and I suppose more could have, but I know of dozens who were killed through intrigues in Mordenhold. Those who tried their own path fared even worse. Outside the gaze of our father, they were nothing more than prey. Some of them were my prey."

Rubbing a hand over his head, Rew asked, "We can agree that our family is horrid, but what's your point? Where are you going with this?"

"I wonder if I would have chosen your path had my father won the Investiture? Would I be high-minded and refuse to participate? I think not. I believe, had my father won, I'd set myself to plotting against my brothers as strenuously as anyone. I think it likely I could have succeeded, and I'd be the one ascending the throne. We both know what would happen then. Vaisius Morden would take me. My soul would be imprisoned, but he'd live on in the shell of my body. If my father had prevailed, I doubt I would have had the time and motivation to study as deeply as I have. I probably would have no idea what would happen during the coronation. Pfah, I didn't realize it then, but it was a blessing when my father died. It gave me the chance to save my life, to save so many others, as well."

Alsayer raised his glass in toast. Rew stared at him and did not respond.

The spellcaster's lips curled into a grin. "But I'm not a prince, and that is in the past. I'm a cousin, and already, history has forgotten my name. Outside of Mordenhold and your brothers, how many of Vaeldon's nobles have ever given me a second thought? I have no title, no lands, no real wealth of my own. I have talent, but none of our family, me included, could stomach serving the lesser nobility. I'm a tool for the princes and the king until they weary of me, and then I'll be dead. That's the way it always is. This isn't even my house. I don't have one. There is no place in this kingdom which I call my own." Shaking his head, Alsayer drank deeply of his wine.

"So what, because your father lost and you didn't get a title, you want to burn it all down?"

"Yes, Cousin, I want to burn it all down."

Rew eyed the man, suspicious. "I don't believe you."

The predatory grin still on his face, Alsayer shrugged. "What could I say that you would believe? If it's a lie, at least my actions bear it out, don't you think?"

Twisting his wine glass in his hands, Rew finally said, "You're right, Alsayer. There is nothing you could say that I would believe."

"You abdicated, but you were trained like a Morden. Trust is a weakness in our family. At least, that's what we're told. It's the milk and bread that's fed to us from the moment we could understand it. That's what Vaisius Morden needs, us at each other's throats so that we don't turn on him. It's worked well for two hundred years. Rew, it is time to put all of that aside."

"There are those I trust, just not you," remarked Rew dryly.

"The girl?"

Rew watched his cousin then slowly answered, "Yes."

"Has she figured out what to do, then?"

Rew didn't respond.

"While the king is focused on other matters, we have a chance. Others have defied him, you know. They didn't have the girl. They didn't have the opportunity we do while his back is turned, and they all failed miserably. We need her to—She does understand what is to be done, right?"

"Of course."

"Blessed Mother, she doesn't, does she? King's Sake, Rew, do you plan for nothing?"

The ranger shrugged. "Things have a way of working out best when I don't."

"This isn't showing up at the tavern and finding a willing lass, you fool. This is challenging the king himself. You know what he is, don't you?"

"A two-hundred-year-old shade inhabiting the body of my father?"

"Pfah. Well, yes. That's what he is. You've got to put a bit more planning into what's coming than some wandering patrol off into the wilderness for a few weeks. People's lives are at stake, Rew, and I'm not talking about ours. Blessed Mother, think of Stanton, Jabaan. Those cities aren't unique in this grisly show. It happens every generation, and it will keep happening until he's stopped. So many others have tried to do just that, but us—you, I, and the girl—we have a chance!"

"She's learned much," said Rew, shifting in his seat. "We, ah, we had some books that she read. We, well, we prevailed against Calb and Heindaw. Once I face Valchon, the king is next."

"Books? What about a mentor, someone who can teach her? What happened to that man, Ambrose? I arranged for him to portal to Jabaan to rejoin you. I figured once you killed Calb, he'd stay with you and teach the girl, but he didn't, did he? None of my sources know what had happened to him, but I learned he was not with you in Iyre."

Rew scratched his beard. "I've tried to find necromancers to help train the lass, but they keep dying. A hazard of the occupation, I suppose."

Alsayer threw up his hands, his wine sloshing and spilling over the edge of his goblet. He glared at the glass then wiped it clean with the linen napkin. He scowled at the stained piece of fabric, blotted crimson with his blood and purple with wine. "I suppose that was ruined already. See, one conversation with you, Rew, and things are breaking."

"You had blood on there before I arrived," chided the ranger.

Alsayer drew a deep breath then released it. "I see that you have no plans, and something must be done, so I will train her."

"What?"

"I'll train the lass," he repeated. "It will mean much of the work I've been building with Valchon and against the Dark Kind is a waste, but she has to know what to do. She has to understand... Rew, for this to work, there will be a sacrifice. We're going to get one chance at this, and there cannot be hesitation. Do you— does she—understand that much, at least?"

"She's figured out what has to happen, if not how," said the ranger quietly.

"And she's accepted it?"

Rew nodded and did not respond.

"Good. Well, the situation isn't good, but if she's accepted that... that there's a sacrifice, then this can still work. I'll start today, but Blessed Mother, there's not much time. How long until you move against Valchon?"

Rew coughed. "I'm not going to tell you—"

Alsayer sat forward and interrupted, "I'm on your side, Rew."

"How can I be sure of that?"

"The fete? It will be public. That makes it riskier, obviously, but it will show the kingdom you're not to be trifled with. That could be valuable when you defeat your father and take the throne. We'll need the nobles lined up behind your banner as soon as the crown sits atop your head."

"The throne? No, no, I'm not going to… the fete?"

Alsayer tugged on his goatee. "Of course. The celebration of the one thousandth anniversary of Carff's founding, though it's beyond me how they figured out the year, much less the exact day. It doesn't matter. It's a party. I'm sure Valchon would avoid it if he could, but how would that look weeks before he thinks he'll be king? If he doesn't go, it will appear he's hiding. If he does go, he'll be drinking and distracted. Even Valchon won't be able to watch everyone coming and going from that ridiculous hothouse he's building. It doesn't hurt that the vintners' guild is sponsoring it all. There won't be a sober breath in Carff by the time things are really underway."

Alsayer stopped fussing with his chin hairs long enough to sip his wine then went back to it. "How are you planning to approach him? A public challenge, one on one? It forces him to face you in fair combat that way, if he accepts. He might not. He'll look pathetic if he puts his spellcasters between you and him, but at this point, does he care? You're all that's stopping him from ruling the kingdom, as far as he knows. He can't drop a maelstrom on you if the entire court is standing around, so you'd limit what he can try if he does fight you fair. The rewards if you're victorious will be substantial. The nobility will have no choice but to believe those rumors your minions have been spreading. It ought to secure all the support you need, which is worth risking much, but… are you certain you can defeat him? The maelstrom takes days to form, so you've an advantage with surprise, but that's not his only spell."

"Leave that to me," grumbled Rew.

"Have you studied the layout of the new building his engineers are erecting? There are possibilities there, and I'd like to hear what you think of them."

"I'm, ah, not sure…" mumbled Rew, looking down into his wine. "When did you say that fete was? And where?"

Staring at Rew for a long time, Alsayer finally said, "Please tell me you have an actual plan to confront your brother. Maybe you weren't sure before you snuck into the city, but now that you're here and you've had several days to reconnoiter the place, you must have come up with a few ideas? Come on, Rew! I helped cover your arrival from Shavroe, so I know how long you've been here. What have you been doing?"

"I've been working on it."

"Oh, really," drawled Alsayer, his tone patronizing, like a parent talking to a child. "Can you tell me what you've worked up so far, then? And don't pretend you won't tell me because you think I'll tattle to the prince. Believe what you want about me, but you know as well as I that if Valchon ascends the throne, Vaisius Morden will take him, and my life and eternal soul are forfeit. I have nothing to gain supporting Valchon past this point."

"More wine?"

"Rew…"

"I've been dealing with the simulacra, first."

"The simulacra? Ah, you mean his children. You killed the one that went missing, I suppose."

Rew nodded. "I questioned one of them, but it was stubborn, and it was a risk, so we had to put it down… We've, ah… I also spoke to Valchon's spymaster, and now you…"

Alsayer crossed his legs and cradled his wineglass with both hands. "And?"

"And that's it, so far," muttered Rew, quickly glancing away, cursing himself for feeling like a scolded child.

"How in the Blessed Mother's Grace have you managed to get so far?"

"You all are playing Kings and Queens," declared Rew. He drew a deep breath then continued, "I've been flipping the board."

Alsayer rubbed a hand over his eyes. "Right. I see we have much to do."

"If you tell me—"

"I'll tell you all I know of Valchon's spawn and where you can find them. They'll be easy enough for you to handle. They have their father's looks and strength, but none of his cunning. There are some scenarios, actually, where I think it best if we leave them to the last, but first, what of the fete?"

Rew cleared his throat then tentatively asked, "Tell me about it?"

"It's a good opportunity, if you think you can defeat him in a fair fight, but there's no forest there, Rew, no trees to hide behind. I don't mean to be rude, but without your connection to the wild, can you actually beat him? All is lost if you don't."

Rew touched the longsword leaning against his chair. "I have my ways."

"King's Sake, Rew," said Alsayer, shaking his head. "I was annoyed at you, but I see now that you need me. All right, we'll make some plans for Valchon's brats. I'll begin tutoring the lass, and… Pfah. First, more wine."

"More wine," agreed Rew.

"I imagine she'll be glad to have someone to teach her," mused Alsayer, his eyes looking off toward the wall, lost in thought. "She's not just a rare talent. She has more potential talent than any necromancer since Vaisius Morden himself. Far more than her father. He had to send her away from the barrowlands to foster with Worgon, you know? Falvar was too close, too fertile. Fedgley worried she'd grow power beyond mortal control."

Rew blinked and opened his mouth to ask a question.

Still staring at the wall and not seeing him, Alsayer continued, "After Jabaan, she'll have realized her strength. She'll be curious as to what else is possible, what an accomplished spellcaster can share with her. She's been stuck with… you, and others whose blood is as pure as a mutt's. Yes, I think this can work. It will work. She will be eager for the knowledge I can impart."

"You know you killed her parents, right? If you think I don't trust you, just wait until you look her in the eye. I hate to admit this, but I think you're right. She needs someone to train her, but

Alsayer, it's quite possible that she's going to try to kill you no matter the logic behind this arrangement. She hates you, Cousin, and if you think about it, I'm sure you'll agree she has reason."

Alsayer closed his eyes and appeared to quietly mouth a very foul curse. He opened his eyes and met Rew's gaze. "I can't believe I am asking this, but what do you suggest?"

Chapter Twenty-One

"How can you trust him?" questioned Cinda. "He's a backstabber and a murderer. King's Sake, Ranger, we watched him working with Valchon. Don't you recall he was the one who opened the portal to Jabaan? He's the one who forced us to confront my sister. He's… evil. I don't think that's an exaggeration. And the only person who knows that better than I is you."

"I know," responded Rew.

"Then how can you be considering this?"

"Because we don't have any other plan. The simulacra are tasked with guarding the palace, and there are three of them. We can't—"

"So says Alsayer," retorted Cinda. "Besides, you faced three of them in Olsoth."

"Not all at once, and not with Valchon standing behind them. Besides, I'm not sure I can use the sword again. I risk losing control of it every time I unleash that power, but even if I did use the sword against them, they'll be prepared now. These things gain power the longer they're out there, and they'll have more knowledge of my abilities every time I face one."

"Don't face them all at once," challenged Cinda. "One by one, we pick them off, just like you planned when we first got here. If we do it right, they won't be sharing anything about you when we're done with them."

Rew leaned forward, putting his forehead against the window of the upper floor of the spice museum. He looked out the dirty glass at the people down below. "Carff is too crowded. Valchon is ready. Alsayer told me—"

"He was lying," interjected Cinda.

"He hasn't lied about everything. Look, I realize how painful this is. I wouldn't ask it of you if I thought there were better choices. We're talking about preparing you to battle Vaisius Morden himself. Do you think you're ready for that?"

For a long moment, Cinda was silent. Then, she asked, "Do you think he's telling the truth about being able to teach me?"

"I do."

"Before I agree to anything, let's find out for sure."

Rew stood up and frowned at the young necromancer. "How?"

"He wants to meet us, right? Instead of us, he can meet with the dead. If, like he says, he can practice necromancy, he'll be able to command them. If he cannot…"

"He could just incinerate the things," mentioned Rew.

"Not if he wants to prove himself, he won't. Ranger, if he can't command undead that I've already animated, then he's less skilled than Ambrose was. He claims to have understanding, so let's make him prove it, and if he can't, we'll be at a safe distance, and we can figure out how to take him down. Ranger, if you want me to sit beside the man who killed my parents and study under him, I have to know it's worth it."

Rew rubbed a hand over his head. "I… You're right. This is asking a lot of you, and there's some merit to making the bastard prove himself. If he can't… we'll treat him like the enemy he is."

"Didn't you tell us once that princes never have the talent for necromancy?" wondered Cinda. "Not just your three brothers, but ever? I thought that was intentional, so they wouldn't realize what the king was doing when he took their bodies."

"Necromancy runs in the blood but not by design. It's not a trait that the king breeds into his children on purpose, I mean, but talent for high magic is not just the blood. It is more than that. It's part of your soul, part of who you are. All of the king's children, even if he wasn't inhabiting the body when they were sired, develop some potential for a variety of high magic. If anyone leans toward necromancy, though, they disappear from the creche. It's known that skill with necromancy comes at ascension to the throne, and everyone is strongly encouraged to focus on their other talents. If Alsayer had a natural ability, he hid it during his time in the creche. When his father died, though, the attention was not on him, and it's possible he learned the art. We know he has some abilities as a conjurer, so it's not a great stretch."

"He hid the ability for decades. Why choose now to display it?"

"What does he have to lose? The king wants him dead. If Valchon defeats us, the king will inhabit him, and I'd guess finding Alsayer would be near the first thing he sets his mind to. The spellcaster's only hope is our success."

"We will test him and see what he's capable of. I'll let him teach me if he proves skilled," agreed Cinda bitterly, "but, Ranger, never forget. He killed my parents. That is something neither Raif nor I will forgive."

"We need him," insisted Rew.

"We need him for now."

The ranger grunted and eyed the necromancer uncomfortably.

"I'll talk to Raif," said Cinda. "He won't understand, but he'll do as I ask. I've done many things I find distasteful, and before this is over, I'm sure I'll do many more. This… This turns my stomach. My only solace is that when it's over, Raif will be there to kill this man."

The girl turned, looking out the window again, up toward the palace. Her eyes seemed to reflect a light that wasn't there, crackling vivid emerald.

———

Rew looked on, his lips twisted in disgust. Before him, shuffling like men kicked out of the tavern hours after it was supposed to close, were ten cloaked and cowled figures. When one came too close, they smelled just like men kicked out of the tavern; of urine, vomit, and worse. They were freshly dead, and hadn't started to decay, but death was a cruel passage, and it'd taken its toll on the shambling undead.

Every third lantern was lit on the streets, providing lonely islands of light and allowing darkness to swallow the rest of Carff. Normally, so few hours until dawn, outside of the main thoroughfares, the cobblestones would be lit only by what light bled from the doors and the windows over the taverns, brothels, and gambling halls. In such a quiet quarter as they were walking through now, it would be as dark as the land outside. It was only because of the influx of visitors to the city, and evidently, someone's decision to keep them a little safer, that there was any light at all.

Rew and Cinda followed the corpses for half a dozen blocks, making sure that as they passed through those pools of light, they weren't identified for what they were. On a street corner ahead of them, standing in the yellow glow of a lantern, were Anne and Raif. Anne scowled at the shuffling pack of undead as it walked by her. Raif looked sick and pinched his nose at their odor.

Zaine materialized out of the darkness and waved her hands as if to shoo Cinda's minions onward. She waited until they were a block away then said, "Gross, but I found a good vantage we can watch from. That tower back there, see it?"

"That's a chapel to the Blessed Mother," mentioned Anne.

"Well, it's unlocked, and the bell tower reaches four stories. That is plenty of height to look over the rooftops and get a good view of Cinda's puppets tearing that rat bastard Alsayer into tiny chunks."

"We're hoping he can command the undead, and that he can teach her necromancy," reminded Rew.

"Are we?" asked Raif. His hand was above his shoulder, clutching the hilt of his greatsword. "Cinda asked me to, so I'll go along with it, but I don't like this."

"None of us do."

"You talked us into it, Ranger," reminded Cinda.

"Believe me," said Rew, "if I didn't think we needed every advantage we can get, I would have strangled Alsayer myself with my bare hands. He—I know what he's done to you. I wouldn't ask it if I didn't think we needed his help."

"So you've said."

"We all are doing things we wouldn't have thought we could stomach a few months ago," said Anne, her eyes still fixed on Cinda's corpses, which had stumbled another block ahead of them.

"Shall we?" asked Zaine, hooking a thumb over her shoulder.

They followed the thief to two ancient, oak doors studded with black iron. Zaine grabbed one of the handles and swung the door open. Despite the evident age of the doors and the punishment that the coastal weather had done to them, they opened with only a short squeal. Zaine led them inside and pointed toward a stairwell shrouded in shadow.

So late at night, the room was only lit by two candles at the front of a long sanctuary. The lights sat on either side of a carved, wooden figurine, a totem to the Mother. As they entered, Raif's armor clanking, a woman appeared from a curtained alcove behind the figurine.

Her eyes were blinking heavily, as if she'd been dozing out of sight. She covered a yawn with the back of her hand and asked, "Are you here for forgiveness?"

"We are not," said Anne. "We still have... Not yet."

"To pray, then? A small tithe, please, and you may approach—"

"I am a fellow servant of the Blessed Mother. We fight on her behalf."

"You… fight?"

"We do," said Anne. "We ask the use of your tower, for a little time. We'll be gone by morning's first bell, and it will be as if we were never here. We only seek your tower for its view."

"I believe you are mistaken," said the woman. "The Mother abhors violence. She—"

"The Mother offers Grace to the world," interrupted Anne. "Grace may be a beginning, or it may be comfort on our journey, but sometimes, it is an ending. We are all called to serve in our way. It seems this is my way."

Confused, tired, the other woman simply shook her head and said, "You will not commit violence on these grounds, will you?"

"We will not."

"Then I'll grant you the use of our tower. There is much about the Mother's ways I do not understand, and I feel no shame saying this is one of those times."

"We thank you, Sister. I understand your confusion."

"Mind your head around the bell. It will hurt if you bump into it, but ring it hard enough, and you won't hear for weeks."

Anne strode to the other woman. Without asking, she put her hands on the woman's head and whispered, "The Mother brings comfort. Do not fret, Sister, because that is what you shall find in her embrace. The Mother is wise, kind, and caring. Feel her peace."

The woman's mouth fell open, and she stared at Anne.

Rew could not be sure, but the woman seemed to be standing straighter than when they'd first entered, and her eyes no longer had the dark circles clouding beneath them.

Anne rejoined them and said quietly, "This had better be worth it."

THEY CLIMBED THE NARROW STAIRCASE UP THE TOWER. THERE WERE no rooms or landings, just stairs and windows, until they reached the top. The top of the tower had a low roof, and it was open to the air. A thin railing surrounded it, and a huge brass bell hung from the center. There was a cord to pull the bell. It would be rung in the morning to greet the sun and again in the evening when the sun fell to hasten its return.

Around them, Carff spread out, dark and pungent. In the sunlight, the red-tiled roofs of the city would have crackled with color, but at night, they seemed to shimmer softly, reflecting the light of the sky above. The tiles were coated in a thick glaze, which Rew had been told reflected the heat and kept the homes cool, but it made the city sparkle like the sea.

The only time Rew had occasion to run across the rooftops of Carff, he'd found the tiles to be dangerously slick. It was a natural deterrent to midnight mischief and might have helped explain how Carff became such a mercantile power. Elsewhere in the kingdom, shopkeepers and the rich feared theft from above. In Carff, it was the man across the table from you that you had to worry about.

The party looked around to orient themselves after several flights of stairs and found the courtyard they were looking for. It was better lit than most, bathing a tinkling night fountain in a low glow. There were people there, drawn to the light like moths. Lovers, taking a late stroll before returning to their separate homes and families. Drunks, sure they shouldn't pass out in the taverns they'd gotten to that state within but unsure where else to go. Youths, old enough their parents no longer watched their every move but young enough they had nowhere to be. A scattering of people who looked to be working, drawing water from the well and then disappearing back into the night. Attendants at hostels, employees at the brothels, bakers' apprentices preparing for the morning's work. And there, at the edge of the square, looking annoyed he'd been dragged out so late and forced to stand in the open, was Alsayer.

The man had forgone the black robes of an invoker and instead wore the embroidered doublet and tight hose of a courtier. It was a ridiculous disguise for the time and the place, and it looked as if it'd been years since he'd donned such fashionable garb. Maybe it had been. Rew hoped anyone seeing the man would think he was one of the drunks. But whatever someone thought, it was unlikely they would guess who he actually was. Even someone who knew Alsayer would have to look twice to believe their eyes. The disguise did risk drawing the attention of the thieves, but Alsayer could handle them.

Rew and the others gathered along the thin rail that circled the bell tower and watched.

Soon, Cinda's small party of animated corpses would stroll into the square. People might notice and panic or they might not. Strange things were known to happen on Carff's streets at night, and both the wise and the inebriated knew to melt away as soon as they did. Alsayer may ignore the creatures, thinking they had nothing to do with him, at least until they got close and attacked. He might see them and strike first, casting his spells and obliterating the things. Or he could understand this was a test, and he would command them.

Rew had never seen his cousin practice necromancy, but he'd never seen him show talents for conjuring either until Alsayer had commanded the Dark Kind outside of Falvar. How had the man learned these things, and what else was he capable of?

They didn't have to wait long to find out. A woman out of sight evidently noticed that something was terribly wrong, and she screamed. Other people began running. Most laughed and went back to their business.

Alsayer glanced over, bored at first. Then abruptly, he stood up straight, his eyes fixed on a dark street that led to the square. He watched, calmly but cautiously, as the corpses shuffled into view. For those not close, it might look like any ten figures bundled up tightly at night. To someone who had a talent for necromancy, it would be immediately apparent what was happening.

The spellcaster stared at the corpses a long moment. He looked around the square and the rooftops. Then, he raised a hand, offered a grand bow, and rose to face the approaching pack of undead. He looked to be talking to himself.

"How's he doing?" asked Rew.

Sounding upset about it, Cinda replied, "His strength is paltry, but he seems to know what he's about. Look, he's got them now. Wait, he missed one. Ah, he's got it again. There they go. That is his doing. King's Sake, he's actually commanding them. He... he's not doing badly. Look, they're all moving at different gaits. They're not in lockstep, bumping into each other awkwardly. It means he's able to issue separate commands to several of them at once. Little power, but impressive skill."

"Satisfied?"

"I wish we'd thought to give him a more challenging test, but even with this small demonstration, it's clear he's more skilled than Ambrose. I had hoped he would fail, and those things would kill him."

"Someone has to teach you, Cinda."

"That's what you keep saying."

"What do we do now?" questioned Zaine. "How do we get in touch with him again? That house of his cannot be very safe for us to approach now that we've contacted him once."

"We follow the corpses," answered Rew.

"YOU REALLY SHOULD LEARN TO TRUST ME," DECLARED ALSAYER, sounding somewhat offended.

"That's not going to happen," responded Rew.

The spellcaster tugged on his goatee. "I keep telling you we don't have to be enemies."

"You killed my mother," stated Cinda coldly. "You imprisoned my father, and when my sister killed him, you fled with my sister, who—"

"She fled with me," corrected Alsayer. "I didn't intend for her to kill your father, and I certainly didn't intend for her to jump through the portal after me. No one could have foreseen that, but it ended up working out well for us all, I think, but—"

"You used her to set us up in Jabaan. She stabbed me, and I nearly bled to death on Calb's rug. That was before he took us prisoner and chained us to a wall. If Anne had hesitated a moment when I'd been wounded, if my sister had landed one more blow, I'd be dead!"

Alsayer threw up his arms. "I gave you an opportunity at the prince! Be fair. How else were you going to get inside of his palace with the element of surprise? I didn't… Well, it was unfortunate how all of the details fell into place with your sister, and how was I to know you'd allow yourselves to be captured, but it worked, didn't it? Calb is dead."

"Tens of thousands of other people as well," reminded Cinda coldly.

Nodding, the spellcaster folded his hands in front of his waist. He held Cinda's gaze and told her, "Lass, you made a mistake. You were the one who killed those people, not me. I am the only one who can teach well enough that it doesn't happen again. If you refuse my tutoring, then the blood is on your hands, and you deserve the guilt you will earn. You attempt grand, difficult things. Do you really believe you are prepared to face the king himself without guidance?"

Cinda's gaze hardened, and her eyes flared green, but she did not speak. She hated the man, with reason, but he was right. She had natural talent but no control. Her ability was unrefined and dangerous. She was quite capable of causing the carnage they claimed they were trying to stop, and without training, further mistakes weren't just possible but likely.

She'd been working at drawing more and more power, and she was getting better, and she'd spent weeks studying the books they'd obtained in the Arcanum and Iyre, but strength and knowledge were double-edged swords. She had the ability to perform more dangerous magic, but she had no practice with it, and she couldn't risk practicing in a crowded city like Carff, particularly when under the threat from Prince Valchon. The danger of repeating Jabaan was too high. With necromancy, there was no room for error, and mistakes meant people were going to die. She knew that. She knew she needed guidance. She would have preferred it come from any other person.

Alsayer, despite the anger she felt toward him, was the only chance they had to sharpen her skill before facing the king. Where else in Vaeldon could they find a tutor? Every necromancer they'd happened across was dead, and Rew doubted any new ones would fare much better. Even the Arcanum had been destroyed. The only other place Rew knew of with necromancers and arcanists who studied the art was Mordenhold itself, and the idea of learning from someone there was laughable.

Taking time for Cinda to experiment on her own wasn't any better. She, or the rest of the party, could easily be killed doing it, for one, but two, they simply did not have the time. Thousands of people were dying every day. Cinda could sense the fleeting passage of their souls. The situation was dire, and they were desperate.

The spellcaster, to his credit, merely tugged on his goatee and waited. He must know which wheels were turning inside Cinda's mind, and he knew his voice would only enrage her. He trusted she would come to the only logical conclusion.

She needed to learn, and he was the only one who could teach her.

"I will not forgive you," warned Cinda.

Alsayer nodded in acknowledgement. "Believe it or not, I understand. I wouldn't—I couldn't, ask that of you. We need not have a good relationship, but for me to train you, we need a working relationship. You don't have to forgive me, or like me at all for that matter, but you have to give me a measure of your trust."

Cinda snorted.

Alsayer glanced at Rew.

"She didn't fling her funeral fire at your face the moment she saw you, Cousin. To be frank, you're doing better than I expected."

Sighing, the spellcaster looked around the room he'd led them to. It was in an expansive townhouse that had fallen into disrepair, quite different than the one Rew had found him in before. Alsayer had explained that the previous owner of this place had perished with no heirs during the last Investiture, and Valchon had never gotten around to granting the property to one of his sycophants. It had space, and no one was likely to be venturing inside, but best of all, the family who had once occupied the home had installed a personal mausoleum in the garden out back. Generations of them were interred there.

The other crypts within the city were public, and it would be difficult to break in and experiment on the bodies without drawing notice. There were places to find the freshly deceased, of course. The beggars' tenements, the back doors of shady physicians, and the muddy stretches beneath the wharves when the tide rolled out, but none of them found those options appealing.

Alsayer nodded around, as if all had been settled, then strode across the room to a table set with a rolled-up scroll and a quill. He unfurled it, dipped the quill in ink, and began making notations on the blank paper.

"While the lass and I practice, and while you wait for Valchon's fete, I'll give you a scouting assignment, Rew. I can make your task easier, but it's not going to be easy. Valchon is formidable on his own, and he's got the bulk of the kingdom supporting him, now. Seems he's more popular than you. Unsurprising. Anyway, I'm drawing out the location his party will be held, making some notes on key points of defense, and most importantly, noting where I expect his children will be stationed. You should take this and go see it for yourself."

"I need to address his spawn before I face Valchon," remarked Rew, peering down at Alsayer's scribbling. "I can't face all of them and the prince at once. If they're there during the fete…"

"Agreed you can't face them all together, but if you slay all of his children now, Valchon will have to react, even if it makes him look bad. He might cancel the fete, no matter how disappointed his nobles and merchants will be, or he could convert it into an extravagant trap. If he feels threatened enough, he could lock down the city and send his soldiers door to door until he flushes you out. You can't give him advance warning because there's nothing he will stop at to kill you. It's the only thing that matters to him, Rew. When you hit him, you need to hit him hard enough that he stays down."

"I already killed one of his whelps in the city. He knows I'm here."

Absentmindedly, Alsayer moved to tug his goatee before realizing he was still holding the quill. "True enough, but you did well taking it quietly and disposing of the body. Valchon can't be certain it was you. These things kill each other when they get the chance, did you know? Pfah. I'd call it awful, if that shameful business didn't come directly from our own family. Don't worry. I'll think of a distraction to make him believe you're elsewhere. A few reports of sightings, perhaps some of his emissaries dying in mysterious circumstances… He has few other enemies at this point, so anything disruptive will be attributed to you."

"I spoke to his spymaster. She knows I'm here. She's the one who told us where to find you."

The spellcaster grunted. "Right. I forgot that. I suppose I owe her… But we don't have time for all of that. For now, I'll convince her we fought, and that you fled."

"Alsayer, he knows I'm not going to run away, and he knows I'm not going to be lurking in far-flung corners of the kingdom killing his representatives. Maybe she'd believe it, but Valchon won't buy that I ran away. Us facing each other is inevitable."

"Are you sure he thinks that?" questioned the spellcaster, giving Rew a mocking look. "You spent most of your life running away, Cousin. All I need do is convince him you've returned to form. He saw me banged up the day before. I can use that."

Rew gripped his longsword, and Alsayer's eyes dropped to it.

"Maybe not running away," conceded Alsayer, "but I'll give him a reason to believe you're not in Carff. If it doesn't work, we're no worse off than we are now. I agree you cannot face him and all of his children at once, but give the lass and I time. If she's a quick learner, I have an idea to deal with the whelps, and you'll be free to face your brother one on one."

Rew grunted, eying his cousin suspiciously, but when Alsayer finished jotting notes on the scroll, Rew accepted it and went to a quiet corner to study it. He didn't think Alsayer was intending on betraying them, yet. If he had, there would have been an army of Valchon's people surrounding the townhouse. The spellcaster was helping, for his own reasons to be sure, but Rew and the others weren't in position to turn any sort of help away.

Chapter Twenty-Two

The prince's palace in Carff seemed a town all on its own. It sat in the midst of the city, overlooking the sprawling harbor, shouldering against the manses of the merchants who inhaled the wealth brought in by the sea like they were drawing perfumed air. Wide boulevards led from the city's spice market to the palace, joined by other thoroughfares like tributaries of a grand river.

Throngs of nobles and dignitaries filed in and out of the palace's gates in a regular stream, some hoping to gain an audience with Valchon, most content to be seen by his administrators. They were overseen by a legion of soldiers and spellcasters who vetted then accompanied them all. Frequently, they were granted time with neither the prince nor his people, but it was good to be observed about the hallways of the palace, even if you weren't doing anything there. It lent one a sense of success and importance.

But while it seemed the palace was drowning in supplicants, there were even more soldiers. Men and women wearing Valchon's copper armor were like grass on a plain. Standing in ranks, lining the walls, clustered around the gateways and corridors. Nothing moved within the palace without them seeing.

Spellcasters bolstered their numbers, stationed at important points where they could guard against magical intrusions or respond to support the mundane guards.

The palace on an initial look appeared to be the heart of the city, but when considered closely, it was apart from the real life of Carff. None of the goods from the harbor made their way through its august hallways. None of the gold that passed from hand to hand was transferred in its reception rooms. Not even the soldiers were barracked within the tall, sandstone walls, though they spent the bulk of their day guarding them. The commoners of the city would never enter the place, never see the extravagant gardens and galleries. All they saw were blank walls and iron-barred gates. The place may as well have been Mordenhold or some far-flung capital across the sea for all the commoners knew of it.

It was fitting. Vaisius Morden and his children did not consider themselves part of Vaeldon. They were above it, and Valchon's palace, like the princes before him, trafficked in a different kind of merchandise than what was traded elsewhere in the city.

The guests of the palace dealt in power—political, military, and economic. It was their blood and their breath, but even they were only visitors. The power they touched behind those walls was not theirs. They could merely borrow it. The power stemmed from Prince Valchon.

The prince lived in a world apart. A world of his and his brothers'. His and his father's. It was their world alone, but the palace in Carff had not always been Valchon's. Rew had visited as a youth, years before Valchon had been given the city. If he hadn't abdicated his position in the family, Carff might have gone to Rew. He thought about that, looking at the outside of the palace, and decided that no, this was Valchon's home. Even if Rew had been granted it by the king, the palace never would have felt comfortable to him. His place was the wild, the trees and the mountains, the streams and the animals. One could never own those, one could only exist alongside of them.

But it was clear to anyone familiar with it, Valchon did own the palace. It had his stamp on it. After years of his residency, it'd been changed by his presence, and it'd been layered with wards and protections he'd fashioned over that time.

Rew, accompanied by Zaine, considered that in the bright daylight two hours after dawn. Those layers of protection made sneaking inside the place quite difficult.

"I still think we should be doing this at night," groused the thief. She looked uncomfortable, dressed in a light, sleeveless tunic with a hood that she'd pulled over her head. She'd left her bow behind with the others but wore her paired daggers on her hips. Beneath the cowl of her tunic, Rew could see her glaring at him. She added, "Doing this during the day is unnatural."

"That's the point," suggested Rew. "Valchon must suspect we're coming. At night, every one of his men is going to be waiting for an attack. In the darkest hours, they'll be at their most alert. Those who aren't sleeping on the job, that is. The streets are quiet, then. The city is quiet. Any noises, any unusual motion, will draw their eyes like dogs to a squirrel. During the day, though, the city is alive. It's loud. People are everywhere. No one will suspect us."

Zaine sighed. "This goes against everything I was taught in the guild."

"Amateurs."

Zaine turned toward him. "They are literal professional thieves. Breaking into places was the one and only thing they were good at. You think you have more experience than the thieves' guild? Entering a well-guarded storeroom and making off with a bag of silver is a lot different than stalking through the forest, Ranger."

Rew smirked. "I wasn't always a ranger, you know."

Zaine frowned at him, her mouth opening to respond.

Before she could, Rew blurted, "Now."

He casually walked out of the alleyway they'd been lurking in and crossed the open street to the wall of the palace. Hanging there were twists of vines, spilling down from one of the score of gardens that dotted the sand-colored fortification. There were gardeners who spent their entire days cutting off vegetation that crept out of its boundary, but the palace was a big structure, and Valchon had the gardeners hard at work preparing for his fete. It wouldn't be until afternoon that the gardeners made their inspections of this section of palace.

Also, the night before, Rew had come by and given the plants encouragement to grow longer, to the point they hung down to where he could reach. Plants weren't like animals, able to hear and respond to specific commands, but all life was part of a whole, and everything sought a connection. Plants grew, and Rew had connected with these vines and helped them fulfill that yearning.

He grasped one of the verdant green lines and, using it like a rope, began to walk up the side of the palace wall. Zaine stopped beneath him, glancing nervously at the other people on the street. There weren't many, but there were some, and not a one of them could miss the sight of someone breaking into the palace. In a moment, Rew reached the top of the wall. He turned and shook the vine he'd climbed up. He didn't need to call to her. Zaine was already on the way up.

The side of the palace they were climbing abutted a small quarter of Carff that was popular amongst the foreigners who visited from the lands across the sea. There were merchants there, ship captains, even a few men and women who'd settled in Carff to provide services to their countrymen while they were staying at the foreign port. But most of all, the quarter was full of sailors, and not one of them wanted to entangle themselves with a foreign government. The sailors owed their allegiance to the sea. They knew if they were brought in, they risked missing their next departure, and besides, there was no profit being questioned by the authorities. That was true in any port. It was a mantra all men of the sea knew. Whether soldiers or serving wenches, don't become involved. Rew was willing to risk his life that none of those sailors would go running to Valchon's guards.

Of course, that didn't mean everyone who walked down the street was a foreign sailor. Like anywhere, Valchon's soldiers would move on patrols, and there were others who did business in the foreign quarter who relied on connections within the palace, and they would curry favor however they could. If any of those people saw them, Rew and Zaine would be off like hares, hoping that they could get lost in the crowded spice market before Valchon's people caught up.

It was a gamble that no one would speak about what they were seeing and a gamble they could get away if someone did. Risks Rew was willing to take, but that didn't mean he wanted to be standing atop the wall all day waiting for Zaine to climb up and join him. The quicker they were out of sight, the lower the danger of discovery. Good advice for a thief at night. Better advice for a thief during the day.

On a tier above the wall they'd climbed, there were pairs of guards on patrol. There were forty-five breaths between each passing. Rew had counted them making a dozen circuits, and it was never faster than that. It was enough time to climb up and disappear into the thick vegetation in the garden, but there wasn't any extra time to spare. At night, those patrols were twice as frequent. They never would have made it up this section of wall without being spotted. He glanced up. Another ten, fifteen breaths before those men reappeared?

Zaine, showing off her dexterity, gracefully hoisted herself up beside Rew, and he led them beneath the thick canopy of a flow-ering plum tree. The tree was carefully manicured, and a lovely-looking little bench sat beneath it in the shade. Above, the foliage was thick and verdant with spring growth. Rew reached up and plucked two plums from a branch. He handed one to Zaine then sat down, stretching his legs out in front of himself and taking a bite of the plum.

For anyone strolling the garden, they would be impossible to miss, but for the guards looking down from above, they would be invisible beneath the shroud of leaves.

Rew chewed the fruit and studied the small garden around them. It was an intimate spot filled with the aroma of new flowers. From the walls, one could look out upon the sprawl of Carff, but the sea was not visible, and neither were any of the city's institutions like the spice market. The smell of the garden was thick with blooms, and Rew found it cloying. It wasn't natural, the way the gardeners had arranged things. He wondered if they acknowledged that, and they'd traded the profusion of flora for the chance to overpower the smell of the spice market.

If that was the plan, they'd been successful, but it hadn't made this particular garden a popular place for functionaries to cool their heels during the day. In Carff, you got used to the spices soon enough, and if you couldn't, you left. More so, instead of the city side of the palace, most of the courtiers would be skulking on the opposite side where the open gardens faced the sea. It was cooler there in the fresh breeze, but most importantly, that side was favored by Valchon. Anyone in the palace who wasn't staff or a soldier would leap at an opportunity to have a chance encounter with the prince. For those who couldn't get an audience with him, they might wait weeks, meandering about the hallways and gardens, hoping to bump into him, at least until his administrators found them and kicked them out of the building.

For the minor nobility and the wealthy merchants, there was no shame in such behavior. It was considered a part of the game, one of the few ways to get anything done with a liege who showed little interest in actually governing his province. Rew imagined the administrators weren't as thrilled with the cat and mouse behavior, but they allowed it because if they didn't give Carff's elite some chance of appealing to the prince, they might face a sort of rebellion. If the nobility and merchants forced their way to Valchon's attention, it was unlikely to end well for anyone.

Rew wondered if Valchon's attack on Stanton had scared off

any of those supplicants for a time, or did they swallow the excuse the Dark Kind had been swarming and there was no other choice? Did they herald Valchon as a hero? They couldn't all believe that was the only reason Valchon had called the maelstrom. He had wanted them to see and feel his power. The nobility was experienced enough that many of them would understand.

Rew frowned. It wouldn't be the first time a Morden had lashed out and blamed it on the Dark Kind. In the moment, the message would be understood, but in the histories, would the scholars faithfully recount how Valchon had defended the Eastern Province against a horde of narjags? How many other cities had suffered similar fates for the same spurious reasons? How often had brutality been portrayed as heroism?

Rew shook himself. It wasn't the time for such meanderings. He nodded toward a doorway that was partially hidden behind a trellis of roses, their fragrant blooms and thorny limbs hanging down where one had to duck beneath to avoid getting scratched across the face.

Zaine pushed back the cowl of her tunic and followed Rew inside of the palace.

The interior of the massive fortification presented a different challenge than the outside. People in the hallways would not be unusual, but heavily armed people in the hallways who weren't wearing the livery of Prince Valchon's forces would be cause for alarm. It didn't matter what time of day it was. If the guards saw them wandering about, they would be stopped and questioned.

Rew doubted there would be more patrols during the day than in the dark of night when assassins were prone to come calling, but there would be far more servants and administrators bustling about doing the work of running the palace and the province. They wouldn't be as suspicious as the guards, but their eyes wouldn't be closed, and he didn't know what part of the palace they'd entered. If it was one used primarily by staff, someone was bound to notice them and say something. That meant they had to act quickly.

"Would have been easier had there been a pair of guards in that garden," mumbled Rew.

Her eyes darting wildly, visibly shaking every time they passed an open door or window, Zaine stalked behind him without speaking.

They turned a corner, and Rew said, "Ah, here we go."

A woman spun. She was dressed in a shimmering silk dress. It was cinched tight on the top and had ample skirts on the bottom. In a glance, Rew assessed there was a lot of lace involved. Far more than anyone needed, he thought, but he imagined there was a tailor somewhere making a fortune on pushing the fashion.

"Who are—" began the woman, but she was cut short when Rew whipped out his hunting knife and clouted her on the side of the head with the bone hilt. The woman's eyes went vacant, and Zaine leapt forward to catch her before she fell to the floor.

"Did you have to hit her so hard?" hissed the thief.

"I had to knock her out, didn't I?" responded Rew, shrugging. He pointed to an open door. "Let's get her out of the hallway so you can change."

"Change into that?" scoffed Zaine. "I don't know how to put on a dress like that."

"You put it on like you put on anything. One leg at a—Oh, right, it's a dress. That ought to be even easier than trousers. Just look at how she did it. You're a smart lass. You can figure it out."

They dragged the woman into one of the quiet, purposeless rooms that was scattered all over the palace—small spaces, furnished with a couch or two, a few chairs, some overly polished tables, and occasionally featuring a fireplace, which was never needed in Carff due to the warm sea breezes. In more peaceful times, the rooms were the haunts of courtiers who were stalking the halls looking for important staff to ambush. If they could scavenge food from the kitchen and find a place to conduct the necessaries, those men and women could last weeks in the palace with no one paying them any attention.

Before he'd become a ranger, Rew had made good use of such rooms, much like the courtiers did. An ambush was an ambush. He figured it would work just as well for their purposes today.

Luckily, the first room they found was empty at the moment. Zaine retired to one corner and crouched over the unconscious woman, fussing with her dress, trying to figure out the complicated system of buttons and laces that had sealed the woman inside of the fabric.

Rew stood by the door, listening.

The hallway was not a well-trafficked one, but it didn't take long until he heard the hard rustle of men walking in armor. Three of them, he thought. More than he'd hoped but not too many. He turned, looking over the room. On one of the glossy wooden tables against the wall, there was a heavy-looking bronze bust of a man. One of his ancestors? Rew didn't recognize the man, but when he picked up the statue of the head, it had a pleasant weight to it. Big heads ran in the family.

Rew waited. Then, he opened the door. Three guards, clad in copper breastplates and Prince Valchon's livery, were marching past, muttering to themselves about a woman they'd seen unescorted. The same one Rew had found?

"Excuse me," called Rew. "I believe I saw the woman you are looking for."

As one, the soldiers turned.

Rew bashed the first one across the side of the head with the heavy bronze bust. The man crumpled in a heap, and the second guard opened his mouth to cry out. Rew whipped the statue back into his face, crunching bone and silencing the outcry.

The third man went for his sword.

Convenient for Rew, unfortunate for the soldier as he was slower than the ranger. The crown of his skull suffered the same fate as his companions'.

Working quickly, Rew tossed the bust onto the carpet inside of the room then began dragging the guards after it. He sized them up then stripped one of them of his clothing and armor. Rew bundled his own clothes into a neat pack he tied to his back, got dressed in the soldier's attire, and slid his longsword into the soldier's sheath. It was an awkward fit, and some of the steel of his blade stuck out, but he wrapped a bit of tunic from another of the men around it and hoped it would pass a cursory glance. The bundle of clothing on his back might draw attention as well, but it was his second-best pair of trousers, and Anne was certain to make him go shopping for another if he lost it.

He knelt and felt at the necks of the guards. Two of them were still. One man's heart still fluttered. The ranger glanced over his shoulder at Zaine then slipped his hunting knife from his belt. He put a hand over the soldier's mouth and thrust the knife into the man's chest, angling beneath the soldier's breastplate and between his ribs, up into his heart. Blood pumped from the wound, but Rew quickly drew his knife from the man and wadded the soldier's tunic to absorb most of the mess.

The dying soldier's eyes had snapped open when the blade pierced him, but with Rew's hands over his mouth, the soldier couldn't cry out. It wasn't long before he stopped struggling.

Rew cleaned his knife and sheathed it then scrubbed his hands as best he could without water or soap. He stood and adjusted the copper breastplate on his chest. He asked Zaine, "Well?"

She was still standing over the half-naked woman, muttering to herself, ignoring what he'd been doing.

"Come on, lass. Stop ogling the lady and get her clothes on."

"Ogling? I'm not... I, ah..."

Rew snorted. He could tell when someone was ogling, and that's what she'd been doing.

Flushing, Zaine's gaze darted between him and the half-naked woman. "I, ah, can't figure out how to get her out of this."

Muttering beneath his breath, Rew came to join her. He knelt and unbuttoned and unlaced with deft fingers.

"How'd you learn to do that?" questioned Zaine, watching in awe.

"With enough motivation, you can learn to do anything," responded Rew with a wink. He held up the dress for her. "All a matter of practice."

"Motivation? What sort of motivation…" replied Zaine before glancing at the woman, who was wearing only her underclothes now. "I see."

"When this is all done, we've got to find you a girl," grumbled Rew, shaking the dress to get Zaine's attention. "Get your head cleared, you know?"

Beet red, Zaine looked down at the dress like it was going to bite her.

Sighing, Rew instructed, "Strip down, lass, and put it on. I'll tie you up. You can face away if you like, and I promise I won't look."

"How are you going to lace it without looking?" demanded Zaine.

Rew raised an eyebrow, crossed his arms over his chest, and began tapping his foot on the floor.

"If we were anywhere other than Prince Valchon's palace…" muttered Zaine. She turned and began removing her clothes. "I swear, I think you found a noblewoman on purpose. Oh, no, not content to let me slip into some chambermaid's simple skirts or, better yet, a short and slender guard's trousers…"

Ignoring the rest of Zaine's complaints, Rew helped the thief cinch the dress tight. Then, he stuffed her clothing into the pack with his. Together, they exited back into the hallway, a noble-woman and her escort.

As they strolled through Valchon's palace, they paid careful attention to the soldiers they passed, the staff and their activities, and the other visitors who lurked in the hallways. Before arriving, they'd taken time to alter their appearances with face paints and rouge like performers on a stage, but they still attempted to keep to the side and move at a steady pace to draw as little attention as possible.

Fortunately, their pairing was common in the hallways. It seemed that instead of valets, all guests were being escorted by soldiers, and while the corridors weren't as crowded as Rew remembered them being, the main passages were still busy. There were scores of well-dressed men and women being escorted by hundreds of guards. As long as they looked like they knew where they were going, no one gave them a second glance.

Valchon might not be interested in entertaining anyone, but they were all interested in seeing him. Perhaps they believed the tales that Rew had tried to spread, perhaps they did not, but the fact was that Prince Valchon was the only available heir to Vaeldon's throne. For those looking to attach themselves to a coattail, he was the only one wearing a jacket.

It must be why he bothered with the fete. Valchon could invite the plethora of courtiers who scurried about his palace and give them a story to brag about to those less important, but he wouldn't have to spend much time with them individually. He could focus his effort on Rew and taking over for their father, while giving the upper crust a sign he still cared.

Rew smirked. What would Valchon think about his brother strolling through the palace unnoticed?

It wasn't the way of Vaisius Morden's children to come alone with stealth. They might send assassins, they might send spies, but the idea of walking an enemy's hallway without a company of spellcasters and sword masters as protection was unthinkable. Valchon would never put himself at risk like that, which is why Rew had thought it worth the try. If the prince was anticipating one thing, give him another, which was the entire purpose of their mission.

They'd gather what intelligence they could, but more than anything, they needed to set up some surprises. At a fete celebrating him, surrounded by his spellcasters and his blades, behind the safety of his own walls, Valchon would never suspect what was coming. He would think he had control of every facet of the evening. It was on his turf, after all, but Rew had plans to change that.

He led Zaine unerringly through the palace until they emerged on the seaward side of the structure. A giant field had been cleared between the palace and the harbor, and on that field, a forest of iron and wood struts was rising into the sky. Swarms of engineers and builders clung to scaffolding, maneuvering heavy pieces of the rising structure with pulleys, rope, and brute force.

A guard turned when they exited, and Rew bellowed, "Lady Petunia, from the Mordenhold Arboretum, here to observe construction."

The guard blinked at them heavily, glanced at Zaine, her attire, and the palace they'd emerged from. He shrugged. The man's task was to prevent strangers from entering the palace from the construction site, not the other way around.

Rew led Zaine into tangled chaos, and from an embroidered satchel, she began digging for fistfuls of seeds.

Chapter Twenty-Three

The remaining weeks before Valchon's fete were spent in periods of frantic preparation and nervous tension. Rew and Zaine moved cautiously throughout the city, studying the layout, making plans for escape and backup plans for the attack, and placing tools and supplies in strategic places in case things went sour.

They didn't enter the palace again, though Rew did make several circuits of the perimeter, observing the security and strengthening his connection with the seeds they'd placed inside the construction of Valchon's new hothouse. Alsayer insisted he had convinced Valchon that Rew had left Carff, but there were more guards around the palace every day. Rew couldn't bring himself to believe it was all because of the party.

Anne and Raif spent their time scouring the city for news of the wider world. It wasn't lost on any of them that if they were successful facing Valchon, the most difficult part of their mission was still to come. The king would be ready for them, and he would be able to focus all of his attention and might on stopping them. They wanted to know as much as they could about what he was up to and how he was positioning his forces. Unfortunately, information was scant, and without the rangers in Mordenhold, there was no one they could trust to get accurate, inside information.

In their free time, they all attempted to monitor Alsayer's comings and goings. The man was as slippery as an eel. He was shuttling back and forth between them and Prince Valchon and juggling who knew how many other balls. If they were his only plot, Rew would have been shocked. Every time Rew accused the man of hiding something, Alsayer smoothly reminded the ranger that he was in fact hiding from the king. If he wasn't operating in the shadows, he would be dead.

Rew grumbled about it, and he imagined Valchon was doing the same on the other side of town, but the spellcaster had a point. The king had to know Alsayer had tricked him about the Fedgley sisters, about Vyar Grund, and so much more. As a child of a defeated prince, Alsayer didn't have the protection that Rew and Valchon did. The king wanted one of the brothers to continue his macabre reign, while Alsayer was merely an annoyance. If the king caught him, Alsayer's soul would be forfeit.

But while the spellcaster appeared constantly busy with his behind-the-scenes machinations, he also found time to tutor Cinda. Within moments, Rew had seen that, despite the distrust they had for Alsayer, he was the best teacher they could have hoped for. Ambrose had stumbled and felt his way through learning necromancy, sharing his wisdom couched in cautions and uncertain warnings, but Alsayer knew what he was talking about.

When he explained a principle to Cinda, he did it with confidence. When he demonstrated a spell, it worked. But he readily admitted, he didn't have the natural talent of Cinda.

"My skill is a… reflection, you could say, of my ancestors' abilities," explained the man. "My blood father was an invoker, and that's where most of my talent lies, but through our bloodline, we've been influenced by the taint of Vaisius Morden. Each of us, Rew and I, Valchon and the rest, were born before the last Investiture completed. Our fathers were not yet hosts to the king's soul.

He tries to avoid… seepage that way, but talent with high magic is about more than blood. That's merely a mental model we use to understand a more complicated process. We are of the line, and the reflection of necromantic power passes down that line."

"So Rew could have a talent for necromancy as well?" wondered Cinda. "Could he… do what is necessary to defeat the king?"

Alsayer pursed his lips and shook his head. "If Rew ever bothered to study, he still wouldn't have the raw power that you do. Neither Rew nor I are as capable as you."

Rew grunted.

Ignoring the ranger, Alsayer continued, "If he made the effort, Rew would be able to develop his talent into something more than a feeling, which I suspect he denies having even now, but to do more takes a stronger talent than the reflection we have. I couldn't have raised the corpses you sent to me in the courtyard, but I was able to command them. That's the limit of my strength."

"Why me?" questioned Cinda. "I understand it's part of my family's legacy, that I got this ability from my father, but how? If there are no other necromancers of talent within the kingdom, how have my ancestors consolidated this strength in our blood? The rangers… they described it as breeding, like horseflesh, but from what I know of that art… it doesn't make any sense. My mother's talent was even less than that fool Ambrose's."

"Breeding horseflesh is about the blood and only the blood. A foal inherits the nature of its sire and its mother. High magic is deeper." Alsayer was silent for a long moment. Cinda waited patiently. Rew frowned, wanting to accuse the spellcaster of being dramatic, but he sensed Alsayer was wrestling with a truth. "The first time you used your powers, it was to banish the wraiths in Spinesend?"

Cinda nodded.

Alsayer cleared his throat, perhaps thinking about what else happened that day, then continued, "Commanding a wraith, particularly one of that vintage, is exceptionally difficult. I wouldn't even attempt it. In Falvar, I had to cheat, to utilize an enchanted device to capture them, but you, without any training to speak of, banished—what—three of them?"

"Yes…"

"That's the secret of your line. Of the king's line. Your family hasn't lain down with the wraiths of the barrows, that would be odd, but you have been… influenced by them. For centuries, the Fedgleys have watched over that land, and for centuries, it has shaped you even as you shaped it. You, only you, are a product of hundreds of years of exposure to those forgotten shades. To continue the metaphor, it's like a horse of superb breeding that was also given the best food and care. All that you lack is training."

"So the wraiths…"

"Were not men and women as you know them. They're from a time before, a wilder time. They're bound by the laws of ancient magic, not the laws of magic as we know it now. Some arcanists suggest that necromancy itself is an art from that time, which is why it's become so rare these days. It could be that, or it could be Vaisius Morden executes anyone who shows exceptional skill, but I'm confident saying, the king… was one of them. I think Morden stock began there in what we call the barrowlands. At some point, I don't know why, Erasmus, or some Morden before even his time, left. They took the strength of that wild nature, and they married it to the power of man—what we think of ourselves, that is. In the fusion between the two lineages, they found real strength. When their people were defeated, and years later when the Dark Kind rose, they used that strength to gain more power for themselves."

Cinda glanced at Rew.

He looked back but did not respond. He'd never heard anything like this, even in the oldest stories that the rangers shared amongst themselves, but he supposed those stories began with Vaeldon. The time Alsayer spoke of was before, before the kingdom, before there was a king.

"You doubt my tale?" asked Alsayer, peering at Rew.

"I… don't know."

"You could find out, you know, if I speak the truth."

Rew frowned at him.

"Your sword," explained Alsayer. "Erasmus Morden. He's not very trustworthy, given none of our family is, but you're a clever man. You could tease the truth from him if you wanted. You have connected with him, haven't you? For a ranger, it should have been easy."

"Yes, I've… connected with him. But it's dangerous to commune with him," said Rew slowly. "I don't do it, anymore. The shade of Erasmus Morden is not stable. Not sane."

"You can control him, though?"

"Briefly. It grows harder each time."

Alsayer nodded. "He's learning from you, just as you learn from him. It's good you can still maintain control. You will need that, for what is coming. Once again, my theories are proven correct. For years I suspected you were the only one of our line who could hold onto yourself and exert control. You're stubborn, and a ranger. For once, that's a good combination. And you do not seek power like the rest of us. The combination of all of your traits, that is the secret, and what's allowed you to survive our ancestor so far. Erasmus, and the knowledge you received from him, is what started you on this quest, correct? It's what you've learned from him that gives you confidence you can face the king?"

Rew frowned at his cousin and did not respond. The man was like scratchy trousers. Constantly irritating. How did he know so much about the sword, and about Erasmus Morden?

The spellcaster stood and stretched. "We don't have time for these discussions, but I suppose you all should know what we're about. Vaisius Morden, my ancestor as well as yours, Rew, is a relic of an age long since passed. Vaeldon, our entire world, cannot move forward while bound by his anchor. He holds us in the past, in a wilder, more vicious place. It is only with him gone that we may move forward. That is why I do this, so we can sever the final tie, so that we can progress. If we're successful, the world will be better for it."

Rew grunted. "That's the reason you help us? Forgive me, but…"

Alsayer offered Rew a wicked grin. "You have my help, Cousin. No matter how much you distrust me, can you refuse it?"

The ranger scowled at the spellcaster but didn't argue. They needed Alsayer for the information he could provide on Valchon's plans, the mentoring he could give to Cinda, and the insights he could provide when they faced the king. It grated Rew like rough rock on raw skin, but every day proved how useful Alsayer could be to them.

Their plan for Valchon was drawn out, Cinda was learning by leaps and bounds, and questions were building up about what was next. What did Alsayer know of the king? What did he know of the Dark Kind, and how had he communicated with them? Big, important questions, but the spellcaster was adroit at fending them off, claiming there was a time and place for everything, and they ought to worry about the next step before leaping beyond it.

There was some wisdom to that, but for a man who complained so fervently about Rew's lack of plans, Alsayer wasn't making it any easier to plot a course to confront the king and deal with the fraemoth, not to mention the army of Dark Kind it was raising.

With suspicion curdling about what Alsayer's true plans were, but confident they were doing what was necessary, Rew waited impatiently.

THE HUM OF THE CITY GREW WITH EACH PASSING DAY. MORE PEOPLE arrived, nobles and merchants, hangers-on and the desperate. Only the wealthiest could afford lodging within the city, and it wasn't long before the sailors and those from beyond the sea began to trickle back to their ships and out of the port. The ramshackle inns and filthy taverns where those men made their temporary homes were unaffordable now, stuffed full of Vaeldon's own.

Shops, and even the kiosks in the spice market, were turned to temporary housing, still doing business during the day but hosting visitors at night. It became common to see men and women sleeping in the streets, in dark alleys, on the doorsteps of townhouses, and anywhere else they could find without being chased away.

Some of them were residents of Carff who'd rented out their apartments and cottages to high-paying guests. In the mild climate of the coastal town, perhaps they thought the several months wages they could earn sleeping on the street was a fair bargain.

It seemed to Rew that little sleeping was being done, regardless of where folks found to lay their heads. The city was crowded and loud. It thrummed with life and excitement, and while housing was in short supply, wine and ale were not. Valchon must have directed his supply masters to purchase all of the libations in the kingdom, and he'd offered it to the vendors in Carff at discounted prices. Drinks flowed like water and at all hours. The usual clamor of commerce in Carff changed to boisterous, frequently slurred sounds of celebration and singing.

There was a rampant surge of crime as well, though it did not seem that Valchon's soldiers rose to meet it. That only emboldened the thieves. Rew wondered whether Rebecca was influencing the prince, keeping his men tight around the palace so her minions could feast, or whether the spike in thefts and killing had slipped beyond her control. So many strangers, so many people on the streets, meant opportunities abounded for those who were not shackled by moral inhibitions.

It was a boon to Alsayer and Cinda. In the morning hours, before the city workers emerged to clear away the dead, they went scavenging. Raif, despite his clear distaste for what they were doing, accompanied them with a wheelbarrow. Each day, they returned to the manor house with several more corpses hidden beneath a dirty tarp. In the secluded back garden, Cinda practiced under Alsayer's instruction.

It was grim, disturbing work, and it sent the rest of them scattering out into the city on whatever errand they could invent for themselves. Rew loitered near the palace, tending to the seeds he and Zaine had scattered, the thief largely disappeared, and Anne connected with the healers she knew and trusted in the city, gaining whatever information spilled off their tongues.

Carff was thriving and wild, overrun with strangers, most waiting for something they couldn't articulate. Ancient magic tugged at the souls in Carff, though few of them would recognize it.

Rew wondered if Iyre had been like this twenty-five years prior when his father had murdered his brothers and become the heir apparent to Vaeldon's throne. In Mordenhold, such celebrations had been muted. They hadn't known the true nature of the ceremony, but Alsayer and others had lost their fathers in the violent clash to determine the successor. Even Rew and his brothers had little reason to celebrate. Their father had ascended, but that only meant opportunity for one of them. They'd all known, for the rest of them, it meant death. They still had a generation to get there, but the course of their lives had been set.

Set for everyone but Rew. He'd chosen differently. He'd chosen the shadows and then the wilderness. He'd chosen to turn his back on it all. Now, the fanfare around Valchon's fete disturbed him. The prince wasn't being named king, there'd been no word from Mordenhold at all on the matter, but for the nobility, they understood what had been happening. They knew what it meant that the princes had gathered forces, and they knew what it meant that Calb and Heindaw were dead. Rew suspected there were those who believed the tales that had been spread about a fourth brother, a member of the king's rangers, but those who were most likely to support Rew openly would be as far from Carff as they could get.

In Carff, it was the bootlickers and lackeys of Prince Valchon that were crowding the streets, and from the revelry and excitement, it was evident they were prepared to name him king, even if Vaisius Morden had not.

The Investiture was a calling, not a proclamation. It was ancient magic cast upon the kingdom. Instead of criers traveling the roads and reading from a scroll, those with sensitivity, those with the oldest bloodlines, would have felt it. They knew. The ritual had been completed. Rew worried about that, as they waited for the fete, for their opportunity. What did it mean that these people thought Valchon had won? What sort of direction did their belief grant that old, natural magic?

When the day of the fete arrived, he supposed he would find out.

Chapter Twenty-Four

After ten more days in Carff, it was the day of the fete, and already they had problems. The first problem was that of the three remaining simulacra of Valchon in the city, only two were standing where Alsayer had claimed they would be. The second problem was that in addition to the simulacra, there were a dozen spellcasters.

Within the hour, Rew got reports from Zaine that there were dozens more spellcasters scattered throughout the incredible ballroom where the party was located. They lined the walls in clusters of twos and threes, adorned in splendid versions of the standard spellcasters' robes like they'd been set on display.

It wasn't a stretch to guess that every surviving spellcaster in Jabaan and Iyre had come flocking to Carff, groveling on their bellies in front of Valchon, begging to be allowed into his service. They might not be rewarded for their late loyalty, but their only alternative was to hope Rew would kill the prince and ignore whatever atrocities they'd committed on the behalf of his dead brothers. There were a lot of things Rew could say about such men and women, but they weren't fools. They'd figured the odds.

"And the other simulacrum?" asked Rew.

Zaine shrugged.

"He's got to be around here somewhere. Maybe we should look again."

"He could have gone to relieve himself," suggested Raif, adjusting his armor, like perhaps he was considering doing the exact same thing.

Rew scratched his beard. It was possible. Valchon's party would last the entire evening, and even spellcasters created by a dreadful breeding regimen must feel the call of nature.

"Shall we wait?" asked Cinda, her eyes fixed on the glittering cathedral that had risen behind Valchon's palace.

The fete, while considered by some to be a celebration of Valchon's pending coronation, was actually honoring Carff's long history. Much had been done in the city over the last months to beautify it, but the crowning achievement had been a final, massive, glass enclosure that would be used to house and grow exotic plants from all over the world.

It was said it would be the only place in Vaeldon where one could find the highly prized fruits that were imported from across the sea, and of course, all of the kingdom's precious flora would be displayed. Half an attraction for visitors, half a practical way to grow rare herbs and produce, it was a remarkable construction. It'd been raised over the space of weeks through painstaking engineering and backbreaking labor, and supposedly, it'd been infused with magic by Valchon himself to allow the profusion of flora to grow year-round.

Valchon didn't have that kind of magic, but it made Rew grin, thinking there was at least a little bit of truth to the story.

But before the place would be filled with pots of dirt and nestled seeds, it was filled with courtiers. Well over a thousand of them, it appeared through Rew's spyglass. It wasn't every important person in Carff, but it was most of them. They streamed toward the open doors of the hothouse like salmon swimming upriver, and then flooded the floor of the glass building when they entered.

Even from afar, Rew could see several of the spellcasters Zaine had mentioned, along with a veritable army of serving staff. They were adorned in bright white robes, and they seemed to sparkle, reflecting the brilliant lights hung beneath the roof of the massive, glass enclosure.

The walls and top of the place shimmered like a jeweler's display case. Delicate music floated on the air, seeming an accompaniment to the intricate fountains and waterways Valchon's engineers had designed to flow through the hothouse for irrigation and then outside in carefully crafted streams to give the entrance a forest-like appearance.

Even from blocks away they could hear the murmur of excited voices rising and falling like the tide. The grand display of the hothouse, the shimmering lights, the ranks of musicians, the copious spread of food and drink, and the spellcasters, were all just a frame for the main attraction. Valchon sat atop a dais at the far end of the glass hallway. They could see him there, barely, through the spyglass. He was dressed in the black robes of an invoker, but Zaine had reported that around his waist was a woven silver belt with a sapphire the size of her fist clasping it. He carried a scepter capped with a gleaming emerald, and on his head, he wore a diadem that was ringed with thumbnail-sized rubies. The robes reflected his talent as an invoker. The gemstones, along with being ostentatious displays of wealth and power, were nods to the other professions of high magic.

The seat he occupied was a massive, carved wooden monstrosity. No doubt, it'd been built for the occasion, and it was padded with plush, purple cushions. Were those meant to evoke the purple robes of his new spellcasters? Rew scowled, lowering the spyglass and handing it to Raif.

With Valchon sitting on the imposing wooden throne it was blatantly obvious that the hothouse had approximately the same dimensions as the throne room in Mordenhold. It had to be intentional, but such obvious symbolism wasn't Valchon's style. What was the prince playing at?

Raif raised the device to his eye and began muttering to himself. Evidently, he was counting spellcasters.

"I know Alsayer said Valchon would be vulnerable," remarked Zaine, "but he's got an army around him. It's true he may not expect us to attack right now, because it's suicide! There are scores of spellcasters and a hundred times as many soldiers, plus who knows how many more within minutes of here, and that's not to mention the simulacra and Valchon himself. We can't fight all of them."

"Not easily," agreed Rew.

"What if we wait?" asked Anne. "Perhaps when he retires for the night? We could sneak into his bedchamber or at least get near it. Surely with so many soldiers around this hothouse, the rest of the palace is undermanned."

"I can go scout around some more," offered Zaine. "If I can spy the other hunter…"

Rew frowned then nodded. "Be careful, lass."

Wordlessly, the thief disappeared back into the night.

In the distance, thunder rumbled, and Rew glanced across the rooftop, past the harbor, out toward the sea. Flickers of lightning lit a looming cloud bank. It was still several leagues offshore, but it'd been growing closer as the sun ducked below the horizon, and it appeared as it approached it was gaining in power.

Storms on the coast were more common in the autumn, but spring was always blessed with one or two tremendous downpours. It was fortune, thought Rew, that they would get one that night. The clouds would hide the moon and the stars, allowing them to move in the dark. Once it began raining, the sound would obscure the noise of their movement and limit the soldiers' and spellcasters' vision. Beneath the cover of a serious thunderstorm, even Raif could move undetected.

And once the action began, the rain and lightning would only add to the confusion and chaos. They were counting on madness, on being able to use the size of the crowd to their advantage, instead of it providing a protective layer for the prince. If they could disrupt things enough that the courtiers panicked, stampeded even, then they could approach Valchon amidst the throng, and with luck, the prince wouldn't see them until too late.

They'd planned carefully and prepared as best they were able, but first, they had to get through the two simulacra and the dozen spellcasters around them, and they had to worry about the missing simulacrum.

Rew grimaced. For all they knew, the simulacrum could have been sent on a diplomatic mission to Mordenhold, or maybe the thing had eaten bad shellfish. It could be anywhere. King's Sake, it could be dead.

It'd been days since they'd last seen Alsayer. He'd set Cinda with one final task, and since then, the spellcaster had been beside Valchon. He was keeping the prince's eyes turned away, he said, and Rew hoped. At the moment, the ranger sorely missed the other man's intelligence updates. Rew would feel a lot better about all of this if he knew where the third simulacrum was.

Sighing, he glanced back out toward the sea again, judging they had another hour before the storm hit. Enough time the bulk of the courtiers would be inside the huge, glass hothouse. Enough time for their party to get into place.

"I don't like that the third simulacra is missing, and I don't like that we've got extra spellcasters there to contend with, but we've got to take advantage of the storm. It's pure luck it's hitting tonight. Valchon can prepare for what we plan, but he can't prepare for what's outside our ability to control. We won't get another distraction like this if we don't strike tonight."

Frowning, Cinda looked back toward the spellcasters and simulacra guarding the entrance to the huge, glass structure.

"Do you think you can take them?" Raif asked his sister.

"If I can't face two of them, then I won't be able to face three of them later," she replied. "None of us like that the third one is missing, but I think the Ranger is right. When else will we get a chance like this with everyone in the open? When else will we get a distraction like the storm will bring?"

Raif drew a deep breath and then released it slowly.

Rew glanced around, waiting for more objections, but no one spoke. He cracked his neck and said, "All right. Let's go."

HE'D CONSIDERED ACTIVATING HIS LONGSWORD, UNLEASHING THE strength of Erasmus Morden. For a moment, a dozen breaths, the blade would be imbued with incredible power. He could whip through the two simulacra, the dozen spellcasters, and force his ancestor back into his prison. It was tempting, tapping into that well of strength.

Was it his own yearning for an easy solution, the strength to prevail against what he truly believed was evil embodied, or was it Erasmus, lurking in the depths of Rew's soul, hoping to widen the wedge between his steel tomb and the life of the world?

Erasmus was always there, like a shadow. He was quiet, most often, a presence that Rew did not feel, but there were other times the ancient spellcaster weighed on him like a yoke on his shoulders. Rew could feel the unsubtle pull of Erasmus's desires. He could feel the need to unsheathe his longsword, to draw blood. It was worst when Rew wanted that blood as well, and now, like Erasmus, he thirsted for it.

Looking at the two simulacra, he knew that hunger wasn't a benevolent desire to rescue the kingdom from oppression or the honorable intent to free the people of Vaeldon. Had the simulacra been boarding a ship, headed across the sea with assurances they'd never return, Rew would still feel that thirst for violence. It was in his blood. A bred desire to kill those like him? A hatred for the pinnacle of what Vaeldon's inbred nobility could become?

"Fascinating, isn't it?" said Raif.

"What?" asked Rew, shaking himself and cursing at how distracted he'd been.

"All of us are a bit like them, aren't we?" continued the nobleman. "My father and mother didn't marry for love, companionship, or some storybook reason. They married because the arcanists believed their magic would mix well, and they hoped to breed that into me and my sisters. It worked, I suppose, with Cinda, but not me. It's the same thing, isn't it? Valchon just did it better."

"Better…" murmured Rew. "If you want to call it that."

Raif's thoughts echoed his own, and somehow, that made it worse. They could kill the simulacra, but those fiendish creations weren't the end of it. All of the power in Vaeldon rested on the same concept. How much of that would they have to destroy before the kingdom was free of the influence?

Two hundred paces in front of them, the two simulacra sat beneath an oilcloth tent. Around them, a dozen spellcasters loitered, looking out over the dwindling stream of courtiers that trekked into the open doors of the hothouse, into the light- and sound-filled party. Outside, the water features tinkled with delicate drops, occasionally drowned out by the ominous rumbling thunder from the storm boiling in from the sea.

The stragglers to the party were silent, unlike those bright souls who'd arrived first. It was as if they were unsure whether they would be welcomed. Recent refugees from Calb and Heindaw's courts, Rew assumed. They must have professed fealty to Valchon, or they wouldn't be there at all, but when short months ago they'd been working to kill the man, it had to feel a little awkward. They had to wonder if instead of welcoming them, the prince would make an example of them.

How did that make the simulacra feel? Even after the last of the guests arrived, they would be stationed outside in the coming storm, beneath the least elegant structure in sight. Did they infer how Valchon truly felt about his spawn from such treatment? Did they discuss whether they would always be left outside, while their father conducted the business of the kingdom away from them? And Blessed Mother, where was the third one?

"How much longer?" asked Cinda, peering over Rew and her brother toward the approaching storm.

"Quarter hour, no more," responded Rew. "It's moving fast."

"They always do, coming in from the sea," remarked Anne. "Nothing to stand in the way, I suppose."

"You're sure about this?" asked Raif, sitting near his sister.

"I think so."

Zaine slipped out of the darkness and crouched beside them. Whispering, she said, "Alsayer is inside now. He's not as close to the prince as we'd hoped, but no one is. There are two dozen spellcasters surrounding Valchon, a couple score of soldiers, and they're keeping everyone else twenty paces back. Your cousin is wearing the robes with that ridiculous pattern embroidered in silver like he said he would be. All is ready on his end."

"Unless he's betraying us," muttered Rew.

"Do you think he is?"

The ranger shrugged. "Probably, but I think he wants Valchon dead as badly as we do, and he's right when he talks about his fear of the king. Vaisius Morden will take Alsayer's soul, given the chance. The only hope the bastard has is to help us or to flee, and so far, he hasn't been running. Knowing his risk is as great as ours is good enough for me. At least for tonight." He glanced at the storm again. "You'd best hurry."

The thief nodded then stalked back into the dark.

Rew put his hand on Cinda's shoulder. "If you start to lose control…"

"I know. We'll call it off."

"I'd feel better if we'd tested this," grumbled Raif, unconsciously reaching over his shoulder to touch the hilt of his greatsword. "I know we couldn't, but still. You saw—"

"I saw," replied Rew. "I understand. Cinda says she can manage it, though. Trust your sister."

Raif swallowed uncomfortably, and Rew felt his hesitation. Cinda insisted she could do this, but the last time they'd used her powers against one of the princes, a city had nearly been destroyed. The last time they'd seen what she attempted tonight, hundreds had died. There were a million people in Carff. If she lost control…

"You'd better get in place," Cinda told Rew. "I'll wait until the rain starts. When it happens, it's going to happen fast."

"Mother's Blessing on us all," whispered Anne.

She met Rew's gaze, and they held the look for a long moment. Then, the ranger moved away in the opposite direction Zaine had gone. He wanted the blood of the simulacra. He could feel that need reverberating through him, amplified by the remnants of Erasmus Morden. He wanted it, but that wouldn't be his fight.

Not tonight. He had a bigger fish to catch.

THE STORM HIT LIKE A PUNCH TO THE JAW.

A roaring wind ripped through the sails and masts in the harbor, pounded down the streets of Carff, tumbled over stalls and kiosks in the spice market, and blasted its way toward the palace.

Rew's cloak whipped around him, and he was surprised at the unseasonable chill the air brought with it. He clutched the tail of his cloak, pulling it tight so as to not draw the eye, but everyone he could see was glancing up at the blistering crackle of lightning and the powerful gale that blew into them like charging cavalry.

The remaining notaries outside of the hothouse's walls tossed decorum to the howling wind, gathered their dresses or their coats, and rushed forward in a tight mass, forcing their way inside. Most of them made it before a hammering rain caught them, beating its way from the sea to the palace in an unrelenting torrent.

Rew flipped up his hood and cursed, but the truth was, the might of the storm would be to their advantage. They hadn't planned it, but it fit like a glove with what they had thought up.

Through the rolling sheets of water, Rew could see heads tilted up inside of the hothouse, as Valchon's guests looked at the interior of the glass building in awe as the rain scoured the outside. The giant glass enclosure, while made quickly, had been made well. It withstood the rain and the wind and offered shelter to those inside. Elsewhere in the city, Rew imagined the denizens of Carff rushing indoors and slamming their shutters closed. They would hunker down, like during one of the powerful autumn storms, except this one had caught them unawares.

The streets would be turned to rushing streams. The houses in the poor quarters would leak and then flood. The spice market and the shops would empty, and only the taverns would see anything like their normal level of business as patrons found somewhere dry to sit and got something wet to drink. Until the storm passed, Carff would be a different city, a quiet one, but the gaiety inside of Valchon's party wouldn't pause for the rain, no matter how hard it was coming down. The nobles and the merchants inside had shelter. They had a veritable ocean of wine provided by the vintners' guild, and the storm would only heighten the excitement they felt at being in such exclusive circumstances.

Rew sauntered farther down the wall of the hothouse, his cloak tugged tight around him, trying to act like he belonged there. A trusted servant of one of those inside, perhaps, but not quite so trusted he was allowed shelter. Rain dripped from the hood of his cloak and was already soaking through on his shoulders and back. Around him, there were still a handful of people darting across the open, trying to find somewhere to get away from the rain. Rew grinned. The excitement was only beginning.

Several hundred paces away, the ranger saw a light spring to life, and an invoker shone a golden glow on his companions and the two simulacra that had occupied the oilcloth tent outside of the hothouse. Their tent was gone, blown off by the wind, but the men and women were still there, huddling together, looking miserable. A dome formed over their heads, and the group was obscured by a sheen of water as the rain poured down on an invisible barrier and then sloughed away.

The wind seemed to roar with anger, flinging missiles of sting-ing, cold water ahead of it. The chill in the air worked in their favor as well, and even Rew was surprised when he heard a more mournful cry carried on that wind. A presence—felt more than seen—drifted in front of him, unaffected by the fury of the storm. Around the spellcasters, the dome dropped, and the golden glow brightened. Rew couldn't see well through the cascading water, but he saw enough to know they'd sensed what was coming, and then, Cinda's wraith was amongst them.

The screams, if there were any, were lost in the sound of the storm and the hubbub within the hothouse. The spellcasters might be barely visible from within the building, and no one would see the wraith through the cascading water on the glass walls. Amongst the revelry and the storm, Rew doubted they would feel it, either.

Only the two simulacra and the spellcasters were left to face the apparition that had floated into their midst. There was crack of a spell unleashed, a flash of light. There was motion, as if some of Valchon's minions had decided to run.

The second wraith tore into them from behind. The creatures could slice through the spellcasters with ease, but Cinda was directing the wraiths against the simulacra. The spellcasters took advantage and scattered like alley cats before a pack of dogs. The two spawns of Valchon would have to contend alone against the spirits of the grave. They were powerful, ancient things, drawn from the barrowlands that Cinda called home, remaining from a time before Vaeldon. She'd spent the entire week pulling the apparitions closer, bit by bit, until they'd lurked outside of Carff, haunting an abandoned graveyard Cinda had sensed out there. Her father had called to ghosts like these before, but he was dead. Now, only she and the king could control these monsters.

There were ways spellcasters could defend against the wraiths that haunted the forgotten parts of the world, but there were few strong enough to stop two of the apparitions at once. It might be that the simulacra were up to the challenge. Alsayer didn't think they would be, because he didn't believe Valchon had trained them in those types of defenses.

The only significant necromancers in the kingdom had been Cinda's and Valchon's fathers, after all. The prince's bannerman and his king. Briefly, Rew had considered that Valchon believed he would be king soon enough, and then he would be the one with power to call upon the wraiths. He'd mentioned it to Alsayer, and his cousin had given him a twisted smile, and reiterated that Valchon wouldn't have taught the hunters to face a wraith.

But just in case, Zaine had prepared the next step and would lead Valchon's whelps on a merry chase if they survived the wraiths. Rew hoped it wouldn't come to that. Despite the obstacles they'd spent weeks putting into place, Zaine wouldn't last long running from those awful ghosts.

It would work. It had to work.

Cinda hadn't slept in a week. Any break in her control, and the wraiths could have slipped her grip and rampaged. She was exhausted, drawn thin, but it'd begun. Just another moment or two, and the fight would be over. It had to work.

She wouldn't have the strength to banish the ghosts. It'd taken too much out of her to get them to Carff and to keep them from straying after the living souls all around them, but she didn't have to send them back home. That would be Raif's job.

Rew could see the fighter's armored form cautiously approaching the battle between the wraiths and Valchon's minions. He held his enchanted greatsword in front of him, ready to rush in when the battle was done and smite the wraiths with the magic imbued in his blade. If he'd been sent forward, it must mean Cinda felt her part in the attack was working. The simulacra would be getting the worst of it.

There were flashes of light, crackles of energy. It was all muted by the power of the storm. Rew couldn't see the simulacra, and the wraiths were near invisible even on a clear day. The pulses of magical energy seemed to be growing less frequent but frantic.

Spells cast without thought, in panic, cast against a foe they didn't know how to fight and that was already dead.

Rew turned. The younglings were facing incredible danger, manipulating power that was best left alone, but he had work to do. It looked like the plan was underway, so he had to trust them to finish it.

Rolling his shoulders, feeling the water beat down on him, Rew began moving toward the glass walls of the hothouse. It looked magical, the water-streaked glass reflecting the brilliance that shimmered within. The structure was a jewel, a massive, sparkling gemstone of light and wealth and power.

He could barely see the vines and plants that intertwined the struts of the glass building, could hardly make out the giant fronds of verdant flora Valchon's people had placed around the building. Exotic plants, grown from afar, unfamiliar to many in Vaeldon. Or grown from seeds housed within Carff's extensive seed museum. Stored just a few floors below where Rew had slept every night they'd been in the city. Many of those seeds had been planted by him and Zaine when they'd snuck into the palace. They'd been nurtured and encouraged by him for weeks now, drawing in nutrients, waiting.

He reached the exterior of the glass wall and knelt, putting his hands on the muddy soil. Water cascaded off the wall in front of him, splashing into already-deep puddles, spraying him with thick, brown sludge.

From a score of paces away, he heard a shout, barely audible over the crash of the storm and the sounds from within the hothouse. Soldiers, even in the torrential downpour, were on duty. They weren't fast enough, though. The rain made Rew's job easy.

He reached out through the soil and communed with the plants inside. They were simple things, life and little more. They did not think, could not understand commands like an animal might, but all life was open to the world. All life could be connected with, and plants, as any life, strived to live, to thrive, and to grow.

Rew poured encouragement into those shoots and twisting vegetation. They drank deep of the moisture in the soil, filling their stems and trunks with heavy water, infusing the nutrients and sun they'd absorbed and held for weeks, building and climbing, and drawing in more. As the vines swelled, writhing and crawling, they began to wrap around the spars which held up the soaring, glass roof of the hothouse.

Chapter Twenty-Five

S teel and stone splintered with high-pitched squeals and sharp crunches. Vines, lashing and crawling like they were having years of growth in the span of seconds, tore at the supports holding together the largest glass enclosure ever built. In other places, vegetation seemed to burst out from within the spars and supports themselves, splitting them like cordwood, thrusting up from below the supports where Zaine had scattered seeds during the building.

Roots shouldered against structure, shifting the wet soil around them. Writhing tendrils snaked higher, grasping, pulling. Fruits swelled, and pods pregnant with seeds dangled from the vines, hanging from supports that had been designed to hold up the soaring roof and little else. The entire building shuddered as the flourishing growth warred with man's recent construction. And then the glass fell.

All other sound, even that of the rampaging storm, was eclipsed by the shattering of several city blocks' worth of glass followed by the screams and cries of panic and pain as that glass collapsed on top of thousands of revelers.

The guard calling for Rew's attention had reached the ranger's side and placed a hand on his shoulder the moment before.

Rew threw himself down into the mud, covering his head, and the soldier was flung backward by a wall of broken glass that collapsed down and exploded outward. Inside the hothouse, people wailed as they were smashed beneath the falling roof.

Lightning burst above, illuminating the scene in stark white. Broken bodies, water, and blood filled the space in front of Rew. The light reflected on tens of thousands of sharp edges. Hundreds of people stumbled about, clutching at cuts and bleeding heads. Hundreds of others lay down, unmoving or rolling on a carpet of glimmering edges. The bulk of the partygoers would survive, but it would be unlikely any of them would walk away unscathed.

Rew stood and pulled a pair of thick leather gloves from his belt. He tugged them on. Then, he drew his longsword and plunged into the chaos. He shoved past confused people, crimson liquid leaking down their faces and arms. Lighting crackled above, accompanied by deep booms of thunder. Cold wind and billowing heat washed over him as the gale whipped back and forth. People shrieked and cried. Rain fell, washing the blood in a growing river that spilled away from the palace.

A malevolent red glow built from somewhere, making it look as if the entire grounds were afire, but no flame could survive the pounding deluge from the storm above. Rain cast a curtain over everything, and Rew could only see a score or two of paces in front of him between the roaring sheets of water that whipped across the now-open space, pounding on the confused bodies that occupied it.

People appeared from the gloom, lit for an instant by lightning then cast back in the dim red glow. They stumbled and staggered, confused and terrified. Some of them called to him, called to anyone, wondering if the storm knocked down the walls, but he ignored them and fought through the crowd. Beneath his feet, the glass was slick, and Rew struggled to keep his footing as he shoved and punched his way forward.

Atop the palace walls, bells rang in alarm, competing with the cacophony of the thunderclaps. Soldiers would be rushing toward the site, but Rew knew with the chaos they would find, he had time. No one understood what was happening, what had occurred. No one but Valchon and his closest advisors would have any idea of the threat in their midst.

Rew forced a man out of his path and found himself in an open space. An eerie red and orange glow illuminated a field of broken glass. It looked like the ground itself was aflame with liquid fire. Several robed men and women lay unconscious. Others stood. One close to the ranger spun, and from an extended arm, a crackling whip of lightning snapped to life.

Rew ducked and felt the heat on his scalp as the spell ripped overhead. It was the same spell Valchon had cast against Calb's imps, but the spellcaster didn't have the prince's talent. As the whip cracked past Rew, the spellcaster turned awkwardly, trying to avoid entangling himself in his own magical weapon.

Darting at the man's back, Rew thrust with his longsword, stabbing deep into the spellcaster's torso. He kicked the man away and dodged as a bulbous glob of liquid flame wobbled toward him. He slipped and fell to one knee, broken glass crunching beneath him. His left hand, protected by his thick leather gloves, splayed on the shimmering carpet. Rew grabbed a heavy piece of the glass and flung it at the spellcaster who'd attacked him.

The man raised his arms, and the glass smashed into him. He fell back, sprawling, kicking, and clawing on a bed of points and edges. He was doing more to injure himself than Rew had done.

The ranger rose and stalked forward.

An imp, apparently recently summoned and unharmed by the fallen ceiling, charged at him on unsteady feet.

Rew met it, rushing forward, swinging his sword hard and severing the imp's arm at the shoulder. It wheeled backward, and Rew struck again, carving a long trough in its chest. He pressed after, but a heavy fist of sound slammed into the back of the imp, crunching bone.

Hurdling the falling body, Rew raced in between two spellcasters, a sodden conjurer and a blood-stained enchanter. He rammed his longsword into one and dragged his hunting knife across the throat of the other.

There was a tremendous blast, and a hundred streaking orbs of crackling electricity exploded toward him. Rew threw up his arm to cover his eyes, but the orbs smashed into an invisible, humming wall, popping in smaller blasts that mirrored the one which had unleashed them.

"I've got the spellcasters!" cried Alsayer.

The black-robed man thrust with his hand, and a dark cloud speckled with shimmering sparks flew toward a green-robed enchanter who, unfortunately for him, was horribly outmatched. The enchanter's body seemed to dissolve from Alsayer's attack, blood and flesh hurtling backward in long, sticky streamers.

There was another explosion of electrical charge, and again, it burst and fizzled on an invisible barrier in front of Rew. Alsayer was shouting, but over the raging storm and the blasts of high magic the spellcasters were directing at his cousin, Rew couldn't hear what the other man was saying. He thought it might be something like, "Hurry."

Rew ran toward Valchon.

The prince stood from his heavy, wooden throne. He lifted his hands, and a glowing sword and shield sprang alight. They crackled with energy and appeared to be made of solid lightning. Rew came close, and Valchon leapt at him, moving with the speed of a striking snake.

Cursing, trying to stop but skidding on the carpet of broken glass, Rew swung up with his sword, deflecting Valchon's blow and then raising his arm to absorb a strike from the shield on his leather bracer.

A charge surged through Rew's body like a hundred years of static had been built up on a woolen jacket. It jolted him, and he stumbled back.

Valchon pressed, his sword streaking at Rew, and when the ranger dodged or deflected, the prince struck with his shield.

Each blow came with a blistering electrical charge and carried the force of a runaway wagon. By the third clash of the prince's magical blade and the ranger's enchanted one, Rew's arm was numb, and he could see his skin blistering in the angry red glow that suffused the scene.

Valchon was faster and stronger than Rew had anticipated he would be. His brother moved like a stalking cat. He used familiar moves, attacks Rew had seen a hundred times before, but he did them at twice the speed and with three times the force that Rew recalled from when they were youths. Valchon hadn't been injured by the falling glass like so many others. He'd been waiting, realized Rew, anticipating this fight.

The lightning shield swung at his head, and Rew bashed it aside with his longsword, the enchanted steel protecting him from the shock it would give if he had blocked any other way. Valchon's sword, snapping like a scorpion's tail and moving faster than Rew could see, gouged a cut beneath his eye. A finger higher, and the ranger would never see again. The charge from the sword was like getting punched in the face by a huge man.

Rew slipped and dropped into a roll across the piercing pieces of glass. Valchon's shield swung overhead, and the prince kicked at him with a boot. Rew caught the prince's foot and stood abruptly, flinging Valchon backward to land heavily on the dais.

The prince swung his feet, nearly striking Rew, then flipped himself back upright.

Rew stared at him, mouth agape. King's Sake, the prince was fighting like…

Growling, Rew stepped back, dragging his foot. Then, with his toe, he flung the pile of broken glass he'd just made toward the face of his opponent. Some bounced off the shield. Others struck Valchon's chest and face. The prince wiped his forearm across his cheek, smearing blood and theatrical paint.

Valchon had used the same tricks that Rew had sneaking into the palace, except this wasn't Valchon. It was the third simulacra.

In the pounding rain and sourceless red light, fighting for his life, Rew hadn't been able to tell.

The younger version of his brother laughed, its voice high and manic. "Expecting someone else?"

Blood smeared its lips where the broken glass had cut it, and its eyes gleamed crimson, reflecting the diffuse glow that surrounded them.

Cursing loudly, Rew looked over his shoulder.

It was as if a giant torch lit a scene of utter madness. Behind him, thousands of people, soaking wet, lacerated and bleeding from standing beneath a rain of shattered glass, scrambled and screamed. Spells blasted back and forth then stopped.

The simulacrum took a step closer. It was... it was lit. In the midst of the lashing storm, Rew could see it easily now that he knew what he was looking at.

Shaking his head, confused, Rew reacted on instinct as the lightning sword struck at him again. He fell back, avoiding the counterstrike from the shield.

There was light to see.

Lightning crackled, and thunder rumbled overhead. Bitter cold and scalding air swirled in bands across the remains of the ruined hothouse. Rew spared a glance up, and through the shifting shroud of rain, he saw burning streaks striating the clouds, like coals smoldering beneath a layer of ash. The sky was on fire.

The lightning sword whistled toward him, and Rew scrambled away, taking a glancing cut on his left arm. The limb went numb.

"Alsayer!" he bellowed.

There was no response. Explosions, muffled by the rain, thumped in sonorous bursts. Lightning crackled, but Rew couldn't see if it was cast by man, or from the sky.

The blazing shield of light swung forward.

Rew dropped his longsword and grabbed it. He spasmed, his fingers clenching involuntarily. His hunting knife felt slick in his other hand. Chopping his knife against the simulacrum's lightning sword, he battered it away. He tore the shield to the side and launched himself at his enemy.

Rew smashed his forehead on the nose of the simulacrum.

The ranger's fingers and palm were blistering, his flesh burning from the heat of the simulacrum's shield. Jagged surges of electrical energy pulsated down his arm. He gritted his teeth, steeling himself against the wracking pain. He smashed his head again against the younger version of Valchon.

He stepped closer and worked his elbow behind the lightning shield. Then, he punched the smug face in front of him, raining blows with his bare fist against the nose, lips, and eyes of Valchon. It was like they were boys, scuffling over the pretty smile of a beautiful girl none of them would be allowed to speak to, but Rew had grown since then, and he hit a lot harder.

Hammering his fist in the simulacrum's face, he beat the thing and absorbed its counter blows as it bashed its lightning shield against his side. The spawn of Valchon, retreating under the attack, slipped, and Rew pressed, knocking the thing onto its back.

He jumped astride it, unable to get room to stab it but whaling on it with a fist curled around the bone hilt of his knife. The lightning sword flickered out, and Rew slapped the shield aside again. He reared up and saw the terrified look of a young man staring back at him.

He brought the bone hilt of his knife down, smashing the butt of the weapon square on the forehead of the simulacrum. He heard bone crunch as the skull was broken. He struck it again and again to be sure. Then, he stood, taking heaving, ragged breaths, his body trembling from the electrical current that had jolted through it. Blood dripped down his face and from his arm. His knees and forearms were covered in dozens of shallow cuts from the broken glass beneath his feet.

He gathered his longsword and turned, raising his arm and trying to block the falling rain. He looked to the sky where sizzling heat was melting away the cold that had come earlier.

Lightning blasted through the clouds, but the light that was cast down was the burning red of a forge. The sky was on fire.

"King's Sake."

Valchon had called a maelstrom over Carff.

Anne and the younglings stumbled out of the dazed, injured press of nobles and took Rew's side, but they didn't look at the ranger. They looked past him to where Prince Valchon stood, holding a steel collar, inscribed with glowing cerulean insets, locked around Alsayer's neck.

"You didn't," croaked Rew. "Tell me you didn't unleash a maelstrom against your own city. Against your own people."

Valchon grinned.

All around them, from the horde of revelers, men began to emerge. They cast aside cloaks and fine jackets, revealing breast-plates of copper and chainmail shirts. They raised swords and began to form a circle around Rew and his companions.

Most of the men were injured, some severely. Valchon had scarified hundreds of his soldiers, knowing they would be in harm's way. Thousands of his... Rew looked up at the sky again. The churning clouds stretched for leagues in all directions. Valchon was sacrificing Carff. All of it. His own people. His most loyal supplicants. The city he'd ruled for a decade and a half. He'd used all of it as bait.

"I had to see your face," snarled the prince, and behind him, a blazing twist of purple and gold formed a vortex and opened into a portal.

There was a keening whistle, and down from the sky came a giant meteor. It burst a dozen blocks from the palace, but even at that distance, Rew could feel the ground shudder beneath his feet from the impact, and heat washed over him.

Cinda gasped beside him. Rew knew it was because she felt a surging wave of departing souls from where the burning missile had fallen.

Valchon shook the collar around Alsayer's neck, and the spell-caster coughed and choked.

"Both of you here to witness my power, to feel it. I couldn't have planned this any better," crowed Valchon. His teeth flashed as another ragged bolt of lightning crackled overhead. "You should have stayed in the wilderness where you belong, Brother. You never should have trusted our cousin, either. He betrayed you, and as his reward, he'll stay with you. He's the last invoker left alive within a hundred leagues of here. The only person other than myself with the ability to open a portal. It's too bad I've dampened his magic. It's too bad only my magic can open this collar."

"Forgive me, Rew," rasped Alsayer, his hands clutching helplessly at the collar around his neck. "I had to tell him. I'm not your enemy, but I had to tell him you were coming. I thought I'd fight by your side, that I could help you, give you answers after, but—"

Valchon yanked the collar again, cutting off Alsayer's words.

Rew scowled at the pair and raised his longsword.

"Erasmus cast the first maelstrom," cried Alsayer, forcing the words from his bruised throat. "He'll know how to—"

Valchon's eyes flashed, and the collar blazed with light. Blood spurted, shooting around the ring of steel and splashing down like a bucket of it had been turned over. Alsayer's black robes were drenched with his blood, and then Valchon yanked the collar through the spellcaster's neck. Alsayer's body fell one direction, his head fell in another.

"Blessed Mother, I've wanted to do that for a long time," drawled Valchon, shaking his arms out to his side and flinging Alsayer's blood from the dripping collar. "It would have been fun imagining the two of you clutching at each other before you burned, but I can't risk that bastard saying whatever he was going to say. Apologies, Brother. You're going to die alone."

Rew stared in horror at the body of Alsayer.

"This is your doing," chided Valchon. "None of this would have happened if you'd stayed out of it. Die knowing all of these people would have lived had you kept in the wilderness."

Valchon took a step backward, and suddenly, a virulent streak of white and green light flashed toward him. The prince raised his arm and used the collar like a shield. The collar seemed to absorb Cinda's attack, the cerulean crystals flaring with each blast of her magic. She struck again and again, and Valchon was sent staggering backward. The collar shattered in his hand, and slivers of broken steel cascaded down.

"A nice attempt!" he cackled, the air shimmering in front of him as he raised a defensive spell. "You are feasting, I can see it. You'll be stronger than I, soon, but I know you can't open a portal. Your moment of greatest power will be your own death. Wallow in the filth of your impure talent, Necromancer."

Another meteor came screaming down from above, landing somewhere near the docks, sending a billowing inferno roaring into the air. Valchon stepped back again, moving through his portal, and the vortex winked out. In the space of a breath, he was gone.

Cinda screamed in rage, her funeral fire burning impotently around her hands.

A third meteor smashed into the city, hitting the opposite side of the palace. They could feel the scalding heat of it and the tremor in the earth as it landed. Debris and dust rose through the torrent of rain, pattering them with wet ash and pebble-sized bits of broken stone.

"Rew!" barked Anne. "What are we going to do? We can't... It'll take us an hour to get outside the city, if we can even make it through the—Blessed Mother, the crowd. What of everyone else? What of... everyone!"

The empath spun, looking at the gaggle of injured nobles and soldiers around them and then at the buildings of the city beyond. A million people were in Carff, and beneath the sound of the falling meteors, the wind and the rain, the raging fire above, they could hear them screaming.

Rew clasped his longsword. He looked down it and felt the darkness within. With both hands on the hilt, he fell to his knees. He drew a deep breath then ripped opened the prison of steel. He was filled with the soul of Erasmus Morden. Power and hate coursed through him in equal measure, a flood of fire and rancor. The rage burned, a counter to the storm above.

Rew allowed Erasmus to flow into him. He didn't fight his ancestor. Instead, he absorbed him. The soul of that ancient spell-caster clawed at his own, eager, greedy. Alsayer said Erasmus had cast the first maelstrom. Erasmus had to know the nature of the spell. He had to know a way to stop it. He had to.

Hate. Raw, utter hate. It fueled Erasmus. It fueled his magic. It had fueled Valchon as well. It echoed in Rew's blood, and like the lightning above had struck him, he understood the vitriol he felt toward his family. The anger every one of them felt toward each other. It was part of their legacy, passed down for hundreds of years, bred and distilled as effectively as their magic.

The spirit of Erasmus felt the torrent of power above them, and it rejoiced. That anger, that spite, once released into the world couldn't be stopped. It couldn't be fixed. The maelstrom was the physical manifestation of the ancient magician's unquenchable anger. The maelstrom was the legacy of Erasmus, his child. And the child was always stronger than the parent.

The storm was unquenchable, unstoppable, and hollow.

There was nothing to the ghost of Rew's ancestor except rage. His spirit, lingering within his steel tomb, had been sifted into nothing but vicious anger. Rew could feel the old man's soul gnashing at his own, but any compassion the spellcaster once had, any empathy, his humanity, had been worn away by his long confinement. He was hollow.

The shade did not want to stop the maelstrom, it wanted it to burn. It wanted all of Carff to burn. All of Vaeldon. It didn't care that its host, Rew, would burn along with it.

Suddenly, like he was plunging into an icy lake, it struck Rew. Erasmus didn't seek power or a return to the world. He sought release, not from his prison, but from existence, and as he left, he wanted to take as many souls with him as he could. That anger could not be salved. There was no succor which Erasmus sought, no fix to the maelstrom swirling above.

Once the storm began, it could not be stopped. The spell could not be broken, but maybe it could be turned. Rew had no talent for high magic, but Erasmus did. Rage, once released, could not be sated, but could it be balanced? There was a connection in all. Everything was a part of the whole.

Rew clawed back at his ancestor. As Erasmus scoured Rew's soul, the ranger ransacked his ancestor's memories. Balance. He had to fill the hollow of the specter's need. He had to connect the power of the storm to the greater world.

"Anne," said Rew, his teeth gritted, his arms already trembling with the strain of keeping the sword steady to prevent it from jerking and plunging between his ribs, to prevent Erasmus from commanding his body and turning that blade on his friends, on those beyond them, bathing himself in blood until a falling meteor finally found him and ended it. Rew gasped, "I can't... alone..."

The empath knelt beside him and put her arm over his shoulder, her other hand grasping his forearm. She began to mumble prayers to the Blessed Mother beneath her breath. Rew felt the tension in her arms. She knew what he'd done. She knew what was happening. She felt it. She trembled. She was terrified. But she prayed.

A fourth meteor hurtled from the maelstrom and exploded with a concussive blast that stirred Anne's hair, the wet strands brushing against Rew's face with the force of the detonation.

Anne was crying beside him. He was crying as well.

The rage of Erasmus Morden clawed at their souls, demanding they feel his hate, demanding they join him in rending the world around them. The inferno burning the sky above and the fire in Rew's soul mirrored each other. He felt like he was being scorched from within. Erasmus pulled at Rew's natural, undeveloped talent.

The spirit grasped that strength and flung it into the storm. Erasmus was expanding the maelstrom, building it, forming a towering, impossible mass of weather. It would destroy Carff and more. Against his will, Rew felt his strength pouring into that inferno, stoking it hotter, bigger.

The ranger felt a soaring singing within his blood. His talent. His magic. Erasmus was calling upon it, drawing on the latent power like Rew never had. The ranger had never felt anything like it. The old magician was feeding fuel into the fire, swirling the maelstrom larger and larger to the point it would sprawl out from Carff, careening across the Eastern Province and perhaps beyond. The momentum of the storm was immense, like a giant vortex, drawing heat and wind from one hundred leagues around, reaching for more.

Rew felt Erasmus's intent. He knew what the old man was doing. He knew how he was doing it. They were together, within Rew's body.

The ranger reached out with his thoughts and he gathered himself around Erasmus, bending his ancestor to his will. Erasmus fought him, and Rew fought back. Rew's power surged. Unlocked by the ancient spellcaster, it tore through him. Like Erasmus had dug his claws into Rew, the ranger scrabbled at Erasmus. He wrestled the old man for control of his body, for control of their surging magical talent.

Anne felt the struggle, and she quaked in agony, but she was there because he needed her. She stayed. She was there.

Rew felt hot tears running down his cheeks as he battled with Erasmus, striving not to lose himself in the ancient spellcaster's thirst for revenge. He fought, using the only thing he had, the only counter to Erasmus's hate, and Anne felt it.

"Love," she whispered. "Rew, I am with you. Feel it. Can you feel it? Love is the answer to—to him. To what he is."

Rew felt it. It was like Erasmus had been struck.

The ranger leapt on the moment. He surged to his feet, pointing the tip of his longsword skyward, toward the back of the boiling maelstrom. He shoved with everything he had, all of his love: for Anne, the younglings, Ang, Vurcell, Tate, Blythe, and the others. For the wilderness, for Vaeldon. Rew released it all, everything he was feeling, had ever felt.

Like Erasmus had shown him, he poured those feelings into the sky, fed them into the storm. Ancient magic. Natural magic. Rew acted on instinct. He channeled the strength of his talent and that of Erasmus, along the blade of the longsword and toward the raging inferno above them.

Erasmus, his spirit thrust from the force of Rew's power, clawed at the ranger's soul, scrabbling for purchase, but there was nothing for him there. There was no hate or anger to latch onto. There was love. Only love. They were opposites. They no longer shared ties. Rew had turned his back on his family, but he had another, and they had him. There was no longer anything of Erasmus in Rew. The hate of the Mordens was gone. Erasmus was empty, but Rew was full.

The ranger pointed his longsword at the center of the swirling maelstrom. He unleashed the power, letting it flow from him, along the blade, and skyward. Erasmus flowed with it, calling to the maelstrom that hundreds of years prior his anger had spawned. It was there. In the heart of that storm, his legacy echoed. Like a knife, the soul of Erasmus rode the well of power directly into the heart of his creation.

It was release, relief, and with a terrific crash of thunder, the power in the center of the storm swelled and tore it apart, as hate always does. The clouds above began to collapse, sundering away from the force of Erasmus joining the power above. Hot wind blew directly upward as the rush of the movement drew the air from the city, pulled in the wake of the ancient spellcaster's passage, driving the two pieces of the spell-cast storm farther away.

The force of Erasmus's arrival had split the storm in twain.

Thunder, lightning, and rain rolled off from Carff, lashing the coast with twin storms that would be remembered for half a century, but the maelstrom was broken, shattered by the inclusion of Erasmus Morden's rage. The old man had been turned against his own spell, the physical manifestation of his hatred. He'd destroyed what he wrought. That was his legacy, the legacy of all Mordens. He'd split the storm beneath the weight of his anger, and it'd shattered what remained of him and the spell.

Like a loaf of bread being torn apart, the storm ripped open, revealing the dark night sky and the sparkling stars above it. Jagged bolts of lightning and screeching meteors fell, like nightmare soldiers marching away from Carff.

The howl of the wind began to fade, and the groan of the injured rose behind them. In the city, bells rang, alerting the citizenry of the conflagration at the palace, or of the fires that would be raging where the meteors had fallen, or simply out of panic as the bell ringers called, seeking to draw others into the madness that they had felt and seen.

The twin storms roared but rolled away. In the gap over Carff, the sky was black, and the rain slowed to a gentle patter, and then nothing. Cold air blew in a steady whistle, replacing the heat that had been drawn into the storm.

Rew stood, shivering, his longsword held trembling in his hand. Finally, he lowered the blade to rest the point on the broken glass at his feet. Anne rose beside him.

"W-What just happened?" stammered Zaine from a dozen paces away.

"We lost Valchon. It was all for nothing," rasped Cinda, staring up at the rumbling, lightning-streaked twin storm fronts that peeled away from the city, thundering in opposite directions down the coast. Her eyes burned green. The stench of power around her was almost palpable, but Valchon had been right. She couldn't open a portal. She couldn't chase him. Her power was wasted.

"He... he..." stammered Raif. The big fighter spun, looking wide-eyed at the soldiers around them, but those men had no interest in the party. They were looking at the vanishing storms above or the angry red flames and rising towers of soot from where the meteors had landed in the city, where their families and friends might have lived. Perhaps unconsciously echoing Zaine, Raif asked, "What just happened?"

"He could be in Mordenhold right now, petitioning the king," lamented Cinda. Her voice was bitter, resigned. "It might be over, already. We've lost before we started. Surprise was the only advantage we had. Now, instead of us stalking him, he'll stalk us. We're the prey. We saw today there's nothing we can do to fight him, but what does it matter? We don't even know where he is, and the king... the king will have felt this, Ranger. He'll already know what occurred here today. Even if Valchon isn't in Mordenhold telling him, the king will know. This many deaths... There is no hiding, now. Blessed Mother, he could be coming. We could—It's over. I'm not ready to face him. Not here, not now. It's over."

Rew wiped the water from his face and looked around the wreckage of the hothouse. If the king knew...

But he wasn't there. He hadn't portaled into Carff the moment he had felt the surge of departing souls. He hadn't come. Rew didn't know why, but he knew they had time. A little. Enough.

"There's one person who may be able to tell us where Valchon went. He betrayed us, and he knew what it'd cost him. He thought... I don't know what he hoped to gain, but he knew what would happen. He—We have to try. He's the only one who might know where Valchon fled."

Cinda looked at the ranger, not understanding.

"Alsayer."

"But he's..."

"Dead," cried Raif. "Alsayer is dead. I thought I'd be happy, but we needed him. Now, he's—"

Cinda spun and staggered forward, falling to her knees beside the spellcaster's body then turning and scooping up the man's severed head. She sat it on his chest and held it between her hands. Her body went rigid. For a long time, nothing happened. Then, Alsayer's body twitched, and he rolled back and forth, like an old man trying to find a comfortable position on a hard pallet.

His hands rose and then fell. Blood leaked from his ruined neck, joining the pool around him.

"Alsayer," demanded the necromancer. "Where is Valchon?"

The body stilled, but the head did not speak. Could it speak? Cinda had tried to capture the soul of the simulacrum they'd taken prisoner, and she'd failed. Could she perform the spell on Alsayer, or had she simply animated him? If she did call him back as the king could do, the man's head was severed. Even if his spirit was returned to his body, he wasn't going to be able to talk.

"Where is Valchon?" repeated Cinda, tilting the head so its face was looking at her.

Rew stepped closer, peering down at the head over her shoulder. Its eyes blinked sickeningly.

Cinda stared hard at the prone form. Then, she violently shook the head. "Where is he?"

The corpse's arms flopped, and Rew gasped. It was pointing a finger at him. Then, it moved and tapped its own chest.

"What does that mean?" demanded Cinda.

Rew frowned. He, Alsayer... What could his cousin mean? The two of them... The corpse's hand moved again, and it was pointing to the empty space where Valchon had vanished into his portal.

"We follow... No. The three of us... The creche! He's gone to the creche, but not Mordenhold. No, his own creche, where Valchon was raising his whelps, but where is that?"

The body fumbled at its belt, clumsy fingers unable to open the neck of a pouch tied there.

Zaine reached forward, eying the blinking head distastefully, and filched the pouch off Alsayer's side. The dead spellcaster stilled. Its eyes were closed now, and its arms did not move, but it was there, still. It wanted to be there. Alsayer's spirit wasn't fighting Cinda's hold, like the simulacrum had. It lingered.

The thief opened the pouch and shook out a tarnished ring. She frowned at it and showed it to the others. "Does this mean anything?"

Alsayer's body thrashed. Its jaw opened and closed, startling Cinda, who dropped the head. No sound came from its open mouth. Cinda bent over it, her hands trembling.

"I don't know how to make it speak. I don't know if it can. It's… damaged. I think, maybe…" murmured Cinda. She grasped the head again, ignoring the blood that stained her fingers, and leaned close to it. She sat, bent over the body of Alsayer for a long time, and then suddenly straightened. "I lost him. He… he slipped to the beyond. I—Was it enough? Did we get enough?"

"It was enough," said Rew, taking the ring from Zaine and studying it. "That emblem on the ring is familiar. It's from Havmark, I think. It's a fortress thirty leagues east of here. Sits at the mouth of the Laxton river. It was destroyed fifty years ago in the war against the Dark Kind."

"An old, abandoned fortress," remarked Raif, staring at Alsayer's body in disgust. "Sounds like a good place to raise an army of evil simulacra, I guess. It, ah, is it bad if I still want to kick that man's head down to the harbor? I know he helped us, but…"

"We don't have time for that," declared Rew. "We can be in Havmark in two days, if we hurry."

"One if we get horses," interjected Zaine.

"Come on," said Rew. He stood, preparing to leave, but then he paused and looked around. "There's one more person we should find."

Chapter Twenty-Six

Havmark sat on a narrow spit of land that thrust out toward the sea, bound by the mouth of the Laxton river on one side and the crashing waves of the ocean on the other. In years past, it'd been an important port, though one that was always overshadowed by nearby Carff. The river was a convenient outlet, though, for cities and towns along its path, which originated near Spinesend. There'd been enough commerce to support a vibrant economy, and at one point, someone had paid for a sturdy fortress, which stood on the tip of the promontory. It offered defense against pirates and served as a convenient place to light a massive fire atop the tallest tower to warn incoming ships of the rocky shore below.

The fortress had withstood the ravages of wind and weather for years, which was more than it had done when the Dark Kind had swarmed over the city at its feet. Of that city now, there was almost nothing left, just lumps where stone buildings once stood and twisting paths that could not have been natural. Eventually, there would be a day when no one remembered what had happened when the narjags had rampaged through the settlement, but fifty years was not long enough to be done with the ghosts that haunted those ruins, so the fortress and town remained empty, though evidently not as empty as Rew had believed.

They stalked closer under the cover of night, using the ruined buildings of the town to hide their approach. Rew and Zaine moved amongst the tumbled structures like ghosts, Anne and Cinda following in their wake, quiet enough that their footfalls were covered by the crash of waves far below and the wind that cried endlessly over the thick tongue of rock. Raif clanked behind, and had they been stalking toward a properly guarded fortress, Rew would have been nervous about the clamor the young fighter made.

But Havmark wasn't properly guarded, and despite the fact they must have known Rew would come, the people there weren't ready. What spellcasters and talents Valchon had, he'd used in Carff. Many of them had died there, and those who hadn't had been wounded. The prince had gambled everything that he'd catch Rew and the others in his maelstrom.

In the aftermath of the confrontation, Rew and the others had left Carff quickly but not before reconnoitering the grounds of the battle. They'd found dozens of dead spellcasters, easily identifiable by their robes. Only a few spellcasters had survived, conjurers and enchanters, all. Valchon truly had made certain there was no one left who could have opened a portal. Several companies of soldiers were in the area, and as a group, they'd fared slightly better than the spellcasters. Rew guessed they'd been smart enough to stay back when the spells had started flying.

Rew had worried the soldiers would still give them trouble, but a gruff captain of the men in the hothouse had told his soldiers to stand down. He'd quietly thanked Rew before advising him it would probably be best if the ranger left quickly. The captain understood what had happened, and in the moment, he was grateful enough he'd allow them to leave, but other soldiers who hadn't witnessed the confrontation and hadn't seen what Valchon intended might not be so generous.

Leaving quickly was good advice. Valchon's hold on the city had been shaken tremendously by the events that night, but some would remain loyal. Power impressed, and there wasn't anything more impressive than a fully formed maelstrom. Even when it'd been called down upon them and even as the rumors spread it was Rew who'd stopped it, some of Valchon's minions would still believe it was always best to attach oneself to the man who could destroy an entire city with a thought.

The survivors sorting themselves out would take time. The nobles and merchants who were wealthy enough to command soldiers had been decimated by the falling glass, the collateral damage caused by the spells that had been flung, and the carnage that the maelstrom had caused. Those who had survived unharmed would be distracted for weeks trying to salvage the power and wealth of their less fortunate peers. Carff was going to be a bloodbath, which was unfortunate for those there, but it suited Rew's purposes.

There were still some centers of power within the city, and Rew had set out to find them. He was surprised when they finally located the remains of Rebecca, Valchon's spymaster and the head of the thieves' guild. She was dead. A heavy piece of glass had fallen from above, slicing deep into her neck. Beside her was the nondescript man Rew had once seen playing Kings and Queens against the prince.

The ranger's hand dropped to his longsword, but the man stood and shook his head, raising a hand to stay Rew's attack. "She was my daughter. Did you know?"

"I didn't."

"I was injured several years ago," continued the man, looking down at the dead woman but speaking to Rew. "I recovered, but I had a limp that's never left me. Slowed me enough I didn't feel I could protect the prince's flank. He didn't think I could, either. My daughter took my place. I knew—We both knew what kind of man he was, but the world is full of such men, and I'd always believed it was best to be at their side, rather than being a victim of their capricious whims." The man gave a short, bitter laugh. "But we're all victims tonight, aren't we?"

Rew didn't know what to say, so he simply responded, "I'm sorry for your loss."

"You're not," challenged the man, but then he knelt, and he unfastened the woman's belt. "Maybe the rest of these people don't realize, but I know what you did. Valchon cast the maelstrom, but you're the one who brought the roof down on us and killed my daughter. You and your brother—yes, I know exactly who you are, Rew Morden—are responsible for much suffering. All of Vaeldon squirms beneath your boots. I suppose you think it means something you act guilty. Pfah, maybe it does. I don't know. Your brother wouldn't have expressed remorse. Your father… He raised you, and you are his son. I blame you for Rebecca's death, but Valchon almost destroyed this entire city, with us inside it, just to get at you. Had she not been killed by your glass, my daughter was going to die tonight anyway. I would have died as well. What to make of that?"

"I… don't know."

"Aye, neither do I."

The man removed his daughter's belt, her two poignards tucked securely into sheaths hanging from it, and stood back up. He looked over the party. He spied Zaine, standing a pace behind Rew, and he tossed her the belt. The silver hilts of the spymaster's weapons swung as Zaine caught it.

"Those stickers will make you a terror if you use them properly," murmured the man. "They carry a cost, though. It all does, doesn't it? There's always a cost. Someone always has to pay."

"You have another daughter? A son?"

"A granddaughter."

"I know you don't think I mean it, but I hope for a better world for her. I'm trying, but it's not been an easy path to get there, so far."

The man shrugged. "You are a Morden. You can't change that."

"I can try."

The man looked at Rew. "Do me a favor, will you? This time, just this one, make sure the prince pays. It can't always be on the rest of us. This time... I want him to pay."

"We'll do what we can," assured Rew. He hesitated then asked, "I understand he's at Havmark?"

The other man shrugged. "He didn't share his plans with me, obviously. I... Blessed Mother, I hope I wouldn't have agreed to this, had I known. Havmark. It could be where he fled. That makes sense."

"What can you tell us of the place?"

"Not much. I've never been. I do know the prince lost most of his strength tonight. All of his spellcasters were here and his most loyal soldiers. My daughter and I... Evidence enough, isn't it, that we aren't what he cared about? A warning, Ranger. He is weakened but not weak. Don't let him see you coming. Kill everything you find at that place."

It was unlikely that Valchon himself was going to be on guard, and Rew believed the prince's former spymaster that all of the spellcasters had been in Carff and were either dead or unable to portal to Havmark, but that didn't mean Valchon would have no protections.

They slunk closer with the expectation they would see someone on guard, that there would be some defense against intrusion, so it was no surprise when they saw a dark form standing atop a fallen piece of the fortress wall. The shape was silhouetted by the low light of the moon and the stars, falling from above and reflected off the sea on the other side of the ruins.

Rew paused the others and frowned at the shape. There were no lights, which might have made sense to not give away a guard, but that person had to be guarding something. If there was a settlement there, it was dark. Abandoned.

"They look short, don't they?" whispered Zaine.

Rew rubbed a hand over his head. She was right. He watched as the figure moved, as if shifting their feet and trying to stay awake.

"A woman?" wondered the thief.

"A child," responded Rew.

"King's Sake…" murmured Raif from behind them. "You don't think… Pfah, it has to be. More of his simulacra. A young one."

Rew nodded and did not respond. Kill everything that you find, the former spymaster had said.

Cinda, her voice barely audible, said, "This was his creche, where he raised the simulacra. It appears he wasn't done. There are more of them, younger ones. We've got to kill that thing, Ranger."

"We're not going to do that," chastised Raif, glancing at his sister.

"They're hunters," replied Cinda. "Just like the others."

"Look at how big it is. That's a child of ten winters, maybe less. It's not a hunter. We're not going to kill children."

Cinda shrugged. "That thing drains the soul from its victims, Raif. It's not a child. It's an abomination."

"What do we do, then?" asked Zaine. "If that was a normal boy up there, I think the ranger and I could slip by unnoticed with little difficulty, but these things hear like bats, and it's dark. Do you think they can see in the dark?"

"Better than we can," guessed Rew.

Zaine grunted. "Take 'em quick, then. Strike before they see us."

"We're not going to kill children," insisted Raif.

"I meant we bonk 'em on the head," claimed Zaine, "but we do it quick. And hard."

"Bonk them, that's all?"

The thief shrugged.

"We have to do something about these things," challenged Cinda. "We can't leave them."

"We can for now," said Rew. He took off his pack and laid it down then checked his weapons. "You all wait here. I'm going to find Valchon."

"You're going to strangle him with some plants or something?" questioned Raif. He patted his greatsword. "Against Valchon, you're going to need us. That thing up there might be a child, but we are not. We work as a team, Ranger."

"Not tonight. I'll have an easier time of it going alone, unless you want to take off your armor," replied Rew. He drew his longsword, running a hand along the flat of the blade. It felt... different. More comfortable in his grip. It was his sword, now, no longer the tomb of Erasmus Morden. It wouldn't have the ancient spellcaster's power, but it was still crafted by an enchanter, still a fine blade. He hoped that would be enough.

"You're sure about this?" questioned Zaine. "I could go with you, at least. This isn't the forest. It isn't your kind of place."

"No, it's not the forest, but the forest wasn't always my home."

LIGHT SPILLED INTO THE ROOM, CASTING WIDE SHARDS OF PALE SILVER across the dark floor. Outside, the celestial glow lit the world with a magical aura. Inside, it barely pierced the black at the heart of the fortress. All around, tumbled walls and shattered stone gave hints as to what the place had once been, but now, it was nothing more than ruins.

When he'd stalked through the grounds of the abandoned fortress, Rew had seen signs of the current residents, and he'd spied a dozen boys on guard. The ones he saw could have ranged between six and fourteen winters. They were on duty, but it was clear none of them knew how to go about doing that. Whatever their training, it didn't involve walking on patrol. The younger ones appeared as though they were confused about what they were even supposed to be guarding.

As a group, they stood in places that were obvious. They

looked with dull eyes, not knowing the difference between the shadow of a piece of masonry and that of a man. None of them stood a chance of seeing Rew as he crept through their midst. They were training to be hunters and killers, he knew, but they were not hunters yet. They were still children. Some part of them were children, he told himself.

In another section, he saw what he guessed were dormitories for the simulacra. There was a courtyard that had been cleared of rubble and was braced with racks of wooden and metal practice swords. Targets lined one end, and even in the dark, he could see they'd been ravaged by more than arrows and thrown knives. There was a mess hall, though no one cooked within it. No morning bread, it seemed. And he found bodies. They'd been thrown or fallen off the edge of the cliff, landing on the rocks below.

He'd been climbing around, high above those rocks, when something drew his eye. It'd taken him a moment to comprehend the shapes he was seeing, but the robed figures below stood out in stark relief when the surf washed around the bodies, pulling on their clothing, trying to tug them to sea.

There was a score of corpses scattered around those rocks. Rew wondered how many more there'd been that had been taken into the sea's embrace. Some were disturbingly small. Some had the size of a man.

Had they fallen, or had they been executed? Were they bodies of the weapons masters and tutors of Valchon's spawn or the simulacra themselves?

His stomach sour, Rew had continued on until finally, he'd worked himself into the center of the fortress and found the remains of what could have been the old throne room for the dead nobleman who had once occupied the fallen city fifty years earlier.

The windows were long gone, along with some of the masonry. The room was open to the elements, and the wind and the waves whooshed constantly as Rew crouched on a balcony just outside. Inside, seated in a chair, slumped over and swilling from a ceramic jug, was Prince Valchon.

The prince wore his signature billowing white silk shirt and his snug black britches. They both appeared to have sustained damage and were filthy with dried blood. From Carff, two days prior? The shirt showed evidence of spilled wine as well, but judging from the loose way the prince cradled the jug, Rew thought that might have been recent. Valchon was talking, or perhaps singing, to himself, in between long quaffs from the jug.

Rew watched him for a long moment then stepped into the room.

There were no magical explosions, no rushing crash of guards. Nothing except the noise of the world outside and Valchon's drunken murmurings. Walking on silent feet, Rew came closer until he was a dozen paces in front of his brother, and the invoker finally looked up.

"Rew," barked the prince, "I thought you'd be here sooner."

Rew tensed, prepared to strike. "Apologies."

"Come to finish it, eh? Think you'll sit the throne better than I?" scoffed the prince. "You're not ready for rule, Rew. Rule, Rew. Ha. Rew... Rue. Rue the ranger. Rew the..."

"You're drunk," observed Rew.

"What are you, my nursemaid?" Valchon snickered. "You, of all people, saying that I am drunk. Pfah, when weren't you drunk, Rew?"

Rew shifted. He ought to lunge, to thrust his longsword into Valchon's chest and get it over with, but... something was odd. This conversation wasn't right.

"What have you done in this place, Valchon?" Rew asked his brother. "These... children, what have you created? Did you think they'd help against Calb and Heindaw, or was it more? You plan to rule the kingdom with your spawn? You'll repopulate the nobility with these horrors?"

"I saw Father," mentioned Valchon abruptly, ignoring Rew's

questions. "One… ah, two days ago. The morning after Carff. I saw him in Mordenhold."

Rew didn't respond.

"He wouldn't crown me," slurred Valchon. "Told me you were still alive, that I hadn't finished it. Guess he was right."

Rew still did not respond.

"Said if I wanted the crown, I'd have to earn it. Then, he laughed. I don't think he believes I can kill you, Rew. I tried my best, you know. I didn't tell him that. I told him I'd finish you. But Carff took everything I had. A storm like that, the subterfuge around it, taking care of that bastard Alsayer, preventing everyone else from portaling out of the city, that'll drain me for weeks. Not even Father could have done it all, but what's it matter? It failed."

Rew stayed silent. He wasn't sure what to say.

"My children… I thought they'd be enough. I thought I'd figured it out, just like Father. Rule the kingdom with my offspring. That's what he does with us. It would have worked, but they started killing each other. Can you believe that?"

"I can," murmured the ranger.

"If I do kill you, do you think Father will proceed with the Investiture?" wondered Valchon. "You think he'll make me king? He has to, doesn't he? It's the way it's always been. He cannot say no. He has to step aside, to allow me to rule. His time is done. It is my time, now."

"That is the way it's always been," agreed Rew slowly.

"He laughed at me, Rew. Did I tell you that? He said we have to be strong, that the kingdom draws power from our strength, and that we draw our power from the kingdom. He said that marriage was the only thing that prevented true darkness. That we—him, he said—are the only things standing between life and death. I thought he was talking about necromancy. I'm not sure now. Or I'm drunk. What do you think he meant by it?"

Rew stared at his brother, unspeaking.

"I didn't know, either," muttered Valchon. "Rew, I think I made a mistake."

"What's that?"

"Stanton… Carff… If we draw power from the kingdom, then maybe Father was trying to tell me… I always brought people to my cause. I always had allies. He liked that about me, you know. I could tell he believed it'd earn me the throne. I thought those allies would win me the Investiture, thought they'd destroy Calb and Heindaw for me, but they didn't. They were worthless. All the nobles, their armies, all my spellcasters, they did nothing. They wanted me to do the work, Rew. They weren't the help I thought they'd be. They only thought of what they wanted."

"People are like that, Valchon."

"You. You were the one who killed our brothers. Your way was the right one all along. No allies, no friends. I figured if all those allies hadn't helped me, maybe they could be some use against you. I figured I'd show Father I could be strong… but Jabaan was you. Father knows that, doesn't he? Why blame me for Stanton when you did the same? I'm not thinking straight, these last days. I thought he'd respect my strength, what I was doing… He told me I had failed."

Rew stood still, studying his brother. He hadn't always been the man he should be, but looking at Valchon, hearing the prince's callous musing about his allies, about whether or not he should have killed a million people to prove his strength to their father… Rew knew he was a better man than that. He understood, finally, knew it as truth. He might not be a great man, but he was a better man than this one.

He was a better man than any of his brothers.

A better man than the king.

That was why he had to do this. That was why he had to raise the banner and finish it. The kingdom deserved a great king, but right now, it needed a better one.

Quietly, he asked Vachon, "What else did Father say?"

"He gave me this sword," responded the prince, gesturing to

the blade at his side. "Told me to cut your heart out with it. I guess he gave me the sword because he knew I've drained my talent. I could barely open a portal to get to Mordenhold. He had to open the one I took back here. Thought I'd hidden that from him when I arrived, covered my weakness. He said that until I did it—cut your heart out, I mean—I ought not to come back."

"And you plan to do that? To cut my heart out with that sword?"

"Of course."

Rew waited.

"After I finish this wine," clarified Valchon. "We can wait, right, then settle things? We're brothers, and there's no reason to be uncivilized about this. You're more skilled with a sword, I know, but everyone makes mistakes. I'm meant to be king, Rew."

"No, Valchon, I don't think we'll wait."

Rew leapt at his brother.

Valchon spluttered, dropping his jug of wine and grasping at the sword beside him, but he was drunk. He was too slow, even if he hadn't been.

Rew slammed the point of his longsword into Valchon's chest and slid the blade deep.

The prince spit a surprised, hacking rasp, but whatever words he meant to say, his final declaration, was lost as the longsword skewered his heart and ended his life. Blood poured from the prince's chest, staining his white shirt, staining Rew's hands.

The ranger waited a breath then pulled the longsword free of his brother's body. Blood poured from the gaping hole in the prince's chest, and Rew wiped his blade on Valchon's sleeve, cleaning the weapon as best he could.

Behind him, he heard the scuff of a boot.

Rew spun.

Standing framed in an empty doorway to the balcony outside was a child. One of Valchon's spawn. A simulacrum.

Rew raised his longsword, but he didn't attack. It was a child.

Just a child. No matter what Valchon had done to it, how he'd twisted the thing, what it might become, it was still a child.

In a thin voice, a child's voice, it said, "No need for that. I'm already dead. They all are."

Rew swallowed. The child wasn't talking about Valchon. Blood pattered on the floor, dripping from its spindly arms, pooling on the stone tiles.

"I always wondered if you could truly turn your back on your nature," said the child in its eerie lilt. Not a child. The king. "I could not, though I never tried."

Raising his longsword, Rew readied himself to fight.

"You won the Investiture, Rew. There's no need for that. Come to Mordenhold. Come see me. Claim your reward. The throne is yours."

Rew didn't respond. There wasn't a response.

"You know what I am, but still think you can stop me?" cackled the child, its voice wet, blood flying from its lips like spittle as it spoke. "You're not the first to defy me. Two hundred years, Rew. There have been many who thought as you do. Many who tried. But come. Make your attempt. We both know you are done running, so let us end this."

Rew started to panic. He shifted his grip on the longsword. He worked his tongue in a dry mouth. Then, he croaked, "I will destroy you, Father. Your evil cannot exist in this world. It must be stopped, and as your son, it's my duty to do it."

The undead child staggered a step closer and asked, "You truly think you can stop me? I didn't think I'd sired a stupid son. You never learned the high magic which is your blood right. Living up to the power in your blood was your duty, if you want to speak of such things. This pathetic rebellion, this childish tantrum… Come to me, Rew, and face my wrath. Stake your pathetic duty, your rebellion, against my might."

"I stopped Calb and his minions. I faced Heindaw's enchantments, and I tore apart Valchon's maelstrom. I don't claim our blood as my right. I claim it as my enemy, and all who have it will be destroyed."

"Erasmus stopped the maelstrom," corrected the king. "You couldn't do it alone. The girl raised the dead in Jabaan. You couldn't have done any of it alone. Every step, he was there, guiding you, empowering you, turning you against me. But he's gone, now. I felt him pass to the beyond. He is mine, now, and you cannot face me by yourself."

"Maybe I can't defeat you alone, but I'm not coming alone, Father."

"I'd wish for more obedient children," squeaked the voice of the child, "but I need your strength. I crave your will. Now, more than ever, I need it. Come to me, Rew. Defy me. I welcome you."

"The blood of our family will spill on the soil of Vaeldon one more time, and then you'll be finished. We'll all be done. Your line will end with me, Father."

"Raise your banner, then. Come to Mordenhold and spill the blood of your family. Cut out the rotten heart of the king. Come. Do it if you can. You know where to find me. I am waiting."

The child teetered for a brief moment. Then it slumped down in the moonlight, dead, killed for the sole purpose of serving as the king's macabre messenger. Its corpse, the mirror image of Valchon when he'd been ten winters, sprawled in the silver light from the sky, in a spreading pool of black blood.

Raise the banner. Spill the blood of family. Cut out the rotten heart of the king. It was time to go to Mordenhold. It was time to go home.

Thanks for reading!

꿈꿈

M y biggest thanks to the readers! If it wasn't for you, I
wouldn't be doing this. Those of you who enjoyed the
book, I can always use a good review—or even better—tell a
friend.

My eternal gratitude to: Felix Ortiz for the breath-taking cover
and social media illustrations. Shawn T King for his incredible
graphic design. Kellerica for inking this world into reality. Nicole
Zoltack coming back yet again as my long-suffering proofreader,
joined by Anthony Holabird for the final polish. And of course,
I'm honored to continue working with living legend Simon Vance
on the audio. When you read my words, I hope it's in his voice.

Terrible 10… Always stay Terrible.

Thanks again, and hope to hear from you!

AC

YOU CAN FIND LARGER VERSIONS OF THE MAPS, SERIES ARTWORK, MY
newsletter, free short stories, and other goodies at accobble.com.

It's the best place to stay updated on when the next book is coming!

If you want more of this story, unfortunately you'll have to wait! The final book in the series, **The Ranger's Lament: The King's Ranger Book 6**, is due out March 31st. It's up for pre-order now, though, so go ahead and get first in line!